M000118810

GOOD NIGHT, SWEET DADDY-O

JOHN A. CONNELL

NAILHEAD PUBLISHING

COPYRIGHT

GOOD NIGHT, SWEET DADDY-O

A NailHead Publishing book

Copyright © 2020 by John A. Connell

This is a work of fiction. Names, characters, places, and incidents either are
the product of the author's imagination or are used fictitiously. Any
resemblance to actual persons, living or dead, events, or locales is entirely
coincidental.

All rights reserved. No part of this book may be reproduced or used in any
manner without written permission of the copyright owner except for the use
of quotations in a book review. For more information:
john@johnaconnell.com

ISBN 978-1-950409-11-2 (hardcover)

ISBN 978-1-950409-10-5 (paperback)

ISBN 978-1-950409-09-9 (ebook)

www.johnaconnell.com

The scariest monsters are the ones that lurk within our souls.

Edgar Allen Poe

I don't remember going to bed, but in the morning, there I was.

Charles Bukowski

There's something twisted about a place that's colder in the summer than in the winter. Just about anywhere else in the country, July evenings are warm and balmy, but on most summer nights in San Francisco, a cold damp fog blows in from the Pacific and drops a shroud over the entire city. But I loved it. You could immerse yourself in it, let it obscure and limit your view so the whole crazy world wasn't more than a hundred feet in front of you.

As I walked through the fog on the way back home, I imagined myself cocooned inside that cold, white blanket where no one could find me. The fog conceals a lot of things too; I didn't see the '53 Club Coupe Chevy as I neared my apartment building. Sickly green in color and beat to hell, the heap was unremarkable except that it was an oracle of my coming misfortune.

I lived on the edge of the Tenderloin near O'Farrell and Larkin Streets. My apartment was on the top floor of a three-story, wood-frame job, wedged between a sex shop and a liquor store where winos did their shopping and addicts robbed at regular intervals. It was two a.m. by the time I had reached my street. The cold had seeped through my clothes, and all I wanted to do was fall into bed. Even this late you could find a few hookers or guys looking to score dope, but tonight there was no one around. The few isolated streetlamps barely pierced the fog for more than a couple of yards, and the only sounds were my footsteps echoing off the buildings. A car door closed ahead of me, but I didn't look up. It wasn't until I saw their legs that I noticed the two guys blocking the sidewalk. A flash of panic ran through me.

"What know, man?" one of them said.

They stood in the shadows, but I recognized the speaker from the round gut that hung over his beltline and the thick New Orleans accent. He was a small-time dealer that I bought reefer from. Daniel Devrees.

"Oh, man, Disease," I said.

"Don't call me that." He sounded like the kid bullied too many times on the playground who could finally exact his revenge. "You know I don't like it. People that owe me money don't get to call me anything but sir."

The initial panic had subsided, but a deeper dread was growing a knot in the pit of my stomach. Daniel took a few steps forward and moved into a pool of light. The frayed edges of the brim of his straw porkpie hat threw a saw-toothed pattern across his diminutive nose and round cheeks. At the age of thirty, he had already lost a substantial portion of his hair, and he tried to hide it by always wearing that same worn hat. I'd never seen him without it.

"I haven't got it," I said.

Daniel motioned for his companion to come forward. My

stomach tightened when I saw the guy was carrying a baseball bat.

"What the hell does he have that bat for?" I tried firm, but my voice quivered.

"Why, this is Mickey," Daniel said, then flashed me a Cheshire-cat grin. "Get it?"

I didn't think he meant the mouse. The punk stood almost six foot four with biceps that bulged from his rolled-up sleeves. His black hair was slicked back into a ducktail with half a can of pomade.

"Ain't it perfect? Mickey? Mantle? Don't you get it? Mickey here is batting a thousand when it comes to people's heads. He was on his way to becoming a home-run king in the minors until he blew out a knee. It just made him madder than hell, and now he likes to take it out on everybody else." Daniel chuckled as he rolled a cigarette around in his mouth.

"What did you bring him for? We had a deal."

"It ain't my money, brother. That's another department."

"What are you talking about? Ernie said it came from you."

"Well, Ernie told you wrong. I'm not allowed to do loans. At least not a two-grand floater like yours. So I referred it to the guys that do. The outfit is always looking for an easy mark like you to hustle."

"What outfit? This is the first time I heard any mention of a damned outfit."

"Not just any outfit. *The* outfit, man. The one that knows where all the bodies are buried, if you dig what I'm sayin'. That's who I work for, and that's who you owe the money to."

"Ernie said nothing about that. If I had known, I would have said no." I heard the fear bordering on pleading in my voice.

"Makes no difference to me whether you knew or not. A deal's a deal."

"Give me a break. Please. Two thousand dollars isn't that much."

"Not that much? Hell, any more than that and we'd have to break both legs and dump you in the bay. Consider this just a friendly incentive."

"I'll pay you back."

"No more whining. Look, I don't want to hustle you, but I've got no choice. They're puttin' the screws to me now, and that's where our friendship ends. I told you last week that trouble was coming if you didn't cough up the dough."

"Give me some more time. I'll borrow it from my friends if I have to."

He took a deep puff from his cigarette and pushed the smoke out of his lungs, letting the smoke hang in a swirling cloud in front of his face. He tried to be menacing with the smoke thing, like some big-time gangster, but his eggplant-shaped face usually inspired me to laugh. I wasn't laughing this time, though. All I wanted to do was wrap my hands around his triple chin. Or run.

"Business is business," he said. "I've got my guys to answer to, and they're not old friends like we are."

"Look. I've got a line on something. One of the cats I played with tonight is going to give me some studio gigs. Give me a few more weeks. We'll make it fifty percent interest."

"This is just a formality, but I have to ask. To make things official and all. Have you got the money?"

"I'll get the money, man. I swear."

"I'll ask one more time. Have you got the money?"

My mind raced. My only chance was to get out onto Geary

Street and flag down a car or hope to catch a patrolling cop. I could outrun Daniel, but I wasn't so sure about Mickey. My survival instinct decided for me. I bolted for safety.

Mickey was ready for me, and despite his supposed bum knee, he was on me in three strides.

My back exploded in an electrical shock. My knees hit concrete, and I went face-first onto the sidewalk, bounced, and rolled, ending faceup. I fought for breath as my mind tried to work against the torment, screaming at me to breathe, to run, to beg. I was only vaguely aware of Mickey and Daniel standing over me. Through the haze of tears, I watched the bat rise, then heard the whoosh of air as it crashed into my ribs. My lungs froze and I panicked. My legs pushed me along the sidewalk, a vain attempt to get away. I'm not sure if I said "no, stop" in my mind or out loud. Mickey grabbed a foot and dragged me back. Daniel's face came in close to mine.

"I never wanted to do this. I tried to talk 'em out of it. I really did. But they insisted on Mickey giving y'all a few batting lessons. I'm sorry, man, but my hands are tied."

Daniel straightened. They waited. Probably allowing some of the shock to subside so I could appreciate the full impact of Mickey's next lesson. I made eye contact with Mickey. He smiled and raised the bat. As it came down, I turned. It hit the concrete with a hollow thud. I got up onto my hands and knees and crawled. Reason left me. The bat slammed into my side and I went down. Mickey grabbed me by the shoulders, lifted me up, and shoved my back against a brick wall.

"One more and we're outta here," Daniel said. Mickey wound up for his swing. "Not the head, man," Daniel added.

Mickey raised the bat for his home-run hit.

I'll always regret what I did then. It was instinct, but it

changed my life. Mickey swung, and I thrust my left arm out to protect myself. The bat smashed into my wrist. A million volts of agony short-circuited my already overloaded brain. I figure that Mickey, angered that he'd hit the equivalent of a foul ball, ignored Daniel's warning and struck me in the head because everything went black.

2

ONE MONTH LATER

Daylight burned into my eyelids. I pulled a pillow over my head and tried to form coherent thoughts through the pounding in my temples and my chest. I peeked out from under the pillow to see if I was back in my apartment. I was. Last night's drunk had erased any memory of how I'd got there. There must be some primitive instinct that takes over and steers me home. I fought the urge to pee, desperate not to move, but there was no way I could put it off. I groped for the bathroom and let loose. I hoped for relief. Instead, my guts clenched.

The hard reality crowded out the night's booze-induced optimism. I was screwed. A month late on my rent—or was it two? A month absent from my day job, down to a few dollars, no food, and a pile of hospital and doctor bills.

I'd borrowed money from my friends to pay off Daniel and save myself another beating, but he'd kept shaking me down for the interest. I opened my eyes and caught sight of my reflection in the mirror. A stranger stared back at me. I raised my left hand. My fourth and fifth fingers were curled up together like a claw, paralyzed from the impact of Mickey's bat. The wrist had healed, but the break had left my ulnar nerve damaged—at least that's what the doc had said. I stared at my fingers and willed them to move. My whole body tensed with the effort.

Move, move, move, move, goddamnit!

I imagined my brain squeezing the idea out into my arm, but the movement came only from the other fingers, opening and closing as if in spasm.

I stopped and caught my breath. Hand still raised, I picked up the pin I kept on a shelf. This morning ritual was an extreme test, but I'd hoped that if there was any feeling at all …

I stabbed the tip of my fourth finger, then the fifth. Nothing but beads of blood. They might as well have not been there. A growl rose from my throat and burst out, and I slammed my good hand against the wall.

I shuffled out of the bathroom and walked past the dirty underwear, full ashtrays, discarded whiskey bottles, and food wrappers, and sat at the beat-up spinet piano. On the floor, around the piano, lay sheets of music where I'd jotted something down, crumpled them up, then tossed them. I wasn't a genius; I couldn't write music I couldn't already play. Everything I'd tried after Mickey's grand slam sounded like "Chopsticks." A music sheet with a few scribbles sat above the keyboard, notes almost unreadable. Streaks of black ink ran down the page from a previous fit of rage and frustration.

The name is Frank Caruso Valentine and, in spite of the

middle name, my parents never dreamed I'd be a musician—
rather, struggling jazz pianist and composer. After a degree in
music and seven years of playing in two-bit dives for pennies,
by my age of twenty-eight, I'd expected to be performing in
high-class nightclubs with a couple of albums under my belt.
But time had slipped by while I'd waited for the break that
didn't come, or written, then rewritten music that never saw
the light of day. Then just about the time I had six tunes I felt
proud of, I met Ernie.

Ernie Bertram, a part-time music promoter and full-time
hustler, had heard me play my tunes last May at a West Coast
jazz competition put on by a local radio station. He'd been
looking for someone to help launch his career as a record
producer and convinced me that if we cut a hot demo, he'd
shop it around to the regional record labels and make us both a
pile of cash. All I had to do was to come up with the whopping
sum of three thousand dollars for the studio time and the four
musicians.

Ernie's promise of fame and fortune had gone to my head,
and three thousand hadn't seemed like that much at the time
because I'd been just *so sure* that I was going to make a small
fortune when I got my record contract. So I'd taken out the six
hundred in my savings, borrowed four hundred from friends,
and—the source of all my problems—made a deal with Ernie
to get the other two thousand from Daniel. There is, indeed, a
sucker born every minute.

Needless to say, the whole thing had gone south real fast.
Ernie pulled together a band he must have found at the musicians' local for hopheads, booked the cheapest recording studio
he could find, cut everybody's rate in two, and skipped town
with most of the money.

The telephone ringing interrupted my brooding.

When I think about it now, I should have never answered it. But I did. It was George Mayhall.

"How you doing, man?" George asked.

"If I could figure out a way to make a living playing the piano with one hand, I'd be in like Flynn."

"Good. Your sense of humor is intact."

I could hear George lighting up a cigarette.

"Did you get your cast off?" he asked.

"Yeah. A few days ago."

"And the fingers?"

"The same."

He blew smoke into the mouthpiece. "What can I say?"

"Nothing to say."

"Are you in another tragic moment?"

"Yeah." My headache returned and I wanted him off the phone. "Look, if you called to collect the money I owe you, I don't have it now, but I can start work at the bra factory again in another couple of weeks."

"Two thousand dollars is about ten months' pay for you, isn't it? Add in taxes and living expenses and you're looking at paying it off in, oh, three or four years."

"My world's crashing in on me and you lay that crap on me?"

"I'm not laying any crap on you. I'm trying to make a point. You can take your time paying me back. I loaned you the money because you're my friend and you needed it bad. I still can't figure out why you didn't come to me in the first place."

"You weren't around, remember? Besides, I don't like borrowing from friends, especially that amount of dough. My mom doesn't have two pennies to rub together. So I let that scumbag record producer talk me into getting the floater from another scumbag, and voilà."

"A loan shark."

"George, we've been through this. I screwed up, okay?" I took a deep breath and tried to calm down. "What did you call for, anyway?"

"I've got something that could make it all better."

"I've got enough pills from the doctor."

"I wasn't talking about pills."

"How about a million dollars, then?"

"Bingo, my brother cat."

I tried to clear enough of sludge in my brain to follow his crazy train of thought. "Bingo what? What are you talking about?"

"I'm not saying anything else over the phone. You want answers, you show up at Sammy's tonight at eight."

He hung up before I could respond. I imagined him on the other end with his sly smile, getting a big kick out of stringing me along. George had been the first person I'd met when my family moved from Boston to Mill Valley. He was the king of the hill among the pack of kids that lived in our neighborhood. I was ten, he was twelve, and, for some reason, he took me under his wing and treated me like a little brother. I'd smoked my first cigarette with George, experienced my first drunk and, later in high school, my first reefer. He was the kind of guy I'd wanted to be but never could: a guy who got things done, who never looked back, and never seemed to be flapped about anything. I had to admit that right then I needed him again.

I pulled a cigarette out of the pack and lit it, glancing at the piano sitting mute in the corner. It seemed to taunt me. To keep my mind from the dark places, I took a long walk up to the wharf and back, and watched the sun go down at Caffe Trieste. I hung there, sipping coffee until it was time to make the pilgrimage to Sammy's and find out what George could possibly offer to ease my dire situation.

3

S ammy's—my favorite realm of the senses. Comforting
odors of cigarettes and old beer greeted me. Through the
haze, on the far side of the room, a jazz trio played "Blue Cee"
by Charles Mingus. Slow and cool. Sammy was there as
always, working behind the bar. He had transformed this once
aging sports bar on Columbus Avenue into a popular art and
jazz venue that brought in the North Beach crowd. Each week
Sammy displayed art on consignment for local artists. Some
weeks it was cool; most of the time it went into the realm of
"I'll dig that when hell freezes over." This week hell had been
saved from another blizzard: along two walls hung sorry
Jackson Pollock imitations, and on a third were three-dimen-
sional wall hangings consisting of some kind of headless-baby-
doll motif. I wanted to be cool enough to appreciate this new
expressionism, but my tastes in art didn't include splatter paint
and decapitated toys.

Half the clientele adhered to precepts of Beat culture, but
were more followers than creators. I put myself in that cate-
gory, or "fringe Beat" as I called it. I was neither a grand poet

nor a Beat philosopher, but I believed in the principles even if I failed to strictly follow them. The rest of the crowd were what's commonly referred to as the fake Beats: Beat wannabes who'd flocked to San Francisco—and Sammy's bar—when the movement had been popularized in the magazines and Hollywood. They were the ones wearing the berets and crude sandals, sporting goatees, and applauding by snapping their fingers.

I crossed the room, nodding to a few of the regular cats, and spotted Roach and Arliss at our usual table. George hadn't arrived yet, so I ordered two pitchers of beer. My friends turned to look at me at the bar. I waved. Roach held up his hand and waved with his fingers. Arliss shot me a bird, then belly laughed.

The two were a picture of contrast. Roach's real name was Roland Rochfort, hence the nickname. He was ex-army gone bohemian: thin, army muscled, a rose tattoo on one arm, shaggy hair, dime-store clothes, and a mustache that blended into his permanent three-day beard. He had this aloof, calm demeanor, which he managed to exaggerate by smoking his cigarettes in a rose-decorated cigarette holder. His dark eyes remained half-lidded, which gave him the air of an intense thinker, although I think most of the time it was to keep the smoke out of his eyes from the three-pack-a-day habit.

Arliss Henriksson was a farm-raised Swede from Iowa. A Nordic blond with faint-blue eyes, he could have been the Nazi propaganda poster boy. His flannel shirt struggled to contain his massive muscles, which he exaggerated by rubbing his short-cropped hair and flexing his biceps. But I couldn't help thinking of him as a dangerous six-foot-three, 230-pound teddy bear, because I knew there had to be a tenderness that Arliss showed Roach only behind closed doors.

Roach and Arliss had been lovers ever since I'd known them, but I knew very little of the dynamics of their relationship except that Roach endured Arliss's occasional heterosexuality. They'd met in an army hospital in Korea, and had broken up, then gotten back together numerous times over the past six years. There was a silent agreement among the group that their relationship should never be discussed, unless they brought up the subject first. The rest of us were content to ignore their odd coupling and talk about a myriad of girls and their anatomical attributes or bedding potential.

Sammy handed me the two pitchers and I took them to the table. Arliss watched me cross the floor.

"Hey, look," he said. "It's James Dean in *Rebel of the Lost Cause.*"

I dropped into my chair and started filling mugs. "Did you just make that up or have you been working on it for weeks?"

"Oh, did you hear that?" Arliss asked Roach.

"Can it, man," I said. "I'm not in the mood."

"See what I mean? All pouty and serious like James Dean."

"I'm not all pouty and serious, just … thoughtful."

Roach studied me with half-closed eyes. "You're not as pretty as James Dean, but you do kind of look like him. Especially the way you're slouched in your chair with that cigarette hanging from your lips."

I didn't respond except to take a drag on my cigarette and blow it in their direction.

"You do look ragged, man," Roach said.

I shrugged my shoulders and transferred my cigarette to my left hand, because I could pick up the mug only with my right. Roach and Arliss looked at my gimpy hand hanging in the air.

Roach nodded at my two curled fingers. "At least the cast is off. Will the fingers ever work again?"

"The doctor said they might. They don't really know. I keep trying to move them, see if the feeling is coming back, but nothing." A long pull on my beer helped wash away the lump in my throat.

"You've got to go easy, man," Roach said. "'Cause there's no other way to take it. Stop embalming yourself. Get something else going."

"Yeah," Arliss said. "You can find something better than working in a bra factory."

"I take pride in my work. I think of all those lovely breasts that will be nestled in those bras one day." My friends returned deadpan looks. "Okay, let me put it this way—I sure as hell am not going to start praying to the false gods of the American dream and get lost in that giant gristmill like my old man did. The man worked as a machinist for thirty-three years of his fifty-two. And for what? It's all an illusion dreamt up by the corporate conglomerates to enslave the masses."

"Did you just make that up or have you been working on that for weeks?" Roach asked.

I laughed. "That's the condensed version. I usually keep an index card handy to whip out at opportune moments."

Roach's and my exchange had been lost on Arliss. He was still trying to catch up. "What's wrong with what your dad did?" Arliss said. "He spent his life taking care of a wife and child. Boy, I bet he was real disappointed when you popped out."

"Isn't there anybody else you can rag on?"

"You're my favorite target."

"Well, I'm glad I provide you with some entertainment."

We all laughed, enjoying this semiweekly ritual of slinging insults at each other. The band took a break and we fell silent as we drank our beers. In the middle of the dance floor, some kitten writhed in a black leotard and turtleneck sweater to the rhythm a guy pounded out on his table. She twisted and stretched as her arms wove together and unraveled, then swirled above her head.

"Write any more screaming death epics?" I asked Roach.

Roach and I had met through George about a year ago. We'd started hanging out together at the Six Gallery or The Cellar for the poetry readings and the Black Hawk for jazz. Roach had gotten up one night at the Cellar to read his poem about war and violence. One stanza in, he'd started prancing around the stage, stripping his clothes off and making war sounds as he simulated bayonet stabs and the screams of dying men. He wasn't asked back. I was never sure if something had snapped or been turned on during his visit to the frozen Korean countryside in '52.

"Obviously, my form of expression is not appreciated by the uninitiated," Roach said. "Now I'm working on a novel."

"It's like his third novel," Arliss said. "Only he don't finish 'em."

"I'll finish this one. It's about going to Tangier and doing drugs. I have to do some research first, so I'll go to Tangier and do lots of drugs. For the research, of course."

Arliss let out a snort. "He's been talking about it ever since he read that in Tangier you can smoke hashish in the bars and find willing young boys on every street corner."

"I've gotta get there before it all disappears," Roach said. "I'm going as soon as I get enough cash."

"Maybe George has something that'll take care of all that," I said. "He's plugged into something. Maybe that's why he made a big deal about getting together tonight."

"What makes you think he's gonna throw us any bones?" Arliss asked. "He don't let us in on anything."

Arliss stiffened like the head schoolmaster had just entered the classroom, and I knew George had just walked in. I turned in the direction of Arliss's stare. George negotiated the tables with his long legs while nodding to those he knew.

George Mayhall exuded true confidence. Even when he was relaxed or thoughtful, he seemed to be observing some amusing irony or plotting a sarcastic remark. You felt that a whole world went on behind that face, and you listened and waited in hope that he might reveal that private world.

"Hello, my fine feathered cats," he said.

Hand slapping all around. George sat, and Roach poured him a beer.

"You do not want to get into this conversation," Roach said. "Turn right around and come in again"—he looked at his watch—"oh, say, in five minutes. Just enough time for Arliss to get bored with character assassination."

"I can take Arliss's ranting as well as the next man," George said. He leaned way back in his chair, crossed his arms, and waited for the big guy to continue.

Arliss suddenly took interest in his beer. George was the only one of the group who could silence him with a look and a smile.

Some women called me good-looking, but it was foolish to compare myself to George. He had the round, chocolate-brown eyes, long lashes, and cleft chin of a movie star. His hair broke in dark, wet waves that swept across his forehead and ended with a slight curl with just enough gel to hold the whole stormy sea in place. Herds of dames melted around this guy.

George kept what he did for a living shrouded in mystery. But he was doing something right. The clothes weren't the giveaway; they were standard department-store brands. It was the gold watch and the Italian leather shoes that cost an average man's monthly salary. A ritual of mine was to probe George about his recent activities.

"Do anything really frantic today, man, like get on the red phone with Khrushchev and divert a fleet of commie subs?"

His wry smile deepened. "The same thing I do every day. Long walks in the park, coffee, and the paper." George lit a cigarette. "And by then, it was time to come and watch you boys get hammered." He held up an empty pitcher, caught Sammy's attention, then pointed at it.

"You drink too, you bastard," Arliss said.

"Ah, but not to excess. I have to keep sharp at all times. You never know what might happen during my evening strolls."

This was George's patent response, and it only amplified my curiosity. After college George had done a whole Kerouac thing, traveling all over the country. He'd decided to use his poli-sci degree and had gotten into politics. It had taken him a couple of years to get going, but he'd finally hooked up with a local representative and helped run the guy's reelection campaign. When the guy won, he took George along. But then something had happened, and George had disappeared. He'd popped back into my life a year ago, but refused to tell me anything about what had happened to him. He would always be the king of hepcats for me, and we'd never lost that closeness from our teenage years, but he'd become unreachable, like something had really gotten to him. He was in a constant state of being cool with an edge, a sharp edge.

"Are you going to tell us why you called us all in here?" I asked.

"You can wait the ten seconds it takes for Turly to find his way to the table," George said, and pointed across the room.

All eyes turned. There he was: skinny, a crew cut, and blue eyes hidden behind thick, black-framed glasses. I felt a pang of regret as Turly crossed the room. I hadn't seen him in his insurance salesman's uniform, a boy in a man's garb, a plastered smile, trench coat, gray suit, fedora, and briefcase. He was an old friend and I loved the guy, but he was stretching the limits of my tolerance with this performance.

"What happened to him?" George asked.

"Turly's a full-fledged insurance salesman now," I said. "His dad badgered him into the business. Insurance. Can you believe that?"

"The poor boy," Roach said in mock sympathy. Puffs of smoke escaped from his mouth as he chuckled. He loved to watch humanity struggle.

Turly dropped the fake smile and stiff walk as he approached the table. He bopped to the beat with his last few steps. So, he hadn't mutated completely, but it wouldn't be too much longer. I instantly mourned the loss of a friend and a good sax player to his father's brutal pressure. He stopped bopping when he saw our faces. Looked down at his feet as he pulled a chair over and sat.

George leaned over to Turly. "What happened to you?"

"What do you mean?"

"You in that monkey suit. I thought you were cool, man. You change sides or something?"

"I never chose sides. At least I'm doing something with my life. I was going nowhere with the music."

"You have to give art time, man," I said. "It just doesn't come overnight. You and I had dreams."

Turly shrank away from the table and squeezed his face with as much contempt as he could muster in his defense. "You guys are sad. No careers, no money. Very sad. I mean, what do you expect to get out of life if you don't do something constructive?"

"Like insurance?" I asked. "I'd rather clean toilets."

"Well, just wait," Turly said with a sneer. "That's what you'll do."

The pitcher of beer arrived and created a lull in the conversation. The band returned to their spot and broke into a frenzied number, while we soaked up the alcohol and waited for George to tell us what he had wanted.

Finally, George cleared his throat and leaned forward. "What do you guys think about doing something together other than sucking down beer?"

"Like what?" I asked.

Arliss smiled and pounded the table. "Yeah, do something together. I've been sayin' that forever."

"I don't think George is talking about the circle jerk, Arly," Roach said.

"You're just too fucking funny. I was thinking about, I don't know, a ball game, pool."

Roach lit up another cigarette. How many cigarettes since I'd gotten there?

"Okay, Georgie," Roach said, "cough it up. What have you got in mind?"

"I'm talking about an enterprise that we all can profit from. Let's say it's something outside the law, but guaranteed to stir the blood. Get your circulation going somewhere other than your butts." George stopped to let that sink in.

Surprise and curiosity crossed everyone's face.

"I don't want to go into details unless I know you guys won't get your panties in a wad. I look around the table and I see a lot of puckered sphincters."

"My sphincter is always puckered," Roach said, biting hard on his cigarette holder, "but I'm intrigued."

"Yeah, me too," Arliss said, and glanced at Roach to make sure he'd said the right thing.

George leaned in closer. "Now, the business I propose doesn't require any capital. Just nerve and a commitment to not turning back. If you sign on, you stay with it until it's over."

He stopped to take a swig of beer while we digested this, then slammed his beer mug down. Turly jumped.

"It's big," he said. "And to pull it off, I need all of you guys. In return, loads of dough. So much dough that you'll never have to work again."

Turly spoke first. "I don't know what could do that, unless it's bank robbery or something." He looked around the table as everyone stared at him. "What? Oh, no, I'm not doing any bank robberies. Count me out."

He'd spoken too loud, and people near our table turned their heads.

George leaned into Turly. "Clam it up, man. I'm not talking about bank robberies."

Turly stiffened and leaned back.

"Do you want a chance to get away from your old man or not?" George asked.

Turly swirled his beer and watched the foam rise, then shrink as the bubbles popped and became beer again. "More than anything. But that's not what I had in mind." He looked up. "Maybe we could find something else."

George turned and surveyed the rest of us. "So?"

Roach's smile made the cigarette holder rise like a needle on his excitement gauge. "I'm in. Stir my blood, man."

"I'm in," Arliss said.

George turned to me. "And you, Frankie?"

I felt everyone's eyes on me. "Outside the law," I said. "Which means something criminal. I'm not sure I'm ready for that."

George scanned my face as if reading the neon sign that said *desperate* on my forehead. "I know you better than you know yourself. You're ready."

"I'd have to think about it."

Arliss groaned. George held up his index finger to him, and Arliss stopped.

"What's there to think about?" George asked me. "You're in a deep, dark hole already, and I've got the solution to get you out of it. I tell you what: you say yes, and I'll forget about the money you owe me."

"How can I say yes if I don't know what it is?"

"I'm not going to tell you what it is 'cause you're going to get all moral on me. Look at me, man. I'm your oldest friend, and I wouldn't steer you wrong. You give me your time, nerve, and commitment, and within a month, maybe less, I guarantee you'll be able to buy your own goddamned studio and cut records till you're blue in the goddamned face. You could get a *real* doctor to fix your hand so you can play again. Whatever you want."

His argument was overwhelming. What would I do for a chance to realize my dream with only a month's commitment? How far was I willing to go? That was something I couldn't answer in less than sixty seconds.

"Give me some time, a day, to think about it. I don't trust my judgment after a pitcher of beer."

Arliss was about to say something, but George whipped up his finger again. Arliss's mouth froze open for a moment. George's smile returned. He gulped down his beer and put his hands on the table like a father at suppertime. "Now, boys, I say we convene to the Aztec. It's twist night and the young *thangs* will be there like a field of fresh flowers, all sweaty, hot, and worked up into a froth."

"Let's go, man," Roach said. "I can't wait to see all of us trying to do the twist."

Everyone laughed, except Turly. "I have to work tomorrow." He looked guilty and ready to take the verbal punishment.

I decided to go easy on him. No doubt his dad had already badgered him enough. I said, "At least use some of that hard-earned money to help yourself ease into the arms of a giving young lady."

George put an authoritative hand on Turly's shoulder. "Turl, it's still early, man. You can't let a little work interfere."

"I can't remember when I seen you with a girl," Arliss said. "You got to use something other than your five fingers once in a while, or your pecker's going to shrink up into a little acorn."

Everyone stood. Roach stepped over to Turly and ruffled his hair. "Ah, leave him alone," he said. "Maybe he likes boys."

Turly turned red. "Okay, okay, I'll go. Just get off my case."

George put his arm around him. "That's right, boys, give him some air. We don't want to lose our little buddy. He's the only one with a working car."

"Where's your ride?" I asked.

"It's in the shop again," George said, and tossed money on the table. "It's on me, boys. Take care of it, would you, Frankie?"

While I grabbed up the money and paid the bar tab, Roach and Arliss pulled a reluctant Turly outside. I rejoined George at the door. He put his arm around me and leaned in close.

"I want you to think hard about what I was talking about, you hear? 'Cause I had you specifically in mind. I'm counting on you."

"What can I say, George?"

He led me outside, his arm still around my shoulder.

"I didn't want to say anything in front of Turly, but something's going down tonight at the club. I'll make you a deal. You help me out tonight and see how it goes, and I'll not only forget your debt—I'll slip you some cash too."

"I pay my debts."

"I can dig that. But how about a little cash? I know you need it, and I need you. I'm going to have Roach and Arliss do something for me tonight too. It's all planned. I've covered all the bases. You cool with that?"

"Sure, George."

We made our way to Turly's car, a beat-up green '47

Packard. Turly fell into the driver's seat. George got in front like our big brother, Roach, Arliss, and I jammed in the back. Turly finally got the engine started, and George snapped on the radio, catching Fats Domino's "Ain't That a Shame." As Turly pulled away, we started singing along.

I'll remember it forever: the five of us packed into that rolling heap, hurtling down Market Street in the fog, buzzing from the beer, and singing our lungs out. Too bad it was the last time we'd do that together. I was amazed we didn't hit anything. It was like fate knew what was coming and gave us a break.

4

W e cruised by the Aztec, noses to the windows, checking it out. The property had changed hands a number of times and become a dance club just after World War Two. It blended in with the rest of the giant brick buildings in the Jackson Square area that had survived the 1906 earthquake —that is, except for the big flashing sign, a beehive of cars, and a long line of girls in poodle skirts, saddle oxfords, and tight sweaters, the guys in hip-tight jeans, rolled-sleeve T-shirts, and leather jackets.

"Ah, they're just kids," Turly whined.

"Listen to you, old man," George said. "They're legal tender. There are three loaded bars in there, so they've got to be at least twenty-one."

Turly parked and we piled out. We'd smoked some reefer on the way over and everyone giggled that silly giggle you get when Mary Jane is in bed with you. Even Turly was snickering. He hadn't imbibed, but the smoke-filled car had worked its charm on him anyway.

"Man, Turl," I said, "your smile's so big it looks like

you're gonna sneeze."

Everyone was laughing at Turly's expense, even Turly.

George made a move to go. "Gentlemen, I think we're about ready."

The Aztec fulfilled the promise of its name: huge faux carved-stone columns broke up the large U-shaped hall, and tacky Aztec friezes decorated the beige brick walls. The bars, the stairs that swept down to the dance floor, and even the stage were all made of faux stone, imitating ancient pyramids. Palm trees and jungle vines added the finishing touches. Onstage, a five-piece band, wearing gold lamé blazers, jittered as they played.

The place was packed. We stood on the mezzanine level, which had flanking bars, at the top of the steps and looked out onto the crowd of dancers. While the perimeter of tables and sofas remained dark for cruising and necking, spotlights illuminated a rotating mirror ball and slashed across the twisting bodies.

I looked back to one of the bars, my taste buds calling for another drink. The guys and dolls stood three deep at the bar, and there were some fine-looking ladies among them. A large lounge area had been set up between the two bars with sofas, chairs, and a forest of palms.

One girl caught my eye. She sat on the arm of one of the sofas, talking to two other girls. I never looked at them; my eyes zeroed in on her. She wore a pearl satin blouse and a red flared swing skirt.

I could tell from where I stood that she was different: the way she held herself wasn't exaggerated, not too girlish, her smile had a genuine small turn and playful curve, and her mouth wasn't moving a mile a minute. Black hair fell in curls that were pulled back to reveal a long, graceful neck. Then, as if she'd felt my stare, her piercing eyes connected with mine. Her smile broadened, and then she looked back at her friends. I was stricken. Something clicked in my brain and I remembered to breathe again.

Turly tapped my arm and brought me out of it. George, Roach, and Arliss had already descended the stairs. We caught up with them, and wandered along the fringes of the dance floor, staying together and following George. Turly stayed close to me, looking like a nervous rabbit.

I slapped him on the back—an awkward attempt to snap him out of it. "I have to admit, this music makes my hips loose and my feet bounce. It appeals to my primitive nature. No wonder it scares the parents and seduces the young."

George took my arm and pulled me aside. "Roach, Arliss, and I have something to take care of. I want you to keep Turly company and make sure he doesn't leave."

"I've got to be the babysitter?"

"He's your best friend, right? Entertain him. I'll let you know when I need you."

We joined the others, and Turly must have sensed his exclusion. He turned away. "Maybe this wasn't such a good idea."

Roach grabbed his belt. "No, Daddy-O, you're stickin' around. You have the ride."

"Yeah, you're sticking around," Arliss said.

George leaned in. "Stay put," he said to Turly, then turned and merged with the crowd. Roach and Arliss followed.

"Turl, come on, relax," I said. "You've got to let your hair down once in a while or you'll burst one day." I put my hand on his shoulder; it felt like we were two kids again, lost in a crowd of strangers. "I bet if we scour the perimeter of this bacchanal, we'll find a few eager young women."

As we merged into the crowd, the band started up "Rock Around the Clock." Along the darkened perimeter a few couples were necking, but there were also a lot of girls waiting to be asked to dance and boys afraid to do so. These kinds of tribal gatherings had always given me a little sickly feeling. Memories of high school surfaced, especially so walking with Turly.

He must have been reminiscing about the same thing. "Remember in high school when we used to hang out at the sock hops?" he said. "We were both afraid to ask a girl to dance."

"I wasn't. I just refused to conform to, you know—"

"Bullshit, you were scared."

"We're talking about the eighth grade here, right?"

"Hell, you were in the twelfth grade before you ever got laid."

"You're wrong, but I'll humor you since you have the car."

I hadn't talked to anyone about it. We had called her Lassie —sweet, nice hair, but a bit of a dog. I was in the tenth grade, and she was a year older. She had stopped me in the hall one day and cajoled me into a maintenance closet. Curiosity and hormones had prevailed over aesthetic judgment. The closet had been dark. She had been warm, wet, and invisible. There was a lot of fumbling around, but it left me convinced that sex was the greatest thing ever. We visited that closet a number of times in the next few weeks. Then one day she disappeared. I heard later that she and her mom had moved to Sacramento to be closer to her dad, who was in prison for armed robbery.

Turly couldn't leave it alone. "I bet you never got laid in

high school."

"What's with your obsession with my sex life? Yeah, I got laid, but I don't want to talk about it."

"So, the rumors of you and Lassie are true." Turly started howling and barking like a dog while humping the air. A couple of girls moved a little farther away.

"Turl, my boy, I'm happy to see you laughing. I haven't seen that in a long time."

The encouragement had the opposite effect and Turly turned somber. Fortunately, he stopped there and didn't sink back into depressing.

We checked out the girls as we walked.

"What do you think of George's idea?" Turly asked.

"I don't know. He's right about one thing—I am in a deep dark hole, and I can't see anything happening but me going deeper."

I spied one girl that looked like Turly's type: not beautiful, but pretty, everything in place. Blonde hair pulled back in a ponytail and just enough makeup. Her pleated skirt, white blouse, and saddle oxfords gave her that put-together girl-next-door appeal. She talked to two other girls, who were facing the other direction.

"Hey, Turl, there's one for you. She has that sweet suburban housewife potential. Let's go over and meet her."

Turly froze. "Let's get a drink instead."

"We will. But if all we wanted was to drink, we could have stayed at Sammy's. Girls were the reason to come here. Right?"

"Not for me it wasn't." In spite of his refusal to move, I had picked a good one. He couldn't take his eyes off her.

"I'll get it started for you," I said. "You just have to keep up the momentum."

"What makes you think you can get it started, single boy?"

"Because when it's not for me, it's easy. I don't chance the rejection. Get it?"

Turly finally took his eyes off her and turned to me. The nervous-rabbit look returned. "What am I supposed to do if you get it started?"

"Dance, my boy, dance."

I walked away before he could object. I tried to be casual so I wouldn't scare off the prey. I did the cool, casual slide-up, met the blonde girl's eyes, and smiled.

"Hi, I'm Frank. What's your name?" I could hear my internal critic: *not a great start, blockhead.*

"I'm Judy." That was it. No help from the future suburban housewife.

"I, uh, saw you over here not dancing and—"

"I'd love to."

One of the other girls turned. I knew it by the way she moved and the satin black hair that flowed with her—the girl I had locked eyes with at the bar. I froze. I had to set things right before they got out of hand.

"I, uh, it's not for me. I mean, you're pretty and all, but it's for my friend over there."

I turned so as not to be hypnotized by the black-haired beauty. I pointed at Turly. He was doing his utmost to blow it by trying to be cool.

The black-haired beauty spoke. "What's wrong with him? You blow his nose too?"

Failure. I couldn't come up with anything. All my education had let me down. That first time we stood together, me staring and mute, has never left my memory. She had perfect proportions; each individual feature on her face had harmony. Heavy eyebrows against creamy skin accentuated those amazing dark-brown eyes that pulled me in and wouldn't let go. Her nose, small and a little broad, ended with a sweep. It highlighted provocative lips—red with lipstick—which invited me to kiss them, feel them wrap mine. I wanted to tell her all this in that instant, but all that came out was "Ehh."

"Well, he's not too bright, Judy, but he's cute. You could do worse."

"But I ..." I stammered and pointed to Turly.

The beauty spoke. "Don't be such a dull cat. You can't come over here, slay the dragon, woo the lady, then ride off on your horse and leave her with a poor substitute." She put Judy's hand in mine—she touched me. "Don't be like all the other creeps in here and cower from your responsibility as the male of our species. Dance."

Judy clamped down on my hand and dragged me toward the dance floor. I watched the dark beauty turn, laugh with her other friend, and walk away.

I stopped Judy in front of Turly.

"I'd like to dance with you, but I've got a bum leg. Korean War." I transferred her hand from mine to his. "He really wants to dance with you. He's a killer-diller on the dance floor."

Judy smiled at Turly, who looked panicked. "Okay," she said. She clamped on to his other hand and tugged him into the mass of twisting bodies.

I stayed and watched Turly's awkward moves for a while. Judy tried to give him twisting lessons, but Turly had two left feet. Ten minutes of that was all I could stand, so I went back up to the mezzanine level to one of the bars and took my place in line to get a drink. I noticed a few enticing girls but had no desire to go through the ritual of meeting them. Crowds like this made me want to go back to Sammy's and drink in secure solitude. The shuffle toward the bar brought me into the middle of the line.

I felt something warm in my stomach like the first sensation of desire. Then I heard her voice.

"Are you following me?"

The dark-haired beauty was standing in front of me. I can't say I actually froze, because everything turned all hot inside. "I, uh, no."

That was it; I couldn't come up with anything else.

"Like I said, cute, not too bright." With that, she turned back around.

I zipped around to face her. "Wait. I normally have a lot more to say. It's just, you know, you—"

"I leave you speechless? I've heard that one before. Nice try, Daddy-O."

"Okay, how's this? I rebel against the usual predatory male dating rituals that discourage my aspirations of finding original and creative ways to gain favor with the opposite sex."

She smiled. Good sign. "So," she said, "coming up behind me in the booze line is your way of being original?"

"No, it's not that. I don't dig the crowds, and believe it or not, this bar had the fewest people."

She looked me up and down. "You don't look much like the rock-and-roll type. You miss the turn for the coffee shop? Or are you just looking for a little skirt action?"

"Man, you don't let up, do you?"

"Call it my rebellion against predatory male dating rituals."

We had made our way to the front of the line. The bartender called out, "What'll you have, lady?"

The beauty turned her attention to him. "Bourbon and water, please."

"I'll buy that." I started digging for the money, knowing I didn't have enough.

"That's okay." She beat me to the cash, got her drink, and turned to me. "You see, my ritual is to test the male predator. Character and intelligence."

"Well, how did I do?"

"Pretty good." She smiled and her eyes conspired to hypnotize me. She turned and walked off.

"Wait."

Someone poked my arm, and I turned to see the bartender glaring at me. "You going to order or just block the rest of the customers?"

"Whiskey on the rocks." I turned back to look for the goddess, but she had disappeared.

I got my drink and went back out on the mezzanine dais. I scanned the ballroom, trying to spot her among the twisting bodies or along the perimeter. No sign. I descended the stairs and skirted the edge of the dance floor. On the far side, between the bobbing heads of the dancers, I spotted Arliss. His large frame and squaresville clothes made him easy to spot among the rock and rollers. He was in a huddle with Roach and George. They glanced toward something I couldn't see, then went back to talking. I descended the stairs and moved toward them. As I crossed the dancefloor, the band broke into a slow tune about twilight time, but I wasn't listening. I fixed on my friends through the swaying bodies and managed to reach the outer circle, when someone grabbed my arm. I whirled around expecting trouble. It was, just a different kind —the dark-haired beauty.

5

"Come on, let's dance," the sultry brunette said.

She looked so beautiful, her voice so soothing, that I couldn't resist and allowed her to pull me out onto the dance floor. The band started to play a slow number as we came together. I drew her in close and kept my left hand on her back to hide the clawed fingers. Her touch, her smell, gave me a flush of blood to the head and the groin. We didn't say a word as we started to dance, our cheeks nearly touching. I remember movies about two people coming together and everything else fading around them. I'd thought that was pretty corny until it happened to me. Better than three slugs of good whiskey and a Chesterfield. I started to get an erection and separated my waist from hers so she wouldn't feel the rock in my pants. I finally had to say something if for no other reason than to quell the royal flush.

"I'd decided to give up on you after our little talk at the bar. You turned me into a knuckle-dragging idiot."

"You didn't do so badly. I'm dancing with you, aren't I?"

"You know, speaking of male dating rituals, I'd decided to give up on women in general."

"Can you make one exception?"

I offered her my most charming smile. "I'm Frank."

"I'm Rebecca."

We went back to our tight embrace. "And to think," I said, "I was about to give all this up."

"It's like the stove thing," she said. When I gave her a puzzled look, she said, "You know, once burned, twice shy."

"So, have you stopped hanging around stovetops?"

I felt her nod in the crook of my shoulder.

"Then what are you dancing with me for?" I asked.

"Umm, practice."

"Practice for what?"

"Dancing." She shot me a coy smile. "And female dating rituals."

"That's hard without a partner."

"Well, here you are."

She held my eyes as we danced. I felt comfortable in her arms and didn't need to posture or prove anything ... or lie like I normally did. We forgot the usual get-to-know-you banter and communicated with our eyes.

"What's a beautiful girl like you doing without a boyfriend?"

"I don't remember saying I wasn't."

"But you didn't say you were either. That means I might have a chance at wooing you."

She pulled back and gave me a long look. I had said too much.

"You can't blame me for trying," I said. I silently cursed

myself for going from devout bachelor to drooling idiot in less than five minutes.

Rebecca looked over my shoulder. Her smile disappeared. Her dark eyes changed from seductive to something else. I didn't know her well enough to be sure, but I thought it might be fear. She made eye contact and nodded to someone behind me. I turned but saw no one.

I turned back to her. Her eyes locked onto mine, and she forced a smile. The smile couldn't hide her eyes, eyes that had flashed fear for a second and now looked simply sad. I couldn't resist and kissed her. Her arms wrapped around me and pulled me in tight. Once more, the world disappeared but for her lips, her breath, her body. We stayed that way, dancing as we kissed, until the song ended. She broke the embrace and opened her eyes. Took a deep breath and stepped back.

"I'd better go."

"What? That was the most incredible kiss I've ever had. I can't let you walk away now. What's wrong?"

"Nothing. I've just got to go, that's all."

"How do I get in touch with you?"

Rebecca pulled out a piece of paper and a pen and wrote something down. She stepped in close and stuffed it into my hand. "My home phone." She kissed me and started to leave. "Call me."

"What time do you get up in the morning?"

She hesitated. Something changed in her expression. It was too subtle to make out, though it would all made sense later when I learned who she was.

"Just kidding," I said. "I'll call you a little later. I'll at least wait till noon."

She started to say something, then thought better of it, just smiled, waved good-bye, and left. I watched her walk away through dancers now hopping to a fast number. Had she been summoned, or had I simply blown it?

I moved off the dance floor and scanned the room for the boys. On the steps leading up to the mezzanine, Rebecca's black hair stood out among the crowds. A tall, gray-haired guy in a snappy suit met her at the top. The odd thing was, he stared at me, not her. If he had some connection to Rebecca, he didn't show jealousy or contempt. He smiled at me as if he knew my whole story; I was the plaything that his mistress was allowed to flirt with, but not touch. He'd given her a ten-foot leash, then reeled her back in before it had gotten out of hand. The impression was only vague—he was too far away for anything more—but it left me cold. Rebecca moved toward the exit and out of sight. He took one more moment to eyeball me, then turned and followed her.

Just as she disappeared from view, a couple of girls off to my right screamed. Turly had just vomited on himself and the floor. He staggered in place, oblivious to the spectacle he'd created.

I forgot about Rebecca and the mysterious guy, and went to rescue Turly.

"You okay, Turl? You tilt any more and you'll fall over." He wasn't really listening. I waved a hand in front of his face. "Hey, you in there?"

His eyes rolled up. I pulled him into a dark corner and eased him onto a sofa.

"Damn, Turl, how much did you drink?"

His eyes focused on me for a second, then disappeared beneath his lids. He pulled a handkerchief out of his front pocket and wiped his mouth.

"You going to be okay?"

"I'm feeling a little better," he said, talking through the handkerchief.

"Puking can do that."

"Judy dumped me."

"You have to date before you can be dumped, and I don't think dancing constitutes dating."

"She dumped me."

"What did you drink?"

"Tequila. I saw George. She dumped me, so George gave me tequila and a pill."

"Turl, we should get you home. I'll go find the others."

"I can't have my old man see me like this. He'll knock my lights out."

I knew it. Now it was confirmed. "Then I'll take you to my place. Just stay here. I'll be back."

"I don't think I'm going anywhere."

I went in search of the boys. George was leaning against one of the columns in a corner far from the stage and the crowds. He was talking to a middle-aged man who kept peeking out from behind the column, scanning the room, then pulling his head back. George saw me and waved me over. I got closer and studied the older guy. He had that tall-man stoop, grayish pale skin, and wide eyes framed by dark circles. George handed him something I couldn't make out, and the older guy gave him a piece of paper and a set of keys. The guy stiffened when he saw me approach.

George said something to him. The wraith slunk along the shadows and slipped out of one of the emergency exits.

I stepped up to George. "Aren't you going to introduce me to your boyfriend?"

George just smiled and drew on his Camel. "Where've you been?"

"Rescuing Turly," I said. "He just puked his guts out. We should get him out of here."

"Not until we do our thing."

"What did you give him, anyway?"

"A couple of yellow jackets."

"What?"

"Tuinal, barbiturates. Look, he was getting in the way. He kept going on about a girl, so I gave him some tequila, but that just made it worse. I told him about the pills I had that would make him relax and have a good time."

"He's a rank amateur when it comes to things like that."

"He was all gung ho about taking them. I didn't make him do anything he didn't want to." George sighed with impatience at my continuing scowl. "Relax. Roach and Arliss took some. They're having a good ole time." He laughed, pushing smoke out of his nose. "They're flyin', man." He arced his cigarette through the air. The smoke left contrails in its wake. "Barbs and booze, nice combo. You should check it out."

George pointed to the dance floor, where the kids were in a slow dance. In the center, a small crowd of people had stopped dancing and were staring at something I couldn't see.

"I asked them to create a distraction," George said. "I didn't care what kind; they came up with how on their own."

I didn't have a good feeling about this. I wasn't in the mood to rescue anyone else.

George's smoke trail swept past my face. "You see that door up there?" He pointed with his cigarette to a dark corner on the mezzanine level above and to the left of the stage. Beside the door stood a couple of guys. Not your everyday bouncers; forty-somethings with well-tailored suits. The type that couldn't wait for somebody to give them trouble just so they could reward the moron with a bloody near-death experience.

"I'm hoping Roach and Arliss create enough of a ruckus to get those guys away from that door. When they do, you and I are going up and in."

"Are you crazy? What is this place? What's behind that door?"

George drew in another puff. His smile slightly crooked from the booze. "You going to work with me or not?"

"What kind of work are you into? There's no way I'll agree without knowing what it is."

"I'm in distribution. Recreational drugs."

The revelation didn't surprise me; I'd suspected he was into something shady, but I'd hoped it was the numbers racket or money scams, not drugs. Sure, I did drugs and had nothing against the guys I bought them from, but I never wanted to be one of those punks like Daniel who roamed the neighborhoods, selling reefer and pills to make quick money, then hiring guys like Mickey to beat some poor sucker who couldn't pay up.

I must have been broadcasting my ruminations because George said, "It's not what you think. I work for a cat that only handles large quantities for wealthy individuals. We're not going to be pounding the streets, selling to kids. In six weeks' time, you're going to walk away with a colossal amount of cash."

A storm of conflicting thoughts rolled through my head. "I'm with you tonight, but I don't know about the rest of it. I don't think I'm ready for something like that."

"You're ready. You just don't know it yet."

I looked toward the dance floor and the growing crowd of spectators. "If Roach and Arliss are that stewed on booze and pills, then they don't know what they're getting into. Those bouncers look like they'd be glad to spill a little blood."

"They're war veterans, man. It's the bouncers who should be worried."

He had a point, but I still felt I needed to warn them. I made my way onto the dance floor and squeezed through the crowd of onlookers. There they were, Roach and Arliss, dancing cheek to cheek as if they were in some bizarre Fred and Ginger musical. Even while dancing, Roach kept his cigarette holder wedged in his teeth, the cigarette smoke swirling as they moved. They swayed to the rhythm, eyes closed, smiles contented. This was too much. Living in San Francisco had exposed me to the homosexual crowd, but I wasn't ready for two of my pals in a slow dance. I couldn't leave them like that.

I tapped on Roach's shoulder and whispered, "Boys, time to break it up. We're splittin' this pop stand."

Roach opened one glassy eye. "You're ruining the moment, Frankie."

This called for a surefire tactic. I waved my drink under their noses. Both pairs of eyes popped open.

"We're flyin' fine, man," Roach said. "Go away. It's not what you think."

"I know what you're doing, and it's not a good idea," I said. "Look around you, guys. You've gathered an audience and it's close to turning into a lynch mob."

They broke their embrace and surveyed the crowd. Glassy-eyed and swaying, they both smiled and Roach bowed.

Arliss growled to the crowd, "What you all lookin' at?" He

was intimidating even in his stupor. No one offered a challenge.

Under his breath, Roach said to me, "Get out of here."

I backed away and rejoined George. He signaled me to follow him and we made our way up the stairs as casually as possible. I kept checking on Roach and Arliss as we climbed. The band started to play Elvis Presley's "Hound Dog." Roach and Arliss undulated to the music. Arliss sang at the top of his lungs. Roach hung all over him, giggling. Some of the onlookers started yelling at them, threatening them. What those two were doing put them in danger not just from the bouncers and the crowd, but also from the cops. The mayor had vowed to clean up the town, which meant busting up the gay bars and browbeating anyone careless enough to display any public homosexual "behavior."

Arliss and Roach finally attracted the attention of the two bouncers guarding the door. They blew past us, descended the stairs, and worked their way through the crowd. Two more came from the opposite direction.

"Come on, let's go," George said.

We stayed against the wall as we made our way across the mezzanine balcony and to the door. George thumbed through the key ring the pale-skinned guy had given him.

I looked down onto the dance floor. Roach had spotted the bouncers. He pulled his cigarette from its holder, stubbed it out, and pocketed the holder. He looked up at me, winked, and turned to meet the bouncers.

George hit me on the arm. "Stay here. I'll be just down the hall, so you give me a clear, loud signal if they start to come back."

I nodded and George moved into the darkened hallway.

Down on the dance floor, one bouncer grabbed Arliss's arm. Arliss spun around, elbowed him in the face. The bouncer recoiled. Two more bouncers jumped Arliss. Roach threw himself into the fray. Cheers and screams erupted from the crowd as my friends fought off the hired muscle. The army training came out in both of them. I'd only seen Roach move in composed, almost delicate movements. Now his arms pumped with the quickness of a boxer.

Arliss and Roach fought like crazy, but they were too numb to handle them all. The four bouncers, plus a few punks from the crowd, had them pinned. They dragged the pair toward a back exit, and my stomach clenched as a large group followed close behind. The band continued to play as the chaos grew. Then one of the bouncers stepped back inside, straightened his jacket, and walked toward the stairs.

"George! One of them's coming."

No response. I ran down the hallway to an open door. George was leaning over a desk, writing something down from an open notebook.

"George. They're coming back."

He slammed the notebook closed, jammed it into a top drawer, and locked the desk. We bolted for the exit and slipped out. We were in luck; the bouncer was standing on the stairs, looking toward the back exit. George locked the door, and we slid down the wall to the tandem bars before the guy turned and returned to his post by the door.

"Get Turly out of here," George said.

"What about you?"

"I'll take care of Roach and Arliss. Here." George handed me forty bucks. "I told you I'd slip you a few. And consider the loan paid off."

"I'll take the forty, but I pay off my loans."

"You'll pay it off if you come work for me."

I started to say something, but he stopped me. "Enough said."

We split up at the bottom of the stairs. People had begun dancing again, and as I wove through them I couldn't help but feel a thrill, an adrenaline rush. At the same time, I had the cold sweats, worrying we'd be discovered before I could get Turly out of there. It was a strange mix of excitement and fear; we'd gotten away with something dangerous.

Turly was on the sofa where I'd left him. I lifted him by his armpits and threw his arm around my shoulders. Four cops rushed past me, and I hoped they'd break up the fray before someone decided that the only good queer—or crippled jazz pianist, for that matter—was a dead one.

6

E verything that had happened the night before at the Aztec club kept playing out in my mind as I shuffled into the living room. I walked up to the couch where I had left Turly last night and shook his shoulder. "Hey. Prince of puke."

Nothing.

I put my foot on the sofa and created Turly's own personal earthquake. That got him to stir, proving he was still among the living. Obviously, I'd have to employ a more drastic measure. "Turl, your dad just called. You're late for work."

It was a lie, but it got him jumping up and flailing around like a beheaded chicken.

"Where am I? Where are my clothes?" When enough pain penetrated his pickled cortex, he stopped and held his head.

"You partied a little too hard last night, my boy."

"You've got to help me."

I found his pants and shirt, which was all I'd been willing to pull off him last night for the sake of comfort.

Turly jumped into his clothes and turned to me as he jammed his shirttail in. "Thanks for helping me out."

"You would have done the same. Right?"

Turly buttoned his shirt, straightened his tie, and retrieved his fedora. Gave me one of those disgusting salesmen winks. I shot him a bird. He laughed, but then something clicked. I could see it in his face, the mental preparation for the upcoming punishment and another boring, mindless workday.

He gave me another weak smile, said, "Abyssinia," then turned and left.

Turly slammed the door closed, the sound like an airtight seal, trapping me inside. I'd forgotten about my own plight while I'd watched Turly struggle with his. Everything about my loused-up life crept back. My brain triggered a desire for alcohol just to ease the pain. It took what willpower I had to push down the urge, and instead, I made some coffee and opened a can of beans. I dropped into a kitchen chair, and as I drank my coffee the memories of the previous night poured back through again: Rebecca, George, and the bedlam Roach and Arliss had created. Daylight's harsh realities were goading me toward accepting George's offer, but surely there had to be another way. Weak-kneed pseudo-intellectuals, no matter how desperate, usually avoided crime as an option, didn't they?

A pounding at the door brought me out of my daydreams. I forced myself to move and stood to one side of the door as if expecting bullets to rip through it at any moment. "Who is it?"

"You know who it is, man. Don't make me yell through the door."

If I'd had a fire escape, I'd have used it. I pulled together what resilience I had left to face him and opened the door.

"What know, man?"

Window light reflected off Daniel's glazed eyes in their

50

eternal doped-up state. He didn't wait for me to invite him in, just pushed past me and stood in the middle of the living room.

I went to close the door, then recoiled. Mickey pushed past me and entered. No baseball bat this time, meaning he might be carrying something worse. I retreated to the sink.

"What the hell is this?" My voice quivered.

Daniel sniffed the air. "Fine smell you got here. Eau de butt-crack, I believe."

"Yeah, morning to you too."

"I reserve cheery greetings for my paying customers."

"I paid you!"

I crossed the room, took a cigarette off the table, and lit up without facing Daniel. My hand shook in spite of my attempts to control it. Daniel came around to face me. He took the pack from me and helped himself to a cigarette.

"Sorry about the hand, man," Daniel said.

"You fucked up the only way I had to pay you off."

"You didn't pay me off. You paid the principal, not the interest. But I'm going to give you a break, since we messed you up. We'll call it two hundred even."

"Two hundred?"

"I'm being reasonable. But it's only going to go up if you keep jerking me around."

"I've got a line on some work," I said. "I can get it next week."

"A job that could make you that much dough in a week? You're stalling. But I tell you what, maybe we can make a deal. I'm gonna give you the week, 'cause I like you, buddy."

"Gee, that makes me all tingly."

He turned away and scanned the room. "What kind of work

you got lined up? You make that kind of dough, I might be interested too. I'm always looking to broaden my horizons."

He returned his glassy eyes to me and studied my face. I had to make up something quick. I usually wore my thoughts on my forehead like a bright, flashing sign.

"I don't have any plans."

"Bullshit. Don't piss on my leg and tell me it's rainin'."

"If I had some big plan, I wouldn't be living in hogsville and owing you money!"

"All right, all right, it's cool. I'll play along." He pulled out a reefer stick like a magician who'd revealed the very card you'd just plucked out of his deck. "A little going-away present."

"You're leaving town?"

"As soon as I tie up some loose ends. Like you paying your fucking debt."

"Who are you running from?"

Daniel didn't say anything. He strutted around the apartment and puffed away. "I'm headin' to Oregon." He grinned, his eyes on the imaginary road. "I've got a friend starting a giant pot farm up there. Can you imagine growing reefer like corn, instead of trying to sneak it across the border? It might be the next big thing, man. You see? I've got dreams too. And I feel bad that I had a hand in ruining yours. I do. I really do."

"I'm touched."

"No, really. Why don't you come along?" he said. "It'd be cool, smoking reefer, checking out the sights and the local poontang. I ain't gonna pay your way, but it won't cost much. Some gas money and food. What d'ya say?"

"You in some heat with the guys you work for?"

"Stop tryin' to pry into my affairs. Worry about your own

hide. My advice to you, get away from here for a while. Take it on the road. You don't know where you are until you can see where you've been, man."

In spite of my wanting to jam steel spikes into his eye sockets, the offer sounded attractive. Maybe that's what I needed. Go on a road trip like Kerouac … "Nah, I'd kill you before we reached Mendocino."

He shrugged. "Suit yourself." Ground out his cigarette. "I've got to agitate the gravel."

He hoisted his pants, but they never quite made it up to his big belly. The gesture looked so comical that I burst out laughing, and he joined me even though he couldn't have known what I'd found so funny. At the kitchen table, he picked up one of my unpaid bills, ripped off a corner of the envelope, wrote down his phone number, and gave it to me.

"I don't give this out to just anybody, so don't pass it around. You keep this and if you want to come along, you let me know. I think you and I could be good pals." He nodded at Mickey.

Mickey swung an invisible bat and made a thwacking sound. He grinned and left.

Daniel opened the door, then hesitated. "Remember. Next Friday. Get me the dough or next time Mickey gets to play ball. You dig?" He winked and shut the door.

I staggered backward and dropped into a chair. My chest and throat tightened, desperation and loneliness welling up. I searched for any whiskey bottles I might have discarded without draining. I located one and sucked the last few drops, with nothing to do but sit, brood, and spin a record. But even Charlie Parker couldn't lighten my mood. I'd already hocked the television and radio, so the only connection to the outside world was the telephone. It sat there, black and mute, taunting me with its silence. What a pointless thing to have in my apartment. It merely amplified my sense of alienation and isolation. Rage and depression surfaced, and I threw the empty whiskey bottle against the wall. It smashed into pieces, prompting the upstairs neighbor to stomp on the floor.

I picked up the phone and dialed.

THE CROWDS AND THE SMOKE INSIDE SAMMY'S WERE AS THICK as the San Francisco fog. There was just enough room at the bar to squeeze in sideways. Sammy spotted me and winked. He always knew what I wanted and came over with the double whiskey.

"How's it hangin', Frankie?"

"Oh, you know. Same old."

"You're usually here a lot earlier." He put the glass down in front of me. "Thought I'd give you one of these. I haven't got a funnel."

Sammy laughed at his own ribbing, winked, and moved on to help someone else. This was obviously Screw-with-Frank day. I turned away from the bar and scanned the room while sucking down the cheap call-brand whiskey. The same jazz trio played some number I didn't know. The bass player walked his fingers up and down the fingerboard and a few couples did some crazy dance between the tables. Back in a dark corner, I spied George sitting in a booth with a girl. I couldn't see her face, just straight blonde hair that hung to her shoulders, and her arms, which extended across the table, holding his hands. George saw me, pulled away, and motioned me over.

As I neared the table, I got a better look at the girl. She had a blonde's complexion— delicate porcelain skin dotted with freckles, the veins just visible beneath bright blue eyes. She had an open face, high cheekbones, and full lips that would make for the most beautiful and endearing smile. A robin's-egg-blue dress and white cardigan sweater hugged her lithe and graceful form.

George got up and rubbed my hair, showing me who was in charge. With him, I didn't mind.

"Park yourself," he said. "Move over, honey, and let the boy sit."

She scooted over. Her eyes caught mine. They were soft, unassuming, vulnerable. A natural beauty. Definitely not one of George's usual big-breasted bimbos.

"I don't want to interrupt," I said.

"Shut up and sit down," George said. "Marjorie doesn't mind."

Marjorie shot him a look, then all smiles for me. "Come sit next to me. George doesn't mind." She shot him another look.

I tried suave, but it turned out sophomoric. "I thought you were Ingrid Bergman for a minute."

She laughed with a shy, self-conscious lilt. "Really? You think so? When did you last have your eyesight checked?"

I liked her polite teasing. "Well, it was more from the back, I guess."

"Yeah, I get that all the time. 'Your back looks just like Ingrid Bergman's.'"

"Touché. But you kind of look like her from the front too."

"Stop. You're just digging a deeper hole." She looked at me a little closer. "You do look familiar, though."

We introduced ourselves, and George added, "Frankie went to San Francisco State too."

"You went to State?" I asked her.

"That's where George and I first met," she said. "I was two years behind him."

"So was I. Maybe we were in some of the same classes."

"Maybe." She scanned my face once more as if searching her memory. The way she looked at me—man, oh, man, it made me want to grab her hand and take her away, rescue her from George, the lady slayer. "I was an English lit major," she said.

"I spent most of my time in the creative arts building," I said. "Maybe we just passed each other on the quad. All that time I spent at State looking for beautiful women and I didn't notice you?"

We smiled at each other, and longer than George liked.

"Now Frankie spends most of his time here at Sammy's," he said loudly. "And by this time, he's a little further along in his drinking."

Definitely my day for character assassination. I let my hormonal rush blunt the sting. She had some kind of magnetism. I swear women must give off some scent that modern man has lost the ability to define. This very ripe plum was a prime example of Mother Nature's drive to procreate, transforming even intellectual snobs like me into drooling, throbbing, sperm donors.

"Frankie!" George snapped me out of it, gave me that *she's mine* look. "You don't seem so good. You okay?"

"I'm fine." At least I wanted to be for Marjorie.

"You on some kind of diet?"

"Yeah, liquid diet," I said.

Marjorie laughed. Her intention was friendly, but behind it I saw a flash of pity.

"No kidding," George said. "You're really skinny. You're starting to look like one of those bums on the street."

"I'm not far from it," I said, and took a gulp of whiskey. I slumped back, feeling small. Time for a cigarette.

George studied me a moment. "Marjorie, baby, could you go powder your nose or something?"

Her eyes widened at his callous request. "I don't need to."

"Just do it, would you? Frankie and me have got some man-to-man stuff."

Marjorie grabbed her purse and shot George another look. She touched my arm and leaned into me. "Excuse me. I might as well go to the bathroom. Man-to-man stuff usually makes me want to gag anyway."

I let her out and settled back down.

George watched her go and shook his head. "You're looking bad, my cat."

"Feeling bad, my cat."

George gave me that amused grin of his. "So, you called and we met. What's up?"

He was done pitching his idea; it was now up to me. Everything had been moving toward this point. Fate had driven me there, and I was just a passenger along for the ride. An inner voice tugged, mumbling some kind of warning, only I didn't listen. I heard the tumblers falling into place.

"I'm joining up."

"Cool, Daddy-O. I have to make a couple of calls and set up a meeting with my contacts. Then we can do this thing." George dropped the hepcat tone. "I'm glad you said yes, buddy. This is gonna be good."

"Yeah." That little bit of sincerity made me feel like I'd done the right thing.

"I'll call you for the time and place."

I felt a rush of relief and anticipation. Working with George and making some quick dough drowned out any apprehension about my newfound career.

"You haven't asked about Roach and Arliss yet," he said.

"Are they still in jail?"

He nodded. "They got slapped with disturbing the peace and a drunk and disorderly rap."

"What was that all about last night?"

"Remind me to tell you sometime, but not now and not here." George lit a cigarette and took a swig of his wine. "The only hitch was that Roach got knifed."

"What? Is he all right?"

"He wasn't cut too bad. Some guy tried to stab him, but he moved at the last second. He's got a pretty deep slash from here to here." He drew a five-inch cut from breastbone to armpit with a finger. "The cops took him to the hospital, then threw his ass in the joint with Arliss. I'm going to bail them out tomorrow."

"I'm going to go see them."

"Forget it. Not now. There's been some buzz about last night, and I don't want you wandering around near any jails now that you're working for me. I want you to keep a low profile. Go home. Get some rest or something. You can see them in a couple of days. I'll take care of them. You got that?"

"Whatever you say, George. I don't get it, but I got it."

He leaned back, a signal that business was over, and waved Marjorie back to the table. As she neared, the hepcat returned. "Have another glass of that turpentine and keep your tonsils wet. It's on me." Which in George-speak meant it was time for me to go. I took the last gulp of my drink and made a move to leave.

Marjorie stopped me with another touch on the arm. "I hope I catch you sometime."

"Uh, yeah, I'd like that."

"Margie," George said, and she turned obediently back to him. He then dismissed me with a wink.

I turned and navigated the crowd, mulling over the events that had added up to one crazy day and my recent commitment to something that would surely land me in prison or a shallow grave.

7

I sweated it out in my apartment the next couple of days. The weather had turned hot and the air was still and dry. I'd tried to call George a few times when the tension got too much. He never answered. I tried Rebecca too, but the same thing. The wait became a blur of frustrated daydreams.

I kept thinking about George and me breaking and entering an office, especially in a place that had felt less like a nightclub and more like gangland central. Any movement in the stairway prompted me to rush to the door and look out the peephole, but other than a neighbor passing in the hallway or the landlord harassing me for the rent, I was left alone. Except for a few trips to buy food, cigarettes, and booze, I stayed put, too afraid to leave in case George called. By the end of the second day, the claustrophobia of the trash heap I was living in was strangling me. Internal voices hounded me until I felt like a burned-out wreck with a cork brain and a volcanic stomach.

Finally, at noon on the third day, George called. I answered with a surly hello.

61

"Get your ass over to Sammy's as soon as you can," he said. "We're waiting."

Rotting in my apartment had dulled my mind. As though I were waking up from a deep sleep, George's words took their time to reach my brain.

"You sober? 'Cause I want you sober for this."

"Yeah, sure, George. I've been waiting for you to call."

"Good. You're meeting the guy I work for, so I need you sharp."

He hung up. I shuffled into the bathroom and checked my reflection. Just as I'd expected: something resembling a two-day-old corpse stared back at me. I did what I could to clean up, then made my way over to Sammy's.

GEORGE SAT AT OUR USUAL TABLE WITH A COUPLE OF GUYS I didn't know. One was a lanky, baby-faced kid with a crew cut and a black leather jacket two sizes too small. The other guy was in his late thirties. Short, muscular body, handsome face, sandy-brown hair, and bushy eyebrows that framed intense green eyes. His square jaw formed a point that was emphasized when he tilted his head back slightly, as if aiming a weapon. He rolled a toothpick around his thin lips—a ritual, I figured, given the small pile of mangled picks next to him.

George stood and waved me forward. "Frankie, come on over and meet some friends." Being the host of this little gathering, he took it upon himself to do the introductions. "This is Paul."

The lanky kid stood and shook my hand eagerly. "How's it hangin'?"

George pointed to the tough guy, who hadn't moved. "And this is Vincent."

I had to bend over to shake his hand. He said nothing. I sat, and we commenced with the masculine ritual of staring at each other.

"You want something to drink?" George asked.

"If you're buying," I said. "I'm clean out."

George tried to look cool, but his eyes danced in their sockets. He yelled to Uncle Willie, who was taking a break from his constant bar-wiping. "Willie, another beer."

Willie wasn't about to move from his stool. "Do I look like a fucking waitress?"

Vincent motioned to Paul to get the beer, and resumed staring, the toothpick still rolling around in his mouth. "What can we do for you?"

This was getting stranger by the moment, but I wanted the job—whatever it was. "Well, I told George I was hoping to hook up with some work."

"You know what kind of work it is?" Vincent asked.

"Something to do with distribution and recreation."

"How do you know you want this kind of gig?"

I looked to George for a clue as to why I was getting the oral exam. He avoided my eyes, and I imagined him praying I didn't spout some blundering error or dangerous insult.

"I trust George. I figured if he's into it, then it's got to be solid."

I chanced a look at George to see if he'd broken out in a sweat from my answer. He was smiling. Okay, so far, so good.

Paul returned with four beers. I liked Paul. He seemed like the good kid enlisted from the family ranks who was still just happy to be there.

"He's good for it, Vincent," George said. "I've known him a long time, and he won't let you down."

Vincent, reposed in a posture of cool, eyeballed me. I summoned all my willpower and held his gaze. This staring contest was the most crucial step in the exam, and if I wavered or showed fear, I was out. My dad and my older brother had possessed this same habit of playing chicken with their gaze; I'd had years of practice. Just forget they were human eyes for a moment. Study the shape, the color; count the blinks. Vincent had amazing eyes, his irises stars of dark green. Each arm of the star folded in upon itself, forming creases and holes in a complex pattern like a forest of sea kelp. Spikes of brown shot through the green like spokes of a wheel. Finally, he took a gulp of beer and leaned forward, signaling the end of the exam.

"Okay, we're looking for some new blood. George, you sure you can vouch for this guy? He's stand-up?"

George looked at me, and said, "I vouch for him."

Vincent rose and Paul followed.

"All right, Georgie, you get him up to speed, and we'll see how he does."

George shook his hand. "You got it, Vincent. Thanks."

I thought I better copy George and shook his hand. "Yeah, thanks a lot."

Vincent squeezed my hand to make a point. "Don't fuck it up."

He walked out, shadowed by Paul.

George turned to me as soon as they'd stepped out the door and gave me a Cheshire cat smile. "Let's go for a ride."

∽

RIDING AROUND WITH GEORGE IN A '42 BLACK BUICK reminded me of college days. Glenn Miller was on the radio and we were tapping out the beat.

"What are you doing driving around in this old clunker?" I asked. "You can't be picking up chicks in this thing."

"You have to keep a low profile in our line of work. Nothing that will attract attention."

"Okay, now that you brought it up, exactly what kind of recreational distribution are we in?"

He offered a cryptic smile. "Grab that briefcase in the backseat."

I put it on my lap.

"Open it."

I popped the latches and lifted the lid. Inside were neatly wrapped oblong and triangular-shaped packets in white butcher's paper. That could mean only one of two things. I slammed the lid and looked around to see if anyone had noticed me.

"This what I think it is?"

"Eighty percent pure heroin, baby."

I felt a cold sweat coming on. I tossed the briefcase in the back and wiped my hands on my pants legs.

"It's a small run this time. Worth about ten thou."

"What if we get in a car accident?"

"Then you better hope it's fatal, 'cause we lose this and we'll be dead anyway."

I had heard enough stories and seen enough movies to feel sure he was right.

"You getting cold feet?" George asked.

It was too late to say yes. "Nah."

"Good, because you're in it, buddy. You stay in and you do

exactly what you're told. And you don't say anything to anyone about this."

"You got it." My gut knew I was stepping in something rotten, but desperation forced me to ignore it.

"You ever do that stuff?" I asked.

"Sure, it's cool. I'm not an addict or anything. It takes more than you think to get hooked. You?"

"No. I'm happy with the booze and the Jane. I never pegged you for a heroin dealer."

George waved his hand, warding off the curse of that word. "Don't ever use that term. I'm a distributor. I don't sell. I'm paid to distribute."

"What's the difference between what you're doing and what I'm supposed to do?"

"I take from the big pile and distribute it into little piles, then you'll take them to the various points of sale. They like couriers with no criminal associations and no police record. You get caught, there's no trace back to them."

"Vincent," I said.

George nodded. He took a left on Church Street, and said, "Butt me." I gave him a cigarette and we lit up. "It's a busy route. Before I got into this, I never knew there was so much H going around." George lowered his voice as if the car were bugged. "I'm working on an angle right now that could really set us up. You stick with me, and we'll be sneezing C-notes."

I let that idea diffuse. Then I hit him with another question. "How did you get into the, uh, distributing business?"

"Sort of like you. I have a few connections and I got recruited."

I opened my mouth to ask another question. George waved

his free hand again. "No more questions, okay? You pay attention, use your brains, and you'll do fine."

We drove silently for a while and crossed over into Noe Valley. A small ridge at Twenty-second Street separated this part of town from the bustle of the rest of the city. The working-class neighborhoods and the suburban atmosphere were not my idea of the heroin-infested flophouses where I'd been expecting us to conduct our transactions. George parked in front of a small library.

"Catching up on your reading?" I asked.

"This is our first stop."

"Librarian junkie or what?"

"Would you quit asking so many goddamned questions? Get the briefcase and pop the lid."

I did what he asked. He reached under his seat and pulled out a folded brown paper sack. He put a packet inside, rolled up the top, and stapled what appeared to be a diner receipt to the top. He handed the sack to me.

"Now roll up your jacket sleeves. That's the sign you're the courier."

I had a hard time rolling up the right sleeve with my dead fingers. My heart started to pound. He must have noticed my nervousness.

"It's simple. Just walk into the library like you're delivering a lunch."

"How am I going to find this contact? Tell me he's not thirteen and in the kids' section."

"The contact will find you. That's what the sleeves are all about. Now get your ass in there and make sure they pay you."

I got out and tried to look cool as I strode toward the library, fighting coat sleeves that refused to stay up. The closer

I got to the door, the harder my heart pounded. I flinched at every shadow, expecting a cop to jump out any minute and handcuff me.

I stopped inside the doors and looked for anyone who would fit my image of a heroin dealer. A handful of people wandered among the rows of books, a middle-aged lady librarian stood at the counter in the center of the room, and another ancient woman shelved books. Two college-aged kids sat at a desk studying, and a *Better Homes and Gardens* house-wife browsed the fiction section. The librarian glanced up at me and then went back to whatever she was doing. I figured I'd better scan the books before she got too suspicious. Off to my left, I noticed a group of parallel shelves that would conceal me while I waited for contact. I sauntered over and ducked in between the shelves, pulling at my sleeves and wiping the sweat off my brow.

I checked out a couple of titles, feigning interest. I was in the religious section: *Twelve Ways to Teach Your Children About Christ* and *Christianity Today*. It was the kind of stuff my mother had spoon-fed me when I was still young enough to believe this philosophical propaganda. I turned and nearly bumped into the housewife.

"What are you doing hiding back here?" she said. "I've been looking for you."

She pointed to the sack in my hooked left hand. "Are they using cripples these days? That's my sandwich."

I hoped she wasn't truly expecting a sandwich, and when she held out a wad of fifties, I knew it. I offered her the sack. She snatched it out of my hand and replaced it with the bills as fast as a gunfighter. Added a condescending shake of her head for good measure. Her serious expression transformed back into happy housewife, and she turned and walked away.

I hightailed it out of there.

George got a big laugh out of my story. It was so genuine that it prompted me to join in. I immediately became more relaxed in his confident presence.

We made several deliveries that afternoon. Nothing quite as ironic as the library, but all stranger than what I'd expected. I'd seen movies where the drug dealer would show up at some hophead party, "Negro" jazz club, or Italian restaurant with the Mafia types. But not us. We'd been to an auto shop, a deli, a Laundromat, and even a dress shop. I always did the same thing—rolled-up sleeves and the lunch sack. It all went smoothly, and with each delivery I gained confidence.

Pity it wouldn't last.

8

I arrived back at my apartment that evening and the full force of my pathetic surroundings crashed into me. Gone was the high from riding around with George and actually doing something for a change. I was still penniless and now in a dangerous game. What had felt like an improvement in my life now seemed like an insane idea. What had I said yes to?

The phone rang. As little as the telephone rang in the last six months, it had apparently decided to make up for lost time. I finally pulled myself away from the window and answered.

"Why didn't you call me back?" Rebecca said.

With my temper still in high gear, the question made me sore, even if it was Rebecca. "I got buried in other things."

"Sounds like a brush-off to me. Is that what this is? Because I'd rather you be direct and just say it."

I calmed myself down before I blew it. "I tried you a couple of times. Then I got tired of trying." I wasn't doing too well.

"You're not your eloquent self. I guess I called at a bad time. Call me later if you want."

"Wait, wait. I'm sorry. I don't want you to get that idea. It's just, well, I'm broke and going a little crazy in this apartment." I took a deep breath and blurted out what I thought would be the death knell for any future relationship with the dark-haired beauty. "I can't afford to take you out."

"You guys are all alike. You think you have to spend money in order to get a girl to like you. Then once you spend the money, you think the girl owes you."

"Most of the girls I've met were like that."

"And you a college man," she said. "Shame on you." She paused, presumably for effect, then said, "Listen, there's a good jazz band and a poetry reading tonight at Chump Change. I thought you'd like to come. It's free, and I'll buy you a drink. That is, if you can forget your male morals for an evening."

"You have to promise me that I get to buy you drinks next time."

"You mean when you find a suitable job that allows you to continue the fine lifestyle you currently enjoy?" She laughed, signaling it was said in jest, but it still cut to the bone. "Meet me in front of Chump Change at nine," she said. "Okay?"

"You'll know it's me 'cause I'll be wearing the sunglasses and holding the tin cup," I said.

"Good, that's more the Frank I remember," she said, followed by a deep, sexy "Bye." She hung up.

Even from manure doth the flower grow.

CHUMP CHANGE WAS ON GRANT AVENUE NEAR BROADWAY, IN the middle of a row of nondescript storefronts. Everyone in the know knew where it was so the proprietor had found no reason to put up anything more than a small sign. The place was used for a bunch of different things: poetry, music, political stuff. A crowd had already gathered out front, some going in, others hanging outside talking and smoking. I couldn't see Rebecca, so I waited against a wall.

A cigarette later, a cab pulled up and she stepped out. She looked incredible with her black hair, dark eyes, and tight black dress that showed off her hourglass figure. She strutted up and kissed me.

"You look beautiful," I said.

"Thanks. You too." She gave me a smile that got my blood rushing. "Come on, let's go in."

We entered and passed through a purple velvet curtain. The place was dark except for a small stage. Primitive tables crowded the floor. Rows of chairs were lined up behind for those coming only for the poetry later in the evening.

"You don't know how much I needed this," I said.

"Things that bad?"

"This is that good."

I went to claim a table while Rebecca got the drinks. I ordered a whiskey and soda—a little cultural elevation from taking slugs directly from the bottle. I got one of the last tables, sat down, and soaked in the music. The band was playing a jazzed-up version of "Moonlight in Vermont." I drummed the table to the beat.

Rebecca returned with the drinks. She had a martini. I knew it would be her drink.

"Looks like you started the party without me," she said.

"I'm rolling with the sounds, baby."

That elicited a smile as she sat next to me. Her arm brushed mine. I reached for her hand, but she reached for her drink. She noticed my crooked fingers while I drummed the table but didn't say anything. I stopped drumming and wondered what I would tell her about how it had happened. She took a sip and watched the musicians while I studied her face, unsure about her silence.

"You got quiet all of a sudden," she said.

"I was trying to read you."

"Don't waste your time. I'm unreadable."

"No one is unreadable. Some just take longer than others."

"So?"

"Not enough time. But, if I had to guess, something's on your mind."

Rebecca looked away and lit a cigarette. I let her take her time with a response.

Finally, she said, "I was just wondering if I'm doing the right thing."

"Seeing me, you mean?"

"It's more complicated than that."

"You dating someone else? Because I'd understand. A beautiful woman like you ..."

"Stop saying that."

"What, that you're beautiful?"

"Yes, it's getting redundant."

"I haven't been accused of redundancy in a while."

"Then stop saying the same things."

"You really don't let up. More rebellion against dating rituals?"

"This isn't a date."

"Then what do you call it? Two good-looking people out on the town, music, drinks ... there're even candles on the tables. I can't stop thinking about that kiss at the Aztec. Man, those lips of yours."

I thought she was going to fall into my arms the way she was leaning into me. All the combativeness in her face melted away. Her eyes and lips looked ready to replay that incredible kiss.

She backed away and fidgeted with the collar of her dress. "I'm sorry. Maybe this wasn't a good idea."

She started to get up. I put my hand on her arm and rose with her. Before she could do anything else, I kissed her deeply. She returned the kiss and we pulled each other in tight, our hips pushing hard. A couple of people applauded and somebody yelled "whew." She broke our kiss, though she kept her face close to mine, her breathing coming hard. Then she put her hands on my chest and gently pushed us apart.

"Stay," I said. "I won't put any pressure on you. Just enjoy. Be here with me right now and don't think about anything else. Okay?"

She looked at me as if she'd been struck, as if this hadn't been part of her plan. I saw the lines in her forehead relax and we sat back down.

"You're just getting more wonderful by the moment," she said, and leaned in once more. "Let's do that again."

I felt my blood rush as our lips wrapped and pulled. The tips of our tongues met and played. We unlocked when the music stopped. It was just the two of us, the table, the room. The people disappeared. We stared at each other and kissed again when a new song began, opening our mouths wide and driving our lips together. The slow, throaty tones of the saxophone urged us to sink deeper into each other's embrace. Rebecca pushed away with her arms even as her lips struggled to remain against mine. She finally broke the kiss. Something in her eyes told me she was fighting some kind of internal battle.

"It's okay," I said. "Take your time."

She sipped her drink. I did the same and watched her. I knew not to press her; I was having too good a time.

Rebecca put her drink down and avoided my eyes. "You're some kind of kisser. You practice a lot or is it a natural talent?"

"Natural, I guess. Not very much practice. It's you—your lips inspire mine."

She leaned in closer, and I could smell her perfume and sweet warm breath. "You're not the same guy I talked to on the phone."

"I was having a little attitude problem when you called. All I wanted to do was get drunk. But that's old news. Stupid and pointless now that I'm here with you."

She sat back and studied her hands. Her expression turned serious. "So, what do you want out of life?"

I was a little surprised by the quick turn. "Well, I played the piano until this." I held up my hand.

"I wanted to ask you how that happened."

"A baseball incident."

I could tell she didn't believe me, but she let it drop.

"I wanted to compose music, but I'm not good enough to do that without ten working fingers."

"Is it permanent?"

"I don't know."

She stroked my cheek. I pulled back.

"I didn't tell you this for sympathy," I said.

"Sensitive, aren't you?"

"Yeah, when it comes to my dreams of a career."

"Well, what about in general? A career's one thing, but how about relationships, maybe getting married and stuff like that?"

"You're moving a little fast for me."

"That's not what I meant." She played with her napkin. "I'm asking for me too. I'm twenty-six, twenty-seven in a month. Thirty is right around the corner and I feel stuck. Like everything is already set for me, and I think ..." She'd shredded the napkin.

I waited for her to finish, but she didn't. I could see the process she was going through to push it all away.

She tossed the pieces up in the air, laughed, and turned back to me. "Forget it. I don't know what I was going to say. I guess part of it is that I can relax with you." She took another moment to think. "And that's why I'd better go."

She made a stronger move to leave and was quick on her feet. I stood, and I knew I couldn't stop her this time.

"You're a wonderful guy." She stepped in and spoke softly in my ear. "You know, I was going to come here tonight to use you, then lose you. I changed my mind." She kissed me quickly, then let out a little moan. "Such a good kisser. Good night."

She pulled back and her eyes had that expression of someone saying good-bye for the last time. She turned and walked away.

I didn't chase after her, not only because I knew it wouldn't do any good, but also from the shock of this strange turn of events. I sat down and grabbed my drink. Took a gulp, and lowered the glass, concentrating on the ice as it shifted and sparkled.

It was either that or throw it across the room.

9

R oach's apartment was on Page Street in the Haight, another area of town where the downtrodden and the bohemian youth cohabited. Some said it was past its prime; others claimed it was up-and-coming: Salvation Army shelters, obscure coffee houses, second-hand clothing stores, and used bookstores shared the area with dilapidated apartment buildings.

Rotten wood, rusted ornamental iron, and imbued with the stench of human waste best described Roach's building. The old wooden structure hadn't seen a coat of paint since the American Revolution. To live here willingly demanded a true dedication to bohemian values. I wasn't close to that kind of commitment.

I found Roach's button, pushed, and waited a long time. I imagined one of them hobbling to answer.

"Yeah?" Arliss said.

"It's me. Frank."

The front door lock buzzed open—not that a lock would have done any good, as the whole doorframe looked like it might come off any minute. I had to feel for the stairs in the dark hallway. Music played somewhere, angry voices echoed in the stairway, all permeated by a miasma of rot, urine, and cooking food.

I reached the third floor; 303 was already open. I stepped in and closed the door. I'd been there before, but the neatness always amazed me. Everything was in place, comfortably decorated. Shelves were laden with books, and art posters lined the age-tinted walls. Cigarette smoke, heavy even by my excessive standards, hung like a thick ether.

"Roach? Arliss?"

Arliss said, "In here."

I figured that meant the bedroom, the only other room in the apartment. Roach lay on the bed, wearing only pajama bottoms. A wrapped bandage covered most of his chest. His knuckles, right eye, and chin sported bruises.

Arliss sat beside him. Stitches ran from midforehead into his hairline, but he looked in better shape than Roach. Arliss's knuckles were swollen and purple as well.

Neither said a word. I grabbed a chair and sat on the other side of Roach's bed.

"How you doing?" I asked.

Roach looked at me with his good eye.

Arliss answered for him. "He's all right. Now. Where'd you go? We could've used a hand."

I felt a flush of guilt. "I tried to get you guys out of there."

"Yeah, you tried real hard," Arliss said.

"What was I supposed to do with one lame hand?"

"Arly," Roach said softly. Arliss's expression became tender.

"George said you guys were creating a distraction so he and I could check out something on the second floor."

"Was it worth what we had to go through?" Arliss asked.

"Haven't got a clue. He wrote something down in an office and then we split up. He told me to take care of Turly, said he would help you guys."

Something private passed between them.

"Well, he didn't show up," Roach said.

"We were putting up a pretty good fight out in the alley until some punk slashed Roach," Arliss said.

He was about to say something else but Roach put up his hand. "It's cool," Roach said. He gave me a weak smile. "We saw you dancing with some girl that night. You meet someone?"

"Yeah, she's great."

"Dig it, man." He lifted his hand and shook mine.

That was why I liked Roach no matter what. He could be happy for me even in his train-wreck condition.

"What did the doctor say?" I asked.

"The usual: bed rest, and they'll take the stitches out next week. I've got a good slash, but nothing vital got cut, so they patched me up. A mild concussion and what you see before you. Nothing permanent. I'll be okay."

I turned to Arliss. "What about you, Bluto?"

Arliss, ever eloquent, said, "I'm okay."

"Yeah? Nice hairline," I said.

"Funny, man."

Roach laughed, then winced. "We need a little humor. Arly's been brooding all day."

"I scraped enough change together to get this on the way over here," I said, and pulled out a bottle of bourbon.

I took a swig and passed it to Roach. He tried to lift his arm but winced again. Arliss took the bottle and lifted Roach's head enough that he could take a drink. For such a big lug, he was playing a good Florence Nightingale.

We sat in silence for a while and passed the bottle around. Arliss lit a cigarette, placed it in Roach's cigarette holder and gave it to him.

"I always wanted to ask you how you got that habit," I said to Roach.

He took a loving draw before answering. "The army beats individuality out of you. By the time I got out of the service, I was so sick of it that I started searching for something that would define my uniqueness. I saw a movie—I don't remember which one now—where this guy, English, I think, was puffing away on his cigarette holder, spouting off something very intellectual. I was so impressed with that guy, I picked up the habit. It makes me feel so …"

"Kooky?" Arliss answered for him.

"That's a good one, Arly," Roach said. "I'll remember that. Kooky."

"He's kooky now," Arliss said, "but when he was in the service, he was real gung ho."

"You wanted to be a war hero?" I said. "I can't imagine that."

"I was twenty and still wet behind the ears," Roach said.

"He was rated expert marksman," Arliss said, like a proud younger brother, or lover.

I tried to imagine Roach in a uniform. "You guys never talk about it much."

"I went in wanting to fight and learned to hate it. Arly went in as a wide-eyed plow jockey and learned to love it."

"I didn't learn to love it," Arliss said. "I saw too much over there to say that. It's just that for the first time, I was doin' something meaningful."

"Meaningful?" I asked.

"You wouldn't know about such things, college fart. I'm talking about being challenged beyond your limits and surviving. Protecting your buddies and going all the way with them."

Roach snickered. "All the way."

"You know what I mean," Arliss said.

This was a whole new perspective on my friends, and I was dying to hear everything. "So you saw some action?"

"Yeah, but I don't like to talk about it," Roach said. "I'm not ashamed of what I did. In the middle of that shit, you see and do things you'd never dream of any other time. At one point I'd had enough. All I saw were young guys on both sides being butchered for all the fucking politicians. I never saw any goddamned congressman or general out there in the field. I hate them all. The only thing that kept me together was my buddies. That's all that mattered. The love I felt for all those guys goes beyond what I ever imagined."

"You survived," I said to Roach. "How'd you get out of it?"

"I got wounded by a shell. Shrapnel in my back, my legs. I couldn't hear for the ringing in my ears. I was stunned, couldn't move. Just felt all the hot fragments slowly burning into my flesh. I still can't see perfectly out of my right eye. It was great. I recommend it for everyone." Roach rolled onto his back and stared at the ceiling.

I passed Arliss the bottle. He looked mellow enough to talk to in some reasonable fashion. "And you, Arliss? What about you?"

"You know, talking to you about it is a waste of time. You weren't there, so you'll never understand."

He obviously wasn't mellow enough. "That's cool. I can dig it." I decided to change the subject. "I signed on with George."

"Cool, man," Roach said.

"What's so goddamned important that he has to keep us in the dark?" Arliss said.

George had instructed me not to say anything, but I needed to talk to somebody about it. "He's running smack for some serious-looking guys."

"Yeah, so?"

"So? You knew that?"

"He didn't come out and tell me," Roach said. "I guessed that's what he was doing, because he wanted us to scare up our old contacts. Arly and I had a little reefer and speed business at the army and navy bases back in '54, '55, until I got popped for possession. That's where I met George."

The revelation shocked me. It explained George's disappearance, but I'd never imagined him in prison. "He got busted?"

"Marijuana possession. Small amount, first offense, so neither of us got much time. But during his stretch, something happened in there that really messed with his mind. He's never told me what. I got out before he did, but we hooked up later. That's about the time he introduced me to you."

My mouth must have been hanging open because Arliss said, "What's with the face?"

"No big deal," Roach said. "Robert Mitchum got busted. And Neal Cassady's in San Quentin as we speak. You didn't know anything about George?"

All I could do was shake my head. My muteness was not from the shock; my mind was otherwise occupied by a whirl of thoughts. That explained George's secrecy, a simmering agitation he kept buried under a surface of cool. But what worried me most was that he was living on a knife's edge to compensate for whatever had happened to him in prison, and we were blithely following him over that edge.

10

The next couple of days passed without a hitch. George and I were getting a good routine down, and the more relaxed I became, the more I was able to look past my apprehensions. I kept putting off asking George about his prison experience. I don't know if I was waiting for the right moment or just being a coward. He spotted me enough dough to get some food and smokes, which put me in a better place, and I felt pretty good about myself. Rebecca never left my mind, but the boost to my ego had given me the backbone to put her on hold. I had taken on an air of excellent cool.

On the third day, George told me we were going to see one of the bigger fish on our route, one of the largest banks in the city. My recently acquired cool kept me from sweating too much as I walked in with such a big order. It was a cinch to sweet-talk my way past the guards and may-I-help-yous all the way to the bank manager's office. I don't know if he handed out little white packets to new loan customers or what, but he was, according to George, "one of our best customers." I mean I had three ounces stuffed in the sack. I'm sure the rest of the employees wondered what Mr. Vitner, the bank manager, was doing with some flunky delivering a sack lunch.

Vitner calmly motioned me inside. The man had obviously been born with the silver spoon already protruding from his mouth. His whole attitude expressed indulgence at having to move among the swine; he hadn't had to grovel or sweat to attain his high position.

He closed the door gently. "The usual arrangements, I assume."

"That's what they tell me."

I put the bag on his desk. He checked the contents.

"Well, you tell them something. I'm providing them with good business, and I want to continue our relationship. However, I've yet to see any initiative on the part of your employers to provide me with an incentive for my continuing patronage. Did you understand what I just said?"

"I dig. You want a volume discount. I'll give them the message."

Vitner said, "A well-educated thug. That's good. We might be able to do business. Brains and crime mix very well. Tell them to keep you on the route; I don't want anyone else."

"Thanks. I bet after I deliver your request for a discount, you'll be able to tell them everything in person."

A little regret passed over his imperial facade. I extended my hand. He handed me a roll of bills, and I left him to his second thoughts.

I met George back at his car. He had a big grin on his face and was snapping his fingers and singing along with Dean Martin. I discovered why when I got in—the sweet smell of reefer.

"You going to share?" I asked.

He passed me the reefer and we finished it while I told him what Vitner had said.

His eyes were just two slits, but I could see them well enough to know he was putting in some hard thinking.

"You and I are good partners," he said. "We have the brains and a foothold in the market. We're going to branch out. Seek new horizons within the affluent drug-abusing community."

"You mean, do this on our own? I like my blood right where it is, inside my body."

"This is all part of the big plan, Stan. We do it on the sly and build up a clientele out of the rich guys. See? We meet plenty of good customers on our little route. Take Vitner, for instance. He's unhappy with the arrangements. I know he'll get nothing but indigestion if we deliver his discount message to Vincent. We keep that under our hats and provide an alternative source, namely, us."

"That's the reefer talking, man. I'm sure Vincent is connected to some bigger guy, who's connected to some even bigger guy, on and on. What happens when we piss them all off?"

"We play it cool and none of that will happen."

George started the car and took off.

OUR NEXT DESTINATION: THE SIDE POCKET. IT SAT IN THE middle of a row of small shops in the relatively quiet neighborhood of Eureka Valley. The pool hall couldn't have been there more than ten years and had probably done pretty well when it first opened, attracting War Two vets who'd flocked to the suburbs. As the vets got jobs, wives, and kids, businesses like this had dwindled. According to George, the enterprising owner had decided to hook up with Vincent to keep his cash flow in the black.

The front door of the Side Pocket was open, probably in a hopeless attempt to cool the place off. We stepped inside and I let my eyes adjust to the darker interior. In spite of the ceiling fans, the place was an oven. A group of six punks in rolled white T-shirts and jeans played at two pool tables near the front window. A Buddy Holly song blared from the jukebox. Behind the bar, a guy in his seventies had his arm propped up and slept with his head in his hand. A rotating fan blew the dozen or so wisps of hair left on his head.

We walked over to the bar, and George shook the guy awake.

"Ed. It's George."

Ed straightened and rubbed his bloodshot eyes. "Marty's in the back." He turned. "Marty!" he yelled, the strength of his voice a surprise coming from such a thin, frail body.

"How you been?" George asked.

"You shoulda asked me that ten years ago. I don't even bother answering anymore."

"This is my partner, Frank." He turned to me. "Ed is Marty's dad."

I gave him a friendly hello, but he just scowled and proceeded to wipe down the bar.

Marty stepped out from a hallway that led to the back. "Gentleman George," he said. Standing six foot five, the man needed only three strides to cross the twelve feet of floor. He shook George's hand.

"Marty, this is Frank, my new partner."

Marty shook my hand with a grip of steel. Early forties and

he hadn't lost the strength of his youth. Everything about him was long and tall; even the anchor and the U.S. Navy emblem tattoos had stretched to accommodate his long forearms.

"Frank will be my man on the scene from now on," George said. He glanced back at the punks playing pool, who were staring at us. "Let's talk in back."

I followed them to the hallway, but George stopped me. "Give me the bag. I've got business with Marty. Why don't you keep his dad company?"

I gave him the bag and returned to the bar. Ed had disappeared. I heard a soft squeak and the pop of a cork from behind the bar. I leaned over. Ed was sitting on the floor, swigging from a pint of gin. He saw me and jammed the cork back in the bottle.

"What are you staring at?"

I straightened. One bony, age-spotted hand grasped the edge of the bar, and with a grunt, Ed hoisted himself upright. His gin breath assaulted me.

"You always sneak around, spying on people?" he asked.

"You do what you want. It's a free country."

"I don't hold much hope for this country when I see punks like you. Probably a commie sympathizer. I bet you don't even believe in Jesus."

"Can't say that I do, but then again, can't say that I don't."

He turned away from me with a harrumph and started wiping down the bar again. "Godless buncha kids these days." He turned back to me, wagging his filthy cloth near my face. "You'll start praying when the commie bastards are dropping H-bombs on your head."

"Can't say I'd have much time for praying."

"That's right. You'll be too busy crying and wishing we'd

had a president with enough balls to drop the bombs on the Russkies first."

"Do you think Jesus would really listen to me?"

"He listens to everybody."

"Then if I prayed to him right now and begged him to make you shut up, you think he'd be up for that?"

Ed threw the rag on the bar and walked to the far end, glaring at me the whole time.

George came back out with Marty.

Marty leaned his elbows on the bar, noticed Ed scowling. "I hope you told my dad to shut up," he said.

"Jesus did it for me."

"Well, I just hope Jesus keeps it up after you've gone."

George and I shook hands with Marty, and I could hear Ed ranting to his son as we walked out.

We got to the car and George said, "We've got one last big stop before we kick back for the evening."

11

George drove us to the Marina District. We pulled up to a row of pastel-colored pseudo-Mediterranean villas, all trying to be elegant and old-world, but crammed together like Italian sardines. Most of them had been built in the twenties and housed well-heeled professionals.

"Another rich guy?" I said. "I haven't been to a dirty old run-down drug den yet."

"That's what I've been trying to tell you." George snapped his fingers, his signal for the briefcase. "We cater to the high-class clients."

"Aren't there any dirty old run-down drug dens?"

George popped the latches and pulled out a bag. "Yeah. It trickles down." He stuffed a packet into my shirt pocket. "Our clients sell to their clients, and so on, until it reaches the dirty old run-down drug dens."

"That's the part that gets to me. Selling to the hopeless."

"We sell dreams, man. You stick with me for six weeks, and you'll have the rest of your life to make up for a few sins."

He opened his car door and started to get out.

"You coming with me?" I asked.

"This one's a little different. You just keep your mouth shut. Don't question what I'm doing. You got that?"

I nodded. We got out and walked down the sidewalk. A few yards later, he stopped, lit a cigarette, and flicked it in a high arc into the street.

We started up again and made for a big hacienda job that had seen better days. There were cracks in the stucco, and the woodwork was void of paint and beginning to rot. Massive marble flowerpots held only dead remnants of what had once been palms.

"His name's Charles A. Malvar the Third," George said. "But, hell, I just call him Charlie. That's all the creep deserves. You saw him with me the other night at the Aztec. He was a hotshot lawyer before he hooked up with some big crime boss, and now he's a patsy lawyer slash devoted heroin addict."

The door opened just as we got there. I realized that George's waste of a perfectly good cigarette had been a signal.

I followed him into the somber, empty foyer. Charlie watched us enter while he hid his body behind the door. The place was sparsely furnished. Lighter spaces on the walls indicated ghosts of paintings past. The telephone, probably once displayed on an antique table, lay on the floor. The only furniture visible in the dim light was a tattered Chippendale sofa, a small barley-twist oak table, and a couple of straight-backed chairs.

In the light, the lawyer's skin looked beyond pale, tending more toward undead. "Who do you have with you?" he asked.

"Relax, Charlie. He's my new partner."

Charlie stared at me for a moment and slowly closed the

door, never taking his eyes off me. He held a pistol at his side. My balls were sucked into my stomach at the sight of it, especially in the hands of such a twitchy individual. He belted the pistol, seemingly satisfied that I wouldn't jump him or pull out my own weapon. What had been slow, lethargic movements became frenetic. He blew past us.

"What took you so long?" he said, and dropped into one of the chairs. "Let's have it." He beckoned us over with a violent wave of his hands. "I need some bad."

George gave him a calculated smile. "I haven't got it on me, Charlie."

Charlie's hands shook and he gripped the arms of the chair. "Cough up the goods, asshole. Don't fuck with me."

George sauntered over to Charlie and took time to check out his fingernails. "We had an arrangement. You gave me the how and where it's coming in, but not the where it's going or when. No deal until I get it all."

Charlie stopped breathing. His eyes widened in silent horror as he sucked in air.

George continued. "Now, I like you, Charlie—you know that. So, I can give you more time, but today's delivery can't happen unless you give me something as a show of faith."

Charlie pulled out his pistol and my balls disappeared again. I thought, *Here we go—first week on the job and I get lead buttons.*

We both backed up.

George put his hands out in front of him. "Whoa. Take it easy, man."

I froze in panic as Charlie lifted the gun. I closed my eyes, anticipating the explosion.

"Charlie, don't do it," George said.

I opened my eyes to see which one of us he might shoot first. The man had the gun jammed into his own temple.

"I'll kill myself, and you won't get anything. Give me the stuff or I'll shoot."

"Look, man, that's not going solve anything."

Charlie jammed the gun hard into his temple, like he was struggling with some invisible force. "No deal. I've changed my mind."

"Then no delivery. Unless you pay up, no dice."

"I haven't got any money," he said. "And I've already hocked everything. Please."

George remained calm and gently delivered his words. "You're an educated man. Now, the best thing to do is use your brains instead of decorating the walls with them. We can work something out."

Charlie stopped struggling but kept the pistol glued to his temple. He worked his face in some inner argument. Man, it looked like his instinct for living and desire for dying were duking it out in some heavyweight bout. His face relaxed a little, as if the debate were resolved.

"All right, I have some info for you. You screwed it all up. They knew someone had snooped around in the Aztec office. You weren't thorough, left something out of place. They changed everything—the ship, the destination. And now they're asking around, checking on everybody that had anything to do with that office. That includes me!" He wiped the sweat from his brow with his free hand.

George's eyes bounced around in their sockets. I knew him well enough to realize he was calculating his next move. A second later, his smile returned. "The deal still stands, information for heroin, and it's all free. You don't have to pay a dime."

George nodded toward my coat pocket. "Look, Charlie."

I pulled out the packet. The crazed lawyer's eyes locked onto it.

"What can I do?" Charlie asked. "I can't keep giving you that kind of information. They'll kill me." He stared at the packet and sucked in air. "Okay, okay. But you've got to promise you won't say where the information came from." He pointed at me—fortunately with his free hand. "That means you too."

I put up my hands in conciliatory surrender. "You have no problem here. I don't know those kinds of people anyway."

Charlie went rigid. "Those kinds of people? What do you mean, those kinds of people? How do you know what kinds of people if you don't know what I'm going to say?"

"You got me. That's why you were the hotshot lawyer, not me."

"*Am* a hotshot lawyer, fuckhead!"

"Well," I said, "let's say you're in court—"

"Frank," George said.

"I was—am—in corporate law. I was never in court for anything other than keeping my pinheaded clients from going to jail for fraud or tax evasion."

George broke in, "This is getting us nowhere."

"Shut up, you," Charlie snapped. He pivoted back to me. He was calmer, probably coddled by the compliment. "You were saying about hotshot lawyer?"

"Well, yeah." I tried to think fast, since I was probably first on the list for being shot. "To be a good lawyer, you have to out-argue the other guy, outsmart and strategize. I bet you could use those skills to figure a way past this."

That got him to thinking again … not a pretty sight. That

burned-out brain of his was trying to cook up some way to get the smack. It was sad to see a guy reduced to obsessing about his next bump, even if he was a stinking lawyer. He finally generated enough heat to stimulate a few remaining brain cells. He closed his eyes. "Ladies and gentlemen of the jury," he started, probably remembering better days in a better court, "it's not that I begrudge these two gentlemen their right to a proper hearing ..."

"We're going, Charlie," George said.

Charlie's eyes popped open; his face blew out in all directions. He renewed his frantic struggle with the gun. "I'm not finished!"

I waved George down. "It's okay. Let him finish."

George glared at me, but stopped his retreat. "Please continue," he said.

Charlie closed his eyes again. "Inasmuch as the jury has heard the case brought before you, I urge you to find the defendants not guilty. They have acted on the behalf of others and, through no fault of their own, performed to the best of their abilities." With a flair, he lifted a piece of paper out of his suit-coat pocket and extended it toward George. "I rest my case."

Keeping his eye on the gun, George reached out, took the paper, and read it.

Charlie brought the gun down and held out his free hand in anticipation of the reward. "That's the new ship and dock." A crooked smile broke across his face. "Pretty good, huh? I'm not as far gone as everybody thinks. I've still got it."

"Thanks, Charlie." George took a step toward the door.

Charlie wiped the gun up and pointed it at us. "No one leaves without giving me the smack. You can keep the secret message, but the smack stays."

"What about the rest?" George asked.

"Don't fuck with me! We had an agreement! You give it to me, or I'll tell Vincent you've been exchanging his heroin for information."

"The trouble with that argument, Charlie," I said, "is that George could impeach you as a witness and get a motion to strike based upon your record as an addict, then accuse you of lying to avoid payment."

Charlie turned his attention to me. My little bit of court-room talk seemed to have calmed him enough that his smile returned.

"Your objection is sustained," he said, and turned back to George. "I'll have another piece for you tomorrow night at Bimbo's, ten-thirty. Bring another present when you come, and you'll have everything you wanted." He pointed the gun at me. "Now, I want my present."

The bore at the tip of the barrel mesmerized me, an experience so bizarre that I couldn't move.

"Frank!" George snapped me out of it.

I remembered the packet dangling from my hand. I walked over to Charlie, holding it at arm's length.

Charlie took it and bowed his head. "Thank you, Frank. You've been nice to me and I appreciate it. I urge you to complete the quest and acquire the information. You'll find it quite exciting."

"Sure, Charlie," George said, and motioned for us to leave.

Charlie stopped me with his haunting, quiet voice. "One more thing, young man. Never get involved with the white lady." He held up the packet. "She'll take all your money, then your soul. Good-bye."

George and I backed out and into the light of the living.

We still had to visit the lion's den before we could call it a day, and my nerves jumped. This would be my first visit to Vincent's.

12

Vincent operated out of a warehouse in the Central Basin area. We drove along the waterfront, passing row after row of warehouses that sat alongside long docks. Many still received cargo or the day's catch from fishing vessels. The warm and humid day thickened the smells of saltwater, old fish, and boat fumes. I had an almost primal attraction to the scent from childhood memories of living near the Boston Harbor.

George turned into one of the alleys that fed a row of warehouses and stopped in front of one halfway down. Chinese guys were carrying boxes in and out of trucks. The two large doors stood open and stacks of crates filled the building.

George put a hand on the door latch then looked at me. "What happened between us and Charlie, we keep that to ourselves."

"What did really happen back there?"

A flash of his salesman smile clued me in; he wasn't going to talk about it. "You did great today. I knew you would, man."

101

He patted me on the shoulder. "We'll go far, my brother cat. Far." He exited before I could question him any further.

We entered the packed warehouse. Guys carried boxes or moved crates with hand trucks among the tall stacks that formed a maze through the building. High above, overlooking the hive, was an office. A goon stood beside the door eyeballing us as we approached. I pointed him out. "That's not obvious, is it?"

George looked nervous. "Quiet."

We climbed the stairs and stopped in front of the goon. This constipated gorilla scanned me up and down.

"He's with me."

"Gee, Georgie, I'm glad you cleared that up for me. I thought he was a big cock-a-roach."

"You're pretty funny," I said. "I hear *The Ed Sullivan Show* is looking for good animal acts." My chuckle was choked off when the goon wrapped my neck with one meaty hand and started frisking me with the other. I looked at George as I dangled from the goon's grip. No one else would notice, but I saw another small crack in his cool demeanor. The goon released me, and I gulped in air.

"Meet Herman the Kraut," George said, as Herman started to search him.

"That's Mr. Vegel to you, pal."

"As many times as you've searched me, we should be married by now."

Herman nodded his all-clear and someone in the office waved us in.

We entered what looked like a real working office: file cabinets, calendar schedules, and papers everywhere. Vincent sat on the corner of the desk. Paul, the younger guy I'd met at the bar with him, was sunk into a plush office chair with his feet up on the wastebasket.

"Come on in, boys," Vincent said.

"Herman was getting pretty fresh out there," George said.

"Things have gotten tense around here lately," Vincent said. "He's just doing what I told him to." He peered at both of us, then stood and paced the room. "Someone put their hands where they shouldn't have, and it's stirred up a hornet's nest. You two wouldn't know anything about it, would you?"

George shook his head a little too nervously.

Vincent eyeballed him. After a long hard look, he seemed satisfied.

"We got half the town pointing fingers and pulling guns. It's gonna get nastier before it gets better. You guys keep your eyes and ears open. You got me?"

"You got it, boss," George said.

Paul gave us a more genuine smile. "You fellas sell all your Girl Scout cookies?"

George forced a smile that didn't quite make it all the way up. "Yeah," was all he could muster.

There was a third guy sitting at a corner desk. Vincent introduced him as Reed. He looked like a regular workingman type, a farm-to-urban import I could imagine walking to his factory job in coveralls and carrying a lunch box. He waved us over. He didn't look so regular when I got closer. It was his eyes. They didn't blink, and it made me stop halfway to the desk. Without a word, he held out his hand and stared at us. George pulled out the wad of cash from the day's proceedings. Reed counted it, wrote down a figure in a logbook, then turned it so Vincent could see.

"You're short," Vincent said.

"Charlie again," George said.

Reed slammed the logbook closed. "You didn't collect from that douche bag? That's the third time. Why didn't you collect?"

George's voice cracked, and with it his facade of cool. "We ain't muscle. We're couriers."

Ain't—I liked that. George and I had both learned you had to talk to primitives in their own language or they wouldn't understand.

George was pulling a sweat, and his eyes flicked from face to face. A slow creep of dread rose from my toes to my scalp. He was hiding something from these guys. I figured it was the deal with Charlie, but I knew George could handle that. So what made him sweat like that?

"Why do you keep supplying him if he's not paying?" I asked. I guess it was the panic that made my mouth move; there was no other explanation.

"Shut up, you," Reed said.

"It's 'cause he's connected, right?" I said, continuing despite the killer glares. "If you can't force the guy to pay, and you can't stop supplying him, chalk it up to business expenses."

To cope with the fear, my mind had turned the whole thing surreal. Nothing in life had prepared me for this bizarre piece of theater and its weird cast of characters. Like some crazy dream, it removed me from reality. I'd lost my sense of danger and, it seemed, the unwritten thug standards of propriety. George had this oh-shit-what's-gonna-happen-now look on his face.

"Who is this guy?" Reed asked him.

"Sorry, Reed, I—"

Reed turned to me. "Who the fuck are you to give advice?"

"I was just—"

"You was just nothing. You think you got bright ideas, then *you* figure out a way to get the money from him. You. And if you don't, you're gonna pay for it in blood. Fucking punk. Get him out of here."

George shoved me out the door and slammed it shut. I came face-to-face with Herman the Kraut. I backed away and retreated down the stairs. A few minutes later, George came out. He raced down the stairs, grabbed my arm, and led me out of the warehouse.

Not until we got in his car and slammed the door did he say anything. "What the fuck was that? Didn't I tell you to shut up and play it cool? I got chewed out in there for something that you did."

"I'm sorry, George. Okay? That was so surreal, I sort of lost track of reality."

"Surreal, my ass. These guys can mess you up so bad your parents wouldn't be able to identify the body. So wise up and shut up."

The lesson was over, but he continued to glare at me. "Today was payday."

He threw me a roll of bills. I unrolled it, and to my joy and astonishment, counted out five hundred dollars.

"Hallelujah," I sang, and danced in my seat.

George slammed the Buick in reverse and backed out. The tires smoked; then the engine stalled. He fumed as I fanned out the bills in his face. He tried not to laugh, but it burst out anyway. He restarted the engine, cranked up the radio, and we peeled out, laughing at our good fortune. It shocked me what that much money could do for my psyche. The world was turning.

George and I had dinner and a few drinks, but I didn't get drunk. I had all the money I needed to get as plastered as I wanted but elected to maintain what I call relative sobriety while we talked. We avoided business and, instead, reminisced about college days and our favorite musicians. We split up after dinner with only a quick mention of meeting up for work the next day.

Coming back to my apartment wasn't like a dreaded walk to a prison cell as it had been so many times before. I opened the door, turned on the lights, and watched the cockroaches scurry without feeling depressed about spending another night in my own little hell. Rather than seeing it as a symbol of my decline, it had become the point of my ascension, the Easter of my life as I arose from the undead to be born again. I set aside my pursuit of truth for the pursuit of wealth.

Never mind that I was now an employee of the illegal drug trade.

THE NEXT MORNING, I HAD A FEW HOURS BEFORE MEETING George. I got some breakfast—no can of beans for me this time. I even bought some new threads. At noon, I waited for George on the appointed street corner, dressed in a new camel-hair jacket, black turtleneck, black gabardine pants, and hand-made Italian leather shoes. The shoes were stiff, but the guy had slick-talked me into buying them. Still, I was glad I had the warm duds, because a mean breeze blew off the water and brought the fog with it.

George pulled up in his heap with the radio blaring Sinatra. It was even louder when I got in. Sinatra was singing that he was gonna have his fling and live till he died. I thought it kind of appropriate. I sang along until George snapped it off.

"What the hell are you doing dressed like that? You're not some prince of the street, college boy."

"I had to get something. The old stinky rags I had were falling off me. And it's better than going to the Laundromat."

"From now on, you dress like that on your own time. Dig?"

George looked at me a moment and drove off. "You've got to keep a low profile. Like this car, you dress pretty off the job. You're gonna stick out like a virgin in a whorehouse."

We drove in silence a while. I checked out his clothes for an example of incognito-drug-dealer attire. Blue collared shirt, black suit jacket with mismatched black cuffed pants, topped off with an old fedora.

George noticed me checking out his clothes. "You go out and buy some poor-boy clothes this afternoon. You got that, ace?"

"Sure thing, Georgie."

We made a number of deliveries that afternoon. Each one floored me more than the one before: an architectural firm, a union rep for the Teamsters, a small-time politician, and, the ultimate wig tightener, an aide buying for a superior court judge. Where did all these H-heads come from? It amazed me that there was such a market in a city that had barely risen above harbor-town status.

Finally, late afternoon, we delivered to the kind of places I'd expected: a massage parlor, a pool hall, and then a crazy guy at a law school. We got a laugh out of that one—a future

Charlie. There would be no recession when it came to the drug trade.

We finished around six and agreed to meet up again at nine at Bimbo's, where we could see Charlie and do a little celebrating. We parted and I went to buy some incognito clothes like George had said, and treated myself to a nice dinner at a real Italian place, not just a pizza joint. I had a gas spending money on something other than rent, rotgut booze, and cigarettes. A little internal voice warned me about being seduced by it all, but I shrugged it off. This was temporary, right? Hell, what was wrong with treating myself, living it up while it was there to be lived?

The phone was ringing when I opened the door to my apartment.

"Seventh Precinct," I said.

"Uh, hello?"

"Turly, don't worry, it's me. It's a joke. See?"

"I've been trying you all day."

He sounded weak and depressed, but he sounded like that a lot.

"Been busy with George." I waited for the reprimand, but he remained silent. I tapped the receiver. "You there?"

"Yeah, sure. I've been thinking ... Well, I've been thinking about what George talked about the other night."

I had dreaded the moment Turly might try to join up. "Are you really ready for that kind of work? It isn't like suckering the elderly into buying insurance policies."

I expected him to hurl insults at me, but all he said was, "I'm ready."

"I don't want you stepping in, then saying, 'Oh, shit, this

ain't right,' or getting some kind of crazy conscience and going loco on me."

"I know what I'm ready for. Is it yes or no?"

"It's okay with me, Turl, but I have to call George."

I told him to meet us at Bimbo's; he could talk to George there. A drip of stomach acid stung me with an inner warning. I wanted him in, but I wasn't so sure Turly could make the transformation. Straitlaced insurance man to dope peddler was an awful big stretch.

13

Things were just getting cranked when I arrived at Bimbo's, a hot joint on Columbus and Chestnut, a dress-up show-and-dine place with named acts. Big flashing sign, big cars pulling up, big bouncer at the front door. The billboard advertised Dick Blaine's Big Band Sounds and two older crooners, with a Lenny Bruce imitator on after that. I was seriously underdressed judging by the rest of the clientele, but I got past the bouncer and stepped into the main ballroom. The room was heavy in old-fashioned—red plush curtains and matching tablecloths, mahogany-stained wood, candles and chandeliers. A small Dixieland jazz band was warming up the diners.

George had told me to meet him in the smaller enclosed bar off to one side of the ballroom. I found a booth and ordered my usual. It tasted stronger than I remembered. Probably because I hadn't been drowning myself in it lately.

When Turly walked in, I knew what had happened. He crossed the bar with a mild limp, sporting the yellow and purple of a fading black eye, a cheek the size of a plum, and a lip to match. He sat down, eyes everywhere but on me. I gave him time to volunteer the information. I'd seen him a lot like this in high school. There was always an excuse, usually a biking accident. He had a lot of bike accidents. He grabbed my whiskey and took a long gulp.

He finally looked at me and gave a lopsided smile usually seen on circus clowns, the kind where you can't tell whether they're smiling or crying.

"Have another bike accident?" I asked.

He looked puzzled then turned red in the places that weren't already. "I fought back this time."

"You did? Turly, my cat, I'm proud of you. You hurt him bad, I hope."

"I got in a couple of good ones. That's when he pushed my face in the dirt until I nearly suffocated."

"The cocksucker. We should get Arly to pay him a visit."

Turly turned away, his face etched with anger, regret, and confusion.

"Why do you still let him hit you?"

He turned back to me with a weak smile of pride. "Not anymore. I'm out of there for good. I'm staying at a friend's place in Mill Valley."

"That's major-league, man. What are you going to do?"

"I need money," he said.

"What've you been doing with the money you've made already?"

"My dad talked me into putting it into his savings. Now he's got it locked up. All I've got to my name is that wreck of a car."

"Man, open your mouth. You took his boot so far up your ass, I want to know if I can see it."

"Remind me to laugh. ... I need a place to stay and I need a job."

"You can stay with me if you like."

A waitress came and we ordered drinks.

She left, and I said, "Have you got some of your stuff with you?"

"I left a suitcase in a locker at the bus station."

We fell silent again, and both of us opted for looking around the room rather than at each other. The waitress came back with the drinks, a beer with a tequila chaser for Turly—very serious for him. Between sips, we watched the crowd or exchanged glances.

Above the rim of my glass, I saw George enter. He was dressed to the nines: a golden sharkskin silk shirt and gray silk suit. He laughed at Turly as he pulled up a chair.

"Man, you stick your head in a meat grinder?"

Turly just stared at the table. George looked at me. I shrugged, and he let it go.

George smiled and nodded toward the bar. "Will you look at that joyride?"

I looked where he'd indicated. A gorgeous blonde in screw-me red was sitting on a stool at the bar, sucking on a margarita, her lips wrapped around the straw. It was the most seductive margarita-sucking I'd ever seen. She glanced at George, then me. She turned away and shifted in her stool. Her hourglass butt had this wicked way of embracing the seat, and each cheek moved independently as it followed her waist around to face the bar.

George snapped his fingers in my face. "Business first, Daddy-O. Then we'll fight for the bedroom furniture."

"I got a girl," I said.

"You hear that?" George said to Turly. "He's got a girl." He turned to me. "Why stop at one? There's a whole world of honeycakes out there."

George stopped the waitress and ordered a highball and another round for us. She left and he leaned forward, elbows on the table, signaling he was ready for business. "So, what happened to the insurance business?"

"I dunno," Turly whined. "It just didn't work out, you know."

"No, I don't know. You tell me."

"It sucks. Okay? That what you want to hear?"

"No, I want to hear why you've suddenly changed your mind. I want to know if you're really ready to work with Frank and me. This isn't like joining the Boy Scouts. If you're in, you're in. There's no out. You got that?"

Turly attacked his fingernails while he stared at the table. He ground his teeth and his eyes blazed. Most of me wanted him in, but a little part of me hoped he would say no. He was too vulnerable and high-strung.

Finally, Turly pulled his attention away from his nails and looked at George. "When you say there's no out, you mean forever?"

"Not exactly. But we don't quit until we're all fat with dough and I say we're done. It's like the army. When the war's over, we all go home. I want to count on you, and not worry whether you'll get a run in your stocking and make for the exit."

The waitress returned with the drinks.

Turly gulped down the tequila. "My reasons for wanting in are my own, but when I say I want in, I mean it. I'm in. If you don't want me, I'll understand, but I won't let you down."

George took a long swig of his drink, then slapped his glass on the table and said, "All right, you're in. You'll handle the accounts and other logistics. We need someone who's got brains for business." He rubbed his hands together and turned to me. "We're branching out, aren't we, Frankie? This is good. We keep our distro job. Turl's not ready to be a courier, but we'll be expanding any day now."

"I need money," Turly said. "When do I go to work?"

"Soon. I've got plans. I can't front you anything. I've got it all tied up, but you hang with Frankie for a while. He'll give you a hand and teach you the ropes."

"What kind of plans?" I asked.

"You gotta have plans to do business," George said. "I'm setting that up right now. That's all you gotta know." He leaned back, finished his drink, and lit up a cigarette. "Charlie should get here soon. But in the meantime …" He looked for the blonde, but she had gone. "Screw it. There're more where she came from." He got up and tossed some money on the table. "Drinks are on me." He waved to the waitress. "I'm going to hit the head."

The Dixieland jazz band finished their set, and more people filed into the bar. The waitress arrived with another round.

Turly downed the shot. He looked nervous in spite of the tequila glaze. "I hope I'm doing the right thing," he said.

"Don't even ask yourself that. You've always been nervous about something. You ought to be used to that by now, so don't pay any attention to it."

He raised his beer in a private salute and swallowed the whole thing in one go.

I leaned back, enjoying his crazy company, my cigarette,

and the whiskey. More people were coming in, all dressed in black ties, furs, and jewels. Gray-haired guys came in with young honeys on their arms and confident smiles that came from knowing they'd screwed over someone to get where they were and loved every minute of it.

Two moose-sized guys stopped inside the front entrance and checked the surroundings. They stepped forward, talked to the maître d', and turned to wait for whoever was their meal ticket.

Then I saw her. Rebecca. She handed a fur over to the coat-check girl. She looked like a countess with her hair pulled back and pinned, her long black evening gown, and a double strand of pearls the size of walnuts around her neck. My heart thumped somewhere in my throat, and my stomach started grinding stones.

She wasn't alone. It was the guy from the Aztec who'd stared at me from the mezzanine dais. I had a better view of his face this time. He was good-looking, sixties, tall, trim, with a long aristo-cratic nose and strong eyes. He oozed class and money. He removed his felt hat and straightened his perfectly styled gray hair still streaked with black. Under the long charcoal-gray cash-mere coat was a tailor-made Italian suit. I had to admit, he and Rebecca were a good-looking couple. He took her arm, they smiled at each other, and he escorted her into the main room.

I felt sick. I couldn't stand the idea of Rebecca having a good time with anyone else, anywhere else, but being in the next room over was too much to bear. I slugged down my drink and went for the bathroom to keep myself from running for the back door. I blew through the swinging door and rested against a wall, trying to calm down.

George and Charlie were talking in the corner near a urinal. You might as well have put a street bum in Charlie's rumpled tuxedo. His hair was splayed out in all directions, his face layered with sweat, and his eyes had sunk another inch or so into his skull. Even though Charlie had set up the meeting, I wondered if his being at Bimbo's had something to do with Rebecca's meal ticket, Mr. Suave.

George turned and waved me over. "Look who I ran into lurking in the stalls," he said to me, tilting his head at our gray-faced associate.

Charlie cowered in the urinal as if he didn't recognize me, then his eyes lit up, and he came out.

"Oh, it's you," he said. "Do you have any, you know, on you?"

"You're out already?" I asked.

"I sold some," he said defensively. "Well, a little."

"We were just talking about that," George said to me but staring at Charlie, smiling like he was his best friend. "He obviously needs more. I mean, look at him."

George lit a cigarette, while Charlie squirmed and rubbed his hands. "It looks like you could use some right about now," he said. "Just guessing, of course. Are we ready to do business?"

George pulled a triangular packet out of his pocket and wagged it in the air.

Charlie grabbed for it, but George pocketed it and backed off. "Not until you come up with the info."

A little shiver ran through Charlie. "They're snooping around and getting too close. Give me a break, please!"

His yelling got the attention of a guy at another urinal and the bathroom attendant, who, up until this point, had been content to wipe down the sinks and replenish the soaps.

"Take it easy," George said, lowering his voice. "I tell you what—you give me the information, and I'll give you the packet *and* cut you in for, say, oh, ten percent. Deal?"

Charlie held his breath and rubbed his face. He expelled his breath and the words came tumbling out with it. "All right, all right! It's tomorrow night."

"Tomorrow night? You said next week."

"It got here sooner. What am I supposed to do, slow it down?"

"Where is it going?"

"I won't know that until tomorrow. They're keeping security real tight because of your bungling at the Aztec."

"The rest of the info I get tomorrow. Right?"

Charlie nodded, snatched the packet out of George's hand, and rushed to a stall.

George nodded toward the exit, and we walked out silently. The bathroom attendant watched us in the mirror.

We stepped out into the bar.

"What the hell is going on, George?" I asked. "Who are *they*?"

He put his finger to his lips, straightened his lapels, gave me one of his classic cryptic smiles, and walked away.

My best friend's evasiveness only added to my frustration and anger. Between his and Rebecca's secrets, I'd had enough. I wanted to shake George, but I wanted to kill Rebecca's beau.

I went into the foyer overlooking the dining room. The curtains opened as Dick Blaine's Swing Band played "Afro-Cubana" in a reasonable imitation of Artie Shaw. Rebecca and Mr. Suave sat at a choice table not far from the dance floor. My heart pounded and stomach churned as I watched them. I don't know what made me do it. I knew better, but my legs just started moving. The swinging music boosted my courage. I walked toward the table with no idea what to do or say when I got there.

About halfway, Rebecca spotted me. Her smile dropped into a frown. Those beautiful bright eyes turned hard as I neared the table. Mr. Suave stared at me.

"What are you doing here?" Rebecca asked, her voice neutral yet cold.

"Hello, Rebecca."

"Who is this, darling?" Mr. Suave asked.

Her eyes flitted from me to him, flashed with a mixture of fear and anger. She recovered as fast as a slap and smiled like everything was cool. "Just a friend. David, let me introduce you to Frank … I'm sorry, I forgot your last name."

"Valentine."

She had the coolness of a receptionist at a mortuary. "Right. Frank, this is David Hanson."

I shook his strong, lean hand.

Rebecca broke the stare Hanson and I had going. "So, Frank, what are you doing here?"

"I'm with some friends, and I happened to see you."

"Nice jacket," she said. "Camel hair?"

"Yeah. I kind of have a thing for camel-hair jackets. That and dancing have become new passions of mine."

Rebecca softened from the under-the-table compliment. I could feel Hanson's eyes studying me. My emotions must have been plastered all over my face in the usual neon.

"Well, it was nice of you to come by," Hanson said, letting the lead-weight hint drop on my toes.

I ignored him and stayed focused on Rebecca. "I haven't seen you in a long time. You doing okay? You look like a countess tonight."

We locked eyes, and Hanson grabbed her hand and squeezed hard. The mood broke and Rebecca flinched.

"You two look very romantic," I said. "I thought maybe this was your dad at first, but then I thought, nah, can't be. Your dad would be a little younger."

Rebecca looked away, her face unreadable. Hanson smiled then nodded off to his side. It was a slight gesture, but enough to bring one of the moose-sized guys up to the table next to me.

"It was nice to meet you," Hanson said. "Now, if you will excuse us, we would like to finish our meal and enjoy the show."

The moose put a hand the size of a porterhouse steak on my arm. I took the hint this time, and gave Rebecca one last glance, trying to a say a lot within that split second. She kept her attention fixed on Hanson, her smile thin, desperate. The moose nudged me.

"Good night," I said. "You two lovebirds have a nice evening."

Hanson ignored me and the moose escorted me as far as the foyer, then released my shoulder from his vise grip.

"My friends are in the bar," I said.

"Why don't you stay in there then, all right?" the moose said. "Then we can all have a pleasant evening."

He gave me one last warning glare and went back to wherever he'd posted himself. The band had broken out into a Glenn Miller number, "At Last," a woman belting out the lyrics. I shifted my gaze to Rebecca, who used her eyes to plead with me to get out of there. I stepped away and headed back to Turly and another three or four whiskeys.

The tequila had done the trick for my friend. His eyes had a glaze like an old varnish. It was a good thing he had two elbows because they were the only things holding him up.

"Where were you?" Turly asked, slurring.

"Looking up an ex-girlfriend."

"Forget girls. It's you and me now, baby."

"Now, why doesn't that make me feel any better?"

Turly leaned back in his chair, listing to one side. His eyes wobbled in their sockets like a man trying to concentrate on at least one of the faces floating before his eyes.

"You look like you feel no pain," I said.

"I'm feelin' good."

Turly's drunken clown face was cracking me up. It made me glad he was there. He kept me from sinking too deep into my own self-pity. I wanted a drink and went for George's lonely martini, but it was empty.

"George come back?"

"Just to finish his drink. He said he had something to take care of. Probably two babes."

"I need another whiskey if I'm to catch up with you."

I fought my way to the bar and had to wedge an arm between drinkers just to flag down the bartender. The guy moved fast, and me waving money at him didn't seem to slow him down. I felt someone behind me, and the back of my body warmed. I turned. Rebecca stared at me.

"Are you following me?" she asked.

"Don't flatter yourself, countess. I met some friends here." I pointed to Turly. "Recognize the guy with the Quasimodo face?"

She looked at Turly and broke a smile. After a quick glance toward the foyer, she glared at me. "That was crazy coming over to the table. You know who he is?"

"No, but he must be hot stuff if he's got muscle as chaperons."

"Don't ever do that again."

"What? Come over to you and your boyfriend's table, because you might actually be in love with me, and anytime you see me, you can't stand being with him—"

Rebecca shut me up by planting a long, hard kiss on my lips. Her tongue, her smell, her taste, played the same trick as before. Nothing else existed, just her and me.

She broke the embrace and pushed back from me. "I've got to get back." I couldn't say anything. She gave me another quick kiss. "Call me tomorrow." She bolted for the ladies' room.

I could only stand there and watch her go. I had just about given her up for good, and she'd done that to me. Maybe she thought I'd made some heroic gesture by coming over to their table. How many heroes had been made just by being too ignorant to know what kind of crap they were stepping in?

Suddenly, the bar felt way too crowded. Turly was about to fall over anyway.

There I was, back to obsessing about Rebecca, when I should have been thinking about her boyfriend.

14

The next day, George didn't show up until early afternoon. He pulled up to the curb and scratched off again before I could even close the car door. He looked ragged.

"What's up, man?" I asked.

He gripped the steering wheel and kept his eyes on the road. "I've been chasing all around town, trying to figure out where the shipment's going to tonight." He hit the steering wheel. "Damn. I've got the name of the ship, the dock, and the time, but if I don't know where it's going, I've got nothing."

"What about Charlie?"

"I went by there already. No answer at the door. Either the creep's hiding or he's passed out."

George never let his anxiety bother him for long, and today was no exception. He relaxed, turned on the radio, and gave me a quick, assuring smile. "We have a couple clients, but first we have to check in with Vincent."

THE HUMIDITY DOWN BY THE DOCKS HAD RESURRECTED AT least a month's worth of odors from dead fish and boat fumes. The heat had forced us to keep the windows down, and I could feel that odiferous cocktail sticking to my skin. I stopped singing along with the radio and turned it off. Our moods turned solemn as we pulled into the alley. George wove a path through the dockworkers off-loading boats and the truckers loading cargo. We drew a lot of stares from the dockworkers, as if we'd crossed some forbidden boundary.

"Do we have 'fuck you' written on the door panel?" I asked.

"A lot of shit goes down on these docks. They see a car and it's usually a cop, a crook, or a union boss who's a little bit of both. Or maybe they're just awed by the fine car and us two handsome cats."

We passed one last truck and came to a halt. Another large vehicle blocked the alley just in front of Vincent's warehouse.

"Ah, what the hell is this?" George said. He honked the horn.

Two thick-necked guys stepped out from behind the truck. One had a shotgun at the ready, while the other walked up to us, his hand inside his coat.

Everything clenched. "Who are these guys? Slam it in reverse—let's get out of here."

"Be cool. They're two of Vincent's yard bulls."

It was a good name. The ox-like one coming up to the car chewed a softball-sized wad of gum.

"I wonder if he could fit any more gum in his mouth," I said.

"Probably the only thing keeping his brain awake."

We both laughed. George's had a nervous edge to it, and mine bordered on frantic.

The gum-chewing yard bull leaned in. "You two little cherries find something funny?"

"We work for Vincent," George said.

"Yeah, I know who you are. I just don't like being honked at. It gives me a nervous reaction. Makes me want to decapitate whoever did it."

"You might want to see a doctor about that," I said.

"A smart-assed cherry. Don't let your mouth start something your face can't stand." The yard bull scanned my features, no doubt memorizing every detail for a later mauling. "You boys packin'?"

"No, man," I said, a little too quickly.

George leaned over and opened the glove compartment. The door dropped down hard from the weight of a .45 automatic. I recoiled as far as the seat would let me. George kept his hands off the gun and in sight.

"Hand it over slowly," the yard bull said. "I'll give it back to you when you leave."

"What's going on?" I said. "You expecting Indians?"

"Whatever you need to know, Vincent'll tell ya."

George handed him the gun. The yard bull waved to a truck driver, who climbed in the cab and backed up enough for us to drive through. George pulled into a space next to the building and angled it for a quick getaway. I looked in the side-view mirror. Two more guys stood at the front entrance to the warehouse.

"I didn't know Vincent had so many guys," I said.

"Maybe fresh hires."

As we approached the entrance, the two guys didn't move.

They weren't showing guns, but they blocked the way like two stone lions.

"It's okay, Jimmy," the gum-chewing yard bull said. The stone lions parted and opened the big double doors.

Nothing moved in or out of the warehouse. Herman stood at his post on the platform next to Vincent's office. We climbed the stairs and stopped in front of him. George opened his coat for a weapons inspection. I did the same, and Herman patted us down.

"You see what I mean?" George said to me. "If only I could feel up girls as much as he does the guys."

Herman gave George a few hard pats, then turned to the window and gave the all-clear. Paul nodded. Herman opened the door, and we entered.

Vincent sat at the middle desk, his feet propped up and a cigar jammed in his mouth. He looked cool and calm, not a bead of sweat despite the stifling heat. Paul shuffled papers at a file cabinet, sweating like he'd just gotten out of the shower. At least I didn't feel alone in the sweat department; it was running down my back and making me crazy. Between my nerves, the heat, and the dead air, I was almost gasping for a breath.

George shook Vincent's hand. "What's up, Vince? Why all the guns?"

"You don't need to know what's up," Vincent shot back. He nodded to Paul, who laid five small packets on the desk.

"That's all?" George asked.

"We're locking things down for a few days, and I don't want too much H out there. You'll get more when we start back up."

"Expecting trouble?" George said.

"You ask too many questions. Take that and get out of here."

"I've got that congressman to see today, and he wanted three ounces."

"Beat it. I don't want to see your pimply asses around here until the day after tomorrow. Have I got to spell it out for you?"

"You guys must be taking inventory," I said.

Vincent jerked his head in my direction. "What?"

"You know, inventory. So you can pay your taxes."

Paul snickered, but Vincent wasn't laughing. "Get out of here."

Yard bulls with guns eyeballed us all the way through the warehouse. George got his pistol back, and we hoofed it to the car. I was ready with my "surreal" excuse again if George gave me grief for the stupid inventory remark, but he peeled out without saying a word. We drove a good ten minutes, George staring straight ahead. I watched the world of San Francisco roll past my window. We were driving alongside Union Square when George slammed the steering wheel.

"Inventory! Hah!" He clapped his hands, then drummed the dashboard.

"It wasn't that funny. Sorry, George, I don't know what came over me again."

He didn't yell at me; he was too busy smiling. He started humming the "The Battle Hymn of the Republic." I thought it was a joke about Union Square, but then he started singing the words.

"Mine eyes have seen the glory of the coming of the load. We are trampling in the backyard where the heroin will be stored. Glory! Glory! Hallelujah!"

He made a quick left and headed for my part of town. "We've got to get everyone together at my place this afternoon. We have plans to make, baby."

"Would you *please* tell me what's going on?"

"It's going to Vincent's. Glory, glory, hallelujah!"

That wasn't exactly the answer I was looking for, but George didn't offer another one.

WE WENT BY MY APARTMENT AND PICKED UP TURLY, THEN rode over to George's place—on the third floor of a wood-frame job with bay windows next to South Park in the South of Market district. Roach and Arliss were waiting for us, and they approached as we got out of the car.

"Hey, you're walking," I said to Roach.

"I get the stitches out tomorrow."

The stitches in Arliss's forehead had been removed, leaving a fresh scar that added to his intimidating demeanor. Faint yellow patches were all that remained of their bruises. Their serious expressions said they knew what was up, and Arliss, for once, kept his mouth shut.

Everyone mounted the stairs and entered the apartment. George had moved into this pad a year ago. The cool George that I knew should have had pretty fancy digs, but it felt more like a flophouse than a home. I'd expected some personal touches, but the only signs that George even lived here were the dirty clothes, cigarette butts, and food wrappers. Nothing hung on the walls; the furniture was shabby and worn. The warped and cracked flooring showed through the holes in two thin rugs. What he did with all his money was a complete mystery to me.

We settled in the living room, Roach and Arliss on the sofa, George and I in chairs. Turly chose the floor, where he proceeded to pick at the fibers protruding from one of the holes in the carpet. The silence was awkward. Cigarettes were lit.

"This is the first time we've all been together without passing a bottle or some reefer," I said.

"Everyone stays crispy for this meeting," George said.

I was about to ask what meeting when someone knocked on the door.

George got up. "Yeah?" he said through the closed door.

"It's me," a man's voice said.

George opened the door and in stepped Marty, the guy from the Side Pocket pool hall. Marty followed George over.

"This is Marty Grimes," George said. "He's the new member of our merry little band."

I looked at Roach and Arliss to see if they were as surprised as I was. They were, it seemed.

Nods and hellos followed, and Marty shook everyone's hands. He then sat in the chair that George had occupied. George stepped inside our circle and scanned our faces with that wry smile of his.

"You guys knew I was planning something big. That's what you all signed up for, and that's why you're all here. I've been working on this for months, and now that I have all my little ducks in a row, we can pull this off and get rich. And it's happening tonight."

"I know you love mysteries," I said, "but are you going to let us in on it?"

George squatted. "We're going to"—he searched for the word—"*redirect* a shipment of heroin."

"We're going to what?" Turly asked.

"You heard him," Arliss said.

"I heard him," Roach said, "but I don't believe it."

"Believe it, brother," George said. "That's why Frank and I have been building up our market." He pointed to Roach and Arliss. "And that's why I had you guys polishing your old army contacts."

"We're going to sell stolen heroin?" I asked.

"No, we're going to shoot it up in one glorious high."

I felt suddenly very sick.

There was a stunned silence.

George's smile transformed into a frown. "Just how many ways do you think we were going to come up with to make it rich in six weeks?" He looked at Turly. "Besides robbing banks." He stood, walked out of the circle, and turned on his heels. "Look. This isn't robbing banks or kidnapping, or selling government secrets to the Soviets, so we're not going to have the cops or the FBI or the CIA on our asses. We're stealing from gangsters. We're going to beat the crooks at their own game."

I cleared my throat and leaned forward. "Don't you think the crooks are going to be just a little bent out of shape?"

"Look around you. Do you see anyone here who'd raise any suspicion? If we go about our usual routines, carefully unloading the stuff on the side, no one's going to be looking in our direction. They'll be so busy pointing fingers at each other, or at crooked cops, that they'll never notice us. We unload it as fast as we can, take our pile of cash, and sail off into the sunset."

Long moments passed before anyone spoke.

"How much H are we talking about?" Marty asked.

George pulled a cigarette out of his pack and lit it. I knew he was using it to mask his own uncertainty.

"I don't know exactly. The shipments vary. My guess is ten, maybe twelve kilos. If we step on it a little and sell only ounces or less, we're looking at a ninety to a hundred and ten thousand dollars apiece."

My head spun with the idea of that kind of money. The problem was living long enough to spend it. I should have run the other way, broken a leg, jumped off a speeding train, anything but stay there, my ass planted in that chair. The only redeeming thing I could grasp onto was that we wouldn't be ripping off the general public. But we'd still be selling heroin, and even though we weren't selling to the hopeless and the forgotten, it trickled down. Besides dying, that was the part I couldn't resolve. Like George had said, I knew I'd have to spend the rest of my life making up for my sins.

"Everybody cool?" George asked.

To my surprise, Turly spoke up first. He yanked off a thread of the carpet and declared, "I'm in."

"Turl! Go, boy!" Arliss said. "I'm in too."

Roach mumbled a "Sure, why not."

Marty gave his ascent. Then eyes turned to me. I looked at George, hoping to find the assurance that we would all be safe. But then I looked away. Neither George nor anyone else could guarantee we'd stay alive, and the chances were that some of us would die. But I was already in too deep.

"Okay, George. I'm in."

George nodded and smiled at me. He knelt by the coffee table. "Okay. The heroin comes in by ship from Singapore or

Hong Kong about once a month. It's off-loaded onto a tugboat and taken to any one of the ports here or Oakland. And tonight, gentlemen, our ship comes in. The tugboat is supposed to rendezvous with the ship around midnight at China Basin."

George nodded to Marty, who dropped a map showing the various city ports onto the coffee table.

"Marty worked for the navy during War Two. He piloted LCIs that landed the marines at Guadalcanal and Tarawa, and tonight, he's piloting a boat that will land us the H. Roach, Arliss, and I will be with Marty to intercept the tugboat." To Marty, he said, "You've got a good boat lined up?"

"A Chris-Craft Runabout with a modified Ford V8."

"Is it fast?"

"It'll pull your ears off."

George pointed to an area of the map. "The tug will head for Central Basin and Vincent's warehouse."

A cold flash went up my spine. "Vincent's? That's who we're stealing it from?"

"No, not exactly. He's the destination point. Then it's distributed from there. They change the destination point each time. That was the only detail I didn't have until we visited Vincent this afternoon."

I understood why my inventory remark had pleased George so much.

"If it's heading for Central Basin," Marty said, "we can intercept the tug about here." He indicated a point on the map about halfway between the two shipyards. "How will we know which one it is? It's going to be running with no lights, and there'll be at least a light fog on the water."

"I got all the details about the tug," George said. "Where

it's docked, what it looks like, the registration number. Everything. We'll find it."

Marty didn't look convinced, but neither did George.

"What will I do?" I asked.

"You and Turly will drive his and my car down to India Basin and wait for us there. I'll tell you exactly where in a minute."

"What if you don't make it?" Turly asked.

George took a draw from his cigarette, then stubbed it out in the ashtray. "Then either we missed the boat, or our corpses will wash up onshore somewhere south of the city."

15

A s Marty had predicted, a light fog rolled along the water of the San Francisco Bay. Off in the distance, the diffused lights of Oakland gave the illusion of a sparkling, nebulous galaxy that hovered above the black water. Turly and I sat in his car with the radio turned down low, listening to big-band music on KRE. Turly had his coat pulled tight against the cold—or a chill from the fear. His head hung low, his chin resting on his chest, coat collar and lapels flipped up, hiding his face.

We had driven his and George's cars down to India Basin and parked in a dirt lot near an old dock. Ahead of us was a line of dilapidated warehouses silhouetted by faint moonlight that had pierced the fog.

"It's almost three," Turly said into his coat. "Where are they?"

"Are you going to keep asking me that? What part of 'I don't know' don't you understand?"

Out of boredom, I started timing the gaps between Turly's questions; fifteen seconds was the longest.

"What are we doing here, Frank?"

"Seven seconds."

"What?"

"Nothing."

"Well?"

"You want me to tell you what we're doing here? We're waiting to see if we make the gangland's ten-most-wanted list, that's what. Then there's the possibility that we'll have to start looking for four floaters downstream with bullet holes in them."

"This is crazy."

"I think you're on to something."

"Why don't we get out of here? You know, you and I just skip town. We always talked about going to Europe or Australia."

"You know the answer to that."

Turly jerked his coat tighter and crossed his arms as he let out a big sigh. Despite his whining, I enjoyed his company. We were the same age, but he was like my little brother, and I felt more in control and protective around him.

"You know what's funny?" I asked.

Turly lifted his face out of his coat and looked at me.

"I'm glad you're here. And I'm sorry you're here. But mostly, I'm glad. Before this, we were both working backward down the negative side of arrested development."

"Speak for yourself."

"Now we're taking a perverse path up the mountain of life. No more express train to Nowheresville."

"Are you spouting this bullshit to make me feel better, or yourself?"

I looked out at the desolate landscape. "Both, I guess."

Turly turned off the radio. "Look."

He pointed toward the water. Not far from the dock, a light flashed twice.

"That's George."

We got out and stood by the car. Just above the hiss of the city, I could hear the rumble of a boat motor. We walked over to the dock and peered into the darkness. A moving silhouette obscured the lights of Oakland; then the boat came out of the fog.

"This is crazy," Turly said.

"Shut up."

A tugboat pulled up alongside the dock, with Marty's Chris-Craft towed behind it.

"Ahoy, girls," Arliss said, and threw me a mooring rope.

Roach threw Turly another. They were all smiles.

"We did it, man," George said.

Arliss dropped a large duffel bag onto the dock. "They weren't expecting a thing."

Marty was the only one not smiling. He killed the tug's engine and checked the mooring ropes.

I boarded the boat, and said, "Where's the crew?"

"They went for a swim," Roach said.

"What if they can't?" Turly asked.

"Jeez, get this guy," Arliss said as he jumped onto the dock. "Don't worry, Mary. We gave 'em lifejackets."

My stomach clenched even tighter when I noticed Roach packing a revolver into another duffel bag that already contained a shotgun, raincoats, and a coil of rope.

"They know what you guys look like," I said.

George held up a black ski mask. "Not with these on."

"Don't forget the guy below," Marty said.

"That's right," George said to me. "Not all of them went overboard. Remember Herman the Kraut? We had the jump on them, had them outgunned, but Herman still had to try and pull out a rod."

"You're fast with that thirty-eight," Arliss said to Marty, who shrugged and climbed over to the Chris-Craft chase boat.

"Is he alive?" Turly asked.

"He is for now," George said.

"I say we dump him overboard," Marty said. "We can't take any chances."

"We're not going to kill anybody," George said.

"We'll see how long that lasts," Marty said. "You guys are in the big time now. You've opened up a whole new set of rules, and if you don't play the game, you're dead."

Marty didn't wait for a response. He untied the towrope and started up the chaser boat. "I'll see you guys tomorrow." The chaser boat roared as he backed it away from the tug and moved out into the bay.

We watched him disappear in silence, the deep rumble of the chaser-boat engine the only sound.

George turned to us, the smile gone now. "Let's get the H off and into the cars."

Turly made a move to board but George held up his hand. He picked up a tarp and threw it to Turly. "Open the trunk of my car and line it with the tarp."

I could tell Turly didn't like being left out, but he did what he was told.

Arliss hit my arm. "Come on. It's all below."

The narrow passageway that led to the quarters below forced us to file down one at a time. With George, Roach, Arliss, and me jammed in the passageway, there was hardly any room to move. I couldn't see anything in front of me except Arliss's broad back. George squeezed his way past us toward the upper deck with what looked like a bundle of laundry wrapped in paper.

"Next time we form a line," he said as he mounted the stairs. "Frank, you're last in line, so you stay below and hand them up."

Roach came through with a bundle; then Arliss went for one. He turned to get a packet, giving me a view of the small forward cabin. On a table to the left sat the pile of bundles. Herman lay on a cramped bunk on the right, his large body hanging over the edges and his legs bent. A ski mask had been pulled backward over his head and his hands were bound in front of him. He was out cold and panted hard; blood seeped from a wound in his shoulder and spread across the fabric of his suit coat.

"He ain't gonna bite," Arliss said.

I forced myself to look away. I'd never seen anyone shot before, and I hoped I wouldn't again.

Arliss exited with a bundle. I picked one up and was surprised by the weight. I took it to George at the base of the stairs.

"We did it, buddy," he said.

I could only nod and force a half-smile. "What are we going to do with Herman?"

"I don't know yet."

"We're not killing anyone."

George shook his head. "He doesn't know who we are. We'll let him go outside of town."

"We drop him at a hospital."

"We'll call an ambulance from a payphone. How's that?"

I shrugged. "That'll do."

I went back and retrieved more bundles, handing them off to George, Roach, and Arliss. Each time, I glanced at Herman to see if he was okay. I grabbed the second-to-last bundle and met Turly at the stairs.

"Tell everybody there's only one more," I said. "I'll bring it up."

Turly nodded and took it topside. I returned to the cabin.

Herman's breathing had stopped.

"Hey, guys, I think Herman's getting worse."

For all his bulk, I didn't hear him get up, just felt the breeze and saw the shadow. I had just enough time to whirl around before his king-sized hands, still bound, slammed into my face. My head snapped. My vision went black, and my ears rang. Shock gave way to a throbbing ache.

Herman grabbed me by my jacket and slammed me against the table. My stomach screamed with the impact of another blow. I doubled over. My lungs froze, refusing to give me air. I choked on blood and vomited onto Herman's shoes. I thought it couldn't get worse. Until he kneed me in the groin. I fell hard to the floor, my body useless.

Everything became a blur. Herman's massive shoes with my vomit and blood splattered on them. More shoes shuffling in front of my face. A chorus of grunts and groans and screams. A *pop pop* sound that made my skull vibrate. Then an explosion that shut my hearing down. Something wet and warm sprayed my face ....

I LAY ON THE BACKSEAT OF GEORGE'S CAR AND LOOKED

myself over in the sweep of the streetlights. My jacket was gone; my hands and shirt had been wiped off. The hum of the engine made me want to go back to sleep and forget everything that had just happened. Arliss was in the passenger seat. George was driving. I sat up and my head spun. A wave of nausea followed.

Arliss looked back. "I cleaned you up as good as I could."

"Where are we?"

"Bay Bridge, heading to Oakland," George said.

"What happened? Where's Herman?"

"He's in the trunk," George said, glancing at me in the rearview mirror. "We put the H in Turly's car."

"Is he dead?"

Neither of them answered at first. Arliss turned back around. "Yeah, something like that."

"You guys didn't have to kill him."

"If you had've watched him a little better, we wouldn't've had to," Arliss said with little conviction in his voice.

George glared at me via the rearview. "He got Roach's gun and fired off two rounds before I got him with the shotgun."

"He nearly shot Roach." Arliss said, his voice quivering. "I couldn't get in there to help. That cabin was so goddamned small."

"Is Roach okay?"

"The fight opened up his wound a little, but he's all right. He's riding in the other car to keep Turly from wigging out."

George glanced at me a few more times and I saw the pain there, no matter how hard he tried to mask it with a smile. You can tell almost everything about someone by their eyes; his were like two pits, black and void of life. I felt sorry for him in that moment. I was the type to let my emotions come out. He kept it all in, and it was eating him alive.

I looked out the back window. Turly's car followed close behind. He and Roach were barely visible through the windshield. I wondered how Turly was taking this; then I realized my concern for him was simply a way of avoiding my own anguish. We'd crossed over the line into murder. George had done it in self-defense, but it was as if we'd all pulled the trigger.

Now we were killers as well as drug dealers. How many sins would I have to answer for before this was all over?

We crossed over into Oakland, San Francisco's ugly little sister. At this time of night, its grimy downtown was dead. The only things the two cities had in common were the waterfronts, the bridge that linked them, and the bay that divided them.

We passed through downtown into an area of run-down row houses originally built for the mill workers but now occupied by the poorest of residents. Then came the warehouses serving the waterfront and the rail yards. It was a forgotten land of ruins and roving gangs of teenagers, and the ultimate destination for most of the heroin we were distributing.

George turned into an alley of decaying garages and storehouses. He stopped in front of a small, single-story brick building. Turly's car pulled up behind us.

"Stay in the car," George said.

He got out, unlocked the dilapidated wooden doors, and swung them open. He came back to the car and signaled Turly to follow him. We pulled into the dark building, the headlights sweeping across the interior. Along the back wall ran a wooden bench with a few rusted tools, some still cluttering the bench, others hanging on the wall above. George got out and Turly and Arliss pushed the doors closed. George threw a switch. A bare bulb hanging from the ceiling threw the corners into shadows and isolated us in a pool of raw light.

I looked over at Turly. Our eyes met, then he looked away, staring into nothing.

"Turl," George said, but he didn't respond. "Hey, Turly!"

He looked up.

"Open your trunk."

Turly fumbled for his keys and popped the trunk. We gathered around, and Arliss pulled over the bulb and lit the interior.

"That looks like a lot more than ten kilos," I said.

"Well, my brother cats," George said, "you are gazing upon twenty-five kilos of eighty-percent, high-grade heroin. About a million to a million and a half dollars in street value."

Roach, Arliss, and I stared into the trunk without saying a word, each of us with his own thoughts. Most of them, I imagined, were of a creeping dread. Turly stood off to the side, obviously not wanting to come any closer.

George grabbed one end of the workbench. "Give me a hand."

Arliss joined him. They lifted one end and dragged it away from the wall. George moved a large piece of plywood, revealing a hollowed-out section of wall.

"Let's get this done and get out of here," he said.

Roach, Arliss, and I stashed the bundles in the hole and replaced the table and debris. George used scales to split up the kilos into ounces. Turly gave him a hand but didn't say a word. He had fallen into a trance—whether from disbelief or fear, I couldn't tell. I was afraid he'd crack and nudged George.

"He'll be all right," George said. "I didn't let him see the body. He knows it's in there, but he's not going to have to deal with it. That's on you and me."

"Me?"

"Yeah, you," George said. "He can't handle it, and Arliss needs to look after Roach, so they're all going back in his car, and he'll stay overnight with them." He turned and picked up two shovels. "You and I are on burial detail."

16

George drove back across the bridge and headed south. We spent the twenty-five-minute trip in silence, passing a bottle of tequila that George had stashed at the garage, trying to numb our minds to the dreaded task. We pulled onto a street of abandoned warehouses south of Hunters Point. Every city has its dumps of refuse and the abandoned, and Hunters Point topped the list of Frisco's most disgusting. We drove past a few bums standing around barrel fires and pulled up behind an old building.

My nerves peaked. I could hardly sit still. My mouth ended up venting the energy. "Why didn't we just leave him on the boat? Then, at least, the cops could identify him. He probably had family. What if he had a wife and kids? How are they going to know if he's dead or not?"

"Shut up. Just shut up!" George said, just a few degrees shy of hysterical.

He got out and I followed. He pulled two shovels out of the backseat and popped the trunk. He stood next to it, staring at me with a blank look. The open trunk seemed larger in the darkness, like the open jaws of hell. From where I stood, I couldn't see anything of the black interior. I had to walk forward and let the trunk lid block out the few distant lights. My mind opened the cold-water valves in my bloodstream when I saw the large shape of a body inside.

"Come on. We've got to move fast," George said, and started to pull at the lifeless form.

I was frozen. This couldn't be happening.

He shoved me. "Let's go!"

I couldn't touch the body at first. George growled as he grabbed me by the shoulder and pulled me forward. That act of rage, frustration, and near hysteria prompted me to comply. We clamped our hands around the dead man's jacket and pulled. The body flopped halfway out, revealing ragged flesh and bone where there should have been a head.

I jumped back and fell to my knees. My stomach convulsed. I forced myself to turn and look. "Where's his fucking head?"

"It's gone." George's voice sounded distant and tortured. "I didn't aim. I just fired the shotgun and then his head exploded."

He stood there, hands on the headless thing hanging down, bent backward in an unnatural pose. That image will never leave my mind: George and the headless body, like a fisherman with the day's catch. His eyes were glazed, and I knew he had mentally checked out.

"I can't do this myself. Please, Frank."

"I signed on as a courier, not an accessory to murder."

"What in hell do you think you said yes to? Delivering newspapers? I told you from the beginning, you say yes, you're in and in all the way." He grabbed my collar. "Now, we are going to do this thing, or we'll be the ones riding in the trunk next time. You dig?"

George pushed me into the corpse and went around to the other side. We tugged again. It came out and bounced as it hit the ground.

I jumped back and shuddered. "This can't be happening."

"Fuck it. I'll do it myself," George said, and grabbed the feet.

He pulled on the body once more, struggling with the weight. Something clicked off in my head like the numbness from a drunken stupor. I walked over and grabbed one of the ankles, and we pulled the body into the deep shadows. Everything else ceased to exist except the nightmare feeling of that cold, clammy ankle, and watching the corpse bounce along the ground, its severed neck like a bloody Thanksgiving turkey.

The body hit a rock and jammed. We gave it a good yank and it broke free. The sudden forward thrust pulled me off-balance. I grabbed the foot to keep from falling, but the huge shoe popped off in my hands and I hit the ground hard. That's when it hit me. Those shoes—the ones that'd once had living feet in them, the ones I'd bled and vomited on.

I started to cry. "No one deserves this."

George pulled me gently to my feet. "Come on, let's do this."

It helps when the mind checks out. The sick job of digging a hole big enough for this guy was a blur of shovels and dirt, a black hole, Herman patiently waiting. The gruesome task was like visiting a level of Dante's *Inferno*.

Exhausted and filthy, we threw the shovels into the car and drove off. I slid down onto the floorboard and curled up in a ball like a kid.

For the next thirty minutes, I listened to the drone of the car and George's constant reassurances that this was the only time, never again.

"We'll leave the state if we have to," he said. "I promise."

I knew he couldn't or wouldn't keep any promises.

~

THE SUN WAS PEEKING THROUGH THE BUILDINGS OF DOWNTOWN by the time we made it back to George's place. We had wordlessly emptied the tequila bottle on the trip back. I was still cradling the empty bottle when we pulled up.

"You can stay here if you like," George said.

I nodded. "Yeah, that'd be good."

We shuffled into the building and up the stairs.

George searched for his keys, and I said, "The tequila didn't do a damn thing. And I'm out of cigarettes."

He bolted the apartment door behind us and stopped. "I've got something that'll ease you into a better place."

I thought he meant whiskey or reefer, but he went to a small desk and pulled out a tin box. He pointed to the sofa. "Sit down."

I did, willing to take whatever he was offering, desperate to escape the images haunting my brain. George sat down next to me and opened the box. He pulled out a length of brown paper folded almost origami-style. He unfolded it and revealed the white powder within. He laid that on the table, then removed a syringe and a spoon.

"Are you sure about this, George?"

"It's cool, man. Just what we need." He wrapped my arm with a large tube of rubber and doled out a little of the powder onto the spoon. I could feel the pulse in my arm pounding harder. I didn't care anymore; I wanted it all to stop.

George added a little water to the spoon and heated it with his lighter. He drew the liquid into the syringe and checked for bubbles. I'd never liked needles, so I held my breath, tensed up, and submitted. The desire for relief was too strong to fight the little voice begging me to stop.

The needle went in, and out poured the juice. A warmth washed over me, like sliding into a tub of warm water. I was overcome by an exquisite sense of "being" without body, a disconnect of self, a melting into my surroundings, highly conscious, but a dream at the same time. I must have slid onto the floor because images of carpet fiber filled my field of vision. I concentrated on the twisted forest of brown threads. Dirt and debris formed a landscape as beautiful as any I'd ever seen. An inner peace flowed over me, and felt a part of something more benign, more benevolent than my everyday life, removed from seemingly petty problems, every worry absurd and meaningless. I didn't want to leave this place.

Maybe the addicts were the sane ones and the rest of us blind.

I RETURNED TO REALITY WITH A TONGUE AS DRY AS THE Mojave and a pounding in my head that made me wonder whether a stake hadn't been driven between my eyes. I stared at the underside of the dining table. I must have crawled under it sometime during the day. The apartment was dark except for a faint glow from George's bedroom.

"George?" I rolled over and pushed myself up onto all

fours. I was beyond hungry, and needed a cigarette and about twelve aspirin. It crossed my mind to simply shoot up again and forget the pain of reality. Fortunately, my stomach won the debate.

I crawled out from under the table and used the chair to haul myself to my feet, steadying myself as my heart tried to cope with the sudden shift in gravity.

"George?"

Nothing. I stumbled to the bedroom, bracing myself with the walls. The bed was empty. The door to the bathroom was open, but he wasn't there either. I couldn't believe he'd gotten up and gone out after what we'd been through. "What an animal," I said to the walls.

I splashed water on my face and gulped down handfuls until my tongue felt more like part of my mouth. I finally got the nerve to look at myself. It confirmed my suspicions; I looked like a lunatic—two-day beard, rat's nest hair, a bruised jaw, dark circles under my eyes.

And a sheet of paper pinned to my shirt.

"For fuck's sake."

I ripped it off.

The note said to lay low until everybody met up here tomorrow morning at eleven. Images of the night before came flooding back. I checked the clock. It was eight fifteen p.m.

I phoned Turly to see if he was okay. He sounded distant but lucid. I told him to stay at Roach's one more night, that I needed some rest. We agreed to meet at my apartment the next morning and have breakfast before the meeting at George's.

After a cup of coffee, I mustered the courage to call Rebecca.

A couple of rings and she answered, her voice warm and buttery.

"I know it's kind of late, and you did walk away from me the other night at Chump Change, but I keep thinking about you."

"Oh, that's sweet," she purred.

Normally, I would have given up by now, but not tonight. "I want to see you."

"I can't."

"Just for a drink."

No response.

"Come on, you choose the place. We'll keep it low-key and you can leave anytime you want. We'll just talk."

There was silence and then, "All right. The Blue Cove. It's on Fillmore. It's just a neighborhood bar, but it's quiet, good drinks. Meet me there in half an hour."

She hung up. It wasn't far, so I took my time, got cleaned up, and put on a white shirt of George's.

The Blue Cove was, as Rebecca had said, a "neighborhood bar," but the neighborhood was Pacific Heights: a ritzy area with uniformed doormen, fine arts boutiques, and French restaurants. I double-checked the address and said to the cabdriver, "There's only one Blue Cove, right?"

"No, there's six of them and I just picked one at random."

After congratulating him on his ability to live as long as he had with his smart-ass mouth, I paid and exited. I strolled down the street and tried to pick out Rebecca through the window. No Rebecca, just patrons in suits and gowns, seated among the carved wood, brass, and marble. I began to think she'd invited me there just to show me I couldn't afford her.

"Frankie."

She'd snuck up behind me. I thought she'd looked great at Bimbo's, but this was amazing. She wore a dark burgundy dress of raw silk and a matching shawl. She really didn't need makeup, but she'd put on just enough to set off her sensuous lips and piercing eyes. I felt breathless and way out of her league. But then she smiled and popped a quick kiss on my lips. *The hell with leagues, anyway.*

"What?" Rebecca said.

I realized I'd spoken out loud. "Nothing. You look incredible."

"Thanks."

We stepped into the light coming from the bar.

"My God, what happened to you?" she said.

"Boating accident."

She gave me a skeptical look. "It looks like sailing doesn't agree with you."

I shrugged. We stopped just outside the entrance.

"This place has a dress code," she said. "Where's that camel-hair jacket of yours? Boating accident?"

I pictured it floating in the bay somewhere. "At the cleaners."

Her mouth formed another killer smile. "Don't worry, they have jackets at the door." She leaned in. "And I'll get the tab. My treat."

I showed her my cash. "It's on me, milady."

"Let me guess; you came into a rich uncle."

I took her by the hand, and she didn't resist. "Come on, let's get me dressed and have a drink."

We entered the Blue Cove through brass doors. A harpist played in a corner among potted ferns. The maître d' recognized Rebecca.

"Good evening, Miss Debernardi."

"Hello, Phillip. I have a friend along. He needs a jacket."

Phillip opened a cabinet and Rebecca pointed at a pinstriped silk number. We were shown to a corner booth and she checked out my new attire.

"Very hot. You should dress like this more often."

"If you react like that every time, I might consider it," I said. "They say that a man compromises his convictions for a beautiful woman."

"Who are 'they'?"

"I made it up."

The waiter arrived. "What can I get for you, Miss Debernardi?"

"Vodka gimlet, please."

The waiter turned to me with condescension in his eyes. "Sir?"

Rebecca flitted her eyes from me to the waiter.

"Whiskey and soda," I said.

The waiter bowed to Rebecca. "Say hello to Mr. Hanson for me."

Rebecca gave him a polite smile. "I will, thank you."

He left and I leaned forward. "How *is* your boyfriend?"

"Skip it."

"No harm, just wondering."

"Well, don't wonder. Let's just enjoy this evening and talk about something else."

"I was hoping I might have a snowball's chance in hell of seeing you again. Like a real date."

"If you keep pushing there won't even be this evening. Now, please, let's talk about something else."

"All right." But I couldn't think of anything else. "Let me

think, I told you you look beautiful and I'm glad we're here together."

She gave me a quick smile but turned pensive. The waiter came back with the drinks. I pulled out my cash, but Rebecca put her hand on mine.

"He'll keep a tab. They do that in places like this."

I asked the waiter, "Got any peanuts?"

The guy was a real pro; he had a whole menu of condescending looks.

"I'll see what I have."

He left us with one last look back.

"I take it they don't have peanuts in places like this."

She smiled at my expense, but at least she was smiling. "No, not really."

Then she opened up, looked more relaxed. My lack of sophistication apparently charmed her, though I'd have preferred irresistible sex appeal.

"So, where'd you get the money?" she asked. "You go from penniless to Daddy Warbucks overnight. What's your secret?"

"You guessed right earlier. A rich uncle."

"You're not very good at making up stories, are you?"

"Now it's my turn not to talk about it. I just want to enjoy the evening, and I wanted you to know that I can take care of you without asking you to foot the bill. Like, how about dinner tomorrow night?"

She leaned in and lowered her voice. "Did you steal it?"

"That's what you think of me? I'm incapable of a legit source?" I knew I protested too much.

"You're a bad liar, but I like that about you. That's a good trait in a man." Rebecca came a little closer. Her scent was enough to give me a deep flush. "You think I wanted to see you again because of your money? My biggest hope is that you have some incredible job so you can buy me jewels and furs?"

"I thought that's what every woman wants, at least secretly."

Rebecca drew back a little. "Every guy I ever met has the same problem. You can't buy a woman's love. Maybe romance, but not love."

"You seem to be doing all right," I said, immediately regretting it.

"What's that supposed to mean?"

"I can't compete with a sugar daddy like your Mr. Hanson."

Rebecca pulled back completely. "That's really low. Just because I date a guy with money, you assume I'm bought and paid for?" There was conviction in her voice, but not in her face. She took a big swallow of her drink. "You think you're the only one trying to get ahead in this life? I've been a hatcheck girl, a secretary until the boss started grabbing my ass, a cocktail waitress until *everyone* started grabbing my ass or propositioned me so many times I couldn't stand it anymore. I met a nice guy that happens to have money and I'm condemned."

"I wasn't condemning you. I'm just a little jealous. Well, a lot jealous."

"Jealousy isn't flattering," she said, her voice rising.

The waiter came back with a small bowl of olives. He shot me a glare and left.

"When I'm around you, I have feelings I've never experienced," I said. "You've turned me from an avowed bachelor to a heart-throbbing schoolkid, and I'm not responsible for my actions. You do that to me."

The love speech didn't seem to penetrate. She just looked at me. I wanted to know where she stood, but her face revealed nothing.

"I'm trying to figure you out, and I'm not getting very far," I said.

"Well, stop trying. Relax. You're not going to figure me out in five minutes, and you can't woo a girl by getting into her head. You have to win her heart." She smiled and stroked my cheek. "You could win mine if you didn't try so hard."

Being with her was an addiction I couldn't control. I think I truly fell in love with her at that moment. I wanted to say so much, but doubt plagued me. All I could do was raise my glass, too vulnerable to do more.

"That's better," she said. "I can see the ridges in your forehead relax. I knew you had it in you."

"So, do I have a chance, or is Hanson holding all the cards?"

Rebecca signaled the waiter for another round. She came close again. "I'll make you a deal. You tell me where the money comes from, because I have my suspicions, and I'll tell you about Hanson, since I know you have yours."

As much as I wanted to, I couldn't. "I wasn't going to tell you because it's embarrassing. I got it from my mom."

"Bullshit. Is it drugs? Huh? Prostitution? You selling yourself to rich old ladies or boys?"

I felt the blood fill my face. She'd struck a guilty chord I'd kept buried, and again, my mouth jumped off before my mind could stop it.

"What do you call what you're doing with your sugar daddy? That's prostitution, just a more elegant form."

"I've had enough." She grabbed her purse. "Don't forget the tab, hotshot." She got up from the table and walked away.

I couldn't let this happen a second time. I wouldn't have another chance. I left more than enough money on the table then tossed the jacket to the maître d' and hurried out the exit.

She was down the block, waiting for a slowing cab. I had no other choice but to run. She saw me when I was just a few feet away. I stopped. The warm light of the restaurant reflected off her tears. We stared at each other until I couldn't stand it anymore. I lunged for her. To my surprise, she did the same and we collided in a tangle of arms, lips, want, and need.

"You want a ride or not?" the cabdriver barked.

We looked at each other and knew. I took her hand and guided her into the cab. I gave the driver my address. I tried to move into her arms but she stopped me.

"Are you sure you want to do this? You don't know what you're getting into with me."

"I'll take my chances."

We wrapped ourselves around each other and dropped all inhibition. The passion was intoxicating, the cab a haven whose soft rumble provided a backdrop to our breathing. My world was her lips, her neck, her body.

The love we made that night started at the front door and wound slowly through the room. Even now, I can remember the hot, exquisite burn pulsing from head to groin, the aroma of lust, the sensation of flesh on flesh, the taste of her in my mouth, and the feel of being inside her.

We lay there for hours afterward, still playing with each

other while the radio DJ spun records during his *Candlelight Hour* broadcast.

Sometime during the night she must have pulled away. I sensed a change; that other life of hers and the secrets she kept from me invaded my dreams.

17

I woke the next morning to a soft buzz that nagged at my ears until my brain decided to respond. My eyes opened. Rebecca was zipping up her dress. She must have been up for a while, because her hair and makeup were in perfect order.

"You weren't going to leave without saying good-bye, were you?" I asked.

"I wanted to let you sleep as much as possible."

"I don't need the sleep. I need to see you again. Why are you sneaking out of here?"

"I'm not sneaking. I was going to say good-bye." She leaned on the bed and we kissed. "I had a wonderful time." She stood, distracted about something. "I just have a bunch of important stuff to do and need to get out of here."

"More important than having the best morning sex of your life?"

She said nothing as she touched up her lipstick. The distance had returned, and I felt like the girl who's tossed aside after a night of sex. She gathered the last of her things and turned back to me.

"You're not going to be the type who lays claim to a girl after bedding her, are you? I just have stuff to do and would like to keep it private. That all right with you?"

"How many types of guys do you know?"

"There are only two types. The guys who think they own a girl after screwing her and those who want to have nothing to do with her afterward. Which are you?"

"I don't do well with trick questions first thing in the morning."

She kissed me and started for the door.

"Wait," I said. "What about tonight?"

She came back to the bed and kissed me again. "If you insist on an answer now, then no. If you can wait, then it's maybe."

Our lips met again, long and hard this time. Rebecca broke the embrace and caught her breath. Then she was gone.

Emotion flooded my mind: the ecstasy of sex and romance, but also a nagging feeling that it would all come to an end as quickly as it had started. I'd only be able to watch her from a distance as she fell into the arms of the rich guy, Hanson. All sorts of fantasies unrolled as I conceived of ways to get rid of the guy. But that's all they were—fantasies. I never expected I'd have the chance.

I TOOK A SHOWER, GRABBED A COFFEE, AND WENT DOWNSTAIRS to meet Turly. He swung by ten minutes later. I knew a good diner near Chinatown, so we headed out. Halfway there, I got tired of his grunts and one-word answers.

"You all right?" I asked.

"I'm fine."

"You don't act fine."

"It's nothing. I was just thinking is all."

Turly found a space near the diner and parked. "You think someone's going to come after us?"

"Yeah, someone might figure it all out and come after us."

"I didn't count on getting killed."

"Me neither, but it's too late, so we ride it out, then get the hell out. You're cool, right? Because I need to count on you and not worry you're going to start trying on straitjackets."

Turly answered with a groan as we entered Gino's Diner. We grabbed a booth and ordered. My friend stared straight at me with that *just wait till I get you home* look until the waitress left.

"I don't like it," he said.

"You're staying in," I said.

"It's starting to stink. What are you going to do when some killers come after you?"

"I don't know."

"You see? It isn't that simple. We'll have the cops on our ass while we're watching for killers to come and hack off our dicks."

"Cute imagery," I said.

"Well?"

"Well, what?"

Turly forced the words so hard through his teeth that his cheeks puffed out and his forehead turned red. "You've got your head so deep in the sand you can't see the shit flying in your direction."

"Turl, it's going to be okay. You just do what George asks and everything will be cool. This won't last more than a couple of weeks and then you can blend back into the suburbs. Okay?"

Whether it was okay or not, Turly leaned back and shut up. Our order arrived, and after the caffeine fix and a little food in my stomach, my mood improved. Until …

"Hello, boys."

I looked up. Daniel Devrees was standing by our table.

"Mind if I sit in?" he said with a big grin on his mug. "Must be fate. We keep showing up at the same places."

Turly moved over for him before I could tell Daniel to drop dead.

"Yeah, fate," I said.

"Aren't you going to introduce me to your buddy?" Daniel asked.

"Turly, Disease. Disease, Turly."

"I told you I don't like that name." Daniel turned to Turly and offered his hand. "Hey, *Devrees* is the name. Daniel Devrees."

My friend moved to shake, and Daniel went for his toast. "Mind if I have a slice?"

I concentrated on my eggs and tried to ignore him.

"You boys are sporting some interesting bruises. Why, y'all are a matching set. What ya been up to?"

Turly opened his mouth but I cut him off. "Rugby."

Daniel looked at us, taking his time chewing. "I get the picture. I won't ask. Just tryin' to be friendly."

"We were having a private discussion," I said.

"You still owe me some money. Two hundred, I believe."

I pulled out the cash, counted it, and threw it in his direction. He picked it up and smiled, then washed down the toast in his mouth with Turly's coffee and leaned in.

"I'd like a little piece of the action myself, fellas." He looked at me with eyes that said he knew. "You forget, man, I'm plugged into the system. I know people who know people, and on down the line. And look at you, throwing money around. It all makes sense. I know you, man. You can't pull the wool over my eyes." He smiled at his own cleverness.

"Get lost," I said.

"What's one more guy?" he asked. "I don't take up too much space. I got a car, and I know the marketplace." He dropped an arm on the table and pulled up his sleeve. There were track marks along the inside of his forearm. "You might say I've got a pulse on the market." He laughed at his own pun and covered his arm.

"Nothing's going on."

"I've seen you and your partner around. That fella with the movie-star grin and the black Buick. I frequent some of the same places you do."

Blood rushed to my face—fear that he knew too much and embarrassment that I hadn't noticed him spying on me.

"That burned-out pile of shit you have for a brain is making you see things," I said.

"No reason to get nasty, man. I know what I know. You and that cat are working for Vincent. And the word on the street is that somebody jumped a shipment of H a couple of nights ago and glommed it from the wrong guy."

A cold sweat popped on my forehead. Turly chomped on his pancakes, avoiding my eyes. He flooded the plate with maple syrup, maybe hoping that with enough sugar everything bad would go away.

"So," Daniel went on, "you see, when my nose picks up the scent, it's never wrong, and I decided to follow you."

Turly gagged. Daniel slapped him on the back. "Man, you gotta chew your food better."

I tried a tough-guy attitude to mask my own panic. "Bullshit. You didn't follow us. You're bluffing to get information."

"I don't want to insist, 'cause you're a buddy and I think that's rude. I'd rather be invited. It makes me feel more at home, relaxed. It's a Southern thing, hospitality and all. 'Howdy' and 'y'all come back, now, ya hear?' You know, shit like that. So, what do you say?"

"I can't say. I'm not the boss."

"I'm sure he'll agree. He'll want to avoid any loose ends. Any trouble, you might say. It'd be plain better just to let me in and not worry about anything. You dig what I'm telling you?"

He leaned back, pulled a toothpick out of his coat pocket and went at his teeth. All with a big smile.

"You've got it all wrong," I said. "What action we got is not worth your time. But I'll talk to my partner and see what he has to say. I'm sure he won't like the loose ends either, but nothing happens without his say-so. I've got your number. I'll call you tomorrow."

Daniel took another swig of Turly's coffee. "Better yet, I think it'd be fun to hang out with you guys. I'd like to go along. I hate being left out, and I hate waiting by the phone. Okay?" He forked the last bit of Turly's pancakes. "I tell you what, I'll let you two think about it." He got up, brushed the crumbs off his belly. "I'll catch you cats outside."

Daniel waddled down the aisle and stepped out.

"I don't feel so good," Turly said. "We're screwed, aren't we?"

"We're not screwed. He knows less than he thinks, but he's too close to brush off. I'd better call George. Wait here."

I slid out of the booth and went to the pay phone near the restrooms. Smoking a cigarette and pacing the floor didn't help; it just gave me time to imagine the worst of George's wrath. I forced myself to pick up the phone and dial.

"What the hell are you doing calling me so early?" George said.

"I've got a problem and I need to talk to you." I hesitated, realizing I should have taken more time to formulate what I was going to say. "I don't know if it's that bad. There's this guy …" I closed my eyes and blurted out the rest. "He's the dealer I borrowed money from. He's been nosing around and found out about us. You know, what we're doing."

"What the fuck? Come on, spit it out fast!"

No matter how hard I tried to explain, it sounded bad. George took only a second to calculate, something I envied in him. It took me decades to decide anything.

"All right," he said, "we let him in, but only as far as we have to. We keep him in the dark about the amount and the place. He helps us distribute, and that's it. And it's coming out of your cut."

I'd known that was coming. "Yeah. I'll see you at noon."

I hung up and walked over to the exit, signaling Turly to follow me, and we left the diner.

It was one of those mornings where the intense, hazy light warned of an oncoming heatwave. I stuck to the shadows to escape the sun, but felt the sweat trickling down my sides. Maybe it was the heat; more likely the heart-thumping stress.

"Here's our boys," Daniel said as we met him on the sidewalk. He held out a half-pint of vodka. "Want some?" He wiggled the bottle with a grin and glazed eyes.

I shook my head. "You're in."

"Cool, my fine-feathered cats. I knew your partner would pick up what I was laying down."

"What'd he say?" Turly asked, a not-so-subtle way of finding out how much trouble we were in with George.

"Nothing," I said, and pointed to Daniel. "Just that he's in and helps with distribution."

Daniel rubbed his hands together. "When do we get started?"

"Now. And you might want to quit drinking till we're done."

"Forget it, baby," Daniel said, using the bottle to make the point. "This is my lubrication, my cushion for the shock my body goes into when I lay my eyes on all that snow."

"It stays in the packets and out of your veins. You start stealing from the stash, I don't think you'll live very long."

"Ooh, the man's talking tough."

"I'm not the one you should worry about."

A slight breeze kicked up and carried an odor of at least a week's worth of Daniel's bad hygiene. I was sure he'd just come off a binge of heroin or booze or both.

We climbed into Turly's car and went over to George's.

I kept ahead of Daniel the whole way up to the apartment to avoid his stink. I didn't have to knock; George opened the door and motioned us in. Marty stood off from the rest, leaning up against the wall at the back of the corner kitchen. Roach and Arliss were sitting together on the sofa. Roach had his normal cigarette-holder grin, and Arliss sat splayed out, legs on the coffee table, arms crossed, and doing his best to scowl. I'm sure George had muzzled Arliss. I nodded a hello, as did Turly. Daniel went up to George and shook his hand vigorously.

"I'm Daniel. How y'all doin'?" he said in his best N'awlens accent.

"That depends," George answered. "Sit down."

Daniel ignored the command and shook hands with Marty, Roach, and Arliss. "How y'all doin'?"

Roach blew smoke at him. "I'd be better if next time you found your way to a bathtub."

"Yeah, I've been sleepin' under the stars. I did this whole morphine, cocaine and heroin cocktail that's …" He shook his body for emphasis. "… that's so gone, man."

"How are you, big fella?" Daniel asked Arliss.

"Uh … hey," was all Arliss could muster, seemingly disarmed by Daniel's enthusiasm. He was more comfortable with guys who cowered under his glare.

Roach chuckled and patted Arliss on the thigh.

"Sit down, cornpone," George said.

Daniel plopped onto the floor next to Arliss and beamed like a kid at the circus, while Turly looked like a four-year-old on the haunted-house ride. I sat in a chair, and Turly took his usual place on the floor by the hole in the carpet. We all turned our attention to George, who stepped up to Daniel and stood over him.

"I don't know you, and I don't trust you," he said, "but you're here, so what have you got?"

"As Frank knows, I'm already plugged into the market. I've got a preexisting customer base. Sure, it's mostly reefer, but I've been meaning to branch out, and now that opportunity presents itself. They're not what you call high-volume buyers, but enough of 'em to keep me busy. I'll keep up with y'all, don't worry."

"I don't want you stepping on anybody's toes. We fly under the radar."

Daniel studied George's face. "I'm diggin' ya."

Arliss leaned forward within inches of Daniel's ear, pulled out a switchblade, and popped it open. Turly gasped, but Daniel didn't flinch.

"Just give me an excuse to use this," Arliss said.

George motioned for him to put the blade away. Arliss slowly closed the knife and leaned back.

"Every day you bring back the money," George said. "All of the money and whatever you didn't sell. That clear?"

"When do we stop fucking around and get started?" Daniel asked.

"All right," George said, "it works like this. Frankie and I take our normal route to keep up appearances, then distribute on the side. Marty's got contacts up north. He's making a run up to Seattle. Roach and Arliss have their contacts at Presidio and Treasure Island—"

"That's cool," Daniel said. "Talk about mass marketing. I always knew Uncle Sam was a junkie."

"Our man Turly will keep track of all outgoing supply and incoming cash."

Daniel raised his hand. "All I need to know is, how much do I get to unload? I've got to get a feel for the supply so I can stir up the right amount of customers."

"How are you going to sell it? Single doses, nickels, dimes, grams, what?"

"How about I start with a quarter pound so I can cut it and package it myself depending on my customers' needs?"

"You'll start with a half ounce," George answered.

"Now that's gonna limit my resources. How much you got?"

"You don't need to know that."

"You got a limited supply? Is this like a onetime thing? Did you just happen to come across a load lying in the street? Y'all don't impress me as hard-boiled professionals with your fingers on the pulse of the overseas wholesale market. That takes time, lots of capital, and balls. I bet there ain't much of that between the five of you." Daniel chuckled.

George squatted down face-to-face with him. "You ask too many questions. I don't like you or the way you got here, so my advice would be to shut up and do as you're told."

Daniel's smile changed from good ole boy to menacing. "That's not a threat, is it? You don't think I was dumb enough to just waltz in here without protection? Because I do have insurance—life insurance, that is—so I'm not one of your boys. I'm, let's say, a business partner. You dig?"

George stood up and walked into the kitchen. I could hear him opening cabinets and setting up the scale. I looked around the room at the faces of my friends. Daniel was right about us not being hard-boiled professionals; it looked more like a fraternity meeting. Daniel chuckled again.

"How do we know you won't just take this half ounce and disappear?" I said.

"I'll be a whole lot richer if I hang around, and y'all will be a whole lot better off if I disappear. Which one do you think is my preferred option?"

George came back and dropped a packet in his lap. "It's uncut. You cut it however you want, but you bring back at least eight hundred."

Daniel weighed it with his hand. "Oh, man, this is chicken-shit. I'll be knocking on your door by tomorrow morning, asking for more."

"You do that," George said. "Now, get out of here."

Daniel cracked a hollow smile, stood, and scanned our faces in a last act of defiance. Behind his cold eyes hid a self-abused addict, afraid and desperate. I felt sorry for him some-how, but mostly I hoped I wouldn't end up the same way. I'd already met too many people in this business that had lived hard and died fast. I looked around the room and wondered when it would be their turn, or mine. Daniel put his back to us and left.

"Are we gonna follow him?" Arliss asked.

"No," George answered. "If he's selling on the street, I know guys that can find him. If he doesn't get pinched or bumped off first."

Roach looked at me. "What's this life insurance he's talking about?"

"I don't know," I said. "I figure he's got some kind of low-level connection. He knows too much just to be guessing. He said he knew where to go with the information."

"I know the guy," Marty said. "He's nothing, but the guys he's connected to are serious business."

"We should take him down before he rats us out," Arliss said.

"We're moving the operation," George said. "From now on, we work out of my car and at different places every day."

"What a pain in the ass," Arliss said, and then turned his wrath on me. "Did I thank you, dickhead, for fucking things up?"

"Forget it," George said. "It's better this way. If Danny-boy keeps his trap shut and unloads some of the stuff for us, the faster it goes and the faster we get rich."

"*If* he keeps his mouth shut," Turly said.

"Well, for once, me and Turl see eye to eye," Arliss said. "We have to take him out."

We all looked at one another, then at George. He waited for us to decide.

"If he gets steamed, he'll squeal," Marty said. "If he gets pinched, he'll squeal. If he gets greedy, he might squeal. It comes down to survival."

"I'll sleep better if he's gone, and I don't care if it takes longer to unload," Roach said.

"I can't believe what I'm hearing," I said. "I mean we're talking about murder."

"You want to take the chance that he squeals?" Arliss yelled. "I sure as hell don't."

"What about his insurance? He's not stupid."

"He could be bluffing," Turly said.

"Yeah, *could* be," I said. "We don't know, and I'd prefer not to add murderers to our job titles."

"You knew it came with the territory," Arliss yelled back.

"Two weeks ago we were just hangin' at Sammy's, talking about sex, money, and social ills. Now look at us. It's bad enough that we're selling smack, but I don't want to have blood on my hands for the rest of my life. Think about it. There's got to be another way."

No one said anything. I wasn't surprised. I didn't feel that convinced myself. I knew sooner or later my survival instincts would kick in, but I couldn't imagine killing anyone, and I was desperate to steer our enterprise clear of any more bloodletting.

George grabbed his jacket. "You finished?" Off my nod, he

said, "Then let's go." He turned to Marty, Roach, and Arliss. "You cats know what to do."

"We're gone," Roach answered. "Let's agitate the gravel, my brother."

"Turly, stay here for now," George said. "There's not much to do until we get cranked up. Start a list of who's got what and sit tight. Don't go anywhere, don't open the door, and don't make any phone calls."

Turly nodded and looked sad … I figured about being left behind. George went to a small chest by the sofa and removed the bottom drawer. He pulled out a .38 revolver, checked the chamber, snapped it closed and held it out. Turly stared at it for a moment, then took it.

"You're guarding the stash," George said. "If that gumbo asshole tries anything, you add a little lead to his diet."

Arliss burst out laughing. "Oh, that's too much."

"I wouldn't laugh too hard," Roach said. "He's got the gun." He turned to Turly. "Remember. Point, then shoot. And wait till they're inside. Good luck, cowboy." He put their heroin into an old army backpack and pushed Arliss toward the door.

I could still hear Arliss laughing as they went down the stairs.

I walked over to Turly and put a hand on his shoulder. "Don't worry, you're not going to need it."

"I'm not worried. I know how to use it. I did some target practicing with my dad. Every time I had one of these in my hand, I thought about using it on him." He lifted the gun and aimed at an image of his father only he could see.

I noticed George trying not to laugh. "Just don't shoot us. We're the good guys."

"Yeah," Turly said.

George pulled on his jacket and grabbed the briefcase like he was ready for another day at the office. We left Turly sitting in the chair, staring at the wall, facing down whatever demons were floating before his eyes.

18

George's and my first stop was Vitner, our friendly bank manager. This time, George came with me, and so there would be no confusion, we both rolled up our sleeves. I carried a paper sack, not with packets of H, but with an actual sandwich we'd picked up at a deli on the way over.

We hung around a small counter in the middle of the cavernous lobby. A few customers flowed past us or waited for an available teller. I feigned interest in a deposit slip as I cased the place for anyone tailing us. One guard was stationed close to the walk-in safe, another behind one of the large marble columns that flanked the lobby, but neither seemed interested in us. High overhead, Vitner's office had a large picture window that looked down upon the lobby. We both kept an eye on the window. Vitner stood by his desk, talking to a short, bald guy who was almost bowing with submission.

"We can't hang out here forever," I said. "The guard by the safe might start to get suspicious."

"About what? He going to bust us for a salami sandwich?"

"Well, maybe mayo on rye is illegal in this bank. You never know."

"That's good. Your sense of humor is back."

"It's that laugh-in-the-face-of-death thing."

"Better than crying," George said, and pointed to the retirement brochure he'd been reading. "Look, you can put away fifty dollars per month at the age of thirty in this fine institution, and by sixty-five you'll have sixty-seven thousand dollars. We're going to make that by the end of the week."

"What are you going to do after we make all this dough?"

"I've got some things going on," he said, his eyes still on the brochure. "I like to live by the seat of my pants. What about you?"

"Find a doctor to look at my hand, then cut my album."

"No chicks for you?"

"Yeah, that goes without saying," I said.

I had an image of George with three girls at a time, popping champagne, while I pined for Rebecca and hung out at nightclubs, hoping to get a glimpse of her and Hanson. Pathetic.

George gave me a light slap and laughed. "I hope you can do it, man. I want to see you riding the big waves, keeping your head up and your feet dry."

I saw movement out of the corner of my eye. The bald guy was leaving Vitner's office. I motioned to George and he looked up. Vitner noticed us and took a moment, probably deciding whether we were there to deliver off schedule or bring threatening news from Vincent. He waved for us to come up, and drew the window shade closed.

We made it past the guard dog of a secretary and slipped into Vitner's office. I closed the door, joined George near the desk, and handed Vitner the sack. He opened it, took a whiff of the salami, and closed it again.

"Next time try and look a little more respectable. I don't want every employee in the bank getting suspicious. Now, what do you boys want? It's not the usual time."

"We've got a proposition for you," I said.

"Go on."

"Mr. Vitner," I began, "last week you requested a volume discount based on your valued patronage. I think we—that is, my partner here and I—can formulate an arrangement that might be quite attractive to you."

"It's a good start. I'm listening."

George took over. "You were paying fifteen hundred dollars, I believe."

Vitner studied George. "You're the one who delivered to me before."

"That's right, and that's why I know it was fifteen hundred."

Vitner's gaze flitted between the two of us for a moment. "This wouldn't be coming from the regular sources, would it? How will that sit with them? Not too pretty, I imagine. No, boys, no deal. I like my body with the number of holes nature has already provided me." He started to move away.

"We're offering twelve hundred," George said. That stopped Vitner. "You buy enough from your other source to keep him happy and the rest from us."

Vitner walked over to a small cabinet and removed a bottle of Scotch. "You boys care to join me?"

My mouth watered. "Sure."

George gave me a reproving glance. I shrugged. Vitner poured three glasses and popped in some ice from a bucket. He handed us our drinks, stepped back, and swirled his drink as he studied us. I sniffed and sipped the fine Scotch—a far cry from the call-brand whiskey I normally abused.

"Eleven hundred and you've got a deal," Vitner finally said.

"Eleven hundred depends on the volume," George countered.

"I can start with three ounces."

"That'll work," George said. "We've got a deal?"

Vitner took a sip and nodded. "Deal."

"All right," George said. "My partner will come at the usual delivery time with three of ours and the one from our competitors."

Vitner looked at me, walked over, and took the unfinished drink out of my hand. "I'll see you in four days. And this time, meet me in the parking lot, twelve thirty. I have a reserved spot. Can't miss it. No more deliveries in the bank. It's raising too many suspicions."

"You got it, chief," I said.

"And get a shave and a bath, for heaven's sake."

"The Lord is my shepherd, sir. He will leadeth me to soapy waters."

Vitner shook his head and turned his back on us. George grabbed my arm and pulled me away. We left Vitner and walked the gauntlet of the bank lobby.

WE HIT ANOTHER BUNCH OF HUNGRY CLIENTS THAT GEORGE had lined up. He'd obviously done some presales before we pinched the shipment, and by early afternoon, we had a wad of cash and a lighter load of H.

George had the radio cranked as we rode around the city. He danced in his seat, snapping his fingers to the beat. A little drizzle misted the windows, and I watched the windshield wipers as I settled back into my natural brooding state. In spite of the good beginning to our new enterprise, my bones were telling me a different story: There would be a slipup somewhere or a misspoken word, and I would be found dead, or the celebrity piece-of-ass in some state penitentiary.

George gave me a shove. "Snap out of it, man. Everything's cool. See how simple that was?"

"I'm superstitious about simple. When everything's cool or simple, it means something bad is just around the corner. I feel more comfortable with pain in the ass."

"Man, you can see shadows in the shadows."

"It's a perverted form of survival instinct. My own brand."

"We're going to work all our clientele the same way we did Vitner, and get this stuff unloaded. You've got at least ten grand in your pocket right now. The way I figure it, the six of us will walk away from this thing with two hundred and fifty thousand smackeroos. Each. I figure more like three hundred if we do this just right. That make you feel better?"

"You're shittin' me."

George shook his head, smiled, and restarted his seat dancing. I felt a flush of blood gorge whatever part of my brain controlled ecstasy and arousal. I screamed out like a cowboy at a rodeo.

"That's my boy," George said. "I thought that might change your outlook."

"That'll change a whole lot of things. Who's next? Let's get this thing going."

"You got it, baby. We have a couple more clients, but first we have to check in with Charlie. I'll give him a cut of the earnings and a little H. That ought to make him happy."

I let out another cowboy whoop and we both danced in our seats on the way to Charlie's.

George parked down the street from the house. He counted out some cash and gave me a packet of heroin. "Just keep it simple and friendly."

"I'll handle it."

I got out of the car and walked through the drizzle. I was near a hedge in the corner of Charlie's yard when I heard the front door open. I had no reason to hide, but some instinct took over. I slipped behind the overgrown hedge and ducked around the side of the house. A man walked casually toward the sidewalk. He crossed the street and stopped at a car. When he turned and looked back toward Charlie's house, I recognized him. One of the bouncers from the Aztec who guarded the offices.

I hugged the ground until I was sure he was gone, then popped up and looked in a side window. I had a view of the dining room and into the living room. No sign of Charlie. I snuck into a small backyard. The ground was strewn with cracked and broken tiles and empty flowerpots. A stub of a porch led to the back door. I crept up and listened for any movement. It was either hightail it or head in and take whatever came. After a couple of deep breaths, I inched open the door. One small squeak of the hinges and I was in.

"Charlie?" I said to the house. "It's George's friend Frank."

I stepped over trash that littered the floor. The only signs of him using the kitchen were the blackened spoons, used matches, and a handful of syringes sitting in a pot of water. At least he was sanitary—no infections when he finally dropped dead. The silence told me he was in a drug stupor or passed out.

"Charlie!"

I took one step out into the living room and froze. Charlie was slumped in his favorite chair, both arms hanging off the sides. A snub-nosed .38 lay on the floor near his open right hand. Blood still seeped from a small red hole in his right temple. His face resembled a wax figure of horror: skin a yellowish white, bulging eyes, gaping mouth, and blood trickling from his ears and nose.

I slammed against the wall and my stomach convulsed, threatening to bring up what was left of my lunch. But the urge to run overruled my belly. I ran through the back and skimmed along the side yard. With one glance at the front of the house, I rushed back to the car.

I told George what I'd seen. In spite of my warning, he wanted to see for himself. I ended up in the last place I wanted to be, standing in Charlie's living room again. George got as close as he could without stepping in the puddle of blood that had formed around the chair.

"It looks sort of fresh, but I can't be sure."

"I'm telling you, it was the bouncer from the Aztec. He walked out of here like he'd just left church."

George looked around the room. "Nothing's been disturbed."

"Let's get out of here," I said. "This is a murder scene, man. I don't want to get caught."

"It looks like suicide to me. That's his gun," George said,

pointing to the .38. "This isn't the first time he's put a gun to his head. Remember?"

"Maybe the bouncer wanted it to look that way."

"I think the guy came by because Charlie hadn't shown up somewhere. If the guy just left, then the blood should still be wet."

Morbid curiosity got the better of me, and I stared at Charlie. That's when I noticed something white stuffed deep in his mouth.

"George, take a look at this."

George came over and leaned in. He reached into Charlie's mouth with his forefinger and thumb.

"What the hell are you doing?"

He ignored me and fished around, trying not to touch Charlie's violet lips. He put his other hand on Charlie's chin and pushed. My stomach turned a few loops as Charlie's lifeless head flopped and George dislodged whatever was jammed inside. A blood-soaked wad of paper came free.

"We can go now," he said. "Did you touch anything?"

"The back door."

"Wipe it down and let's get outta here."

We made it back to the car. George unwadded the paper with bloody fingers. I could see writing, but not what was written.

"*I can't take it anymore. Charlie.*"

"That's it?" I said. "Charlie was more verbose than that. He'd have used two pages."

George crumpled the paper and threw it on the floor. He started up the car and drove off. Neither of us said anything, but George kept wiping his hands.

"George, who did we steal from? Who is *they*? You always refer to 'them' or 'they' and never a name."

George watched the road a moment. The windshield wiper blades rubbed against the glass, a metronome counting off the seconds.

"It's a business conglomerate."

"You mean businessmen? I thought this was gang stuff like the Mafia or something."

"Mafia is New York, Chicago, L.A., but San Francisco is a sort of forgotten backwater compared to her big sisters. I'm sure it ultimately leads back to the Mafia, but, aside from the Chinese gangs, most of the actual operations have been left to a syndicate of businessmen, investors, lawyers, politicians, public officials, even some of the founding families of this grand city. They call the shots in most of the rackets from here, and north to Canada."

I tried to wrap my head around the whole idea. "We stole heroin from a bunch of guys in business suits?"

"Don't let that fool you. They're just as ruthless."

"I've seen their work."

"It might be even slicker than the Mafia, because you've got legitimate guys in places of power buried in the system."

"Is Vincent a part of this group?" I asked.

George shook his head. "It's not that simple. The best I figure, he's supplied by the syndicate, and allowed to run semi-independently, but he doesn't know their identities, except for some lower-level guys. He and some other independent operators are left alone to do business as long as they don't stray from syndicate directives. They're the smoke screen, the first line of defense. They give the cops someone to bust, so the politicians can brag about cleaning up the city during their next campaign, all the while collecting on their share of the profits."

I had to ask even though I knew the answer and didn't want to hear it. "And Charlie?"

George nodded. "He was one of their principal lawyers before his downfall."

We'd stolen from a powerful syndicate. My guts churned.

"What if they tortured him? He definitely would have talked."

"I'm telling you, it was suicide."

"You think they're on to us?"

"Impossible. I've been covering my tracks the whole time. There is no way they could trace it back to us. No way!"

He was done talking; I wouldn't get any more out of him. He flicked on the radio, settled back into his seat, and watched the road. Probably plotting the next move. That should have given me some comfort, but each time George furrowed his brow, I had the feeling we were sinking a little deeper into our own graves.

19

W e spent the rest of the afternoon making more deliveries. We sold more than we'd expected, which lifted some of the anxiety, but I still couldn't get the image of Charlie dead in his favorite chair out of my mind.

"Aren't you the least bit sorry about Charlie?" I asked.

George stopped his dancing for a moment. "Sure I am. But you might have noticed, dear buddy, that I tend to laugh in the face of adversity. It's my way of dealing with the crap of everyday life."

"Is that how you coped in prison?"

George's smile faded. "How did you know about that?"

"Roach. Why didn't you ever tell me?"

"Those were some dark days. I don't like to talk about that. Ever."

"Is that why you quit politics?"

"You think this is bad, you should try politics. I got screwed and tattooed, man. I got popped for possession because I was getting reefer for that scumbag politician I was working for. Can you dig that? It wasn't even mine. And when it came time for him to help me out, he was nowhere to be seen. I spent eighteen months in San Quentin for that motherfucker."

George fell quiet for a moment. Then his hands started tapping the steering wheel to the music.

"I saw things in there. Some things happened to me in there … You grow a crust, or you don't survive. So, when you think I'm not feeling any pain, think again."

We fell back into silence. George tapped to the music and sang softly, and I understood his demeanor a little better: that smile of his and the devil-may-care posturing had a whole lot of hurt behind it.

One bright point of that day overshadowed everything else. I was carrying my usual lunch sack through the lobby of a savings-and-loan building to the elevators. A large real-estate investment firm occupied the penthouse offices, and I was delivering four ounces of H to the codirector. To push the elevator call button, I had to transfer the bag to my left hand. A sting—just a pinprick—surprised me and I dropped the bag. Alarm bells went off as I watched it fall, imagining its contents bursting open and heroin spilling across the floor.

But the bag remained intact. I snatched it up and breathed a sigh of relief. Then I realized why the pain had surprised me. The staple had stuck my fourth finger. The elevator arrived but I ignored it. I bent back the staple and gave my finger a good jab. The bite triggered my reflexes and my hand recoiled. The few other people nearby must have thought I was crazy, because I let out a cheer and repeatedly struck my fingers, yelling, "They're alive!"

On the ride up, I prodded and poked. The tips were sensitive, farther up my hand less so. I tested for movement, but the fingers refused to move. Still, this small victory had given me hope, and that's why Mr. Markham, the codirector of the firm and buyer of our wares, would have to explain to his partner— and co-buyer—why the guy delivering their sack lunch was singing "Mack the Knife" all the way through the suite of offices.

THAT EVENING, I CALLED TURLY AT GEORGE'S AND TOLD HIM to meet me at an Italian place I knew on Mason. Over a giant pizza and pitchers of beer, I recounted some of what had happened. And even the part I told him was half lies. He heard about burying Herman's body, but I left out Charlie and much of the detail about the syndicate.

I told him to hang out there for an hour, and went back to my apartment so I could call Rebecca in private.

She picked up on the third ring.

"It's me," I said.

There was an unnerving pause. "I can't talk right now."

"Oh? You got Gramps over there?"

"No, smart-ass, I don't."

"You told me to call and that's what I'm doing. Man, you run hot and cold. It's enough to give a guy the flu."

"Why are you making this so difficult?" she asked in a sharp tone.

"Me? What's the matter? You're not allowed to go out and play with kids your own age?"

She didn't say anything. Soft music wafted in the background. What she could do to me with those long pauses.

"Please, just an hour," I said. "A drink or something."

"Meet me by the north side of Coit Tower. It's not safe for you. That adolescent bravado of yours has gotten you attention from the wrong people. David is asking a lot of questions about you."

She hung up.

I took a taxi to the end of Lombard and walked up the hill to Coit Tower, just in case I was being followed. It was a little after ten p.m. by the time I got there. The park was empty except for a few lovers. I waited in some bushes away from the tower lights, enjoying a view of the Golden Gate Bridge and the lights of Marin County on the other side of the bay.

Up here with the trees and the crickets, surrounded by rooftops and above the traffic noise, the city felt more benign. I loved this place, but I could no longer look at it with innocent eyes. I'd seen too much the past few days. Now the city seemed like its bay, alluring when viewed from the shore, but underneath the surface lay a dark heart and dangerous currents.

I'd finished most of a cigarette by the time Rebecca arrived. She was most of the way across the circular drive when I spotted her. In a long black coat and with that dark hair, she blended in with the night. I walked over to meet her near the circle of light.

"You look like you're going to open one of my arteries," I said.

She didn't say a word, just marched up to me, grabbed my shoulders, and pulled me in to her. She kissed me hard and released whatever she had in her saliva that immediately intoxicated me. She had pulled back the curtains and granted me a glimpse of heaven.

She broke the kiss. "Why do you do this to me? I've got to

be crazy seeing you." She turned and walked back the way she had come.

I caught up to her. "I'm the one that's got to be crazy. I keep trying to see a girl with a split personality and a megalomaniac boyfriend."

We stayed in the shadows down the Filbert Street steps. After a short walk down Montgomery Street, we stopped at her car, a nice new Chevy Bel Air. We got in, and I slid across the bench seat. I leaned in and smelled her breath, her lipstick, her perfume. Our tongues met, and I wrapped my arms around her.

She pulled away and caught her breath. "Let's get out of here."

We ended up in a corner bar in the Marina District. It could have been named The Dive, but that would have been too elegant. There were more holes than leather in the booth seats; years of ammonia-scented cleaners and mildew had soaked into the woodwork and now competed with the stench of old beer. But none of it mattered, not with Rebecca sitting across from me. We ordered our drinks and gazed at each other without a word. It wasn't so much romance as sizing each other up. The waiter left our drinks and she leaned in.

"What are we doing?"

"A guy wooing a girl," I said. "A little love, a little romance. That's what it's really supposed to be about."

"You *are* a romantic."

"Well, isn't it?"

"Not when I'm expected to put my heart on the line. I don't know who you really are or what you're doing. I'm supposed to look past all that for romance? You're more of a babe in the woods than I thought."

I swirled the whiskey in the glass, watching the liquid form a whirlpool. There was something prophetic about the way the swizzle stick became caught in the force of the spin.

"If I tell you, you might not like it," I said.

"Not knowing is worse."

I had no good way to tell her, no patent phrases or defensible ways to explain how I'd gotten where I was. I wanted to apologize, qualify, deny, promise to do better, even before I'd begun. Instead, I continued to swirl my drink. I felt the pull of her dark stare.

"I know it's not legal," she said. "I know you're in deeper than you intended. I know you're promising yourself to stop as soon as things improve, or you figure out who you are or what you want. It's something that's going to get worse before it gets better, and you have no idea what 'better' is. Does that help?"

"That's good. Then you also know I got there one step at a time."

She didn't respond, just took a sip of her drink and waited. Lighting another cigarette was all the time I had to delay the truth—at least a half-truth.

"A friend, one of my best friends, got me into the heroin business."

"Goddamnit, Frank."

"Just for a few weeks, then I'm out for good."

"I've heard that one before. I'm looking at a dead man. What a waste."

"I said you wouldn't like it."

I was ready for her to leave. Instead, she took my hand, leaned across the table, and kissed me.

"Is that a sympathy kiss, or are you attracted to bad boys?"

"You can be a real jackass. You're doing just what jackasses do when they think they're smarter than everybody else. I kissed you because you told me the truth. I did it because now I know you're a good guy just being a jackass."

"I don't know whether to say thanks or good-bye."

She didn't answer that one.

"Now it's your turn," I said. "You don't want any love in your life because you're afraid you'll like it too much and risk the cushy thing you've got going with Hanson. You're mad at yourself for falling in love with me, and mad at me for showing you how empty your life really is. But what you're really terrified of is that Hanson will tire of you one day, and you'll wind up in the street again. You can't choose between easy living and passionate love, so you hide in your swanky apartment and avoid everything. You're just delaying the inevitable."

"You're not so bad yourself." She looked down at her drink and played with the ice.

I sensed she was struggling with something.

"You missed one thing," she said, and looked up at me. "I was also wondering if I could have it both ways."

That hit me in the gut. "You mean Daddy Warbucks and me? Together? No dice. I don't play that way." The cramping turned to nausea as I felt any hope for us fade away. I slugged down the last of my whiskey and let the burn take away some of the anger.

Rebecca gave me a melancholy smile. "I didn't think so."

She went for her purse, but I got the money out first and dropped it on the table. She gently took my hand, pulled me out of the booth, and led me to the car.

She drove west, away from the Marina, and headed down Clement Street with the Golden Gate Park on one side and a string of oriental restaurants on the other. We hit the wall of fog and I knew we were on Point Lobos Avenue. The head-lights pierced the damp curtain as the car sliced through the fog and made it swirl around the windows. Rebecca turned into Sutro Heights Park. On rare clear moonlit nights, you could find lovers strolling and families watching the waves high on this perch, but tonight, even if there were other people around, they weren't visible. Tonight, the cold wind blew in from the Pacific, and with it the sound of the ocean pushing the waves into the rocks. We found a place to park beside a tree and slid into the backseat.

We made love with the sad passion of lovers trying to drink up every last drop of desire in a farewell performance. We kept our clothes on and rolled down the windows to let in the fog and the sound of the waves. A distant foghorn added to the bittersweet union.

Afterward, we held each other for a while, avoiding each other's eyes, then rearranged our clothes in silence and drove back to Coit Tower. There was nothing to say. We didn't make any small talk or feeble promises. When she stopped the car, our only good-bye came in the form of a final long, hard kiss.

I walked away, my back to the car as she drove off, fighting the desire to run after her and recant everything. Feeling alone and hollow, I made my way to my apartment.

20

Three days had passed since the theft of the heroin, and besides Charlie's death, things had gone well: Marty had returned from Seattle one kilo of heroin lighter, Roach and Arliss had cranked up a burgeoning market at the military bases around the region, and George and I had unloaded another kilo. Turly had fallen into the routine and proved to be a natural-born accountant of the illegal-goods trade.

Daniel was our only problem, which was becoming more evident each day. George had called a Sunday-morning meeting at a construction site in the Financial District. We were all there, sitting on piles of cinder blocks, smoking cigarettes and passing a box of donuts.

Daniel was talking with half a donut in his mouth. "I can't sell this stuff at the same price as y'all. I sell to a poorer clientele. That's all the cash I could get for what you gave me. Now, if you were to see your way to letting me have more, then I can find some volume buyers."

"Bullshit," Arliss said. "You're keeping the profit and putting half of it in your veins."

"It disturbs me that you don't have better trust in me."

"You're holding out on us," George said. "We're all selling small quantities because that's all we have."

"Now who's the one bullshitting? I know you boys are selling beaucoup quantities. The word's around town. I've got people asking me questions. I've kept my mouth shut, but I think I should be rewarded for the risks I'm taking."

Marty had strategically placed himself beside and a little behind Daniel, who glanced back and slid as far as he could on his pile of cement bags. I saw a glint of light as Marty pulled out his .38 and pointed it at the back of Daniel's head. I sucked in my breath and felt Turly recoil next to me. Daniel stopped chewing.

"I won't take a fall because of you," Marty said.

"Put the gun away, Marty," I said.

He ignored me. "I say we put him down and let the construction guys find him Monday morning."

Daniel swallowed, and he spoke a pitch higher. "Did y'all forget about my insurance? I've got you cocksuckers by the tinies, so don't try pulling muscle on me."

"Marty!" George said.

Marty put the gun back in his belt. Daniel shot up and backed away. His hands shook and he panted. "If you guys keep pullin' this crap, I'll take care of y'all. I mean it!"

"Relax," George said. "It's not going to happen. We're cool, okay? You hold up your end, we'll hold up ours."

I stood and stepped over to Daniel with the box of donuts. He helped himself. "You've got to understand," I said, "when you only bring back maybe sixty percent of what you should, then we're going to get mad."

"That's the best I could do!"

194

I said in a soothing voice, "This is about making money and getting out, not killing. You stay quiet and we'll keep supplying you. It's as simple as that. If anyone asks you questions, say a guy from L.A. came up here with a onetime supply. Okay?"

Daniel cracked a feeble smile and took a bite of the donut. "You keep him away from me," he said, pointing to Marty.

George walked over and held out a sack to Daniel. "Tomorrow, eleven a.m., Dolores Park."

Daniel took the sack, looked up at me, then left.

George and I sat down.

"He's not going to hold out much longer," Roach said. "He's going to make what he can out of us and squeal. We've got to unload this stuff fast."

"Why don't we go to New York?" Arliss asked Roach. "We've always wanted to go there."

"We'll be pegged in ten seconds flat," George said. "Then we'll have the mob on our asses. We stay here."

"Who elected you bossman?" Roach asked. "We've got our lives on the line too."

"We stay here," Marty yelled.

"Ah, now look who's calling the shots," Arliss yelled back.

"That's enough!" George said. He pointed a finger at Turly, who recoiled at the force of it. "How much have we sold, Turl?"

"Four and a third kilos." Turly checked his notepad. "We have 194,347 dollars."

That brought a hush to the crowd.

"You see?" George said. "Where else are we going to do that? Frankie, what's your opinion?"

"We stick to the plan and we stick together."

"Shit, Frank, you always do what George wants?" Arliss said.

"We've been lucky so far," Roach said. "But it's not going to last. I say we give it five more days and we get out of here."

"Do you know how many times I've wanted to run away from this thing?" I asked. "We see this through until the end. That's what we signed up for and that's what we agreed on. I'd say the additional hundred thou apiece is worth the extra few days."

No one argued. George regarded me with a look I hadn't seen from him before … admiration.

The meeting broke up. Roach and Arliss left for their deliveries, and George and Turly went to Oakland to pick up two more kilos. I stayed behind and wandered over to George's place. Under clear blue skies and zero wind, the early-afternoon sun had kicked up the temperature to the low nineties. By the time I got to his building, I was soaked in sweat. George's apartment would be an oven, so I relaxed in the park across from his building.

Splayed out on a bench, I watched a few people that had braved the heat to enjoy the park: two girls with hula hoops, a mom with a stroller, and a couple talking and laughing as they walked. The couple made me think of Rebecca. She was rarely out of my mind, but the past few days I'd been able to put aside the yearning and resolved to woo her after all this was over.

A graceful blonde headed toward George's building. It was Marjorie, so I got up and intercepted her.

"Hot enough for you?" I asked.

She turned and smiled. "Well, hello there."

"Frank." I felt self-conscious and shoved my hands in my pockets.

"Yes, I remember."

"George isn't here. I'm waiting for him too, but it's an oven inside. I'm out here hoping for a breeze to come along."

"I'll wait with you."

I motioned toward the bench, and we walked over and sat down. She had the same effect on me that she'd had at Sammy's. She looked sexy, yet open and unpretentious. She wore a sleeveless blouse that tied up around her neck and a white, pleated skirt. Her bare arms and what protruded beneath the folds of her blouse made me fidget. Her long neck gave off a slight scent of roses.

She glanced at the remnants of the bruise on my jaw, turned my head lightly, and brushed the skin with her finger. "What happened to you?"

Her touch had my mind flying in different directions. "I guess I got someone mad."

She searched my eyes, probably reading the neon sign on my forehead, but didn't press me. "Does it hurt?"

"Not anymore. But thanks for the sentiment."

She looked away and laughed. "Forgive me. I get a little too motherly sometimes."

"My mother would have said, 'What did you do to deserve it this time?'"

"I can't believe your mother was that awful. Guys like to mock their mothers because it makes them sound tougher."

"Wow, that stung."

"No, really. Was she that bad?"

"Not all the time, but her main motivations for living were

guilt and shame, and she tried to pass on the legacy to me as often as she could."

"Do you see her very much?"

"When I can. She lives in a trailer park in Reno with her sister. She moved there when my father died a few years ago."

"I'm sorry."

"I think she's happier with her sister than she ever was with my dad."

"What makes you think that?"

"The last few years they hardly spoke. My dad did anything he could to avoid my mom. Two years before he died, he got it into his head that the commies were going to attack any minute. He was the first one on our block—come to think of it, probably the first in the metropolitan area—to have a bomb shelter. When he was finished, he'd stay down there. He'd close the door and ignore my mom's screams when she tried to get him out of there. The last thing my mom did before she moved away was pour gasoline down the trapdoor and throw a match in after it." I laughed at the memory.

Marjorie had listened patiently, smiling and laughing at the right moments.

"Sorry," I said. "That must have been boring."

"Family is never boring. What about brothers or sisters?"

"I had an older brother, but he was killed at Okinawa. George has been my surrogate older brother since then."

She looked away, then down to her hands, as though some burden had reentered her consciousness. I thought it better to change the subject.

"What brings you to George's?" I asked.

"I ran a few errands for him."

"He's getting his girlfriends to do errands for him now?" I

laughed but stopped when I realized she wasn't finding it funny. I cleared my throat and tried to think of a way to pull my foot out of my mouth.

"Don't worry," she said. "You didn't say anything I didn't know already."

I felt like a real heel. "Well, if I were George, I'd treat you different. If George needed anybody, I'd think you'd be the best thing for him. What I meant to say is, you're great. Uh, you know, different from anyone I've ever seen with George. If I were him, I'd grab on to you and not let go."

She smiled, then stood. "I'd better go. Tell him I'll come around later on."

I got up too. "Wait. Don't listen to half of what I say. I run off at the mouth when I'm nervous."

"Are you nervous the same way I am?"

Without waiting for me to fumble through another idiotic response, she left the way she'd come.

GEORGE AND I GOT SOME SANDWICHES AND BEER AT A SMALL market on the way over to Marty's. We'd left Turly behind at George's to guard the stash and were bringing a half kilo for Marty to make another run up north. George moved through small streets in a roundabout route just in case we were being followed. When we got to the pool hall, the front door was open again to minimize the heat. But no one played at the six pool tables and no one tended the bar.

"I guess it's too hot to play pool," I said.

"Anyone could come in here and clean the place out."

We walked deeper into the room. George knocked on the bar. "Ed! Marty!"

I followed George into the hallway, past old black-and-white photos of war buddies in the Pacific.

"Marty was at all these battles?" I asked.

"Yeah, wounded on Tarawa. He came back hooked on morphine, then switched to heroin. He and his old man are probably back in his office, sharing a syringe."

George stopped in front of the office door and knocked. He waited, giving Marty enough time to do what he needed to do. George opened the door and jumped back. "Shit!"

I knew it would be bad, but I had to look. I poked my head inside. Marty was at his desk in front of a fan, leaning back with the kind of ease that only comes when you're dead. Blood trickled from three small holes in his chest. The bullets had gone in clean but exploded out his back, spilling blood onto the floor and puddling in the chair. Whoever had done this hadn't been satisfied, and had put one in his forehead for good measure. Marty's dad lay facedown on the floor in the far corner with a bullet in the back of his head.

"Don't touch anything," George said. He rubbed the office doorknob with his shirt. "Let's get out of here."

We walked as quickly and casually as possible out the door and to the car.

George gunned it and spun out of the alley, gravel banging against the wheel wells. We hit asphalt and took a series of lefts and rights to get out of the neighborhood.

George slammed the steering wheel. "Shit." He pounded it again. "Shit, shit, shit." He spun around another corner, his face frozen in fury.

My head whirled as we raced from the scene. *Who's next?*

Are we on the radar? Already been made? I wanted answers, but knew better than to ask George. I didn't want to elicit another explosion, and I sensed the same questions were burning in him.

"Maybe it was some addict or armed robbery," I said.

"They were executed. That was a professional hit." George shook his head as if waving off an unpleasant thought. "Marty took his chances like everybody else. He wasn't selling Bibles. Everyone in this goddamned business is trigger-happy, and suspicion is enough to drill somebody. We pissed some people off, but we didn't pull the trigger. You keep that in your head. You got that? We didn't pull the trigger."

"This won't go away, George. They're not going to stop until they find out who did it."

"We stick with the plan. Unload it as fast as possible and get the hell out."

"We should go back and warn the guys."

"We've got one more stop."

"George, we've got to get Turly out of your apartment. He's a sitting duck."

"Okay, we get him out of there and then unload this stuff. We'll be fine, man. Right now, we're a small blip on the radar screen."

"A small blip is still a blip."

21

George's apartment looked peaceful enough as we took a slow turn around the building.

"Okay," George said, "let's give it a shot."

George took a right, went down three blocks, and parked. He pulled the .45 out of the glove box and stuffed it into his belt.

"I'm beginning to like that cannon of yours," I said.

"Maybe it's time you start carrying one."

"That might be a good idea if I had the know-how or the balls to use one."

"You'll use one when the time comes. I can just see you, Mr. Nonviolent, plugging holes in a bunch of guys while they're screaming for mercy, and you with this crazed look in your eyes. Bang, bang, bang. 'Take that, you dirty rat. Yeah.' That'd be a real gas."

"I hope I never get to that point."

"It might be sooner than you think. Come on, and keep your eyes peeled."

The walk back to the apartment seemed to take forever. We scanned the shadows, the sidewalk behind us, even the windows for faces behind the curtains. I wondered what the ulcer rate was among guys who did this all their lives. I followed George into the alley behind the apartments and into the rear entrance. We stepped into the long, dark hallway, which was a straight shot to the front door. Two steps in, George shoved himself against the wall. I did the same and followed his gaze. On the porch outside, a tall, skinny guy was partially concealed behind a potted bush, smoking a cigarette and watching the street.

"You think that's a lookout for us?" I whispered.

"I don't recognize him, and I know most of the people in this building."

"There's probably someone upstairs."

George hissed a curse under his breath. "I should have moved the stash this morning. What do you think, Frankie-boy?"

"We can't leave Turly up there."

George nodded. We slid along the hallway with our backs to the wall. My kneecaps started their little jig as we slipped around the banister and up the stairs. A television from an apartment on the first floor echoed in the stairway and covered the sound of the creaking stairs. George looked ahead, his hand on the .45, while I kept tabs on the skinny guy on the porch. Just before I lost sight of him, he stamped out his cigarette and lit another, taking one glance inside and returning his attention to the street.

"That guy outside is definitely on the lookout," I whispered.

"Two more floors to go," George said.

"What are we going to do if there's another one upstairs? We can't just say hi, then blow his head off."

George looked at me and motioned for us to keep going. We moved up to the second floor. A radio blared some episode of *The Lone Ranger* with horses running and gunfire. We took one step at a time, straining to hear any sign of a guy waiting for us. We neared the landing for the last flight to George's apartment, and peered up through the stairwell. Nothing. George took another step and I saw a hat, then a head moving toward us in the hallway above. I grabbed George by his coat and pulled him back. Gestured upward. We retreated down a few steps and ducked out of sight. George pulled out the .45 and gently fed a cartridge into the chamber.

"Wait," I whispered.

I took a deep breath and walked up the stairs, whistling. My heart pounded, my throat clenched, and my kneecaps bounced like needles on a Geiger counter. I hit the landing and saw the hat. As I climbed the last flight, I could see the guy's moon-shaped face, then his three-hundred-pound body as he leaned against the wall next to George's apartment door. I hoped the sweat pooling on my upper lip wouldn't give away my fear. He watched me closely as I topped the stairs. I returned the stare as I approached him. Took two steps past him and turned.

"Can I help you?" I asked.

"You can help yourself by minding your own business and keep moving."

"I don't know you, and I don't appreciate strangers threatening me in my own apartment building."

"Leave it, Mac."

"I won't leave it. I want you to get lost. I live in three C there," I said, pointing to a door down the hall, "and I'll call the police if you don't leave."

The guy dropped his arms, lifted off the wall, and faced me. "I wouldn't do that if I were you, Mac."

Just beyond the guy's massive arm, I saw George sneaking up the stairs.

"Is that a threat, buddy?" I asked. "I can tell that to the police too. Louses like you belong in the street."

The guy had taken enough. He clenched his fists and moved for me. He managed only one step. George brought the butt of the gun down on his head. The impact made a sickening, hollow *thwack*, but it wasn't enough to bring him down. He buckled, then whirled around. George fisted the .45 and slammed it into the goon's face. The guy fell against the wall and tried to shake it off, but George was on him again and jammed the barrel into the guy's stomach. The goon doubled over with an *oomph*. George brought the gun down hard on the back of his neck and the guy went down.

George unlocked the door and grabbed the guy's foot. "Come on. Help me before he starts to leak out here."

I grabbed the other foot and we dragged the limp body into the apartment. We dropped him just inside the door, and I slammed it shut.

I looked around and sucked in air. The place had been ransacked: kitchen cabinets open, cushions cut apart, shelves torn down.

"Turly!" I yelled.

I ran through the apartment, tripping over objects strewn

on the floor. George ran into the kitchen while I surveyed the bedroom, the closets, and finally the bathroom. No Turly. There was no way to tell if there had been a struggle.

"Shit!" George cried.

I ran to the kitchen. He was by an empty cabinet where the stash had been. "It's gone."

That was the first time I really saw George lose it. He started kicking things that had been tossed on the floor. A large pot clanged across the linoleum. He stopped to catch his breath.

"Turly?"

"He's gone too," I said.

His foot got to work violently rearranging his stuff again.

"Maybe he got out of here and took the stuff with him," I yelled over the noise.

"It took four good hits to bring that bull down. There's no way Turly could've gotten past him."

"He's not stupid. He could've gotten out of here." I noticed the open kitchen window. "Fire escape."

George raced into the living room and fell to his knees. He fished a car key out of his pocket and pried at a floorboard. A small section popped up; he lifted the piece of wood and pulled out a key lying underneath. He pocketed the key and stood.

"I've got to get some things," he said.

While George banged around in the bedroom, I surveyed the living room floor. George didn't have much in the way of personal stuff. Most of the debris consisted of stuffing and fabric ripped from the sofa and chair. Something colorful caught my eye. I picked it up. It was a postcard of a beach scene with flowers in bloom and two sunbathers lying on the sand. There wasn't any writing on the other side, just a title in the upper corner, *Half Moon Bay*. George came back in with his suitcase. I tossed the postcard down. I didn't want him to think I was riffling through his things.

"Okay, let's go," he said.

The phone rang as we started to leave. George and I looked at each other. It clanged again.

"What if they're checking to see if you're here?" I asked.

George walked over to the phone. "I gotta pick it up."

It rang a couple more times and he answered.

He said hello, listened. Grunted a few responses, wrote something down, and hung up.

"That was the library lady, Mrs. Ivers. She wants six more ounces. I'm to meet her tomorrow night."

"She has your phone number?"

He picked up the suitcase. "Yeah, a few contacts do. She's reliable. She's been a regular of Vincent's for a while now, but she's never bought in quantities like this before."

He looked around the apartment, loss etched all over his face.

"George, let's go. Come on. Down the fire escape." I put my hand on his shoulder.

He batted it away, went over to the unconscious guy, and gave him a swift kick in the ribs. The guy groaned and moved slightly.

"Feel better?" I said.

I took George's coat and shoved him toward the bedroom. He let me push him to the bedroom window and the fire escape. I peeked down the fire escape; no one else was waiting for us, so we climbed out and down. We slipped through the alley and ran for the car.

I didn't care how suspicious running flat out down the street might seem. The adrenaline pushed me faster than I'd thought I could run. The hairs on the back of my neck stuck out like some crazy radar device trying to detect anyone on our tail. I listened for the crack of gunfire, although I've been told that you don't hear anything before the bullet hits. It's more *smack, bang* and lights out—comforting thoughts as we sprinted like two pucker-assed juvenile delinquents on the run.

We made it to the car and dove inside. George collapsed onto the steering wheel, breathing heavily, his cool demeanor lost. I should have been upset, but I kept my cool and gave him time to recover. I knew what we had to do.

"We didn't find Turly's body like we did Marty's," I said. "There's a good chance he's still alive."

"Yeah, in some empty warehouse, getting tortured, squawking his head off about us."

"We've got to find out, and the first place to check is my apartment."

"Your place could be crawling with goons too. We can't go back there."

Something hit me. "George, the scales. I didn't see them."

"So?"

"If those guys found the stash, they wouldn't bother with the scales. We'd have seen them in the cabinet or on the floor somewhere."

George lifted his head off the steering wheel, revving up his gray matter.

"If Turly got to the stash first, he would've taken the scales," I said. "He's that way. Screwy but tidy. That's got to be the only explanation."

"That's a big stretch."

"It fits with the screwy-tidy scenario. He'd go back to what he thought was the proper rendezvous point."

"That's not just screwy—that's fucking stupid. If he hasn't been pinched by now, he will be."

"If he's not pinched, we're home free and can get back to selling. If he was, then we'd better get out of town as fast as we can with what we've got left."

"We're going to waltz into your pad and right into their hands."

"I know how to do it without us risking our necks."

George looked at me with what I hoped was a newfound respect—or was it incredulity?

"We need a public place with lots of people and phone booths. Train station," I said.

George looked skeptical. I snapped my fingers and motioned for us to take off.

WE DROVE SOUTH TO THE SOUTHERN PACIFIC TRAIN STATION. Inside was a bank of phone booths. I chose one and dialed Rebecca's number.

"Hello, Rebecca. It's me."

"Well, hello, lover boy. We called it quits, remember?"

I was afraid she'd hang up, and said, "Wait! I'm in trouble, and I need your help."

"You need my help? What about your boys? They dump you already?"

"That was nasty."

"What do you expect? We had a good thing going and you walked away from me."

"Walk away from *you*? I didn't want to be your damned houseboy!"

"And I didn't want to lose everything to become your little housewife," she said. "You know, just forget it—we've been over this already."

"I still need your help."

"Why me, Frank? You ever think for one second that I might be trying to forget you? That seeing you might do a number on me so bad I can't stand it?"

"I can trust you, and you have the brains to stay out of a jam."

"Are you being screwed to the wall like I predicted?"

"With your help I won't be. It won't take more than thirty minutes. Will you do it?"

"Only if I do it and then you let me walk away. I'm not going to hang around and get hooked on you again."

"It's a deal. I'd give you back the hook you put in me, but I don't think it'll ever come out."

She let out a throaty chuckle. "Cut out the romance and give me the scoop."

I told her where to find us, and that I'd give her the details when she got there. The call left me feeling like a guy who'd been smacked around but had come back for more. I was a little like Turly when it came to Rebecca.

George and I waited for her by the phone booths, reading newspapers. There was nothing about Charlie or the bloody tugboat. I guessed a story about a dead junkie or a gunsel gone missing had been too insignificant to warrant printing. How often had this kind of thing happened before I was even aware it existed? There were invisible bloodstains on every street corner.

I looked up from my newspaper. A couple of guys were frozen in their tracks. I followed the direction of their stares and found Rebecca walking through the crowd, dressed to the nines in an all-black suit and wide-brimmed hat. Heads turned as she passed. Watching her had my heart thumping a crazy beat. She was the only person I'd ever met who could give me stomach knots and a divine flush at the same time. She reached the bench, sat, and gave me a peck on the cheek. The smell of her perfume and lipstick worked their magic. I was gone.

George looked up from his newspaper, and his eyes widened. "This is your girl, buddy? Wow, I have a whole new respect for you." Double his normal charm. He came over and leaned in, his smile as wide as San Francisco Bay. "How are you doing, beautiful?"

"Let's get one thing straight. I'm not his girl … anymore." She gave me a glance.

He sat down beside her. "I'm sorry for Frankie. You're as drop-dead gorgeous as they come."

"I'm not interested in becoming one of your trophies, tiger."

George made the sound of water on a hot coal. "Don't worry, gorgeous. I wouldn't step in on Frankie. That is, unless he gave me the okay."

"He's all romance, isn't he?" she said to me, then looked at George. "Are you the louse who got him into this?"

He didn't flinch, but he did lean away from her a little. "I just showed him the keys, kitten, and he took it for a spin."

Rebecca turned back to me. "Nice guy if you like the zoo."

George gave me a wink behind her back.

"What do you want me to do?" she asked.

She seemed satisfied with the grief she'd given George,

and her frown disappeared. Her lips parted slightly and I fought the urge to stare at their curve, to forget their taste. She must have known what I was thinking and smiled. I offered one back and almost forgot what she was there for.

"It's about my friend. The one with the Quasimodo face."

"The sad sack?"

"That's the one," George said.

"He might be hiding out in my apartment, but things are too hot for me or George to get him ourselves. I just need for you to go up to my pad and see if he's there. His name's Robert Turly."

"How much trouble are you really in?"

"Enough to need your help."

"Being cryptic? I won't turn you in."

I hesitated, trying to formulate how much to tell. I was making a practice of half-truths with her. "There's some kind of turf war or something. The whole town seems to have heated up and everyone is a target. Turly was staying in George's apartment while we were out doing errands."

"Errands. I like that. Cute word, like cutting the grass or grocery shopping."

"You done?"

She was.

"How big a stash and how much money?" she asked.

"What difference does that make?"

"If I'm going to put my butt on the line for you, I need to know. The bigger the ocean, the bigger the fish."

"It was nothing, a few ounces. This is just a precaution. It's probably nothing. They wouldn't bother with Turly and me. George is a little higher on the food chain, so his place was on the top of the shopping list of places to toss."

"Who is 'they'?"

There was no way I was going to tell her. "I don't know. Whoever's on the other side of this turf war. You want to or not?"

"You're a lousy liar, Frank." She studied me for a moment, and gave me a resigned smile. "Okay, lover boy, I'll do it."

22

George split off, hoping to intercept Roach and Arliss, while Rebecca and I took her car over to my place. It was early evening and the sun hovered above the fog bank that would shroud the city once night fell. We drove in silence, neither one of us able to make small talk, and found a parking spot across from the apartment building.

Rebecca checked her makeup and straightened her hair and her hat, then gave me a peck on the cheek and headed for the building. I watched from the passenger's seat as she dodged traffic and waved flirtatiously at drivers who stopped and let her cross. She had a way of walking that demanded attention. I was like the starving man watching other people eat through the restaurant window. I could see but not touch, get close enough to overwhelm my appetite but not devour her.

She made it through the traffic and a maze of hat-tipping men, and into the building. My nerves wound themselves in knots as I waited for her to emerge with Turly. Or come out alone and all that would imply.

To stop myself pacing the sidewalk and risk being spotted,

I bit my nails, shifted in my seat, and chain smoked. Worst-case scenarios played out in my head, and once the cigarette pack was empty, I couldn't stand it anymore. I exploded out of the car and raced to a corner liquor store for a carton and a half-pint.

I fumbled for a cigarette as I walked back to the car. Halfway there I noticed him. He was leaning against the hood of the car, facing the street, staring at the apartment building. I stopped. Took in the Neanderthal profile. Daniel.

He said without turning, "I went over to George's and nobody was home."

"Where'd you come from?"

"I've been watching your pad, waiting for one of you to show up." He turned and came around the car to face me. "You boys aren't tryin' to lose me, are you?" He took the cigarette pack from my hand and helped himself. "Well?"

"When George and I got back to his place, it'd been tossed and Turly was gone. You have anything to do with that?"

"No, man, of course not." It didn't sound very genuine. "I went over about two hours ago, knocked on the door, and when there wasn't any answer, I came over here."

"How'd you get past the two lookouts?" I asked.

I saw a quick shift of his eyes. It was a fast recovery. "What lookouts? I didn't see any. That mean we're out of business?"

"No."

I took the pack from him and lit a cigarette for myself. I didn't like the way he was acting, and suspected he'd had something to do with those goons tossing George's apartment. I kept one eye on the apartment building while I thought of a way to get him out of there before Rebecca came back.

"You waiting for your girl?"

That shocked me and it must have showed because he smiled.

"I saw you two drive up. She is a honey, man, a real pants steamer."

I stepped forward, fists ready. Daniel stepped back and kept on smiling. I hated myself for not throwing a few good punches, but I was afraid my left wrist wouldn't take the punishment—at least that was my excuse.

"You're wandering into some dangerous territory, my friend," he said.

"You're laying something down. Now pick it up and hand it to me."

"You know who she runs with. I wouldn't say it's a healthy idea to hang out with that tomato."

"I'm not afraid of that guy."

"You don't know, do you?"

Rebecca came out of the building with Turly in tow. She had her arm around him and was carrying my suitcase. Turly had his own case and a large grocery bag tucked under one arm. Daniel looked at Rebecca, and turned back to me.

"Her boyfriend is this town's eight-hundred-pound gorilla. There's nothing that man doesn't have his hands in." He winked. "I mean everything and everybody." He threw down his cigarette and glanced at Rebecca. She was struggling with Turly and the suitcase as she wove between cars. "You dive into that muff, and you'll be swimming with the sharks."

Rebecca looked at Daniel and hesitated a moment, letting some cars go by.

"Ask her," Daniel said.

"Get the fuck out of here before I break your neck."

He laughed. "I love it when you talk dirty."

I moved for him. He backed off and pulled his coat back, revealing a pistol stuffed in his belt. I stopped.

"I'm outta here, but I need more … you know, fairy dust. I sold everything your partner gave me."

"Eleven tonight. Right here."

Rebecca reached the car, stopped by the driver's door, and glared at Daniel. Turly came around and stood next to me, dangling on the ragged edge. He eyeballed Daniel and held tight to the bag like a traumatized kid with a stuffed animal.

Daniel studied the bag, then Turly's face, and smiled. "Hey, Turl. What know, man?" He turned to Rebecca. "Miss." Daniel slipped in a heavier Southern accent, and I could almost imagine him tipping his rebel kepi.

"What are you doing here?" Turly asked.

"Just sayin' hello. I'll catch y'all later. Have a good afternoon." He left with a smile.

Rebecca got in the car and slammed the door.

"You okay?" I asked Turly.

"Yeah." He gestured with the bag. "I got the stuff."

I patted him on the shoulder. "Good job, man. Say nothing about it. Come on, let's go."

We put the suitcases in the trunk and got in. Rebecca peeled out.

"I thought the whole idea was to stay out of sight," she said. "I'm taking a chance rescuing your friend, and you're outside the car, shooting the breeze with that creep."

"You know him?" I asked.

"Indirectly."

"He knows your boyfriend." That just elicited more anger

and more speed. "He told me your boyfriend is dangerous, but he wouldn't tell me why. He said to ask you."

"You listened to that asshole?"

"I'd like to know if I've got to watch out for him or not." I knew the answer, but I wanted to hear it from her, see if she'd come clean with me.

She looked at me between glances at the road. "You made him sore the night at the club. He's very possessive."

"Possessive means he thinks he owns you. Does he own you, Rebecca?"

"Shut up and leave it alone. I hope you've got someplace to go. I want to get this over with and you out of my hair."

"Any cheap hotel."

We drove in silence as Rebecca headed south and out of the city. We stuck to the highway and passed a number of hotels and motels, but I didn't feel comfortable until the buildings flattened out and suburbia stretched out before us.

"Here, this is a good one," I said, pointing to a real dive. "The Tiki Court Motor Inn. Perfect."

Rebecca pulled in and stopped the car. We stared at each other. I searched for something to say other than good-bye, and I imagine she was doing the same.

Turly got the hint. "I'll leave you two screaming lovebirds alone and check us in."

Rebecca and I didn't answer.

"Right. Thanks, Rebecca, for everything. I can't say how much I appreciate what you did, and I hope I can make it up to you one day."

"You're welcome, Robert. I'm glad I could help *you*."

Turly exited, and Rebecca and I continued our stare.

"Well?" she said.

"Well." I put my hand on the door handle but couldn't bring myself to get out. "I guess I'll go."

"Yeah."

"Well, goddamnit, there are a million things I want to say."

"How about thanks and good-bye?"

I started to open the door and she put her hand on my arm. I turned to her, hoping for one last passionate kiss. Instead, she pulled a revolver out of her purse.

"This is yours, I believe," she said. "Turly almost left it behind."

"Damn." I shook my head and rubbed my face. "Thanks," I said, and took the revolver.

I retrieved the suitcases and handed back the keys.

"Frank, get out of town. I don't want to see you get killed. I don't care so much about the lie, but I'm angry that you're doing something so asinine. I can't hang around and watch it happen. Please don't call me anymore unless you're living in some quiet small town and out of this business."

"Would you come if I called you from Nowheresville, U.S.A.?"

Her eyes were pleading, but she didn't say anything.

"No, I didn't think so. Good-bye, Rebecca."

I turned away and headed for the motel. This was the second time I'd walked away from her. It wasn't any easier.

THE TIKI COURT MOTOR INN WAS ONE OF THOSE HASTILY built single-story roadside motels in pseudo-Polynesian architecture. No more than two years old, it was already a flea-bitten dive with dirty plastic flowers and equally plastic palm trees festooning the entrance. I found Turly in the lobby, talking to the guy behind the counter—less Polynesian, more white trash. However, in keeping with the island motif, his hair had the consistency of coconut fuzz, his teeth were black as lava, and the multicolored stains on his white button-down shirt resembled, if you squinted, tropical flowers.

We weathered the stares from our colorful host and checked in. Our room was at the end of an L-shaped building featuring a parking lot and a great view of the highway. We unlocked the door and were hit with the odor of rot just below industrial-strength cleaning fluid. There were twin beds with overused, bowl-shaped mattresses, and furniture rejected by the Salvation Army.

"Agh," Turly whined. "Couldn't we stay in something better?"

"Low profile and easy escape."

Turly threw down the bag and tested one of the beds. I tried out the other one and faced him. "Talk to me," I said. "What happened?"

"I did like you said—I waited. And then waited some more. It was driving me crazy, Frank."

"Forget the intro and spill it."

"Well, around three o'clock, Daniel started knocking on the door."

"Three? He told me he'd gone by there a couple of hours earlier, which would have made it around five or five thirty."

"I know it was around three 'cause I kept looking at the clock. I just couldn't believe how slow it was moving."

"You didn't open the door, did you?"

"No. I didn't say anything either. He kept knocking, then pounding, calling my name, saying he knew I was in there and to open up. He said if I didn't, he'd have to break in. I panicked. I didn't know what to do."

"You didn't have to panic. You had a gun."

"I know, but I couldn't shoot him or anybody else. I said all those things about killing him, but when it came down to it, I was chicken." Turly looked at his shaking hands.

"It's all right. I couldn't have done it either. A fine pair of gangsters we are."

"I figured if I couldn't shoot him, I'd better get out of there. I didn't want to wait and see if he'd break in, so I grabbed the stuff and the scales and climbed down the fire escape."

"You did the best thing possible," I said, and told him what George and I had found at the apartment after he'd left.

The narrow escape was too much for him. He lay down on the bed and covered his eyes.

We had some time before I called George, so I went to a market and bought us some sandwiches and beer. Back in the hotel room, I checked my haggard mug in the bathroom mirror; I didn't look much better than the guy who'd checked us in. The bruises were almost gone, but the shadows under my eyes had deepened, and my cheeks had hollowed from the stress and lack of food. A hot bath washed off three days of dirt and sweat and exactly one ounce of the ten pounds of stress.

By the time I had finished all this, the sky had turned a dark blue with streaks of pink. A sandwich and a couple of beers later, my head was clear enough to call Roach's place. To my relief, George had managed to intercept him and Arliss. I got George on the line and told him about Turly's rescue, the surprise meeting with Daniel, and the lie he'd told.

"All right," George said, "you keep the stuff for now. We'll be over there in an hour."

"I'll get some more booze."

"You sit tight. We'll get the booze. I don't want you to let the H or Turly out of your sight. I'm not taking any more chances."

"I'm supposed to meet Daniel at eleven."

"I'll have Roach and Arly take care of him."

"Cool with me. He's gone way too far for me to give a shit."

I gave George the details of the meeting and hung up. I roused Turly and gave him some food, which brought him back to the land of the living. Neither one of us was in the mood to talk, so I used the time to rewrap the remaining heroin and hide it behind the access door for the bathtub plumbing. After that, there was nothing to do except wait. Turly and I sat across from each other, sipping on the last of the beers and peeling labels off the empties. The minutes ticked by. George and the others were thirty minutes late.

"You think everything's okay?" asked Turly.

"Yeah, they had one thing to do before they came over here."

"Daniel?" he asked.

I nodded.

"What are they going to do?"

"I could give it a wild guess."

Turly went back to his label peeling. "It's strange, the idea of killing somebody. I can't help but think he's got a mom and dad, you know?"

"In Daniel's case, I bet his parents couldn't care less."

"Would you pull the trigger?" he asked.

I shook my head. "I don't know what it would take for me to kill someone in cold blood."

There was a knock at the door.

I opened it, and George burst in. Arliss came next, dragging a bound-and-gagged Daniel. Daniel was bleeding from the nose and left eye. Air wheezed through his one unblocked nostril and the blood-soaked gag. Roach slipped in last and closed the door. Turly backed away from the table.

Arliss slammed Daniel into a chair. "He had this on him," he said, and held out a .38 revolver.

George went to the bathroom and rinsed his face. Arliss pulled out more rope and tied Daniel's arms and feet to the chair.

"What did you bring him here for?" I asked. "I thought you were going to kill him."

"We thought we'd let you do it, since he's your pal," Arliss said.

My stomach clenched.

Arliss and Roach burst out laughing.

"He's kidding," Roach said.

I was sickened by Daniel's suffering, and they were yukking it up.

George stepped back into the room. "We couldn't kill him on the street, and I want to find out what he knows." He looked around. "Nice pad. You're coming up in the world."

More chuckles all around.

I shrugged. "You said low profile."

"No, no, it was a good choice. I like noxious Polynesian. We'll operate out of here for the next few days. It'll give us time to enjoy the finer nuances of the decor." He turned to

Turly, who stared at Daniel with wide, unblinking eyes. "You okay, Turl?"

"Yeah, I'm fine."

"You did all right today," George said. "You saved us at least fifteen grand's worth of heroin, not to mention your own ass. You see, boys?" he said, addressing Arliss and Roach. "He's made a valuable contribution."

Turly half smiled and went back to staring at our captive.

George stood over Daniel. "Now, asshole, we're going to ask you a few questions. You give us the answers and we'll let you live."

23

"He'll spill his guts if we let him go," Arliss said, glaring at Daniel.

"Why don't we keep him until we're done?" I asked. "Once we've cleaned up any evidence, and we're out of town, we call someone and let him go."

"You hear that, cornpone?" George asked. "You talk, you live."

Daniel looked at him with his one good eye, then turned away. George shot around the chair. He grabbed Daniel's chin, forced his head back, and pinched his nose shut. Daniel jerked. Desperate moans gurgled deep in his throat and rose to muffled screams. His chest convulsed and his body spasmed. I looked away, nauseated by the guttural screams and the creak of the chair as it strained under the force of his frenzied twitching.

"Oh, God," Turly muttered, and slid up the bed away from the mayhem.

"George!" I yelled. "That's enough!"

George released Daniel. He backed off and wiped his hands on his pants. Daniel arched back in the chair, his chest heaving. I thought his one working nostril would nearly collapse with the effort. George looked at the rest of us. Roach, Arliss and Turly's sickened expressions must have mirrored my own. George tried a defensive smile, but it was way off-kilter—the kind that's a mask for pain or shame.

I involuntarily gasped for air, sweet air, as I watched Daniel struggle. His body was demanding more oxygen than he could deliver. Watching him fight for it was almost worse than witnessing his earlier deprivation.

George sat on the bed and rubbed his head as if trying to exorcise a demon, then jumped up and charged Daniel, his face twisted in anger.

"You fucking pig. You see what I've got to do for us? I don't want this shit. I just want to do some business, make some money. Why is it that I have to go and do this?" He got in Daniel's face, spat the words. "Why do assholes like you always try and fuck things up?"

Roach stepped forward. "George," he said softly.

George stopped. He ran his fingers through his hair and went into the bathroom, leaned against the sink, and stared at the drain.

Roach leaned into Daniel's face. "Dying can be pretty ugly, can't it? Especially something like suffocation. To me, that's got to be one of the worst ways. That need for air is so instinctive that a tiny, primitive part of your brain takes over. It's like going insane. And it's ugly, man. You can avoid any more of it by giving us answers. Are you ready to do that?"

Daniel nodded between heaves.

"Arliss is going to take the gag off," Roach said. "You make any sound other than answering our questions, he'll make sure you never talk again."

Daniel nodded once more. Roach signaled and Arliss untied the gag. Daniel's throat rasped as he pulled in air.

"What the fuck did y'all do this for?" Daniel yelled. "I was just waiting for Frank so I could get some more stuff."

"That's not how we see it," I said. "You went to George's pad this afternoon, pounded on the door, and screamed for Turly to open up. Then, right after you left, two goons came by and broke the place up. They knew what they were looking for. Your lie about when you were there tipped me off."

Daniel froze. His eyes shifted from face to face. "I've still got my insurance, remember?"

"We're all curious," Roach said. "Does your policy cover just death or is there a maimed and dismemberment clause?"

Arliss snickered at that.

"If a certain person doesn't hear from me by tomorrow morning, he sends a letter to our buddy Hanson, explaining everything. You don't know who has it, and I don't know where the letter is, so there's no way you can beat that out of me."

"Well now, this dog turd just gave me a challenge," Arliss said.

Daniel leaned away as far as the ropes would let him. He stared at Arliss's fists as Arliss squeezed them, left then right.

Roach snapped his fingers, drawing Daniel's attention. "Who are you working for?" he said. "Did you rat us out?"

"I'm not working for anybody and I didn't rat you out. You're my meal ticket, man."

"You're lying. You brought those two goons to George's apartment this afternoon, and you thought Turly was dumb enough to let you in. You tried to sell us out."

"I went there around three. I sold everything George gave

me, and I came back for more. I pounded on the door, and then I heard your boy banging around in there, then use the fire escape. I ran down to catch him, and that's when I saw those two goons and skedaddled. I swear I didn't say anything to them. I didn't want any part of those two."

"You know them?" I asked.

"Yeah, a little. They're mean sons of bitches, and they work for an even meaner son of a bitch."

"You lied to me then, and you're lying now."

George came back into the room.

Daniel recoiled as he approached, and the words spilled out. "I was trying to keep you from suspecting I had anything to do with it. I don't give a rat's ass what happens between you and those guys. If you're still in business, the better for me. But if y'all get whacked, it's no skin off my nose. I shoulda told you the real time, but I wasn't thinking too clearly. You can't trust a burned-out junkie, man."

Arliss hit him hard across the jaw.

Daniel's head jerked as he cried, "He's full of crap. Why do we have to listen to this cracker?"

George stepped behind Daniel again. Daniel panted and whined as he struggled with the ropes.

George leaned in. "I say we dump this lump of lard in the bay."

"No!" Daniel screamed. "Okay, okay. Maybe I hinted to someone that Marty had something to do with it."

"You sack of shit." Arliss hit him again.

"Arly," Roach said, and Arliss backed off.

Daniel looked like he was ready for a straitjacket; his eyes were wild, his face stretched and distorted. "That asshole wanted me dead! So I turned him in. But I didn't tell them about you guys. Just Marty, I swear. They must have put a tail on me. I guess they followed me back to George's apartment. I didn't tell them anything else."

"Who do those guys work for?" I asked.

"Your worst nightmare," Daniel said with a sneer. Arliss got ready to hit him again. "Hanson," Daniel screamed. "They work for Hanson and the syndicate." He looked at me. "Just like your little muff-doll."

I made a move to hit Daniel, but Arliss grabbed my arms and pinned me.

I yelled, "You say something like that again and I'll throw you in the bay, chair and all."

Arliss froze and turned to George. "Syndicate? What syndicate?"

"I can't believe you ignorant assholes don't know," Daniel said.

Everyone turned and looked at me with a touch of suspicion. I'd given up fighting Arliss. He let me go but stood next to me, just in case. Daniel had taken control of the interrogation, deflecting some of the suspicion and anger onto me.

George must have seen it too, because he waved an arm and said to Arliss, "You'll get your history lesson later." He then turned to look at Daniel and winked at Roach. "But first we kill him."

"No!"

"Wait a minute," Roach said. "If he tells us the truth, then we let him live. I'd like to hear everything. We need to know who we're dealing with."

"All right," George said, and walked around to face Daniel. "Spill it."

Daniel calmed slightly and seemed relieved that he'd transferred suspicion onto me. "Hanson is amazing. He's got the legit side of town licking his boots, thinking he's some great civil leader and patron of the arts. All the while he's one of the captains of the organization. He answers to the syndicate, but he's the one who pushes the buttons. Prostitution rings, numbers rackets, gambling houses, and most of the drug market. If the syndicate is the head, Hanson's the muscle."

"How do you know him?" Roach asked.

"I never met him, but I worked for one of his main guys. That's where I got the loan for Frankie. When Frankie was able to pay me back too easily, I got suspicious and followed. And when word got out about the stolen H, I put two and two together and figured y'all for the heist."

"What do they know about us?"

"Hell, if he knew about you, do you think you'd be standing here right now? That proves I didn't say anything. But you boys better not relax, 'cause he's got his army going around town, turning it upside down looking for who did it. I thought about turning y'all in, but I like a good sporting event. I'm laying odds on how long it's gonna take them to find y'all and cut you up into little pieces. If I told them, I'd spoil my own game."

He paused for effect, studying our reactions, and gave me a broken smile.

"If there's been a leak of information, it's your pal, here. The girl Frank's been hiding the sausage with is one of Hanson's high-class whores. Frankie screws her, then he whimpers in her lap, telling her all his little woes."

I moved on Daniel, but Arliss grabbed me from behind. I stomped on Arliss's foot, then threw my head back, slamming it into his mouth. He cried out and released me. I charged for

Daniel again, but Roach and George caught me and pushed me against the wall.

Arliss didn't take his revenge. Instead, he looked at me and smiled. "Good moves, buddy. You can fight back if you have to." A little blood trickled from his lip.

"Shut him up," George said.

Arliss walked up to Daniel and stood over him.

Daniel looked up at the big man. "A deal's a deal. Remember, brother?"

Arliss's muscles flexed; he twisted his upper body like a home-run hitter winding-up for an oncoming fastball, and swung his fist. The punch landed with a hollow thud. The bones in Daniel's face cracked, and his head flopped forward and hung still. Then all was silent, except the sound of our breathing.

Everyone looked at me. No one needed to ask if I'd known about all of this; my expression must have given it away. The flood of adrenaline nauseated me. My ears rang and my throat closed. I was both exhausted and frenzied.

"Let me go," I said.

Roach and George released me. I doubled over to catch my breath and avoid the looks. My thoughts whirled as fast as my spinning head, each one demanding attention. I couldn't fix on anything. I straightened and turned away from everyone.

George fished a bottle of whiskey out of a bag and shoved it in my hands. I tilted the bottom straight up and let it pour down my throat. The heat of the whiskey percolated in my stomach and radiated its numbing warmth into my veins. I caught my breath again and sat on the bed.

"Is that Hanson's smack we're selling?" I asked George.

"It's the syndicate's." He took a puff off his cigarette and scanned our long faces. "Who cares? It doesn't change anything. The plan is the same no matter who it came from."

"It matters when it's the biggest players in town," Roach said.

"You guys going yellow on me? Who the fuck did you think we would get quantities like that from?"

No one answered.

George turned to me. "Is there something we should know that you haven't told us?"

I shook my head. "I knew Rebecca was dating Hanson, but I didn't know he was connected to all this."

"Does he know about you?" George asked.

"I went over to his table at Bimbo's the night you met Turly and me. I made a scene and he got miffed, but if he'd known what I was doing, I'd have been dead by now." I took a long pull on the whiskey bottle; the pain needed more anesthetic. "I know the next question. I told Rebecca I was a bagman, nothing more."

"Now that we know who it is, who wants out?" George said, scanning the room.

No one answered.

"Okay, we continue as planned. At least now we don't have that fat turd to worry about."

"What about the girl?" Arliss asked me. "You still seeing her?"

"We broke up."

Roach examined me as he jammed another cigarette in his holder. "If it's not Daniel spreading the news, then we've got to wonder who is."

"She doesn't know anything!"

Roach turned away from me and took a long draw on his cigarette. "We've got to dump this stuff."

"We keep going!"

Roach didn't answer.

George turned to Turly. "Did she see the stash?"

Turly gulped and looked around at everybody. "Rebecca? She might have. I don't know."

"Might have?" Roach said.

"I had it in the sack the whole time. I laid it on the floor by the bed. I went to the bathroom while she packed Frank's clothes. I hadn't peed all day because I kept imagining them breaking through the door, and me with my thing hanging out, so I went to pee when Rebecca got there and—"

"We get it," George said. He nodded toward Daniel. "So, what do we do with this turd?"

"Keep him here," Roach said.

"What about the maid?" Turly asked. "She'll find him when she cleans the room."

"Don't let her in," George said.

Turly looked unconvinced.

"Now, remember, Turl," Arliss said, "when the maid knocks, don't wig out and jump out the window." He got a big laugh out of his own joke.

"Arly, careful," Roach said. "I bet he's a tiger when you get him going."

"Yeah, Frankie too," Arliss said, touching his swelling upper lip. "You got me good."

George sucked back the last of the whiskey and threw the bottle across the floor. "I'm staying with you boys tonight. We're going to have a little pajama party." He pulled a second bottle out of the grocery sack, followed by a box of baking soda. He took the empty sack and put it over Daniel's head. "I can't stand to look at him."

I got up, opened a window, and closed the curtain. "I'm sick of his stink."

Roach laughed. "He's gonna draw flies. You cats have a good night's sleep."

Roach and Arliss left, chuckling—their usual exit. Daniel hadn't moved since Arliss had knocked him out. I decided to make sure he was still alive and pulled off the sack. There was a swollen crimson bruise where Arliss had hit him.

"I think his cheekbone is broken," I said. "He'll be screaming when he wakes up."

Turly cringed. "You think he needs to see a doctor?"

"Hell, yeah," George said, "but we're not gonna bother. The pain from going cold turkey will probably hurt him worse than the cheek."

Daniel's pathetic face sickened me. A part of me screamed to take pity on the guy and take him to a hospital. But fear and survival won out. I put the sack back on his head.

"We're taking a chance on this insurance thing of his," I said.

"He's bluffing."

"What if it's legit?"

"You're looking at a burned-out junkie. He didn't have some big plan."

"He was smart enough to track me down and hold us all hostage. We should take this insurance thing seriously."

"Are you going to torture him until he squeals, or let him go because you're afraid of his bluff?"

I didn't have an answer. I looked at Turly, wondering if

he'd have anything to say about it. But he was mute, and went into his corner, where he'd already laid out a makeshift bed.

"I'm going to try and get some sleep," he said.

"Wait," George said, and held up a small packet. "How about a nightcap?"

Turly pulled his knees up tight against his chest.

"It's not going to bite," George said, and wiggled the packet.

Turly needed something. His nerves seemed shot, like he was teetering on the edge of a breakdown. I thought it might do him some good. At least chase away the demons while his brain visited the chemical wonderland.

"You might like it," I said.

"That's what I'm afraid of. I don't want to be an addict."

"One night does not an addict make," George said. "It takes a lot more than you think. This used to be medicine. Before it was outlawed, drug companies sold it in over-the-counter kits. You could go to your friendly neighborhood pharmacy and buy vials of heroin complete with a syringe. People took this stuff like soda pop. Some scientist developed heroin in the 1890s to get people off morphine addiction. Whoops! The man does not get a Kewpie doll."

Turly looked from us to the packet. He reminded me of one of those traumatized dogs I'd seen at the pound when I was eight.

"Are you guys going to have some?" he asked.

"The work is done and it's time to play," George said.

Turly looked at me.

"Yeah, me too," I said. "It's cool, man. A beautiful escape." I'd encouraged him; now I was regretting it. I could see him becoming seduced by the white lady's charms. "Ah, forget it, Turl. Someone has to be sober in case there's any trouble."

"What trouble?" George asked. "We all need a break and this stuff is our magic potion."

George was like the drinker that needed someone else to share in his intoxication.

"Then do Daniel," I said. "I don't want him waking up in the middle of the night screaming."

"All right," George said. "It's not like we don't have enough."

George prepared the dose and Turly edged over to watch him. "It's not going to hurt him in the state he's in?"

"You know Bayer aspirin, right?"

"My mom uses it like candy," Turly said.

"Well, there used to be Bayer heroin." George swept his hand through the air like he was reading a giant banner. "Got some pain? Put this in your vein." He chuckled as he checked the syringe for bubbles, and walked over to Daniel with Turly in tow.

He showed Turly how to wrap the large rubber tourniquet around Daniel's arm and look for a vein.

"Damn, he's popped himself so many times, I can't find one. Squeeze his arm really hard."

Turly took Daniel's arm and gripped. His face creased with the strain.

"There we go. I've got one." George stabbed in the needle and pushed the plunger. "You can let go now."

Turly released his grip. George walked over to the table and changed the needle. "You ready?"

Turly's gaze shifted from the syringe to the two of us. "Yeah," he said, barely audible.

"Cool, my brother. Follow me to never-never land."

Turly watched in quiet fascination as George melted some heroin in the spoon with a little water.

"Sit on the bed. I don't want you crashing to the floor. That'd spoil your first voyage."

Turly did so. George drew the liquid into the syringe, wrapped the younger man's arm, and looked for a vein. Turly looked away as George pushed the needle in. He flinched and, a second later, his facial muscles collapsed and his eyes gazed at some unseen apparition.

"Jeez," was all he said, and fell back on the bed.

"I haven't seen Turly that relaxed, ever," I said.

George helped him up and laid him on his makeshift bed. "Good night, sweet Daddy-O."

He went to the table and began preparing another dose.

"Not me, man," I said. "Somebody's got to be alert in case of trouble."

"Don't clutch up on me now."

"I'm not. I just don't want to do some right now. We've got a half-dead guy tied to a chair, goons sniffing for our trail, and Rebecca mixed up in this somehow. I still want to figure out this insurance thing."

"What makes you think one night's going to make a difference? You're one of those guys that watches life through the window, above it all, like if you don't touch it, don't do it, you can stay all pure? Well, surprise, you're not. You're in the sewer with the rest of us."

George was on some kind of slide down, and he wanted company. In one of those rare moments since Mickey had broken my wrist, I didn't want to escape through intoxication.

"A lot of shit's happened to me in the last few days, and I haven't had time to just lie down and think things through."

I could tell George had stopped listening to me halfway through; his gaze had gone somewhere else, somewhere inside. He prepared the syringe, his hands shaking slightly, and sat on the bed. I helped tie off his arm. He found a vein and took the juice. He shuddered once and slumped. The syringe swung freely, still stuck in his arm. I pulled out the needle, undid the band, and helped him lie down. He turned on his side and stared at the tiki wallpaper.

I surveyed the room. George looked peaceful, Turly cadaverous, and Daniel like a torture-chamber victim at the wax museum. I stood in the middle of this bizarre three-ring circus, listening to the cars pass by, watching shapes from headlight beams sweep across the room. I thought about Daniel's insurance policy and wondered if it had already fallen into Hanson's hands.

24

I looked at my wristwatch in the dim light. It was four a.m. No sleep for my wired skull. I lay there in the dark, assaulted by my internal voices, regretting the missed opportunity for the chemical escape. I could have been skipping peacefully through fields of poppies like George and Turly. Minute by minute, the early morning hours conjured up nightmares as I tossed and turned. Every course of action became a stream of tragic images.

Giving up on sleep, I settled for pulls from the whiskey bottle and my cigarettes. I sat at the table across from Daniel, my eyes reluctantly drawn to that bizarre shape in front of me. The occasional passing headlight beam played tricks with light, twisting his form and giving it illusory animation. I loathed him and felt sorry for him at the same time. How had he gotten to that point? How could I avoid a slide into the same dark hole? I played through everything I could remember about him, what he'd said, what he'd done.

An image popped into my head. I jumped up, switched on

a light and found my pants in a corner. I dug out scores of folded papers from my wallet, stuffed in and forgotten. Buried within the stack was Daniel's phone number.

I pulled on my clothes and went out to the pay phone in the parking lot. I dialed the number. After five rings, I got a groggy "Hello."

"I need some stuff, man," I said, trying to do my best imitation of a desperate junkie.

"It's four in the fucking morning," the voice said, and hung up.

I had to let it ring ten times before he picked up the second time.

I burst out, "I need it bad, and I'm not going to stop calling until I get some."

"Daniel's not here, and I don't know where he is."

"I know. He's with a friend of mine. He sold everything he had on him, but he told me there's some at his place. He gave me this number and told me to call you."

"Why didn't he call me?"

"He's flyin', man. He's in the ozone. I've got plenty of cash, and I can buy everything you have left. It'll be quick, and you won't be bothered again."

There was a long pause. I was beginning to think he'd fallen asleep. "Hello?"

"Fuck it. Meet me at the corner of Geary and Fillmore. I'll be wearing a navy peacoat."

"I'll be there in thirty minutes."

I hung up and ran back to the room. A quick search through George's pockets produced his car keys and the .38. I stuffed the pistol in a front pocket of my coat and filled the other with a wad of cash.

The streets were empty, and I got there fast. I parked fifty feet down from our meeting place, got out, and took a wide detour of the corner, watching for cops, or a trap by my contact. I ducked into a dark doorway and waited. I had a clear view of all four corners. All the stores were dark except a bakery getting ready for the morning rush. An occasional car passed, but no cops.

August, and I was freezing. A cold wet wind blew off the water and cut through my clothes. The next ten minutes seemed like an hour. I constantly checked my wristwatch and tried to stay warm as I thought about how crazy this was. Maybe he was a professional killer and would spot my charade in an instant and gun me down in the street. I had charged into this thing without thinking. What was I doing?

A tall, muscular guy lumbered up to the corner and stopped. Bile rose in my throat. It was Mickey, the punk with the baseball bat. So, he was Daniel's roommate. His peacoat was pulled tight against the wind. I watched him for a few seconds. He didn't look very dangerous at that moment, just half-asleep and growing edgy. I stepped out onto the sidewalk. He spotted me at the curb and raised his hand. I crossed the street and followed him toward an alley. The gun banged against my thigh as I walked, and I figured he'd have one hidden somewhere in his coat too. We stopped inside the alley.

His eyes narrowed. "You?"

"Yeah, what of it? I told you I know Daniel."

He took a moment. I figured he was deciding whether I was legit, and I did my best to look junkie-like.

"You got the cash?" he asked finally. He looked at me carefully. "You don't look like a guy that's needin' a fix."

"I need it and I've got the cash. That's all you have to know." I pulled out the wad. "How much have you got?"

"Four grams. That's three hundred for everything."

"Three hundred?"

"Listen, Mac, you called me in the middle of the fucking night, got me fucking out of bed, and down here on this fucking corner 'cause you were desperate. Now you show up expecting charity? Take it or leave it."

"All right, chum. I'll take it." George had used "chum" when making a deal, and I thought it might sound more authentic.

We exchanged the drugs and the cash. He counted the money while I checked the contents of the bag. The ritual complete, he opened his coat and showed me his gun.

"Don't try anything stupid," he said.

"Too late, man. I just paid three hundred for four grams."

He turned and left. I waited ten seconds, then slipped out of the alley and rushed the short distance to the intersection. I peeked around the corner. He was gone. I panicked. Could he have disappeared that fast? The street was long and straight; nothing obstructed my view. I looked around wildly. The sound of an engine starting up drew my attention. In the middle of the block, a car pulled out, made a U-turn, and drove away.

I ran back to George's car and fumbled with the keys. "Shit, shit, shit." Precious seconds raced by as I fought with the door and located the ignition in the dark.

I gunned it out of the parking space.

Mickey was way up the street. His brake lights lit up as he turned left. I hit the gas and ran a red light. I suppressed the fear of being caught with four grams of smack and a .38 and followed. He crested the hill and disappeared as he went down the other side.

I tore forward, ignoring the speedometer. Dark sky filled the windshield as George's heap became airborne at the summit. A second later, the wheels hit asphalt. The cheap tires and ancient suspension couldn't absorb the force, and the car swerved all over the road. I fought with the steering wheel, slammed on the brakes, and skidded sideways. The car came to a halt in the middle of the street.

Mickey had vanished again. I took off, but slower, scanning the side streets as I passed. Three blocks later, I spotted him walking up steps to an apartment building. I parked, got out, and raced down the sidewalk. I couldn't let him get inside his apartment. Without the last name or an apartment number, he'd be gone for sure. I sprinted up the small front lawn, dodged kids' toys and trash, and dove into the lobby.

I heard him on the steps and rushed up the stairs. The footsteps stopped as I reached the second floor. I ducked down in case he'd heard me. Everything was quiet.

Keys jingled. He had to be on the third floor, unlocking the door. I whipped out the .38 and bounded up the stairs, my steps echoing off the concrete. He could be waiting for me with his gun, and it took everything I had to push through my fear and speed up the hallway. Just as he stepped inside his apartment, I jammed the gun in his neck.

"Hands up."

Grabbing him by the shirt collar, I pushed him into the apartment. My gun hand was steady, but my left wrist throbbed, and I didn't know how long I could hold on.

"Goddamnit, goddamnit," he said. "I knew it was a setup."

I pushed the barrel into his neck and kicked the backs of his knees. He went down on his stomach.

"Hands out straight. Now!" I knelt with one knee on his back. He grunted as he stretched out his arms.

"Palms down and spread your fingers."

I checked his coat, found his gun, and stuffed it in my back pocket. Sweat dripped off my face and onto his peacoat.

"Where's Daniel's letter? I want the letter."

"You're the guy he's been dealing with? Oh, shit, did you kill Daniel?"

"Yeah, he's at the bottom of the bay. Give me the letter or you'll join him."

To my surprise, Mickey started bawling. "Don't kill me, man. You can have the fucking letter."

It was freakish what I was doing. I was trapped inside another body, able only to watch in horror as a maniac in some film noir jammed a gun into a person's neck. "Tell me where the letter is."

"It's under my mattress," he said between gasps and sobs.

"Get on your knees." I pulled him up. "Hands on the back of your head."

He complied but he was shaking so bad his torso wobbled all over the place.

"Now, we're going to get that letter."

"On my knees?"

"You can do some praying while you're down there." I'd borrowed that from some gangster film.

The guy shuffled across the floor, me behind holding the gun in his neck. A lamp with a naked bulb threw exaggerated shadows across the living room. A ratty sofa and coffee table were buried under beer cans and food wrappers. In one corner, he and Daniel had stacked radios, televisions and other appliances; obviously, robbery supplemented their income.

Mickey whined all the way, begging me not to kill him. I silently pleaded with him not to do anything, because I knew I couldn't shoot him. I didn't even know if the damn gun was loaded.

We finally made it into the first bedroom off the hall. A thin mattress with rumpled sheets lay on the floor.

"You're going to use one hand. Keep the other where it is. Slowly, and I mean slowly, reach for the letter."

He bent low on his knees and wedged his hand under the mattress. I tried to keep the sweat out of my eyes while he groped for the letter. My finger pulled at the trigger in spite of what my brain was telling it. My head whirled and my heart thumped. Exhausted from the adrenaline rush, I dreamed of the sanctuary of the Tiki hotel and a bottle of whiskey.

"I got it," he said.

"Pull it out real slow. You broke my hand, asshole, and I'm hoping you'll give me an excuse to blow your head off. I don't know what I'll do if you make any quick moves."

"Be cool, please be cool. I'm sorry about your hand. Really. I don't want to die for that cracker bastard." He pulled the letter from the mattress and inched it back behind his head.

"Lie on the floor."

"Oh, man. Oh, man."

"Shut up!"

He lay on his stomach and extended his arms. I grabbed the letter, stuffed it in my pocket, and pulled out the $300 from his pants.

"You're going to take that too?"

"This is my smack Daniel was selling. He tried to rat on us and now he's dead. Don't try anything." I leaned into his ear. "I know where you live."

I backed out of the apartment, sprinted to the car and peeled out. The sun was just below the horizon, as I raced back to the hotel. A strange kind of laughter burst out and tears pooled in my eyes. The relief, elation, and exhaustion brewed a hysterical cocktail. I hated and loved what I had just done, what I was becoming, college boy turned gunsel. The emotions fought it out in my head. I imagined Bogey saying, "You did all right, kid. It's too bad you're not going to live long enough to tell the tale."

By the time I got back to the Tiki, it was six a.m. I slipped into the room. George and Turly were still unconscious so I fell into bed. Raw emotions screamed inside my skull until exhaustion won out and washed over me, dousing me with sleep.

DANIEL'S GROANS WOKE ME. I CRACKED MY EYES OPEN TO THE glare of daylight. Turly was at the table, gnawing on some bread. He stared at Daniel with an empty expression, his hair stuck out in all directions; the circles under his eyes were darker than his fading bruises.

"He's been doing that for a half hour," Turly said.

"Where's George?"

"In the shower."

I fell back onto the bed, not wanting the day to begin. How much more could I take? My body felt like I'd just come off a three-day binge of bennies. "There any coffee?"

"Yeah, it tastes like crap, but at least it's cold."

Turly got up and brought me some. I slugged it down and lit a cigarette. Daniel groaned louder. His head, or rather the sack, lifted and dropped again. A finger, a shoulder, a leg twitched occasionally, as if trying to wake his brain.

"You have sweet dreams last night?" I said.

"Bizarre dreams."

"How'd you like the white lady?"

"I don't know. It was kinda spooky."

"Spooky. That's probably a first. Why? Did you feel all warm and fuzzy, at one with the cosmos?"

"Yeah," he said, more to himself.

George came out of the bathroom, wrapped in a towel. "You look like crap."

"Feel like crap," I said.

"Where'd you go last night?"

"How'd you know I went anywhere?"

George pointed to Mickey's gun. It was sticking out of my pants pocket where I'd dropped them on the floor. I got out of bed, grabbed my pants, and pulled out the letter. I hadn't looked at it closely before. The envelope had an address and a postage stamp.

"Daniel's insurance policy," I said.

George looked dumbfounded. "That's his letter?"

"I convinced Daniel's buddy to hand it over."

George opened the envelope and read the contents. "It's addressed to Hanson. 'Et al.'?"

"Remnants of his college education."

"He's got our names, addresses, descriptions, the works. You're featured rather heavily, my friend."

George looked up at me with a mixture of shock and respect as I told them the story of how I'd come by it.

"You're a regular fucking Sam Spade."

He went back into the bathroom with his clothes. "I don't think this was an insurance policy at all," he said. "I think he was planning to double-cross us after he extracted what he could."

George came out, buttoning his shirt. "Get your shit together. We've got things to do." He slapped Turly on the shoulder. "Our man, here, and I took a trip to never-never land and came back revitalized, evangelized, and energized. Right, Turl?" George slapped him on the shoulder again. "You have been baptized into the church of Our Lady of the Poppies."

Turly gave a half smile, his eyes drawn to the heroin paraphernalia.

After a shower, a few pieces of bread, and another cup of cold coffee, I felt a little more human. George gave Daniel another dose of heroin to keep him sedated, and we left Turly to mind the store.

Our first stop was Dolores Park and our rendezvous with Roach and Arliss. The "park" was a dust bowl with intermittent patches of brown grass and a couple of neglected ball fields clustered around a dilapidated turn-of-the-century clubhouse. The packs of kids crowding the fields didn't seem to mind the neglect. Neither did the mothers with their toddlers, or the old men playing horseshoes.

Roach and Arliss were at a picnic table next to one of the few trees. Roach sat with his back against the tree, puffing through his cigarette holder. Arliss was splayed out on the table.

He must have heard us approaching because he sat up.

"Next time, pick a closer park. This one's a pain in the ass to get to."

"In a few more weeks, you can buy a car and stop worrying," George said.

"You kids have a restful sleep?" Roach asked.

"Sure." George handed him a lunch sack. "You've got four in there. That enough?"

"At the rate we're going, we'll need more by the end of tomorrow."

"Everyone's whining about it bein' dry," Arliss said.

"Am I not brilliant?" George asked. "Steal the supply, create the demand, then turn around and sell the goods. That's capitalism."

"I knew you were a capitalist at heart," I said.

"It's using the system, but playing outside the rules. That's revolutionary, brother cat."

"Speaking of demand," Roach said, "I got a call from an ex-army buddy. He's looking for big quantities. He heard Arly and I were dealing and wanted to know if I knew someone who could supply him in bulk."

"Do you know this guy?" George asked.

"Since basic. He's a good guy. Get this, he's a supply sergeant at Presidio. That wild or what?"

"Can you trust him?"

"Sure, I trust him."

"We were going to keep this low profile. We can't afford anyone getting even a hint of how much we've got."

"You want to sell this stuff or not?" Roach asked.

George tensed, ready for a fight. Roach just smiled, but his eyes were like two intense beams.

"How much is he talking about?" I asked, trying to defuse the standoff.

"Maybe as much as a kilo," Roach said.

George shook his head. "No, no way."

"If we're in this together, then I think we have a say," Roach said. "You said it yourself—we've got to unload it fast. We say yes."

"Goddamnit, don't you get it? We're supposed to be small-time operators. If we cough up that much dope at one time, to one guy, the word will get around, and whoops, there go the alarm bells."

Roach's good-natured smile faded. He even pulled the cigarette holder from his mouth. "You don't know that," he said. "I say the longer we dick around, the greater the chances someone's going to fuck up, or Hanson will look under the right rock. They already found Marty. Who's next, man?"

"You starting to lose your nerve? We stay low and take our chances. We do it as planned."

Roach looked at me, then Arliss. "You guys aren't saying anything. What do you think?"

"I'm with you, buddy," Arliss said. There wasn't much conviction in his voice, but he would never go against Roach. The two of them looked at me.

"I'm with George," I said, with no more conviction than Arliss. Off Roach's groan, I said, "I want to get rid of this stuff as fast as you do, but sending up a red flag is a really bad idea."

Roach made fists, and muscles that normally remained hidden popped out. The most detached cat I ever knew was losing his cool over money. Or fear.

"Then we split it down the middle," he said. "Arly and I

will get rid of ours the way we want, and you guys can do the same."

"The fuck we will!" George said. "I engineered the whole thing. What makes you think you guys get half?"

"Hold it!" I shouted over something Roach was yelling. "Everyone shut up!"

George and Roach did double takes.

"The worst thing we could do is break up this partnership. If we start talking about dividing it up and who gets what, we'll be at each other's throats. We can't fight about it. We're dead if we do." I stood between George and Roach. "We'd better break this up." I nodded in the direction of a group of mothers staring at us.

Both guys backed off. Roach joined Arliss on the picnic table, and George leaned against the tree.

I stayed in the middle like a ref in a boxing match. "George, what do you think is the maximum we could sell to this guy?"

George thought a moment and pulled leaves from the tree. "Ten ounces."

"Shit," Roach said. "We've got a little over twenty kilos left and you want to dribble out ten ounces?"

"We start dealing in kilos and all of a sudden we're big-time. Where were we supposed to come by kilos?"

Roach recovered his cool and took time to reload his cigarette holder. He lit up and drew in some smoke, mulling it over. "All right, ten ounces. I'll call him. But if we start getting any more heat because we're dickin' around with small quantities, we split up. Arly and I will take our share and go east." Roach looked at me. "And that's what you should do."

I didn't say anything.

"Let's get out of here," George said. "We'll drop you guys off."

"We'll go our own way," Roach said. He tapped Arliss on the shoulder, and gave George one last glare. "Noon, tomorrow, my place."

My stomach sent me an acid-drip warning as I watched them leave.

25

George fumed; his eyes remained fixed on the road as he drove. "I don't trust those guys. I'm moving the stash."

"If we don't stick together, everything's going to go to hell."

"Maybe they're thinking they can be richer. Cut us out of the deal and have it all for themselves."

"Damn, George, are you going to shoot them too?"

"You're fucking naive."

"I'm not naive. They're our friends."

"If there's one thing you learn from this, it's you can't trust friends when it comes to a million dollars. Man, pull off those rose-colored glasses."

That capped it. It was bad enough worrying about the syndicate and the cops, but now our alliance was dissolving. I could feel the whole thing falling apart.

WE SWUNG BY THE BANK TO DELIVER VITNER'S FOUR OUNCES.

I met the banker in the parking lot; we made the swap along with another order for four more next week.

George and I made a couple more stops, delivering an ounce each. But for all our success, I calculated it would take two more months to get rid of it all, not the six weeks George had promised. Two more months like the week I'd had would make me a good candidate for the loony bin. Or the morgue.

We still had to make a visit to Vincent's. A shiver ran through me as I wondered how long we could keep up our front before he or one of his cronies got wind of our selling behind his back.

By the time we arrived at the pier, the wind had changed, and fog assaulted the city. The light-gray veil built up and dissipated over the sun. It was business as usual on the pier: dockworkers and trucks, fishing boats and seagulls ... and the same suspicious stares. We wove through the crowd as before, and cleared the last of the workers and trucks.

George stopped suddenly. The area around Vincent's warehouse was empty. No truck blocked the way, no yard bulls, nothing. Two hundred feet beyond, the work continued. It was like Vincent's had experienced an outbreak of the plague. The two large doors stood open, a few boxes strewn on the ground.

George parked on the edge of the emptiness.

"Give me the thirty-eight," he said. I did so, and he dropped out the cylinder to see if it was loaded. He handed it back to me and checked his .45. "Let's go. Follow me. Keep your gun hidden, but your hand on it. Just in case."

"Are you serious? I don't think I could hit a damn thing with this."

"Just duck, point, and pull the trigger. You won't kill

anybody, but it might keep their heads down while we make our getaway."

We hovered close to the building, edging up to the door but trying to act casual. I had the .38 jammed in my pocket, my hand wrapped around the grip. My heart pounded and the sweat beaded, a condition I was becoming used to. We slipped up next to the door. I checked behind us. A couple of workers watched from a distance.

George hit me on the arm to bring my attention back to him. "We go in slowly, but don't make any sudden moves that might draw fire."

The idea of drawing fire conjured up a wave of panic. George moved first and stepped inside the door. "Hello? It's George."

No response.

I was right behind him, looking over his shoulder. The only illumination came from the skylights above, which grew brighter and darker with the intermittent fog. Nothing moved inside.

We stepped around the fallen boxes and went deeper into the warehouse. The upper office looked empty.

"Vincent, Paul," George yelled. "It's me, George."

We slipped down the first aisle, listening for any noise, any movement. At the end, an open space lay between us and the staircase. We waited for the sun to pop out and illuminate the dark corners. Cries of the seagulls and the distant voices of the dockworkers echoed in the warehouse. A few moments later, the room brightened. No one in the shadows. We crossed the open space and started up the metal stairs. George reached the landing and his foot slid. We both looked down.

George was standing in a pool of blood.

His face screwed up and he hissed something I couldn't hear from the pounding of my heart.

We stood on the stairs, recovering what nerve we had left. He pulled out his .45 and continued. I held on to the rail and stepped over the pool of blood. I felt something sticky beneath my palm and jerked it away. Blood and bits of tissue were stuck to my hand. My head and my stomach whirled. My brain screamed for me to wash it off.

"You all right?" George whispered.

I nodded, took a couple of deep breaths, and started up the stairs with my hand out in front. We reached the landing outside the office. More blood had pooled there. Red-and-white spots dotted the window and the walls.

"Looks like shotguns," George said, and stepped into the office.

There was no reason to go in other than morbid curiosity. I knew what we'd find, but I had to see for myself. My legs took me across the threshold. The room had been torn apart: drawers from the desk and file cabinet lay upside down among the papers, files, and notebooks strewn all over the floor. The wood in the middle of the desktop had exploded from the inside out. Blood and bits of flesh were plastered against the wall behind.

"Vincent had a gun taped to the underside of the desk," George said. "He obviously got at least one shot off."

I pointed to the file cabinet. Half the side was blown inward. Above, a large hole in the plaster wall exposed pitted brick coated in blood.

I didn't wait for George. Backing out of the room, I took one last look at Vincent's remains decorating the wall, then turned and hurried down the stairs. I leaned against a stack of boxes and recovered from my swoon. George came rushing down the stairs a few moments later. We hurried through the warehouse and hesitated by the double doors.

George pocketed his gun and took a deep breath. "Be cool when we walk out of here. We smile, we talk, we laugh, anything, just like it was a regular day."

My stomach fluttered, my hands shook. I looked to George for reassurance, but a wigged-out smile was all I got in return.

"You look like Howdy Doody when you do that," I said.

We both faked our laughs and walked out into the foggy daylight. George slapped me on the back and guffawed.

"Anyone watching?" I muttered.

"I don't know. Just keep it up."

"I wonder how our brains will look on the Tiki wallpaper."

We howled theatrically.

"I can just see Turly's bits of brain and those big, black glasses plastered on the wall after he gets one in the face," George said.

"Or just Roach's teeth with his cigarette holder still stuck in them."

Another backslapper and we made it to the car. We forced one more laugh and got in. George flicked on the radio and cranked up the tunes. Bobby Darin was belting one out as we drove down the pier. Faces turned, so we smiled, waved, and sang along with our own lyrics.

"Oh, the shotgun, and the switchblade, they will slice us both in two," I sang.

"And the fishes, will have dinner, when they throw us, in the bay," George sang back.

We got past the curious eyes and stopped singing.

"Hanson's running out of rocks to turn over," I said.

"Oh, yeah. We're next in line, baby."

TWO BLOCKS FROM THE PIER, GEORGE TURNED OFF THE RADIO. He swerved into a side street and parked.

"Shit!" he screamed. He slumped in his seat and rubbed his face.

"It's time to get out of the city, George."

He didn't answer, just stared straight ahead, fighting off the inevitable decision.

"We can go to L.A.," I said, "even New York, and unload this stuff in bulk. We've got at least a hundred and ninety-five grand in cash already. Even split five ways, that can take us as far as we want to go."

"How are we going to unload twenty kilos in those towns? The mob's got them locked up."

All I wanted to do was run; the hell with the rest of the money. But I knew the only way I could get George to leave town was sell him on the idea that we could make our fortune somewhere else.

"We stay here, we're dead. Look, we go to L.A. and hang for a while, check things out, start asking around. We'll find a buyer. We might not make the same kind of money, but at least we stay alive and enjoy what we do make."

George kept his gaze locked in front of him, but he was listening. "We could maybe get three hundred thousand for the rest," he said.

"That's another sixty grand if we split it five ways. Add in what we already have, and that's about a hundred apiece. I don't know about you, but I'd be sittin' pretty on a hundred grand."

"That's minimum too," George said. "If we find the right source, we could make even more."

"There you go, man. Roach and Arliss should be happy with that."

"What about Turly?"

"He'll be unhappy, but being unhappy makes him happy."

George lit a cigarette as he mulled it over. "All right, let's do it. That means finding Roach and Arliss in time, covering our tracks, and deciding what to do with Daniel. We still meet Mrs. Ivers tonight, then leave in the morning. Now let's go see if Turly's jumped out of another window."

W e got back to the Tiki and made one pass before parking. The hotel looked quiet, and the curtains were still drawn in our room. We parked next to the room and got out.

I knocked on the door. "Turly, it's us."

A moment passed with no response. I unlocked the door and we went in. Daniel was in the same position as before, but no sign of Turly.

"He better not have hightailed it again," George said.

The bathroom door was closed. I went up and knocked. "Turl? You on the can?"

No response. I knocked harder.

"Turl, I'm coming in. Don't shoot if you have the gun. It's Frank."

I opened the door. Turly was sitting on the toilet, rocking back and forth, his face buried in his hands.

George called from the other room, "Turl, get your ass off the can. I've gotta use it."

I stepped in, put a hand on his shoulder, and shook him

gently. "What's wrong? What happened?" I crouched down. "Turly, you've got to answer me."

He stopped rocking. "He's dead. I think I killed him."

"Who? Daniel?"

George listened from the bathroom door.

"I fell asleep after you guys left. I'm sorry, but there was nothing to do …"

"We don't care if you fell asleep," I said. "What happened to Daniel?"

"He started screaming and woke me up. He was cussing and crying and yelling for help. At least the gag in his mouth kept him from being too loud, and his 'helps' were more like 'el', 'el,'" Turly said, trying to imitate the sound.

George thought that was amusing, but to me it was too pathetic to be funny. All I could do was rub his back and tell him everything was okay. Turly started rocking again.

"He wouldn't shut up," Turly continued. "I kept yelling at him, telling him I was going to hit him if he didn't shut up, but he kept on screaming. So I took the gun off the table and hit him on the head. I missed him the first time because of the bag, so I pulled it off and got him the second. I thought I'd knocked him out, so I put the bag back on and sat down."

"That shouldn't have killed him."

"It didn't. A couple of minutes later, he started screaming again. He was jerking so hard I thought the chair was going to break and he'd get loose. I panicked and hit him again real hard."

"You did the right thing, Turl," George said through a half-suppressed laugh. "I'm sure he's just knocked out. I'll go and check."

"No! He's dead!" Turly gulped for air, while his eyes

stared at nothing. "I checked him after that, and he was still breathing." Turly's face twisted at some unseen horror. "I couldn't take it. If he screamed like that one more time, I knew I'd shoot him. I just wanted to shut him up, Frank." He started crying.

George stopped smiling and turned his head away. He could stare at mangled corpses all day, but he couldn't watch Turly cry. "I'll go check him out," he said.

"He's dead!"

"All right, man, I believe you. I'll get some ice from the lobby and pour us some drinks."

I kept my eyes on Turly and heard George close the door a moment later.

"I gave him some heroin to shut him up," Turly said. "I don't know what I did wrong. I watched George do it, and thought I could do it myself. I put on the rubber tourniquet and found a vein. I was careful with the bubbles and everything."

"Did you mix it down?"

"No."

"How much did you give him?"

"A full syringe."

"The whole thing? Pure?"

"Yeah. I thought I knew. I just wanted to shut him up. He was real still after that. I thought he was okay because I could hear him breathing inside the bag. Then he stopped. I didn't know what to do, so I hit him on the back a couple of times. Then there was this noise, kind of like when all the air leaks out of a bicycle tire. And I knew. I just knew. I pulled off the bag and ..." Turly's mouth widened in a silent wail. "His face was blue. It was blue!" He buried his face and cried.

I patted him on the head, washed the dried blood off my

hands, and left him alone to cry it out. I left the bathroom and pulled the bag off Daniel's head. He was blue, all right. His eyes were closed. His blue-black tongue protruded from the gag over violet lips. A few days ago, this would have had me puking.

George came back in with the ice bucket and some paper cups. "Damn, he's blue." He walked over and inspected Daniel. He held up the bucket. "How about a shot?"

"How about two or three?" I said.

George dropped ice in three cups and poured the whiskey. I put the bag back on Daniel's head and joined him by the table.

"How's Turly doing?"

"He's about to snap, if he hasn't already."

He gave me a cup. I swigged it and held it out for more.

"Don't go too fast. We have a lot to do tonight." He poured me another.

I stepped over to Daniel's body, lifted my cup to him, and drank. "The hard part is getting the body out of here without being spotted."

"Then we leave him here for the maid to take out to the trash tomorrow."

"Remind me to laugh when they slap on the cuffs."

"We don't have time to bury him."

"I say we dump him in an alley somewhere with a syringe and a little smack," I said. "The cops won't suspect anything. It'll look like an accidental overdose."

"What do you mean, look like? That's what it was." George got a chuckle out of that one.

The light in the room changed. I turned. Turly was standing in the bathroom door.

"Look at you," he said to me. "Standing over a dead man,

casually planning to dump him in the street like a sack of garbage. No emotion, no sympathy. That was a human being! What's happened to you?" His face was stretched in a crazed expression, his eyes wild and bloodshot.

He was right and it hurt. What was happening to me? I resorted to the worst kind of self-defense. "You killed him, not me. I'm just trying to figure out a way to cover up what you did."

Turly charged me and grabbed my throat. We tumbled on top of Daniel, knocking him and the chair over with us. George jumped in and pulled at Turly, but the depth of his madness had amplified his strength. George couldn't get him off. I yanked at his hands as red-and-white spots flashed in my vision and my lungs started to burn. I was fading when Turly stopped.

His eyes focused on mine and his grip loosened. "Sorry, Frank."

I pushed him away, and George lifted him from behind and shoved him onto the bed.

"Get a fucking grip!" George yelled.

As I struggled to catch my breath, I realized the chair had broken in the fall, and Daniel's stiff legs were tangled in mine. The bag had fallen off his head, and I was inches from his bloated, blue face. Revulsion propelled me to my feet, and with a shudder I wiped myself off. Turly fell back, took deep panicked breaths, and stared at the ceiling.

"Give him some smack," I said.

George studied me for a moment, then went to the table and prepared a dose. I pulled the bedspread off the other bed and threw it over Daniel.

George checked the syringe for bubbles. "He's going to be useless tonight with this stuff in his veins."

"He's useless now." I sat next to Turly. "Turl, we're going to give you some heroin. It'll help you relax. That's all you need to do right now, relax. Okay?"

He didn't say anything. His eyes remained fixed on the ceiling. George gave him the dose. His eyes fluttered and his breathing slowed. We made him comfortable and covered him with a blanket.

"He's not going to feel much better when he comes out of it," George said. "Are we going to keep pumping him full of this stuff?"

"He'll do fine once we get him out of here."

Daniel was beginning to secrete a vague smell of death. I pointed to his covered body. "Well? Shall we?"

"Now? Are you crazy? It's still daylight out."

"He's going to stink up the place, and it's not doing Turly any good."

George just sneered.

"Are you losing your nerve?" I asked.

"No, and I'm not losing my head either."

"Indulge me. I don't want him lying around, rotting in the middle of the room. I've done a lot of things lately, but I'm not going to put up with that. We can do it, and I'm willing to take the chance."

George remained inert.

"I can't sit around a motel room with a stinking blue corpse!"

He held up his hands in mock surrender. "Okay, chief, we'll do it now."

AFTER A FEW BELTS OF WHISKEY FOR COURAGE, WE COCOONED Daniel in one of the sheets and a bedspread. George backed the car up to the door, popped the trunk lid, and slunk back inside.

I poked my head out. The parking lot was empty, and the coconut-haired manager was nodding off in front of the television.

"All right, it's clear." I turned back; George already held the feet. "I get the heavy end?" I asked.

"Somebody has to." He winked and we lifted.

The ends came up, but the middle remained on the floor. The deadweight strained at the bedspread and my lame left hand could barely hold on.

Daniel's ass was so enormous that it didn't leave the ground. In spite of the gruesome task, George and I cracked up. I lost my grip, and Daniel's head thudded to the floor. The sickening, hollow sound sobered me.

"Turly was right," I said. "Here I am, yukking it up over the dead body of someone I knew."

"You do what you have to, man."

"That's bullshit." Anger at myself, at our predicament, gave me strength and I grabbed the bedspread and dragged Daniel toward the door. "That's your excuse for doing crap like this without any guilt or regret."

George caught up with me and hoisted the feet. "Well, it works for me," he said between grunts. "You can whine and cry all you want about humanity, but when you're faced with the me-or-him idea, you're right alongside me, putting a corpse in a trunk and dumping it in an alley for the rats and the flies. Stop intellectualizing so damn much and just do it."

We got Daniel to the door, peeked out one more time, and dragged him as fast as we could to the car. After an eternity of tugging and shoving, we managed to jam him into the trunk. George slammed the lid closed and we hurried back into the room.

"Nice of him to be pre-bent like that," George said between gasps. "It made it easier to fit him in."

"How heavy do you think he is?"

"Two thirty, two forty."

"I can't wait to see how we get him out."

George just looked at me.

"I know," I said. "We should have left him for the maid."

In case Turly came out of it sooner than expected, I wrote him a note and left it on the table. George grabbed a couple of beers for the road and we took off.

We drove up to the Tenderloin, sipping on our beers and searching for an appropriate dump site. The tough part was finding one that wasn't already being used by some junkie or a prostitute turning a trick. After cruising a bunch of the usual junkie spots, we found a hidden T-shaped alley. George backed up the car.

We opened the trunk and jumped back. Daniel's bowels and bladder had let go, and the heat in the closed trunk had cooked up a mean stench.

It took five minutes to unwedge Daniel. I kept glancing up the alley, checking for squad cars and drifters. We dragged Daniel behind some trash cans and unrolled the bedspread and sheet. His body tumbled out, the skin now ashen and waxy.

"Let's get this over with," George said. He fished a switch-blade out of his pocket, popped it open, and held it out.

"Does everybody have a switchblade except me? Did I miss that part of the course on thuggery?"

"Cut the rope around his wrists, and the gag."

"Me?"

He wiggled the knife. I took it, held my breath and bent down. The knife easily sliced through the rope, but strands of fiber stuck to his swollen wrists. I had to peel the rope from his wrists while the last bit of air in my lungs ran out. Finally, I jumped back and sucked in air.

"Don't forget the gag," George said.

I glared at George, leaned in again, cut the gag, and tried not to touch Daniel's cold skin as I pulled it off. The cloth retained the ghastly impression of his flesh and tongue.

"His arms. Try and straighten his arms."

"Are you kidding me?"

"You want it to look like an overdose? I don't know any junkies that shoot up with their arms behind their back."

"All right, but you do the legs."

George looked around the corner, then joined me in a bizarre kind of taffy pull on Daniel's stiff limbs. The legs were impossible to straighten completely. While George worked on the lower half, I took one of the arms. I couldn't get it around his big belly, which had begun to swell. I gave it one last yank. The shoulder gave, snapping like a broken chicken leg, only louder. I let go of the arm, as a wave of nausea forced out whatever was left in my stomach. I vomited next to Daniel and jumped back as soon as the heaving spasms ceased.

"That's good," George said. "The puke adds authenticity."

I wiped my mouth and regarded our work. Legs bent oddly, face distorted from the gag, one arm still behind his back. Hardly the victim of a self-inflicted overdose.

"He doesn't look too convincing," I said.

"Come on, let's get out of here."

As we drove back to the Tiki, the image of Daniel's broken body played in my mind like a looping movie reel, the snap of his shoulder the soundtrack. I shook from colossal fatigue, but not revulsion; I'd turned off the emotion faucet. Now my brain was like my damaged fingers—numb.

I felt hollow and lonely, but at least it didn't hurt so much.

And that helped prepare me for all the things to come.

Not more than ninety minutes had passed since we'd left for our dumping mission. Back in the Tiki, I showered under the hottest water I could stand, then sat at the table with George where we disinfected our insides with whiskey. Stress and exhaustion numbed the effects of the booze, and the strain was showing in George's face. His confident grin was gone, and his eyes had that faraway look I'd seen the night we'd buried Herman. After thirty minutes of rapid-fire talk and lame jokes, we immersed ourselves in our own private worlds.

George broke the lull. "I saw you looking at the postcard this afternoon."

"Yeah, the one of Half Moon Bay? That would be nice right about now."

"This time of year, the fog in Half Moon is as thick as cotton. It hangs on the coast every day, then clears just in time for a beautiful sunset. You feel all alone and cozy-like, you know? It's just you and the cliffs and the waves."

He fixed his gaze on a spot on the table. I let him walk the cliffs in his daydream while he puffed on a cigarette and played with his lighter.

"You were wondering what I did with my money," he said. "I bought a beach house down there." George pulled out his wallet and handed me a photograph. It was a black-and-white image of a two-story house overlooking the ocean. "It's just south of town on the cliff that forms a point. You almost feel surrounded by the ocean. It's off the highway, so there's no traffic noise, just the waves. There's a little curio store just before the turnoff to my place that I was hoping to buy one day. Can you imagine me running a little local store?"

I didn't know what to say at first. I'd imagined him buying a nightclub or something, wearing fancy outfits, driving fast cars, and ladies lining up to jump his bones.

"You surprised?" he asked.

"Well, yeah, but it sounds great. I just don't picture you in a small, sleepy town, hours from civilization."

"Something happened and, boom, things changed. I'm still the same guy—I just kinda looked around the corner and there it was."

"What happened? A brick fall on your head? You were nearly killed by a train? What?"

George offered his knowing, secretive smile. "I'll tell you once we're on the road. We're going to stop by there on our way to L.A."

"What the hell are you still doing up here, standing knee-deep in shit, if you had such a spiritual awakening?"

"I don't plan to live like a Tibetan monk high on a mountaintop. You can't make money down there. This deal is my big meal ticket. I can get out of here and take up beachcombing for a living."

"There you'll be, years later, wearing one of those fisherman's hats, wiggling your toes in the sand, and puffing on a pipe while you build miniature ships in wine bottles."

We both laughed. Me at the absurdity, George at his dreams.

"We'll get out of this, and you'll have your beach house," I said.

"You're pickin' up my wavelength, Daddy-O."

Our false bravado gave me a sense of foreboding. The more we dreamed of a safe haven, the farther away it seemed.

I got George to show me everything about the .38 and his Colt .45: loading, cleaning, dismantling, and, most important, aiming and keeping track of the shots so I wouldn't end up with my shorts around my ankles, holding an empty gun. He brought in the shotgun he kept in the trunk of his car and showed me how to handle it. The shotgun unnerved me; unless you were shooting at birds, the idea was to blow a giant hole in somebody. The lessons had a calming effect though—I imagined Hanson in my sights as I practiced aiming and pulling the trigger.

We finished around eight p.m., and I checked on Turly. He was stirring from his coma, but not yet conscious. A knock on the door startled me. George and I looked at each other. He took his .45 off the table, put it in his lap, and nodded. I grabbed the .38 and put in my belt, then went for the door. I cracked it open with my foot, ready to slam it closed.

The coconut-haired motel manager looked at me suspiciously and sniffed the air. "You sure you don't want me to have the maid clean the room?"

"No, no, we'll be fine. We're checking out tomorrow anyway."

"Good." He gave me one last eyeballing and started to leave. He stopped and turned. "Oh, a lady called. Wants you to call her right away. A Miss Debernardi. She said you knew the number."

I thanked him, found some coins on the dresser, and ran to the pay phone. It rang at least ten times. I was about to hang up when Rebecca answered.

"Rebecca, it's me, Frank."

"Frank, I need you. Can you come to my place? Please." There was a flutter in her voice. She sounded like she was crying.

"What's wrong?"

"Just come. I'll tell you when you get here."

She gave me the address. I called a taxi, hurried back to the room, and told George where I was going.

"We've got that meeting at nine," George said. "You going to make it for that?"

I told him I didn't know. He agreed to go alone if I didn't make it back in time.

"Watch yourself, man," he said.

"You don't trust her, do you?" I said as I grabbed my jacket.

"No. And you shouldn't either."

"I'll be careful."

"Be here by midnight. Don't let me down."

"I'll be here."

I went over to the bed and checked Turly. He glanced at me and looked away.

"Turl, I'll be right back. George is going to look after you. Just stay calm. We're going to get out of town. You hear me? We're going to get you out of here and someplace safe."

276

The taxi pulled up and honked. George put his hand on my shoulder. "Be careful, man. I need you."

I nodded, smiled, and left.

I HAD THE CAB DROP ME OFF A BLOCK AWAY FROM REBECCA'S apartment. Like George advised, I wasn't taking any chances. Rebecca had directed me to Russian Hill, a really swanky part of town—not as swanky as Nob Hill, but close. I walked up the hill from Jones Street and connected with Green. Her apartment building was an art deco number mixed in with Victorian mansions and other luxury apartments. I wondered if Hanson lived nearby so he could keep an eye on his prized kitten.

I made a wide arc around the building, searching the shadows and making odd turns to see if anyone was following. I hurried up the rosebush-lined walkway to the front door, found Rebecca's name, and buzzed. The door responded and I went in. The lobby was covered with baroque wood carvings from floor to ceiling. At the far end was an ornate brass and wrought-iron self-service elevator— no walk-ups for the wealthy. I rode to the seventh floor, exited, and found her door. She opened it before I could knock.

My heart jumped into my throat. Her hair was disheveled, her lower lip swollen. And she had the makings of a black eye.

I rushed in and tried to hug her, but she backed off. "Are you all right?"

She allowed me to take her arm and lead her to a chair. She sat, and I knelt next to her.

"I'm okay." She started to tear up. "I know you're mad *

277

me, but I couldn't help myself. I'm sorry, Frank, but I didn't know who else to call."

She looked up at me with sad eyes. I wanted to comfort her, but she stiffened as I got closer.

"Can you make us both a drink? It's in the cabinet behind me."

The wood-paneled walls, the architectural finishes, plush furniture, and antiques oozed of money. I opened the cabinet and found every kind of liquor among the crystal glasses and decanters. I poured two brandies and returned to her chair.

"Thanks," she said. She winced when the alcohol touched her cut lip.

I pulled another chair up next to her. "What happened?"

"I don't want to talk about it."

"What? You're beat up and you won't tell me why?"

Her hands trembled as she lit a cigarette. I wanted to shake it out of her but held back, letting her take her time.

"Did Hanson do this?" I asked, my tone softer. Her sad eyes turned hard. "I'm going to kill that son of a bitch."

"You and what army?"

"Thanks for the vote of confidence."

"You're not a killer, and he's about as untouchable as they come." She leaned in and stroked my face. "I know you want to be my knight in shining armor, but not that way."

I leaned away from her hand. "Then what way? You won't let me be anything more than a good lay." I jumped up and paced the room.

Rebecca played with her glass and watched the brandy as it swirled. "David had someone tailing me. He knows I went to get Turly, and that I was with you."

"Christ. Does he know that's where I live?"

"He would have been there by now."

"Did he beat you up because he's jealous or to get information from you?" I stopped pacing and stood over her. "What did you tell him?"

She jumped up and backed away. "You're so worried about your own hide, you couldn't give a damn about how I'm feeling!"

I moved to take her in my arms, but she backed away again.

Her voice fluttered with emotion. "Your self-centered, holier-than-thou attitude is what got you into this asinine mess."

"It's called self-preservation."

"I know about the stolen heroin."

"I don't know what you're talking about."

"I knew something was up with David, but I didn't figure it out until today. He's been meaner than I've ever seen him." She rubbed her cut lip. "While he was slapping me around, he kept asking me what I knew about the stolen heroin, you, and your buddies." She paused. "You stole David's shipment, didn't you?"

"Is that what Hanson told you?"

"Goddamnit, Frank, stop playing games."

"That's enough!" I grabbed my brandy and took a gulp.

"Frank, I don't care. I'm not going to run and tell David, if that's what you think."

I didn't answer.

"That's what you think, isn't it?"

I couldn't look at her. I was ashamed of my suspicion. "I don't know what to think."

She looked so vulnerable and lost that I forgot the barriers between us, stepped over, and hugged her. She returned the embrace. We stayed that way, her crying softly. She felt wonderful in my arms. The anger melted away, and I decided to confess. I broke away and held her at arm's length.

"All right, yes, it's Hanson's heroin."

She jerked her arms free and put some distance between us. "I knew it. Of all the stupid things to do."

I had no argument.

"Get out of town now, tonight."

"We're leaving tomorrow morning." I studied her face, trying to predict the answer to my next question; she revealed nothing. "Come with us?"

She took another step back and turned away from me. That told me everything. She wasn't going anywhere.

"So, you're going to stay with that asshole and receive your beatings like a good little girl?"

"I can't go with you, and that's all I'm going to say. If you love me, you won't ask me anything else. Just go quick and don't look back."

"I do love you, but I want to understand."

"I just can't, that's all."

"What do you mean, you can't? No one's got a gun to your head. Or do they?"

She didn't answer.

"Tell me!"

She turned back to me and looked into my eyes. "I … just go."

She walked over to a table and lit a cigarette. I followed her, grabbed her shoulders, and turned her to face me.

"Tell me. Why you're staying with him. What's he got on you?"

She struggled to free herself and took a swing at my face. I caught her arm.

"Daniel told me you're his high-class whore. Is that true?"

She caught me in the face with the other hand. The shock of the slap made me stop. She glared at me through her tear-soaked eyes. I let her go. She went back to her chair and sat down.

"I'm sorry," I said. "I didn't really believe him, but you're not making any sense."

She looked at me. There was a change in her expression and I hoped she'd charge into my arms, but she stayed in the chair.

"Sit down," she said softly.

I hesitated. I was wound too tight to sit.

"Please."

I pulled a chair away from her, sat, and grabbed the arms, bracing myself.

"Dave Hanson is my boyfriend. Well, sort of boyfriend, more like his mistress now. Only I thought it was real at the beginning. My father was a business associate of his. I don't know if it was legitimate or not. Dave came to our house a few times. I could tell my father was afraid of him, but that kind of attracted me. I was a messed-up kid, rebellious. Dave wooed me, and I fell in love. He was exciting and sophisticated and showered me with affection. More love than I'd gotten from anyone else, ever." She paused and studied me as if working out my reaction.

I did my best not to show her one. "Do you still love him?"

"Part of me does. It's like loving your father. It doesn't stop, but you start seeing him differently. I didn't know what kind of business he was in until much later."

"Why didn't you leave him?"

"It's not like I haven't thought about it. It doesn't matter anyway; once he has you, he never lets you go." She gave me a weak, resigned smile. "I wanted to tell you before, but I was afraid you'd hate me."

I made a move to go to her, but she raised her hand.

"Now it's your turn to tell me the truth."

I told her everything: Herman's burial, Charlie, Daniel, every demented detail. I waited for her to scream and stomp off in disgust. It had the opposite reaction. She softened as my story unraveled. I tried to be the tough guy, but my voice quivered, and my eyes teared when I related all the death and disposal of bodies. The confession exhausted me.

Rebecca held my gaze and came to me. She bent over, kissed me hard. I got up and wrapped myself around her. Our tongues met and explored. She broke off the kiss but held me tight. I could feel her breasts, her hips.

"I wanted to forget you," she said. "I tried, but I've given up trying."

She put her hand on mine and led me to the bedroom. We lay on the bed and took our time removing each other's clothes. Our lovemaking was slower and softer this time, graced now with the intimacy that comes of secrets revealed.

I OPENED MY EYES, UNSURE WHERE I WAS. A TIFFANY LAMP glowed on the bedside table ... the sheets beneath me were ruffled. Then I remembered. I turned to Rebecca, but she was gone. The stress and chaos flooded back, and I thought of George. The clock read 11:22: just enough time to jam on my clothes and get over to the Tiki by midnight.

I got dressed and stepped out into the hallway. I didn't know if I could walk away again and leave her to Hanson. Maybe I could persuade her to come with me. The bedroom was at the end of the hallway. Somewhere at the other end, I heard Rebecca's voice. A few steps farther: "Please not here, David."

Then Hanson's voice, some remark I couldn't make out.

I froze and went for the gun but it was still in my coat, which I'd left on the sofa. A thousand emotions assaulted me in those few seconds: anger, panic, the urge to run, and another to kill Hanson.

I crept into the dining room. Rebecca was carrying a drink toward a part of the living room hidden by the dining-room wall. Her burgundy silk robe billowed as she walked. I took a deep breath and stepped into the room. Hanson removed his cashmere overcoat as Rebecca gave him the drink. When she saw me, she took a half step back and dropped her arms with an air of defiance. Hanson noticed me a moment later. He threw his coat on the sofa with a flourish, gave me a politician smile, and loosened his tie like he'd come home from a hard day at the office.

"Hello, Frank. I see you've made yourself at home."

"David, please," Rebecca said.

Hanson ignored her and sat in one of the plush chairs that formed a half-circle around the fireplace.

"Sit down, and we'll talk," he said.

"I'd rather stand."

"I insist," he said with threatening congeniality.

I walked deeper into the room, evading his stare, and stole a glance at my coat.

"What are you doing here?" I asked.

"Why, you talk as though I'm the guest. I own this place and its occupants. You're the one trespassing."

I looked at Rebecca, expecting some kind of reaction, but she wrung her hands and avoided my eyes. Hanson studied me as I crossed the room and stood behind one of the chairs.

"You've become quite an annoyance, Frank."

I sat down on the sofa next to my jacket.

"I've been looking for you and your friends. It's a good thing Rebecca called me to tell me you were here. It saved me some trouble."

"That's a lie!" Rebecca yelled.

"Watch your mouth, young lady."

"I didn't call him. He just showed up a few minutes ago."

Her eyes pleaded with me to believe her. I wanted to, but I wasn't certain. I broke her gaze before I betrayed my doubt.

Hanson shifted in his chair and addressed me. "You two would have made a cute couple. That's not going to happen, of course. She's mine, you see, and I'm known for being very possessive. She works for me, and she knows she has to tell me everything, or she'll find herself in serious trouble." The last part he delivered hard toward Rebecca. He turned back to me. "I know about your little venture with George Mayhall. I'm embarrassed it took me this long to figure it out."

"You don't know what you're talking about. George and I work for Vincent Rousseau. We're distributors, that's all."

"Really? My mistake. The one thing I can't figure out, then, is how I put Vincent out of business two days ago and yet you boys are still selling. As a matter of fact, while everyone else is complaining it's dry in town, you're throwing around good-sized quantities."

He paused and I felt my face turning red. My palms started sweating.

"I had no idea who was selling the dope until I started eliminating the possibilities. It was just a matter of deduction by assassination."

I spun through the escape options. The number came up: zero.

"We didn't steal anything from anyone," I said. "We had a little stashed away, so we thought we'd profit from the dry market and dumped it all. We sold the last couple of ounces last night."

Hanson took a sip of his drink, apparently enjoying my predicament. "The only reason I don't shoot you where you stand, other than ruining a rather expensive carpet, is that I want to know where you've hidden the shipment. I'm guessing you have a substantial portion of it left, and I want it back. You see, you boys have put me in a tight spot. I know that Charlie supplied you with the information. And that makes *me* responsible. I don't work alone. I have others to answer to. I run the show but we have, let's say, a board of directors and a group of investors, and they're very unhappy. Since Charlie was my employee, I have to get it back. And I will get it back one way or the other."

Rebecca moved toward the door.

"I wouldn't go far, my dear. This concerns you as well."

She'd made it into the dining room. Her footsteps ceased,

and she took one step back into the living room. "What do you mean, me?"

"You don't think I consider you innocent in all this, do you?"

She folded her arms as if her blood had just run cold. Hanson hadn't bothered to turn and look at her; he kept his glare on me.

"If we can't get to Frank directly," Hanson said, "he might be persuaded through you."

I slid my hand as nonchalantly as possible underneath my jacket, my fingers searching for the gun.

Hanson pulled out a Walther pistol from inside his suit coat. "If you have something hidden in your jacket, I'd advise you to stop right now."

My breath stuck in my throat, and I slowly retracted my hand. He took aim, peering down the sight, targeting my head, then my heart.

"No, David, stop." Rebecca moved to Hanson's chair and knelt beside him. "He'll give you the heroin back and leave town. You and I can start over."

Hanson cupped her chin with his hand. "Maybe I don't want spoiled goods."

Rebecca stood and backed away. She turned and walked toward the liquor cabinet.

"I told you to stick around."

"I need a drink."

"Get it quick. You two are coming with me. I'm getting tired of this."

"Where are we going?" Rebecca asked.

He looked at her and smiled. She stopped breathing for a moment then turned and hurried to the cabinet.

Hanson stood and stepped forward. "Get away from the jacket." He gestured with the gun.

I stood and backed away. He reached for the jacket.

"Are you going to kill us both?" I asked.

"I may simply have you crippled and your face cut up. Let you hobble around back alleys, thinking always of me. There's a certain Greek-tragedy motif to that, don't you think?"

Hanson examined the jacket as Rebecca poured her drink.

"Do I have to resort to torture to get the location of my heroin out of you?" he asked me almost nonchalantly.

If I hadn't been concentrating on the gun barrel pointed at my chest, or the idea of being tortured, I might have noticed the odd way Rebecca moved back across the room.

She stepped up to Hanson and stuck a gun—my gun—against his head. He flinched. She pushed the pistol harder.

"Please don't move." Her hand shook as she spoke. "Don't make me shoot, though I will if I have to."

"Oh, now, Rebecca, you don't want to do this."

She shushed him, then said, "Not a sound. Put it on the table."

Hanson didn't move. He forced a smile, but it came out crooked. A bead of sweat formed on his forehead. "You have one chance, baby. One chance to change your mind. You can give the gun to me right now, or step across a line that you can never recross."

"I didn't step over the line. You pushed me. Now, lower the gun."

"You're going to have a difficult time getting out of here. I didn't come alone, but I'm sure you knew that. You're giving up a great deal, my dear, and for what? Think about what you're doing."

"Did you think threatening me would make me want to stay?"

"You didn't believe what I said about using you to get to Frank, did you? I was just scaring him."

"You've finally pushed me too far."

Hanson raised the gun to my face as he spoke to Rebecca. "If I shot your young lover right now, would you really kill me? Put down the gun. You'll receive a minor reprimand and go on with your life."

It was up to Rebecca. I had no idea which way she'd go, and I wondered how it would feel to have a bullet slam into my face. Would there be excruciating pain, or would the lights just go out? Three or four seconds of eyes and gun barrels expanded into moments I couldn't measure. Then some part of me spoke. My own voice startled me.

"You want to take that chance?" I asked as calmly as I could. "What if, when you shoot me, she pulls the trigger out of vengeance or even reflex? *Bang* will be the last thing you hear. You might even feel a prick of pain before the bullet smashes through your brain. Is it worth that chance? I don't think she'll miss."

The smirk disappeared from Hanson's face. More endless moments passed before, almost imperceptibly, the barrel of his gun lowered.

"Put it on the table in front of you," I said.

He leaned forward; Rebecca kept the .38 against his temple. His gun touched the table, and he released his grip and straightened. I grabbed the gun and pointed it at his head. Rebecca gasped, turned away and covered her face with her hands.

"I wouldn't say she's happy with her decision," Hanson

said. "Did you see her hesitation? Would you call that entirely trustworthy behavior?"

"Shut up."

Rebecca leaned against the doorframe between the two rooms and took deep breaths.

"You okay?" I asked.

She kept her back to me and nodded.

"We've got to get out of here. Get some clothes on and grab what you can. You've got two minutes."

"Don't kill him."

"Only if I have to."

She rushed out of the room.

"Do you love her?" Hanson asked.

I didn't answer. Concentrating on the gun and my target was the only way to keep the panic and self-doubt at bay.

"If you do, you'll leave her behind. She'll slow you down. She'll change her mind anyway. I know her better than you. After a few days, a few weeks at most, she'll regret her decision. She'll forget you."

He pointed to a silver cigarette case on the table next to his leg. "May I?"

I nodded. He took a cigarette and lit it.

"She *did* call me, by the way. She's more like me than you. I've never stopped her from leaving. She's stayed because this is all she ever wanted, and she really didn't care how I got all my money as long as I shared it with her. You're always going to wonder how such a beautiful and bright girl could stay attracted to such a deadbeat, gutless lad like yourself."

I rammed the gun barrel-first into his stomach. He growled, doubled, and fell to his knees.

"Frank!" Rebecca cried. "You're hurting him."

"Keep it down," I whispered. "He's probably got guards on the door. We've got to get out of here before they come looking for him. Is there another way out?"

"There's a service entrance. It's not used anymore."

I yanked Hanson to his feet and prodded his skull with the gun barrel. Rebecca led us down a narrow stairway in the kitchen. Hanson put up a fight, but I shoved the gun into his head with enough force to push it sideways. Rebecca sucked in her breath, which seemed to convince him that I meant business.

We exited out a back door and made it to the street. None of Hanson's men were waiting by his cars. That surprised me.

"Rebecca, see if the keys are inside."

She ran to the first black Cadillac and jumped in the driver's seat. "Yeah."

"Take them. Now go to the other car and open the trunk."

"Frank, what are you going to do?"

"Putting him in with the spare tire."

"No, Frank, please."

"Do it!"

Rebecca grabbed the keys from the second car and popped the trunk. She avoided looking at either of us as she sat in the passenger seat and slammed the door.

I dragged Hanson over to the trunk.

"You're dead," Hanson said.

"Shut up and get in."

He climbed over the edge and lay down.

"Now, watch your fingers," I said sweetly.

I slammed the lid closed and hopped in the driver's side. The tires squealed as I raced away from the curb.

29

W e pulled up in front of the room at the Tiki motel.
The lights were on. Rebecca slumped in the seat and
stared straight ahead.

"Are you all right?" I asked.

"How am I supposed to answer that, Frank?"

"I don't know. Yes or no, maybe."

"No, of course not."

"Things will look better when we get out of town."

"Cut the bull. It's going to look the same tomorrow, and the
next day, and the day after that."

That put another one-ton rock on my shoulders, but I
shoved it to the back of my mind along with everything else
that had nothing to do with survival.

I'd been so fixated on Rebecca that I hadn't noticed
George's car was gone.

"Damnit, George didn't wait for me."

I jumped out and unlocked the motel room door.

She called after me, "Frank, what about David?"

I ignored her and rushed inside. Nothing had changed

except Turly's position on the bed. George's stuff was still piled where he'd left it. I went over to Turly and shook him awake. He opened his bloodshot eyes and took a moment to focus on me.

"Hey, Frank."

I heard Rebecca come and close the door.

"Did you see George tonight?" I said to Turly.

His reactions were slow. "No, I don't think so."

I felt my guts just about drop around my ankles. Had he decided to skip town without us? Grabbed the stash and left us high and dry?

Turly saw Rebecca and perked up. "Oh, hi."

"We're getting out of here," I said. "You think you can get up?"

Rebecca came over to the bed. "What's wrong with him? Are you okay, Robert?"

"I'm not sure," Turly said a little dreamily.

Rebecca looked at me.

"We gave him some heroin."

She opened her mouth, but I put my hand up.

"I'll tell you the rest later," I said, and gave a slight nod toward Turly.

She got it and helped me pull him to his feet. I then made a beeline for the plumbing access panel and popped it open. Relief and puzzlement both hit me. The stash was still there. George hadn't left for good, after all. So, where was he?

Rebecca walked Turly around the room and I jammed clothes in suitcases.

"Let's go." I jammed the door open with a suitcase and left the room without looking back.

I settled up with the manager and went back to the car.

Rebecca was already up front. Turly lay in the back, using the bags for a pillow. I got in and heard Hanson pounding on the trunk lid.

"David needs some air," Rebecca said.

"It's a Cadillac. Have you seen the size of that trunk?"

"Frank, please, just open it for a few seconds. The noise will attract attention."

With a groan, I exited and moved around to the trunk. I looked around for witnesses. All was clear. I pulled out the gun and opened the trunk. He breathed heavily and made a move to get out.

"You're not going anywhere."

"I'm suffocating."

"Take smaller breaths."

He eyeballed me as he took in the fresh air. "When am I getting out of here?"

"I might let you rot in there."

"You're not just going up against me. You have no place to hide." He gave me a calm, calculated smile. His eyes were playful and friendly. I started to close the lid, but he held up his hand. "Oh, by the way, I knew about your partner's meeting tonight. Drive carefully on the way over there, would you?"

I froze. His expression told me he wasn't bluffing, even though I prayed he was. I fought the impulse to empty the gun into his body. He just grinned.

"Have a nice life and good luck with Rebecca." His hand formed the shape of a gun. He simulated the recoil and the crack of a gunshot. I slammed the trunk closed and dove into the car.

"Is he all right?" Rebecca asked.

I slammed the car into reverse. The tires squealed as I shot out of the parking lot.

"What did he say, Frank?"

I wasn't ignoring her; if I opened my mouth, I would have screamed.

I raced across town heedless of the cops and Rebecca's shouts for me to slow down. The constant battering of stress, exhaustion, and horror—all of them caved in on me, and I lost my grasp on reality. For a brief time, hallucinating from the shock, I watched myself drive like a maniac: beams of head-lights and street lamps whizzed by, muffled honks of narrowly missed cars, Rebecca's screams, Turly cocooned in his mental coma, swinging from side to side as I made crazy turns.

I didn't come out of the trance until I turned on Ellis, a half block from where George had set up the meeting with Mrs. Ivers. Rebecca's screaming became more distinct as I edged up to the turnoff for the alley.

"Tell me, Frank! What's happening?"

"Shut up!"

I rolled past the entrance and looked down the alley. George's car was still there. Any notion of hope vanished. I wanted to collapse. I wanted to run. I wanted to cry out for relief, for forgiveness. But I kept it together, functioning from heartbeat to heartbeat.

I backed the car up and entered the alley. It ran along the rear exits of small shops on one side and the loading docks of a large furniture store on the other. Streetlights illuminated both ends but nothing in between. I took it slow, watching for a trap. The gravel popped under the tires; a guard dog barked somewhere nearby. The headlights splashed across George's car, and I prayed for some movement, some sign that he might still be alive. I stopped a couple of car lengths behind George's. My hands gripped the steering wheel as I gathered the courage to face the inevitable.

"Is that George's car?" Rebecca asked quietly.

All I could do was nod.

"What is it, Frank?" Turly asked.

"Nothing, man. Just one last stop before we meet up with Roach and Arliss."

The latch released and the door opened. One leg stepped out, then the other, the nightmare playing out as my body moved toward a place my mind begged me not to. I went around the back of George's car to the driver's side. The window was up; all I could see was the windshield—a web of cracks leading to a large ragged hole blown out in front of the seat.

I reached the driver's side door, my body blocking the light reflected off the window.

George sat behind the wheel, head hanging forward. His right arm lay across the bench seat, the .45 still locked in his grip. Blood soaked his chest and stomach. I didn't count how many holes had torn into him. I fell against the car with my head on the roof and shuddered from horror and sorrow. But my eyes remained dry. I couldn't cry. My anguish found no release.

The sound of a car door opening snapped me back. Rebecca had stepped out of the Cadillac.

"Is he dead?"

"Don't come over here."

She came slowly at first, then took quick strides, her eyes never leaving mine. She put a hand on my shoulder and stroked my hair. Seconds passed. Then she looked. With a soft gasp she put her hand to her mouth.

My mind dissociated while my body went through the motions. I opened the door, went through his coat pockets, pulled out the packets of heroin stuffed inside; then, in his hip pocket, I found the single key he'd pried from the floorboards of his apartment. I took the wallet, the cash, the wad of keys from the ignition, and, holding back my urge to cry, the .45 from George's stiffening fingers. Tears blurred my vision as I leaned in to say a silent good-bye and touched the back of his neck, but it was so cold that I recoiled.

I walked to the rear of the car and pulled the shotgun out of the trunk. As I reached up to close the lid, I noticed a body splayed out about five yards in front of George's car. I moved toward the contorted shape highlighted by the distant streetlight.

Mrs. Ivers lay on the asphalt, her back flat to the ground and her arms stretched out like wings. Her lower half was corkscrewed around on her right hip. Her face and eyes, frozen in the last moment of shock, pointed to the stars. Her chest had exploded outward, revealing bone and tissue, colorless in the cold light. She had been a pretty woman, a mother, a wife. Now she was a corpse. A revolver lay near her knees. I picked it up and stuffed it in my belt.

"Who is it, Frank?" Rebecca called from behind me.

I whirled around and marched back to the Cadillac. I pulled out the .38. Rebecca grabbed for it, but I pushed her away. I popped the trunk lid and pointed the gun with both hands. Hanson saw my fury. Fright spread across his face for the first time.

"Get out!"

"Frank, no!" Rebecca screamed.

My rage boiled up, but the harder I focused on pulling the trigger, the more my hand shook. The idea of killing someone disgusted me, but a primal hatred and desire for revenge pleaded with me to pull the trigger.

I couldn't do it. No matter what he'd done, I couldn't shoot a helpless man lying in a trunk, looking at me with his hands in the air. And yet, the instant my finger left the trigger, I knew I would regret my act of humanity.

Rebecca held my shoulders from behind, begging me to stop. I pushed her away again, grabbed Hanson by the collar, and pulled him out of the trunk. I dragged him toward George's car, the barrel embedded in his cheek, and took a fistful of his hair. I threw him against George's car door and shoved his face into the window. "You did this."

He fought to escape, but rage gave me strength. I slammed his head into the roof. He recoiled, and the fight went out of him. Rebecca screamed and slapped my back and neck. I slammed his head again and again until his legs buckled, and he collapsed to his knees. I lifted him and forced him to look in the direction of Mrs. Ivers.

"That's the killer you sent after George. A housewife and a mother. She's dead too. How many more, huh? How many more?"

Rebecca stopped on my mention of Mrs. Ivers, just stood and watched as I dragged Hanson to the trunk of George's car and shoved him toward it. His head hit the lid, and he fell in. I kicked his legs inside and he writhed. I pulled out an ounce of the heroin I'd taken off George, broke open the packet, threw it in his face, and spread it on his clothes. The white powder mixed with his blood and created a pinkish sludge.

"I don't know what fucking crazy idea keeps me from pulling the trigger!"

I took in gulps of air to bring down the burn of my rage, so I could think clearly. Rebecca stood off to my left. I felt her stare, her silent pleading.

"George?"

I turned to Turly. He was standing by the passenger side of George's car, his hands on the door, steadying himself.

"Get back in the car, Turl."

"But … George."

"George is dead. We're getting out of here." I pulled Mrs. Ivers' revolver out of my belt, wiped it down and threw it in the trunk. "You can use it to make air holes," I said to Hanson. "You'll leave fingerprints, but if you don't use it, you'll suffocate. It's up to you."

I slammed the trunk closed, retrieved the shotgun, took Turly by the arm, and led him to the Cadillac. Turly crawled in the back. I was halfway in open the driver's door and looked at Rebecca. She didn't move; we didn't speak.

I started the car. We stared at each other across the alley; then I reversed and rolled backward. She rushed over and got in.

Just as I hit the accelerator, a loud bang echoed in the alley. I stopped and looked at the trunk of George's car. Two more bangs followed; two more bullets penetrated the trunk lid.

Hanson had used the gun for air.

I backed out—away from George forever—and sped toward Roach's apartment, praying I wouldn't find the same thing.

30

Turly sat up, and we traded looks through the rearview mirror.

"Give me the whiskey, Turl."

He dug for the bottle and handed it to me. I tried to pull the cork with one hand while driving with the other. Rebecca swiped the bottle from me, got the top off, swallowed a mouthful, and handed it back to me without looking. She shuddered and pulled her coat tight around herself.

"You cold?" I asked.

She didn't answer. I turned on the heater and took a swig of whiskey. No smoky burn, no flavor, nothing. I took another and swished the alcohol in my mouth to see if I could release the flavor that usually sent a signal of comfort to my brain. Nothing. One more try ... a hint of warmth, the tang of sour wood. Rebecca grabbed the bottle, took a mouthful, corked it, and handed it to Turly.

"You've got way too much to do without letting whiskey get in the way," she said.

I found an open spot a few buildings down from Roach's apartment and parked.

"Frank?" Turly said.

I looked at him in the mirror. "Not now, Turl. I'm going to get Roach and Arliss."

Turly pointed at my hands, which still grasped the steering wheel. "Your fingers."

I looked down and lifted my left hand off the wheel. My once crooked fingers were straight. I told my hand to make a fist, and all five fingers complied. At any other time, I would have screamed with joy, but the elation didn't register. I opened and closed my hand, still not believing my eyes. Perhaps it was an illusion, a desperate attempt to sweep away the sorrow. Then it began to sink in and some of my strength returned. The celebration could wait; now I had to get us all out of town and away from danger.

The cold, wet wind seeped through my clothes as I walked to Roach's apartment building. I plodded, numb and empty inside. One step in front of the other. I pushed the door buzzer a couple of times and he answered.

"It's me, Frank."

"For fuck's sake, it's two fifteen in the morning."

"Open the door, Roach."

The latch buzzed, and I entered. I took the stairs one slow step at a time, limiting my attention to the empty, echoing world of footsteps on stairs. I knocked on the door and Roach answered. His eyes were half-lidded with sleep. His pajama bottoms were twisted and inside out, as if he had just slipped them on in the dark.

"What the fuck, man. Come in."

"You'd better get Arliss in here. We've got to talk, and we don't have much time."

Roach returned to the bedroom, and I could hear him rousing Arliss. A moment later, he came back in. Arliss waddled behind him, dressed in his bathrobe, rubbing his eyes and yawning. I sat in a chair and waited. They got the hint and dropped onto the sofa.

"Here's the fast version. Daniel's dead, Turly's temporarily insane, Hanson knows everything and his gang's after us, I've locked Hanson in the trunk of George's car, and"—I forced it from my throat—"George is dead."

Roach jumped off the sofa. "What? Are you sure?"

I nodded.

"I knew it, goddamnit! Goddamnit!"

Arliss looked stunned, watched Roach kick furniture around the apartment, and looked at me as if I might be making the whole thing up.

"I stole one of Hanson's cars. It's downstairs with Rebecca and Turly. Hanson's goons might still be at Rebecca's apartment, but it won't take them long to figure what's up."

Roach grabbed Arliss's arm and pulled him off the sofa. "Come on. We've gotta move." Then to me, "We're half-packed already. Give us five minutes."

As they ran around pulling things together, I yelled out more details about Rebecca and my escape and picking up Turly.

"Why didn't you just kill the bastard?" Arliss asked from the bedroom.

"I couldn't kill him in cold blood at point-blank range."

"It would have made things a whole lot easier," Roach shouted.

"I'm not going to justify why I didn't murder somebody. It wouldn't matter anyway; he's just part of the syndicate. I give it a few hours before they're alerted, and then the whole syndicate will be coming after us."

Arliss came out and dropped an army duffel bag on the floor. "You were at Rebecca's apartment? I knew you'd screw it up somehow. I'm telling you, she still has it for that guy, and I don't trust her."

"Hanson had the jump on me," I said. "She's the one who put a gun to his head and saved my butt, which means she saved yours."

"Bullshit. Not mine."

"I'd be at the bottom of the bay, and they would have come up here and shot you in your sleep."

Roach came out with a large suitcase. He saw me looking at it. "What? I don't plan on coming back, and I'm leaving behind enough as it is."

The call button buzzed. Roach went to the intercom. "Yeah?"

"You guys better get your butts down here," Rebecca said through the loudspeaker. "A sedan just parked down the street with four guys in it. No one's getting out."

"We're coming," Roach said.

I pulled George's .45 out of my belt and held it up. "Anybody want this?" I looked at Arliss.

He shook his head, unzipped his duffel bag, and removed an odd-looking submachine gun. "This is all I need."

My confusion must have shown because Roach answered, "An M-3 Grease Gun."

I still didn't understand.

"It's a submachine gun. It sprays out forty-five-millimeter

caliber rounds like a garden hose. And, yeah, it looks like a grease gun; that's why they call it that. Arly's been waiting for an excuse to use it. I just wouldn't want to be too close to him when he does."

"You don't do anything small, do you?" I said to Arliss.

I threw the .45 to Roach and grabbed one of the bags.

The three of us poured down the stairs. Rebecca was in the lobby by the door, wringing her hands.

"This is Rebecca," I said.

I introduced everyone, and she nodded, her expression neutral.

Roach walked up to her, cigarette holder clenched in his teeth, and offered his hand. "Charmed, I'm sure."

Rebecca shook his hand, then glanced at Arliss at the base of the stairs. He nodded.

"Where's the sedan?" I asked.

"To the left, a few cars down on the other side of the street," she said.

"You sure those aren't your buddies out there?" Arliss said.

"Now, what would I be doing in here if they were?" Rebecca said.

Roach didn't give the big guy time for a rebuttal. "You two start out first," he said to Rebecca and me. "Take as many of the bags as you can. We'll take up the rear and cover you."

We gathered the bags. Roach readied the .45, and Arliss pulled back the charger on his submachine gun.

"Ready?" Roach asked.

I nodded. Laden down with his suitcase and Arliss's duffel bag, I pushed through the door. Rebecca followed me with a couple of smaller canvas bags. We were on a slight rise from the street level and had a clear view of the sedan. The four guys were still there. We hurried across the small yard toward the Cadillac. I heard the building door open again as Roach and Arliss followed. A tree hid our view of the Cadillac until we reached the sidewalk.

A rush of adrenaline hit me.

A thug had Turly against the car and was delivering blows to his stomach. I dropped the duffel bag and charged, holding the suitcase out in front of me. Rebecca screamed. The thug turned, pulled his gun, and fired. A sledgehammer force surged through my hands when the bullet impacted the suitcase. It blew out the other side, bringing with it a cloud of fabric. That's all the thug had time for. I crashed into him, suitcase first. He fell, stunned. I lifted the suitcase and brought it down full force onto his forehead. He cried out and writhed on the ground.

A gunshot cracked from the other side of the street and hit the high tail fin fender of the Cadillac. I ducked. Concrete shattered near my head with the second shot. I jumped back behind the car. Roach raced up, took a bracing stance over me, and fired the .45. It sounded like a cannon. I didn't see what happened, but he didn't need to shoot again.

He pulled me up. "You all right?"

I nodded as Arliss let loose with the submachine gun. The sound was terrifying. Rebecca dove into the backseat of the Cadillac. Roach and I looked in the direction of the firing. Arliss stood on the street, spraying bullets into the black sedan. The other four guys must have come out with the first gunshots because they were either diving behind the car or scrambling under it. Windows shattered. Tires blew out. Metal buckled under the torrent of bullets.

"Arliss!" Roach screamed, and to me, "Get in."

I ran around the car as Roach fired the .45 to cover Arliss. I started the engine. Arliss jumped in the front. Roach emptied his .45 and leaped in the back on top of Turly and the bags. I spun out and passed the other sedan. The guy that had tried to shoot me lay half in, half out of the sedan, motionless.

Arliss screamed, "Go, Frankie, go!"

Roach and Turly grunted and groaned as they fought for space. I glanced in the rearview mirror to see if we were being chased. It was clear. For the moment. Turly had ended up between Rebecca and Roach, and they checked him over.

"Is he all right?" I asked. In the rearview, I could see him nodding amid the sweep of streetlights.

"He got worked over pretty bad," Rebecca said.

"He's used to it," I said. "Right, Turl?"

Turly nodded again. Rebecca shot me a sneer.

"You know where we're going?" Arliss asked.

"We're heading south," I said. "That's the fastest way."

"Are you forgetting about the twenty kilos?" Roach yelled. "We can't leave that behind."

"Are you crazy?" Rebecca burst out. "We're in a stolen car, and you just shot up a neighborhood. Hanson's entire network will be looking for you, not to mention the cops, the highway patrol, and by tomorrow morning the FBI."

"You shut up!" Arliss yelled. "Who asked you?"

"She's right," I said. "We'll be lucky if we get out of town."

"We're not leaving it behind," Arliss said. "I didn't risk my neck for a few lousy couple of grand."

"Look," Roach said, softening his tone, "while everyone's still scrambling, we shoot over there and make off with the stuff."

"Oh, that's real smart, Einstein," Rebecca said. "I know these guys. They're well organized. It will take one phone call from one guy to get things moving."

"It'll work," Roach countered. "We're never going to be able to come back here. Ever. It's now or never."

Turly flew forward and grabbed the back of front seat. "I want to get out of here!" He groaned and held his stomach, pushing the words through clenched teeth. "Please, let's leave with what we've got. I don't want to see any more dead bodies."

He threw himself back and covered his face with his hands. Rebecca rubbed his neck and glared at me through the mirror.

Roach leaned forward, his mouth not far from my ear. "You're driving. Where to?" His voice was calm and low, like the cartoon devil with the angel on the opposite shoulder, each whispering contradictory advice. "If we leave it, we'll never get it back."

"Yeah, maybe," I said.

"Go ahead, Frank. It doesn't matter," Rebecca said. "I give us all one day, two at the most, anyway." She turned her body away from us.

"We'll dump you at the curb," Arliss said. "How's that?"

Roach started again, his soft voice of reason next to my ear. Angel or the devil? I couldn't tell.

"Once the cops find George, they'll be checking everything out. They'll find the warehouse, if Hanson doesn't get there first. We've got to get it, now or never."

"All right, we'll get over the Bay Bridge fast and go south from there. Together, right?"

"Together," Roach said.

"Now you're talking," Arliss said. "You did good back

there, Frankie." He hit me on the arm. "Did you see what I did to that car with the Grease Gun? Goddamn, that was a gas."

I looked at Rebecca in the mirror. Arliss continued to prattle, but I didn't hear what he was saying. Rebecca and I talked with our eyes: mine begged for understanding; hers burned with resentment. I was losing her at the moment of her rescue. Headlights bounced off the rearview and across the backseat, sweeping across Turly and stopping on Rebecca's eyes for a moment, then moving away. She broke our mutual stare and shifted her gaze out the window.

Turly uncovered his face and stared at the roof. His deadman's eyes made me shudder. As we made our way to the Bay Bridge, I tilted the mirror so I didn't have to look at either of them.

31

Crossing over into Oakland affected me more than I'd expected. This time, I was leaving San Francisco, unsure whether I'd ever see it again. Maybe I'd never want to go back after everything that had happened. The profound relief at our escape and my now-working fingers did nothing to relieve the festering core of regret and loss. The parade of corpses rolled through my mind until it reached George. I tried to imagine him alive, but the image of him slumped in his car amid the blood and broken glass had superimposed itself on my memory like a permanent burn on my retinas. In spite of every step I'd taken to the contrary, I'd been sucked deeper into the mud, as if bound by some Hadean force. I'd asked it a thousand times, *How did I get here?* And a thousand times received the same answer: *One step at a time, man. One moronic step at a time.*

~

WE WERE CLOSE. JUST A FEW MORE SMALL STREETS, THEN THE

alley and George's garage. The three o'clock shift of neighbor-hood denizens was out: the bums, the punks, and the forgotten. Back in this web of warehouses and machine shops, no one wandered except a few alkies or junkies who had already gotten their fix and were searching for some abandoned corner to pass out.

I parked next to the garage and took the key off the chain. Arliss got out and stood by the car with the Grease Gun at the ready. I handed Roach the key. He got out and opened the garage door, and I pulled forward.

Roach closed the garage door as Turly and I got out. Rebecca growled and slumped in her seat. We moved quickly. Arliss and I tugged at the workbench. Dust billowed as it rumbled across the cement floor. We rushed up to the plywood panel that covered the hole like three guys waiting for a trea-sure chest to be opened. Arliss threw the plywood aside. I froze in disbelief.

Arliss muttered, "What the fuck?"

The hole was empty. Denial was my first reaction: this couldn't be happening. In a long string of "this couldn't be happenings," George's betrayal was the least expected. Maybe he had changed his mind about the partnership when things went down the toilet, or maybe he'd gotten paranoid about Roach and Arliss. I'd wanted to believe in him, trust him, but looking back, he had done nothing to assure me he wouldn't run out on us.

Roach jumped back and kicked the plywood. "Goddamn that asshole! He was going to skip out on us."

Arliss remained on his knees, peering at the hole, as if by black magic the stash would reappear.

"Maybe he just got paranoid and moved it," I said.

"You didn't know about this?"

"Why would I have agreed to come here if I knew about it?"

"You've been with him the whole time."

"Do you think I sat in his back pocket? It only takes a few hours. He could have done this anytime. I'm as surprised as you are."

"Surprised?" Roach said loudly. Then louder still, his pitch an octave higher, "This isn't what I call surprise. This is being fucked over. All that crap in the park about keeping us together. He was going to skip out on us. Leave us with our thumbs up our asses."

"I can't believe he'd do that," I said.

"You'd better believe it."

Arliss shot up with a roar and slammed into the workbench with his shoulder. The bench lifted up on two legs, teetered for a moment, and crashed down with a bang, raising a cloud of dust. Turly dove out of the way and disappeared in the cloud.

Arliss's heavy breathing slowed; his shoulders slumped. "I don't want to do this anymore. I'm sick of cheats and liars and killers. I want to take our share and go far away from here."

Roach got in Arliss's face, his tone soothing. "I know, man. We're going to do that, okay? It just isn't going to happen as soon as we'd hoped. It's the same old thing, you know? We get kicked around by all the assholes of the world, and we have to fight back. But not after we get the stuff. Not then. Then we'll be livin' above all the assholes. They'll be listening to us. It'll be their turn to jump."

I'd never seen Arliss this unhinged or Roach so edgy. I wasn't sure what the two of them would do if I couldn't come up with some way to divert their anger. I racked my brain for a clue as to where George might have stashed it. Something this valuable and dangerous had to be hidden carefully, somewhere out of the way that no one knew about. I thought of all the possible places and eliminated them one by one.

Until the postcard popped into my head.

"George has a beach house in Half Moon Bay."

"What?" Roach said. "What are you talking about?"

"He told me about it this afternoon. He bought a beach house and said he wanted to move there after this job was over. He even talked about stopping there on our way to L.A."

"What has that got to do with us?"

"I think that's where he's stashed the stuff."

That's grabbed Roach's attention.

"It's perfect," I said. "Far enough away but not too far, and it's in the sticks. It's the logical place. Where else could he hide it? It wasn't in his car, and he wouldn't have hidden it in his apartment. That leaves the beach house."

"That leaves about a thousand other places."

"I'm sick of all this," Arliss said to Roach. "Let's just go, get out of here. I wanna go to New York."

Roach spun around to face him. Arliss took a step back. "Have you forgotten what a half a million dollars can buy us? Don't you think it's worth a few extra days? Hold it together until we find the stash, get our share, and cut out of here. You think you can do that?"

Arliss looked at the floor and nodded.

Roach turned back to me, flushed from his anger. I expected his cigarette holder to snap in half the way his teeth were clamped together. "I'm in no mood for a wild-goose chase. I don't like the idea of leaving town without knowing for sure. Is this some kind of setup?"

"Oh, yeah, me and the rest of my cutthroat gang are going to knock you off. You wouldn't know it, but Turly's an animal."

All eyes flashed on Turly. He stood next to the car, shifting from one leg to the other. He didn't cut a very threatening figure, and I had to stifle a chuckle in spite of my wigged state of mind—or maybe because of it.

"Goddamnit, Roach," I said, "we've got to stick together, think together, and do together. We've got to get out of town. We don't have time to search the entire city. I say we go to the beach house. If it's not there, at least we have time to figure out our next move."

Roach lit another cigarette and mulled it over. "All right."

His former amiable detachment, from the days before George's business proposal, had disappeared. A predatory gaze had taken its place. He spun away from me, turned off the light, and walked to the car. He got in, leaving me standing in the dark. Arliss moved to the garage doors, facing the alley. They were all just silhouettes, shaded figures.

"We're waiting, Frank," Arliss said.

Whatever had connected us was disappearing, and in its place, distrust and a loose partnership held together by nothing more than the fragile bonds of survival and a common purpose.

TWO AND A HALF HOURS OF TWO-LANE HIGHWAYS AND country roads stretched south to San Jose, then north again to Half Moon Bay. That was the only route possible if we were to avoid going back through San Francisco. The drive was a blur of cigarettes, small towns, train stops, marshland, farms, and then the rolling hills and mountains that divided the San Francisco Bay from the Pacific coast. Driving with these guys made me think of Jack Kerouac's *On the Road*, but we weren't on a wild Beat ride through the country in search of truth, unless you counted the truths that came from murder, guns, and dealing heroin.

I drove. Arliss navigated. Roach relaxed in back in his own cloud of cigarette smoke. Turly and Rebecca dozed shoulder to shoulder, head to head. Arliss stayed awake only because I shook him for directions on occasion. I was too wired to feel drowsy in spite of only six hours' sleep in the past three days.

We stopped outside San Jose for gas. While the attendant pumped the gas, I went to pee. Halfway to the bathroom, I heard the car door close behind me. Rebecca hesitated, then walked up to me, her arms tightly crossed.

"It's time to call the cops and tell them about David," she said.

"Nothing doing. They'll find him anyhow, and we need as much of a lead as we can get."

"Then I'll make a call." She turned and marched for the pay phone.

I ran after her and grabbed her arm. "If you tell Hanson's pals where we are ..." I couldn't finish.

Rebecca jerked her arm away. "You'll what? Kill me? You're just as bad as they are." She picked up the phone and dialed.

I didn't stop her. I could only stand there and watch as she talked. A couple of moments later, she hung up and turned back to me. She was no longer angry; she was scared. I walked up to her, but she stepped back.

"He's out already," she said. "The cops discovered George's car a couple hours ago."

"They didn't arrest him?" I already knew the answer but prayed I was wrong.

She sneered. "Are you kidding? Hanson owns half the town."

She blew past me without another word. I knew what she was thinking: Her life was now in danger and it was my fault.

I drove the rest of the way to Half Moon Bay with a sense of the clock ticking. Before the call, things had been unfocused and confused. But Hanson was out of the trunk; he would rally his army of thugs and crooked cops to track us down.

I'd opened the first page of the last chapter.

WE ROLLED INTO THE OUTSKIRTS OF HALF MOON BAY AROUND six in the morning. The sun had crested over the mountains, but the incoming fog was rapidly swallowing up the orange glow that sprayed across the one- and two-story buildings. We crossed over a small bridge and connected with Half Moon Bay's main street. A few of the locals milled about or opened their stores. An old guy, who knew of the beach house from my description, gave us directions, telling us it wasn't more than a few miles south of town.

Five minutes driving south took us to a cluster of houses on both sides of the highway. I found the gravel road after the curio store that George had talked to me about, the one he'd dreamed of owning one day. A minute later, the road ended, a stone's throw from the cliff and the ocean. Four houses were spread out along the cliff with at least a football field's length between them. The cliff turned out toward the water, then bent back in again, forming a point. It was exactly as I'd imagined it when George had described the location.

The fog was even thicker near the cliff, and we could see only a vague outline of the house as we turned on the dirt driveway. To our left, a few cows grazed among the sage and juniper. With the brown hills rising immediately from the highway on one side and the ocean on the other, the area gave me a sense of supreme isolation.

"I'd call this the middle of nowhere," Roach said.

"What would George want to be here for?" Turly asked.

"He tried to explain, but I still don't get it," I said.

The house took shape as we neared. I recognized it from George's photograph: two stories, 1920s folk-Victorian style with white clapboard and a low-pitched pyramid-shaped roof, front gables, and a long front porch of spindle work and pseudo-Victorian details. Yellow flowers and gray-green bushes dotted the area around the house. Tire tracks led to a garage built sometime in the recent past. An arbor connected the garage to the house, and a climbing rosebush clung to the lathing.

I parked in front of the garage. We climbed out and took a moment to examine the building. What puzzled me were the signs of occupancy: a broom left on the porch, freshly trimmed bushes around the steps, a wheelbarrow of potted geraniums near a flower bed that had been partially dug up.

"Did George say anything about renters?" Roach asked.

"Not to me," I said.

"If somebody lived here, wouldn't they have been out here to greet us by now?" Turly said.

"It might be another trap," Arliss said.

"There's no way Hanson's guys could've found out about this place that fast," I said.

Roach drew his .45 and said, "Arliss, stay back with Rebecca and Turl. Frank and I will check it out."

I did the same with the .38, and we edged up the creaking steps of the porch. A light breeze and the sound of the waves accompanied us. Our feet clumped loudly on the porch planking and I hoped the crash of the waves would cover the noise. Roach stood on one side of the door and peered through the cut-glass windows. He shrugged and motioned for me to go ahead.

I took out the single key I'd taken from George's pocket, pulled back the screen, and unlocked the door. The bolt retracted with a clunk. Roach rolled around between the door and me, and turned the knob. We stepped inside.

None of the interior lights were on, though there was enough soft gray light emanating from the lace-curtained windows to show us we were in a large living room. The furnishings were thrift-store quality but clean and comfortable-looking. Stacks of books covered the fireplace wall and lined the mantel; a few moving boxes were neatly arranged against a wall. We crept across to the dining room, where three large picture windows looked out to the ocean. A picnic table and benches apparently served as the dining table.

I paused a moment to take in the view. The ocean was beautiful in spite of the haze turning everything shades of gray.

Roach signaled he was going toward the kitchen, and for me to go the other way. Portions of the flowered wallpaper had been torn away. I thought of George down here making plans for redecorating and still couldn't get my head around it.

I entered what would have been the sitting room when the

house had been built. Another set of windows looked out onto the ocean. A sofa with no legs and draped in an old bedspread sat against one wall; more moving boxes were stacked against another. A throw rug lay in the middle of the room. The toys strewn across the rug stopped me: a metal dump truck, building blocks, a flying saucer that spun if you pushed the plunger in the middle.

I went back through the dining room and into the kitchen. Roach asked me with his eyes. I shook my head, pointed upstairs. We pushed through the swinging door that fed back into the living room and crept up to the second floor.

A hallway led to two rooms, then a bathroom at the far end. The first door stood open. Roach stuck his head in and moved inside. The floorboards snapped and groaned as I snuck down the hallway toward the second bedroom. This door was closed. Whoever was in the house was behind that door. My nerves started to jump as I got closer—so, I wasn't so numb after all. I reached for the doorknob.

There was nothing but my hand, the knob, and the sound of the waves.

I heard the creak of floorboards from inside the room. Raised the .38, hand shaking. I looked behind. Roach inched up the hallway toward me, both hands on his .45.

I turned the knob and pushed into the room, gun first. A woman let out a yelp, and drew back to the wall. Her arms were wrapped tightly around a little boy.

"Please don't shoot," she said.

Roach was right behind me, and asked over my shoulder, "Is there anyone else in here?"

"What do you want? We haven't got any money."

It took me a second to register her face.

I lowered my gun. "Marjorie?"

Her face scrunched in confusion. "Frank?"

"What are you doing here?" I asked.

"What do you mean? We live here."

"You live here?" I had to repeat it just so it would sink in.

"Are you renting it from George Mayhall?" Roach asked.

"No. I'm his wife."

Roach looked stupefied.

"Would you please put the guns away?" she asked with the slight twang of ranch upbringing. "You're scaring us. That is, if you're not planning to rob or shoot us."

"Sorry," I said. "We didn't expect anyone."

We did as she asked.

"Is that how you normally enter a house when you're not expecting someone?" The question was defiant, but she looked everywhere but at us, and clung tightly to her kid. "Is George in trouble? Is that why you're here?"

"When did you last see him?" I asked.

"Last week, when I saw you at the park."

"I knew it, goddamnit," Roach said, his voice a low growl.

"And he hasn't been down here since then?" I asked.

"Not since I moved in, which was four days ago. He was supposed to be here today. I thought you were him until I saw the car."

"Oh God. What's wrong? Why do you have guns? What are you planning to do?" Her pitch rose with each new word.

"Everything's okay," I said. "We were supposed to meet up with George and leave San Francisco together." It wasn't really a lie. "We were going to stay here for a few days, then move on. We didn't know anyone lived here and thought you might be someone setting a trap. I'm sorry—we've been through a lot these past few days."

An embarrassing silence hung in the room.

Marjorie wore a simple flowered sundress and a light-blue cardigan sweater. She looked beautiful. She caught me staring at her, and I felt my face flush.

The boy, who seemed to be around four, looked like his mother, blond and full-lipped, but with George's strong jaw and big brown eyes.

"I'm sorry. I'm being rude," Marjorie said. "You scared us. You can wait for him here. He's coming down today."

Roach and I looked at each other; neither one of us wanted to tell her the bad news—not like this.

"Okay, thank you," I said. "We'll tell our other friends they can come inside."

"Nate, honey, you stay up here and play with your toys. Mommy is going to make some coffee for these nice people."

Nate stared at us. Those eyes, that expression ... one hundred percent George.

"They're not nice," he said. "They scared you, Mommy, and they've got guns."

I squatted down. "You want to know something funny? You scared us too. We thought you might be bad guys wanting to hurt us or your dad."

Nate hugged his teddy bear and pushed deeper into his mother's thighs.

"Come on, Frank," Roach said. "Let's get everyone inside before Arly comes in here with his gun a-blazin'."

Marjorie lifted Nate and put him on the bed, then straightened her dress. The slight disturbance of air released the scent of roses. She held out a long, thin hand to me and we shook; hers was warm and soft.

"I'm happy you guys are here. It's so lonely without someone else around. I can't wait for George to get here."

She turned to Roach. "And you are?"

"It's Roland, but everyone calls me Roach."

"I prefer Roland," she said, "but if everyone calls you Roach ..." She shrugged and offered one of those irresistible smiles that prompts everyone else to do the same.

"Sorry for not introducing myself," Roach said, "but I was surprised to hear that George was married."

"Yes, I get that a lot." She turned wistful and said, "Shall I make you guys some coffee?"

"That'd be nice, thank you," I said.

We went downstairs and outside. Roach stopped at the porch and signaled for Arliss. I went straight to Rebecca.

"What took you guys so long?" Arliss asked as I passed.

"There's somebody in the house. Roach will tell you more."

Turly intercepted me, expectation in his eyes.

"I've got to talk to Rebecca," I said. He didn't take the hint. "Alone for a minute. Roach will tell you."

Turly pouted, picked up a bag, and walked to the house. I took Rebecca by the elbow and steered her around the other side of the car.

"What is it, Frank? Who's in there?"

"George's wife."

"What? He was married? Does she know?"

"No, we couldn't tell her."

"Oh, God, Frank."

"I was hoping you could do it, sort of woman to woman."

"Coward—"

"She's got a son."

Rebecca froze.

"Can you tell her before Arliss blurts it out or she hears it from Turly?" I asked.

"That bastard. It's one thing for him to screw up his own life, but they didn't have a choice." Her expression turned from sad to contemptuous. "Goddamn you." She walked off toward the house.

Roach came out as Rebecca entered. He held the screen door for her and tried a smile, but she blew past him. He shrugged at me and stepped down off the porch. He met me by the car as I removed a bag from the trunk.

"What's she doing here, Frank? Do we have a time bomb on our hands?"

"She's just wigged out like all of us. She'll be okay."

"Is she going to tell George's wife?"

I nodded. Roach grabbed a bag and started to leave. I put a hand on his arm. "We should leave her George's share."

He yanked his arm away. "What are you talking about? We have to keep her in the dark about what's going on. We find the stuff, then slip out of here."

"Pulling out guns and tearing up the house won't give her a clue?"

"We keep her in the boy's room until we're done. It won't take that long to search the place."

"This is George's wife and kid we're talking about. They'll be left with nothing. She probably doesn't have a job, and she's got to support a kid. I wondered what George did with all his dough. Now I know. He bought this house and planned to support them off his earnings."

"He knew what he was getting into. If he was willing to take chances, and maybe leave his wife and kid with nothing, why should we do any more?"

"That's the most screwed-up reasoning I've ever heard. George was our friend. We've got to help out."

"Then it comes out of your cut. I didn't risk my life to support George's widow."

He turned and walked toward the house. I stood alone, face-to-face with George's white, clapboard dream. I felt a mixture of emotions—sadness certainly, but something else too, and it surprised me … envy. For all of George's misguided notions, he had touched on something real, something I'd failed to do. Why he'd hidden it from me, I don't know. Maybe, like he'd said, he would have revealed his mystery when we got out of San Francisco. I shrugged it off, grabbed a bag and the shotgun, and headed for the house.

Inside, the search had already begun. Roach hadn't waited for Rebecca to tell Marjorie. He or Turly had thrown the cushions onto the floor, and Turly had his fingers wedged inside the sofa. He stopped when he saw me. I shook my head in disgust. Turly nodded toward the dining room. Arliss was holding a box. He put it on the floor, and began to pull out objects wrapped in newspaper. Arliss tore at the wrapping and tossed the objects on the floor.

I charged in. "Take it easy with that stuff."

"We're going to be here all day as it is," he said, but his handling became gentler.

I heard Rebecca in the kitchen with Marjorie. Obviously, she hadn't told her.

"Where's Roach?" I asked.

"In there," he said, pointing to the den.

Roach came out with a box before I reached the door. He ripped it open and dumped the contents on the floor.

"I thought we were going to wait until Rebecca had a chance to talk to Marjorie."

"We haven't got the time," Roach said, rifling through the stuff.

"You going to put it all back?"

He didn't look up. "I'll take care of it. Why don't you start helping?"

"I don't want her to see all this stuff getting thrown around. It's going to be bad enough telling her the news."

"You want to find it or not? Stop worrying about George's widow and worry about your own ass."

The announcement of coffee stopped us. Rebecca stood with a tray of cups, milk, and sugar. Marjorie held a pot of coffee and had stopped in her tracks. She looked at the three of us standing among the chaos. Turly came in and fidgeted when he saw Marjorie's shocked expression. I looked around at the guilty expressions. Rebecca stepped past her and laid the tray on the dining room table.

"Break it up, guys," Rebecca said. "Grab some coffee."

"What's going on?" Marjorie asked.

Rebecca took the pot from her and set it on the table. Marjorie turned to me, her blue eyes begging me for an answer.

I walked over to her. "Can we talk upstairs?" I said.

"I want to know what's going on."

Rebecca came over and stood close to Marjorie. "Frank and I want to talk to you. I think it's better if we do it in private."

She looked at Rebecca, then me, took a deep breath, and headed for the stairs. It was like a marching to the gallows. I wanted Marjorie to be okay, whether out of sympathy, charity, or obligation, I wasn't sure. But the desire to take care of her and Nate was keen.

Marjorie topped the stairs and entered her bedroom. She turned in the middle of the room and locked her attention on me. I had to look away before those blue eyes got the better of me. Rebecca sat on the edge of the bed and motioned for her to sit.

Marjorie sat down next to Rebecca and stared at the floor.

"I think I know what you're going to tell me. I can see it in your faces."

"Do you know what George was doing in San Francisco?" Rebecca asked.

"A little. I knew it wasn't a legit job, that he could go to jail if he got caught. I asked him to stop, but he kept saying, 'One more time, baby, one more job.' He wanted enough money for us to live well. I went along with it because I wanted to get out of Stockton and be with him down here." She looked up. "The way you're both looking, I don't think he's in jail."

She looked at Rebecca, then me.

"He's dead," I said softly. "He was killed last night."

She turned to the window, tears streaming down her cheeks, the fingers on her trembling hands weaving in and out of each other.

"I'm sorry, Marjorie," Rebecca said.

"Why did he die?"

Rebecca opened her mouth to speak, but there was no way to justify his death, no excuses that would make any sense to someone who hadn't been sucked in step by stupid step.

"We were dealing drugs," I said. "George had a meeting in an alley and the contact shot him." I tried to make up for the senselessness, but only compounded it by adding, "He managed to kill his murderer, though."

Marjorie hung her head and sobbed quietly, her body spasming gently. Rebecca tried to rub her arm, but she moved away.

"I want to be alone now," Marjorie said.

Rebecca stroked her hair. "If you need anything, I'll be downstairs." She stood and left the room.

I took Rebecca's place on the bed, wanting to comfort her but not knowing how. "I'm sorry" was all I could offer.

I stood to leave. She jumped up, wrapped her arms around me, and buried her face in my shoulder. Her sobs, her touch, the scent of roses brought up every tear I'd buried. I tried to control it. I didn't want to cry on her shoulder. I wanted to be her comforter. But I couldn't hold it back. We held each other tight and wept together.

Long minutes passed. Then she lifted her head and kissed me on the cheek. Our tears mingled. She took some tissues from the bedside table and wiped her face.

"I have to take care of my son."

"I need to tell you one more thing before you go."

She turned to me, the blue of her irises accentuated by her bloodshot eyes.

"My friends and I entered into a partnership with George. Together, we stole a large quantity of heroin from a gang, and George was killed because of it. But now the heroin is missing. We don't know for sure, but we think George hid the heroin here, in this house."

Marjorie slapped me. The slap didn't hurt, but her anger did.

"So that's why your friends are searching through my things?"

I nodded, ashamed.

"That's great. That's just great. And you might have led those killers to my house?"

"No, they know nothing about this place. We're only here to find the drugs, then get out of your life. I'm sorry for all this. I didn't want any of this to happen."

"Yeah, me too. Only you made those choices. I never asked

for any of this." She pushed down her anger and wiped her eyes once more. She reached up and touched the skin where she'd slapped me. "Sorry."

"I deserve more than that."

Marjorie started to leave.

"I'm going to start searching up here," I said. "But I'll check up on you later."

She thanked me and left the room.

I DECIDED TO START THE SEARCH IN HER ROOM: THE BRASS BED, the closet, the dresser, behind and under everything. Nothing. On the dresser, she had made enough space for a black-and-white photograph of her and George. They were arm in arm, standing under a California oak with a picnic basket and a blanket at their feet. They looked younger, him in a white shirt with rolled-up sleeves and jeans, her in a flowered dress, in about her sixth month of pregnancy going by the bulge beneath the dress. She looked straight into the camera with the same compelling gaze that had held me earlier. A big smile told a story of happiness and hope. George beamed, seemingly more relaxed than I'd ever seen him. He stood straight, his pose almost triumphant. The one noticeable oddity was his expression. Some preoccupation the camera had caught. It summed up George—you'd feel great around him, his personality big enough for everyone, but there'd always be a sense of his being distracted, no matter how much he wanted to be there.

I put the photograph down and searched through the boxes: books, magazines, jewelry box, sewing kit, and makeup, but no packets of heroin. I felt certain we were wasting our time digging through boxes and ripping up floorboards. George would have hidden it in some clever place that hadn't taken much time to conceal. There would be no secret doors or tunnels, just some obvious, in-your-face hiding place.

I left Marjorie's room and headed down the hallway. Nate's door was closed, but I could hear Marjorie talking gently to her son. I stopped and listened to her melodic voice as she read a children's book about a family of cats and dogs. A floorboard creaked under my foot. The voice stopped for a second, then continued.

I went into the bathroom and searched to the backdrop of Marjorie's and Nate's gentle chatter. Would I ever have a family of my own? Perhaps—if I wasn't dead by the end of the week; even then, I'd always be on the run. My soul ached in that moment, and I resisted the urge to smash my fist into the mirror. *Focus, Frankie.* I took once last look around and headed downstairs.

Turly stood by the fireplace, looking out the window. I followed his gaze. Rebecca sat on the porch, staring across the field. My first thought was to comfort her as I had Marjorie. Instead, I chose to search the kitchen to keep myself from thinking about either of them.

I checked the den first. Empty boxes, their former contents, and wadded paper were strewn across the floor. Arliss knelt beside one of the cartons. I didn't have the heart to get into it with him and went into the kitchen. I leaned against the counter and tried to imagine George standing in the middle of the room, deciding on the perfect place to hide twenty-two kilos of heroin.

Marjorie didn't have much stuff stored away, so the process went quickly. The obvious hiding places produced nothing, and I stood by the sink, smoking another cigarette, imagining the less obvious.

Turly stepped in with a cup of coffee.

"Nothing?" he asked.

I shook my head. "Pull up a countertop—it looks like you want to talk."

Turly brought the coffee over and handed it to me. He leaned against the counter next to me.

"I'm really happy about your hand, man," he said.

I held up my fingers and wiggled them. "Thanks. They're not perfect yet, but they'll get there."

"You can go back to your music if we live through this." He'd meant it as a joke, but the comment sobered us both.

We didn't say anything for a moment. Then Turly asked, "Is Marjorie all right?"

"I don't know. I guess."

"Does she know what's going on?"

"I had to tell her." I said it as flatly as I could, but the emotions welled up anyway.

Turly put a hand on my shoulder. "It's okay, buddy. That means you're not such a heartless shit after all."

His touch of kindness jolted me; I'd expected animosity. Thoughts of us escaping this whole crazy scene flashed through my mind. I wanted to save him, and regretted ever recruiting him into this madness.

He sipped his drink and sighed. "I'm afraid of what will happen if we don't find it. But the funny thing is, I'm more afraid of what will happen if we do."

"I hope you're not waiting for me to have any ideas."

"What about Marjorie? Are we just going to leave her here?"

"That's up to her. I already talked to Roach about leaving her George's cut. She's George's wife. She's entitled to it."

"Roach isn't going to go for that."

"You're probably right."

Turly stared at the floor, wiggling his feet. I sensed he was pulling up the courage to talk.

"Roach is scaring me. I've never seen him like this. I think this whole thing has got him kind of crazy."

"We need them, and they need us. It'll hold together long enough."

"Yeah? What's going to happen when the big money starts rolling in? I'm not going to be able to sleep at night."

Turly scared easily, but this time he had a point. My own worries boiled up. "Shit, Turl, what am I supposed to say?"

"Okay, man, take it easy."

"We've got to see this thing through. None of us has come this far to run scared now."

"I know. Look, I've been a pain in the ass, and it looked like I was going Looney Tunes there for a while, but I'll be all right."

He started to leave, his expression dejected.

"Turl." He stopped and turned. "I hope we can stay together after this whole thing is over with."

"I know you worry about me, and I appreciate that. You probably saved my ass a couple of times too, and I've been wanting to thank you for all of it. I just wanted you to know that."

I walked over and put a hand on his shoulder. "Come on. Let's find this stuff and get out of here."

Roach and Arliss looked up from their ripping at boxes as Turly and I entered the den.

"You cats hatching some kind of lame plot in there?" Roach asked.

"You're the ones who wanted to break up the partnership,"

Turly said, jabbing his index finger at them. "We should be the ones in a cold sweat."

"This was a ridiculous arrangement anyway," Roach said. "You guys can do what you want. Just don't go getting any ideas in the meantime."

"Yeah?" Turly said. "I bet if we stayed with you guys, we'd find a knife in our backs."

Arliss stepped toward him. "I'll put another bruise on your jaw if you don't shut up."

I stepped in between them, and the big man stopped. He looked as hurt as he did angry.

"Why did he have to say that? I'm not going to knife you guys."

"Then lay off me," Turly said. "I'm tired of you putting me down."

Arliss ignored the comment. "You two are going to be pretty funny trying to sell eleven kilos on the streets somewhere." He imitated my voice. "Hey, Daddy-O, you wanna buy a kilo?"

He and Roach laughed.

I had to admit, it *was* going to be pretty ridiculous, but their mockery made me crazy. I looked at Roach and pointed at Arliss. "Time to call off your ape. He's bugging me."

Arliss's right fist struck me across the jaw and everything went black. I staggered and fell, my ears ringing.

"Arliss!" someone said, probably Roach.

My vision cleared and I looked up. Arliss loomed over me.

I struggled to my feet and ran my tongue around my mouth, feeling for a loose tooth and tasting blood

Arliss backed off, his flash of anger gone. "Why do you say things like that to me? It makes me crazy."

Roach held my chin and checked my jaw. "Anything loose?" he asked.

I shook my head.

"Arliss pulled his punch. You'd have been seeing a dentist otherwise." He looked back at his partner. "No one's jaw gets broken until we get this over with."

He smiled, as if it were a joke. I wasn't laughing.

He backed off and his sneer returned. "I don't care what you cats do after we find this stuff."

"All right, Roach," I said, "if that's the way you want to play it, we'll split up. You watch your backs and we'll watch ours."

"Guys, does it have to come to this?" Turly said. "It's like you're spitting on George's grave. What would you be doing if George hadn't come along with a plan? Sitting on your duffs, growing older, and collecting vet benefits, that's what."

I couldn't believe what I was hearing. Where had the balls come from?

Arliss took a step toward Turly, then backed off and looked away.

"Let them cry, Arly," Roach said. "They're lost without Georgie-boy, and they'll wind up like he did, dead in some alley until the city sticks them in an unmarked grave."

A faint gasp made us stop and look toward the living room. Marjorie was standing next to Rebecca, her hand clasped to her mouth, tears in her eyes.

"Nice going, boys," Rebecca said. "How about some more words of wisdom from you morons?"

Marjorie turned and walked away. I could hear her sobbing. Roach went back to his ripping at boxes. Arliss didn't. He looked in Marjorie's direction. I think he wanted to say something, but he glanced at Roach's cold stare and returned to his box.

I walked past Rebecca, ignoring her angry eyes. Marjorie was draped across the sofa arm, staring out the window. I sat down next to her.

"I hadn't thought about what would happen to George up there," she said. "He's going to be processed like a piece of trash."

"Those were cruel things to say and I'm sorry. The four of us have lost what it takes to be human. I hope in my case it's temporary. You just have to ignore what we say and chalk it up to us being pinheads. Having to leave George like that has hurt me more than you can imagine."

"I should go up there and take care of him, but I'm afraid."

"You don't have to be. No one's after you."

She stopped crying and turned to me. "The wife of the guy who stole drugs? Drugs that are still missing? You told me those gangsters were desperate. If I go up there now, the police or the drug dealers are going to find out and grab me."

She had a point.

"It's sad," she continued. "I loved George and I'll miss him, but he was gone so much of the time that it's hard to feel like I'm really a widow." She shook her head and buried her face in her hands. "I don't know what I'm saying." She looked up at me, held my eyes for a moment. A few deep breaths and she was on her feet and heading upstairs.

Rebecca took the armchair next to me and studied my face, reading the fine print. A little of her anger had subsided, but something else simmered beneath the surface.

"What do you want?"

She crossed her arms and looked around the room.

"You got something to say, say it," I said.

"I've been trying to imagine what's next. Where do I go from here? It doesn't look good to me, Frank."

"I have a feeling you decided that a long time ago."

"Not really. I'm just seeing things clearly for the first time. And I don't like it."

"So, you're giving up before you get started."

"What am I supposed to think? You've been involved in at least one killing that I know of, maybe more. You're selling heroin. Then there's kidnapping, assault with a deadly weapon—"

"What about your sugar daddy, huh? Did you forget all the things he's done?"

"Are you trying to erase everything by comparing yourself to him?" She took a breath. "It was supposed to be different with you. I wanted to get away from all that, but I've just ended up in the exact same place. Except now I'm with rank amateurs who can count the days before they're all dead."

"All right, you made your point." I lit up a cigarette while we looked at everything but each other. "I never wanted it to be this way. Cut out if you want. I won't stop you."

I immediately regretted my remark. Her nervous jiggling stopped, maybe even her breathing. She was fighting back tears. She had made a decision right then and there, but I felt too empty to care. She walked over, touched my cheek, then backed away. I tried to understand what that meant, whether she'd just said good-bye or that she'd stay. I wasn't sure which I preferred.

"I need the keys to the Cadillac."

I looked up and she shook her head.

"It's not that. I'm not going far. Marjorie and I are going to the store to buy something for lunch. I thought it would be better for her to get out of the house and away from all this."

I gave her the keys.

IT FELT GOOD TO GET OUT OF THE HOUSE, AND I DECIDED TO take advantage of the fresh air and search the garage. I walked across the yard, revived by the cool, wet air; calmed by the sound of seagulls and breaking surf. It crossed my mind to stay here for a while and take sanctuary. Marjorie's face kept popping up in my mind. Maybe it was just a reaction to Rebecca's rejection, or perhaps Marjorie and I had been drawn together by George's death. Or was there something else?

The garage doors creaked open on rusty hinges. There wasn't much inside: gardening tools, large bags of planting soil, an ancient push mower, cans of paint, and sacks of cement. It wouldn't take long to complete the search, just enough time to keep away from the women until they took off for the store.

I kicked things around, pushed cobwebs, sand and dust away with the toe of my shoe. Nothing appeared to have been touched in a long time.

I heard the Cadillac start up and the engine rev. I stepped out of the garage. Nate came up to me, his curiosity seemingly overriding his apprehension.

"Whatcha doin' in here?" he asked.

"Just looking."

"My name's Nathan, but everyone calls me Nate."

"Hi, Nate. I'm Frank."

"You going to do some gardening? Mommy said the house needs some gardening."

"Well, I hadn't thought about it, but maybe you and I can do some together later."

"Okay," he said, and stared up at me.

I didn't know what to do next.

"Nathan," Marjorie called. She stood by the open car door.

"Something's wrong with Mommy. She never calls me Nathan."

"Women can just get that way for no reason sometimes," I said.

"She said Daddy isn't coming home."

I felt a pain in my insides, and I didn't know what to say. I hoped a four-year-old kid couldn't read my face like everyone else seemed able to.

"He might never come home, she said." With that, he turned and ran to the car.

He jumped in. Marjorie smiled and I returned the gesture. Rebecca was barely visible through the reflection on the windshield. She stared straight ahead, then turned to me. I tried to read her expression. It was as if she was apologizing for something, and I had the distinct feeling she wouldn't be coming back. A sense of loss overwhelmed me, and I looked away before it surfaced. The car door slammed and the engine roared. The Cadillac backed up and drove off.

To keep my mind off it all, I shifted dirt around with my feet, looking for an indication of digging or a trapdoor. The pushing became kicking. The kicking wasn't enough, and I pounded the walls.

Turly was on his knees, crawling along the living-room floor. He would rap a floorboard, shuffle a few inches, and repeat the process.

"What are you doing now?"

Turly sighed and growled at the floor. "Roach told me to look for hollow spots. Then I've got to do the walls. This is crazy. He says it's in here somewhere, and he's going to start tearing up the floorboards and knocking holes in the walls to find it."

"He was the one convinced it wasn't here. Now he's going to rip the house apart? Where are they?"

"Arliss is in the den and Roach is up in Nate's room."

"That asshole is going to destroy the kid's stuff."

I raced upstairs and down the hall. Roach had Nate's mattress on the floor. He popped open his switchblade.

"What the hell are you doing?"

"What the hell does it look like?"

"You're not going to find it in there. Marjorie said they moved in four days ago and she didn't see George, so how was he supposed to sneak in here, stuff it in a mattress, then sew the whole damn thing up while the kid was sleeping?"

He pointed the switchblade in my direction, and I backed up.

"You trust everything she says? What if she's hiding it? What if she's waiting for us to leave and sell it all herself?" His eyes narrowed. "Or maybe you're in on it with her. You give us a bum steer—then you and she make off with the stuff."

"Come on, Roach. Think about that for a second."

He studied me a moment, his breathing slower. He closed the switchblade and dropped the mattress.

"You don't seem too hot on finding it," he said.

"I don't want to tear up the house to do it."

"With the money you'll make, you could buy them a whole new house. What am I supposed to think when you spend more time with George's wife than you do searching?"

"Damn, Roach. Calm down. I'm not going to double-cross you."

He started riffling through the boy's dresser. "I don't like being hunted, and I didn't get into this shit for some lousy chump change." Beneath his anger, sadness or some buried anguish peeked through. "I deserve more," he said. "We deserve more, and I'm not going to worry about the asshole's house to find it."

Roach was losing his mind. Yelling was the only way to get through to him. "Keep searching, and I'll do the same, but don't tear up the kid's room! He's just lost a dad, for Chrissakes. Give it a rest."

I went downstairs. Arliss was standing by a front window, looking out into the fog. I followed his gaze. The Cadillac was just about visible on the gravel road.

"They're back," he said.

He turned from the window and looked at me. I could tell from his expression that he'd overheard everything. His eyes showed more sadness than anger.

"God, I'm hungry," he said, and opened the front door. "I'll be checking under the house. One of you call me when the food's ready." He went outside, crossed the porch, and disappeared around the side.

Turly went back to knocking the floor. "This is ridiculous."

"Then stop it. You don't have to do what Roach says."

Turly got up and brushed off his pants. "You saw the look in his eyes. I don't want to get him any angrier than he already is."

"It's not under the floorboards."

"What makes you so sure?"

"Keep knocking like a fool if you want, but George didn't have time to build a secret hiding place. It's more obvious than that. There must be an attic. Try there."

He came to the window and stopped next to me. "What's with you?"

"Sorry, but I don't know how much more of this bullshit I can take."

Turly slunk away from me and mounted the stairs with slow, deliberate steps. The front door opened. Rebecca came in with a grocery bag, glanced at me, threw me the car keys, and headed for the kitchen. Marjorie came in, a bag in one hand and Nate in the other. They smiled at me.

"Keeping a watch out for pirates?" she asked.

"Just waiting for you to come back."

Her smile widened. "That's nice."

She crossed the living room. I watched her walk, watched her smile.

"Can I get you anything?" she asked.

"No, thanks," I said. "Just let us know when it's ready."

"Nate told me you and he were going to do some gardening."

I thought of Roach violating the boy's room and decided to keep Nate away until Roach was done. "Yeah, that was the plan."

"Don't you have something else to do?" Marjorie asked.

"I can't think of anything better right now."

I could see why George had been so taken with her. Her face was open and bright, and I didn't feel so alone when I looked at her. No wonder George had dreamed of her and Nate and this house. It was too bad he hadn't come up with a better plan for taking care of them.

"You want to do some gardening with me, Nate?"

"Okay."

"You could show a little more enthusiasm," Marjorie said.

"What are enthususims? Are they in the garage?" Nate asked. "'Cause there's lots of things in there. We keep everything for the garden in there."

I walked over next to him. "I'll tell you what, we'll both look for the enthusiasms. Maybe we'll find some and plant them in the flower bed."

I held out my hand. The boy looked at it, then up at me.

"That's okay. I can walk by myself."

"Then let's go."

We walked out onto the porch and crossed the yard toward the garage.

"So, Nate, when did you see your daddy last?"

"I don't know."

"Has it been that long?"

"I don't know. Maybe."

"Maybe? What's that mean?"

Nate pointed to the shovel. "Mom uses that for the flowers."

I picked up a trowel and gave that to him. "You can use the little shovel, and I'll take the big one." I grabbed one of the bags of planting soil. We walked over to the wheelbarrow near the front porch.

Being with this little kid made me forget, just for a moment, what had happened and where I was going. This boy, with his delicate hands, wide eyes, short legs, and waddling gait, took me back to my childhood. It had the same calming force as Marjorie's eyes and Rebecca's embrace. I felt more like an adult with this four-year-old than I ever had in my years after college, more comfortable with being a man.

Nate attacked the geraniums in the flower bed with his trowel, flinging dirt into the air and on his shoes.

"Whoa there, Sir Lancelot. You don't want to kill the earth. Just move some aside so the flowers will grow and make the earth happy." I dug a hole, added planting soil, and put one of the geraniums, pleased with my demonstration of flower-bed etiquette. "Keep your fingers and toes out of the way."

I dug into the flower bed with the shovel. It was soft and easy to move. Something had been planted there before. I wondered—had George buried the stash here? I went to work with the shovel again until I hit hard clay a couple of feet down.

"Hey, Nate, when did your mom plant these flowers?"

"Yesterday. I helped."

Paranoia invaded my thoughts. What if Marjorie had found the stash and buried it under the flowers? What if she was deploying a skillful masquerade of innocence while she waited for us to give up? Nah, I thought. impossible. Still, I dug around the bed ... just in case.

"Did your mom find anything funny in the ground when she was digging?"

"Yeah, a big fat worm. She screamed when it stuck to her hand. It was funny."

The screen door slammed. I looked up. Roach stood on the porch, staring at me.

"I hope you're digging because you think he buried it there," he said.

"Just dirt and worms. Right, Nate?"

"Yeah, worms," Nate said with a face of delightful disgust.

Roach didn't seem to find that as cute as I did. I walked over to him.

I pointed to Nate. "I didn't want him to see you tearing up his things, so we're out here doing a little gardening."

"More delaying tactics?"

"Christ, Roach, just stow it, all right? That sneer of yours is becoming permanent."

"We didn't come down here so you could play daddy."

"Just trying to do my part. If we get killed down here, our graves might as well look nice."

Roach grunted through his cigarette holder.

"Where's Arly?" he asked.

"He's searching under the house."

Rebecca stepped out, looked at Roach and stopped mid-stride. They glared at each other for a long, malicious second;

then Roach climbed down the steps and disappeared around the corner.

Rebecca tapped the top step with her foot and stared out to the road and the mountains. She shivered and wrapped her arms around herself. I offered her my jacket. She put it across her shoulders with a soft "Thanks." Avoiding my eyes, she lit a cigarette and took quick, hungry puffs.

Nate caught my attention—he was attacking the flowers with the trowel more vigorously than before.

"Hold on, Nate. You're killing the flowers and hurting the earth." I went over, bent down, and showed him again how to take a little soil out of the bag and mix it with the sandy clay in the flower bed.

"You're good with him," Rebecca said. "Probably better than George ever was."

"I'm sure George loved him. He's a good kid."

I chuckled at Nathan's delight as he stuck his hands in the dirt and rolled them around. He got as much dirt on himself as he mixed in the hole. I stood back up and caught Rebecca looking at me.

"What's wrong?" I asked.

She turned away again and tapped her foot even faster. Her hand held the porch rail so hard that her fingers turned white. Her face was drawn and sad. She was as beautiful as ever, but her defiant energy and wild playfulness were gone.

"What's up with you? You're about to jump out of your skin."

She opened her mouth, and I thought she'd speak, but she stuck her cigarette in.

"You gotta calm down," I said. "We had a really good thing, and it can still be that way. Every time we got together, it was like fire. Intensity like that doesn't happen every day, and it's crazy to ignore it."

"Fire burns, Frank."

We locked eyes. Hers were dry.

"The best thing you could ever do for yourself is take care of George's family."

Her look was so resolute that it threw me.

"This is a lousy way of breaking it off between you and me."

Rebecca flicked her cigarette into the yard. "You're a great guy, Frank, but I want you to forget me and get out of here. Get away from all this craziness. Take Marjorie and Nate with you ... as fast as you can and don't look back. Forget the drugs, forget the money, and just go. Go now."

I had not time to absorb it, never mind respond; she'd already stormed inside.

35

The screen door slammed behind Rebecca. I watched her silhouette fade from sight. It felt as though Nate had planted my feet instead of the flowers; they wouldn't move. Rebecca was the most confounding person I'd ever met, the most confounding I would ever meet. The paradox left me stunned.

I felt something patter across the tops of my shoes. Nate had flung dirt on them but I couldn't react. The sense of loss was too profound. My only solution to the rising pressure was to hack at the ground with the shovel. Nate's voice broke through the rage.

"You're hurting the earth, Frank. You're hurting it."

I stopped and looked down. The shovel had cut large slashes of earth all around the flower bed. "Sorry, Nate. I guess I'm just tired."

"Mommy says the same thing when she does stuff like that, only she doesn't take a nap after she says it."

"Oh, yeah?" I tickled Nathan's ribs. "You're just too smart for your britches." I brushed off my pants and shoes. "Why don't you wash your hands and go help your mom with lunch? I'll go tell the other two guys that the food is ready."

I lifted him to his feet. Nate imitated me, brushing off his own pants. "Can we do more gardening after lunch?"

I assured him we would, and watched him go, then forced my legs to move around the side of the house. Arliss was sitting on the ground with his back against the building, throwing pebbles over the cliff. The access door to the crawl space was next to him. He took one look at me, and continued to chuck stones.

"Roach still under there?" I asked.

"He didn't think I looked hard enough. He's looking in the same places I did." He threw a pebble with more force.

"Lunch is ready by now."

"It ain't fair."

"What isn't?"

"Well, you know, life."

"Yeah, and it's getting screwier all the time."

Arliss looked out over the ocean. It felt awkward standing quietly with him.

"Sorry for hitting you on the jaw," he said, and switched his gaze to me. "I didn't want all this. It's got me all wound up inside. Roach wanted it real bad, and I didn't want to let him down. He's the most important thing to me ..." Arliss took a moment. "But this whole mess has changed him."

"He'll be all right after it's all over."

He shook his head. "It's bad for Roach and it's bad for me. He's the one guy I feel good with, and now this shit's come along and fouled everything up. I just wanted things to be like they were, but it keeps changing on me. Why is it that if you find a good thing, it has to go and change on you?"

"Like you said, it ain't fair."

Roach popped his head out of the crawl space and hauled himself out. "Nope, nothing."

"I coulda told you that," Arliss said. "I did tell you that."

"I had to see for myself," Roach said. "No one's interested in finding this stuff but me."

Arliss sauntered toward the porch steps. "I'm interested in eating."

Roach looked at me with a plea for some support. I turned and left him standing there, hands on his hips.

"You guys are actually going to stop for lunch?" he yelled after us.

I called back, "Take a powder and get something to eat."

We did actually stop for lunch—filled paper plates with food laid out on the table, buffet style. Turly naturally gravitated to Rebecca, who sat on the sofa and ate with a sullen stare at the carpet. Roach never came in, though Arliss didn't seem to mind for once. He carried on a conversation with Nate while they played with their food. It made me smile to watch Arliss become such a gentle bull with the boy.

I took a seat at the table near Marjorie. We remained silent and looked out the picture window at the fog and the waves. I would steal looks at her, and she would shyly acknowledge them, then go back to eating or the window. I felt comfortable in our shared silence—and a bit guilty for being attracted to her.

"I know you and George met in college," I said. "Did you guys start dating back then?"

"College sweethearts," she said, and laughed. A flush rose on her face. "Can you imagine? After college, we broke up and got back together a number of times. The last time we split, I moved back to Stockton. I thought he was gone for good, but he showed up again and proposed. Well, make that: he found out he'd gotten me pregnant; then he proposed. We got married in Stockton, but I guess he couldn't stand the small-town living, and about a month later he went back to San Francisco. For business, he told me."

"It must have been hard having him gone so much."

"I knew he was unreliable when I married him, but I loved him too much to care. He was a great romancer … when he was around."

Yep, I thought, *that was George.* "What were you doing in Stockton?"

"Living with my parents and working in a drugstore. They would take care of Nathan while I worked. It was supposed to be a temporary arrangement until George sent for us. That temporariness lasted three years."

"The only time I saw him really relaxed or starry-eyed was when he talked about this place. He never told me about you, but I'm sure you were really what he was dreaming about. I don't get why he left you alone for so long."

"It's a long story."

"He told me about being in prison."

"He never wanted to talk about it, but I could see how it changed him. That's when he got involved with selling reefer, and eventually heroin, through the contacts he'd made inside. I still loved him, but prison had changed him so much. That and the heroin."

"Do you know why he kept you such a secret?"

Marjorie seemed stung by the question. She looked down at her plate. "He told me it was because of what he did. He didn't want anyone to trace anything back to me. But I don't know why he kept it a secret from you. You were his best friend."

It shocked me hearing that. I would have never known it. "He did promise to tell me about everything when this was all over," I said. "He really couldn't wait to come down here. I'm sure that was because of you, not some old house."

She smiled and put her hand on mine. "I'm sure he did, and thanks for telling me that, but he obviously enjoyed the double life. I knew about the girls on the side too." She fought back the tears.

"We should stop talking about this," I said.

I put my other hand on hers. She gave me a shy smile, pulled away and folded her hands in her lap.

"It's okay," she said. "Four years of this kind of arrangement hardened me a little. I still loved him but got used to him not being there. Then when he got into the heroin business, I tried to prepare myself for him going back to prison or worse. Nate has never really known his father. You've been more of a father to Nate in a couple of hours than George was in a year."

I looked to see if the boy had observed any of this. By the way he held his head and halfheartedly played with his food, I figured he was getting the gist of the conversation. He must have sensed me watching him, because after a dramatic car crash with his sandwich and a pile of chips, he looked at me. I smiled and he returned it. I saw a flash of George. He jumped up and ran over to me.

"Can we do some more gardening?" he asked.

"Why don't you go out now," Marjorie said. "Frank will come out a little later."

Nate looked between his mother and me.

"All right, let's do some digging, man," I said, and pushed

my plate aside. Maybe digging with the kid would put things in a clearer light. Or so I hoped.

NATE DROPPED TO HIS KNEES AND PUSHED HIS HANDS INTO THE flower bed. A racket in the garage told me Roach hadn't trusted my search and was tearing through everything I'd already checked. I was feeling more and more uneasy about our fragile alliance. I touched the handle of the gun with a growing sense of paranoia.

"How you doing, kiddo? Got all the geraniums planted?"

"I want more dirt," he said, and pointed to the bag. "It's too heavy."

I chuckled, walked down the stairs, and lifted the large bag of soil. "Look out, Nate. I'll dump a bunch in there and you can mix it all up."

I turned the bag upside down and shook it. The brown-black dirt tumbled out into the flower bed. Something tan and oddly shaped flashed in my field of vision and dropped in the bed, disappearing under the dirt that followed. I put down the bag.

"What was that?" Nate asked.

"You saw it too?"

I dropped to my knees and plunged both hands into the mound. I found the object and pulled it out.

It stopped my breath.

It was one of the kilo packets of heroin.

"What's that?" Nate asked.

"Something we've been looking for," I said absently. I

jumped up and tipped the rest of the bag onto the ground. A couple more packets fell out. "Wow."

"Is it like a treasure?" Nate asked.

"Yeah, kinda."

He jumped up and ran for the front porch, yelling, "We found it, we found it."

Anticipation and fear exploded inside me. I'd found the very thing I'd hoped we wouldn't.

I yelled after him, "Nate, wait."

It was too late. He was already in the house.

36

I dumped the contents of another soil bag on the ground and picked up the packets. Roach came running out of the garage, grabbed up a packet from the ground, and hollered like a crazed fool.

I heard the screen door open.

"Where'd you find it?" Turly asked.

I looked up. Everyone had come out onto the porch. Rebecca and Marjorie looked on grimly.

Nate popped out from behind his mother. "We found it in the bags of dirt."

"There are two more bags of soil in the garage," I said to Arliss. "The rest must be in those."

Arliss leaped over the rail and ran to the garage.

Marjorie gave me a cold glare before leading a protesting Nate into the house. Rebecca followed.

Turly stepped down and helped us. Arliss came back and emptied another bag onto the ground. More packets tumbled out. Roach picked them up as fast as they fell. The rest of us did the same, but with less enthusiasm.

With the bundles cradled in our arms, we went into the house.

We piled the twenty kilos on the picnic table in the dining room and brushed off the soil. Turly and I stood on one side, facing the picture window, Roach and Arliss on the other.

"Now what?" Arliss asked.

The moment I had hoped to avoid unfolded in front of me. Turly looked at me. I turned to Roach, whose eyes drilled into mine. I searched for a glimmer of the friend I'd once known, something, anything, that could dissipate the rising panic.

Arliss looked back and forth between Roach and me. "This ain't that hard," he said. "We split it four ways and skedaddle out of here."

"Is that what we're going to do, Roach?" I asked.

"What are you asking him for?" Turly said to me. "Of course that's what we'll do. If we stick together, great, but if we don't, there's no questions about who gets what."

Turly eyeballed Roach and me, just like Arliss had.

"I don't think that's what Roach has in mind," I said.

Rebecca came in and headed toward the kitchen, then stopped. Maybe she felt the tension in the air because she started to back out the way she'd come.

Roach whipped out his .45. "I'd prefer you didn't leave. Come around where I can see you."

Rebecca moved in next to Turly.

"What are you doing?" Arliss said. "Are you crazy?"

"These guys don't really want any," Roach said. "They said so themselves. And Frank wanted to give away some of the profits to George's wife. Now, is that any way to run a partnership?"

"Roach, please," Arliss said. "This ain't cool."

"Are you with me or them?"

The big man had a pained expression as he looked around the room.

"Arly! You with me or not?" Roach said.

Arliss looked down, his face twisted in indecision. "Sure. Yeah, sure," he said softly.

"Well, then, get your ass in gear. Get one of the suitcases and load it in."

Arliss left the room.

"You're not really going to do this, are you?" Turly asked roach. "Come on, we're friends."

"That stopped when we went into this kind of business together. It's not like I'm stealing it from you guys. It was stolen to begin with. You guys would've just messed it up. So, I'm saving you the trouble, maybe even your hides. You ought to thank me. I'll even leave you some of the dough. Where is the dough?"

Roach turned to Turly, who froze.

"Turl?" I said.

"Uh, in a box on the sofa," he said. "There's 205,231 dollars with what you guys sold yesterday."

Arliss came back with my suitcase. He opened it and dumped my stuff on the floor. "Sorry, man," he said.

I shrugged. I'd gotten used to guns being pointed at me, and I didn't think Roach would kill us in cold blood, unless we tried to separate him from his treasure.

Arliss loaded the heroin into the suitcase, closed it, and stepped back.

"Now, go get the box on the sofa and bring it in here," Roach said.

With a heavy sigh, Arliss went for the box. I looked at

Rebecca. She stared ahead, her eyes blank pools, and trembled slightly. Maybe it was Roach and the gun; it had jangled my nerves. Or was something else going on?

Arliss came back and put the box on the table. Roach opened it and pulled out two large bundles of cash. He threw them on the table next to me.

"Give it to the widow if you want," he said. He turned to his partner. "Shall we, darlin'?"

The big man stood there with his mouth open.

"You don't have to do everything he says," I said to Arliss. "Let him go. It's not cool what he's doing, and I think you're only following him because you think you have to. Well, you don't."

"He knows when he's got a good thing," Roach said. "He's not the brightest bulb in the box, but he knows." He turned to his partner. "You're a good piece of ass, darlin', but I'll leave you too if you're not on my side."

Arliss looked stunned and hurt.

"What are you waiting for?" Roach yelled. "Take this suitcase and our bags to the car."

With a look of resignation, Arliss grabbed the suitcase. He gave Turly and me one last look and walked out.

Roach smiled. "You're not going to come after us, are you?" he asked.

"Hell, yeah," Turly said. "You're stealing from your friends. It's the lowest thing you could do."

"The lowest thing would be to kill you so I wouldn't have to look behind me wherever I go."

"We won't go after you," I said. "That shit has ruined everyone it comes in contact with, including you. Good-bye, Roachie. Vanish before the stink gets too bad in here."

Roach edged around the table, maintaining his aim. He snapped his fingers. "Car keys."

I fished the keys out of my pocket and threw them to him. He caught them and backed into the living room.

"Follow me so I can keep an eye on you," he said.

We did. The screen door slammed. Arliss was back.

"What are you doing?" Roach snapped. "Get in the car. I've got the keys."

Roach glanced over his shoulder. Arliss hadn't moved. He stepped back so he could see everyone at the same time, waving the gun back and forth with his rising panic.

"What are you doing?" he said to his partner.

"I … I'm not going," Arliss said. "I don't want you to go either. Not like this. Please, Rollie."

I'd never heard him use the pet name before. It was an intimate, desperate plea.

"You fucking dope," Roach said. "Do you know what you're doing? No, of course you don't."

"Put the gun down, Rollie, and stay. Stay with me. Everything'll be okay. We do just like we planned. I don't want to do it this way."

Roach stroked at his hair with a shaking hand. His face turned red and his eyes widened in fury.

"Arliss is smarter than you are," I said to Roach. "If you put the gun down and change your mind, we're not going to jump you. We'll split it like we said and go our separate ways. Listen to your friend. He's making a lot of sense."

"Shut up!" Roach said. "You're the ones who brought in Daniel. You're the ones that brought along Hanson's girlfriend. How many times can you fuck things up and expect to stay alive? Now you've got this gorilla on your side, whining about the right thing to do? The stupidity is contagious, and you're all infected." He looked at Arliss, and screamed, "I don't need you. You need me."

Arliss crossed the room and stood next to Turly and me. Roach edged to the front door. He and Arliss stared at each other, each offering silent pleas with the other for a change of mind. I could feel the big man shaking next to me. Roach gave us all one last look and backed out of the door.

We stood frozen a moment. Arliss's shaking became worse, and a moment later he blew out the front door. The rest of us rushed out onto the porch and watched him run across the front yard. Roach had reversed the Cadillac to the end of the drive-way. He stopped. But Arliss didn't get in. Instead, he went to the driver's window.

"Don't go, please, Rollie. Don't go."

Roach slammed on the accelerator, throwing dirt and pebbles as he spun out, leaving his lover standing alone. Roach got to the road and disappeared into the swirling fog.

Arliss's head hung low as he did a slow march back to the porch. He walked up the stairs without looking at any of us and went into the house.

I turned to Rebecca. Even without the threat of the gun, she was still crazed. She met my eyes. I thought she was about to say something but she ran inside.

"You got your wish," I said to Turly.

"This wasn't my wish," he said. "I don't even know what my wish was. We've all been idiots."

He turned away from me and went in.

Despite the shivers up my spine, I stayed and sat on the top step. I tried to envision the warm sun just across the mountains, away from the fog. The landscape didn't help—too far away, too obscure.

ARLISS WAS STANDING AT ONE OF THE REAR WINDOWS IN THE dining room, staring at the ocean. Turly sat at the picnic table and leafed through a stack of money. I took a seat next to him.

"We'll split the money three ways. I'm going to leave some for Marjorie. I might even hang out awhile and make sure they're okay."

"What about Rebecca?"

"I don't know what Rebecca wants."

"She can have my share," Arliss said without turning from the window.

"Who?" I said.

"Marjorie. I don't give a damn anymore."

"I don't want it," Marjorie said from the base of the stairs. She came into the room. "Keep your trash money. I lost my husband because of it. I don't want any part of it." She fired off a glare in my direction.

"I thought I'd hang around awhile and help out," I said.

Marjorie started clearing the table. She stopped and stared at me with her soft eyes for a moment, then went back to her task. "I'm making some coffee. Anyone want any?"

I nodded. Turly muttered a "Sure." Arliss said nothing.

Marjorie turned for the kitchen, and the pocket doors of the den parted. Rebecca came in, stared at the floor, and took a deep breath. She rocked on her heels and raised her head. There was a wild look in her eyes. The words tumbled out.

"I don't know what I'm doing anymore. I'm sorry, but

maybe it's going to be okay. I mean, with the heroin gone and everything."

"Honey, what are you talking about?" Marjorie asked.

Rebecca began to wring her hands so hard I thought she'd take the skin off.

"When we went to the store earlier"—she took a step back —"I called David."

I went stone-cold. "Hanson?"

Turly jumped up as if he'd received a jolt of electricity. Arliss spun around. "You dumb bitch!"

"What'd you tell him?" I asked.

"I'm sorry, Frank." She started to shake, and her tears returned. "I told him where we were."

She took another step back and lifted her hand as Arliss charged at her with a roar. Turly and I intercepted him. He could have easily blown through us, but his move had been halfhearted.

Rebecca backed up against the wall. "I'm sorry!" she yelled, as if the force of her appeal might hold Arliss back.

"Goddamnit, Rebecca, why?" I said. "Why?" I grabbed the back of a chair, more to stop me going for her neck.

"I begged him to take me back. I told him that George tried to skip out on you, and you couldn't find the heroin. I was sure it was still up in San Francisco, and that you guys didn't have it."

"That's a lie," I said. "You made a deal with him to save your own skin. We were the payoff."

"He made me tell him where you were. He swore he'd kill me if I warned you. But I couldn't do it. I tried. I tried to hold out on you until he got here, but I just couldn't. You've got to understand—I need to go back. I couldn't stand being poor and on the run. I knew it wouldn't work. I couldn't take it. He said it was the only way."

Arliss spun around and pounded the table over and over. It jumped with each impact.

"We'd better get out of here fast," I said.

"Oh, good, without a car?" Turly said. "Are we going to run all the way to L.A.?"

I turned to Marjorie.

"I don't have one," she said. "I came here by bus."

"We've got plenty of cash," I said. "We'll go to town and buy one."

"Hell, we'll just steal one," Arliss said.

"Yeah," Turly said. "No reason to get all honest now."

"We get the guns ready in case they show up before we can get out of here," Arliss said. He aimed his fist at Rebecca. "I ought to kill you."

He moved into the living room. Turly and I followed, but Rebecca grabbed my arm just as I made it over the threshold.

"I can make a deal with him," she said. "I'll tell him to leave you alone. He'll have me back. The heroin's gone. What else could he want?"

I jerked my arm away. "Us, Rebecca." I let that sink in.

She coiled into a ball.

"How many other things did you tell him?"

Rebecca looked away. Her face was wracked with misery and remorse.

"You called him when I was at your apartment, didn't you? The only reason you came along was because he threatened you."

She didn't respond, and I knew the answer. The betrayal was like someone stabbing me in the gut and turning the blade.

"Why didn't she tell us earlier?" Arliss said. "We would've had time to get out of here. Maybe Roach wouldn't have run out on us. Crazy bitch!"

"That's enough!" Marjorie said.

Rebecca ran to the den. The pocket doors slammed closed behind her.

"I left my stuff in the garage," Arliss said, and went out the front door.

I grabbed my jacket and pulled out the .38. I looked back at the dining room and Marjorie. Her gaze shifted from the doors of the den to me. Her eyes expressed rage and terror. I tried to smile, to give her some reassurance, but it came out wrong. She spun on her heels and headed for the kitchen. I joined Turly and piled the bags by the door.

"How are we going to run around town, lugging all this stuff while we try and steal a car?" Turly yelled to no one in particular.

Arliss blew back in and threw his bags on the floor. He opened one and pulled out his submachine gun.

"What about me?" Turly said. "I don't have a gun."

I gave Turly the .38 and grabbed the shotgun.

Marjorie came back out into the dining room. "You're safer if you stay here. I'll go."

"We don't have time for all this," Arliss said.

"One of the neighbors has a car for sale across the high-way. It won't take me more than an hour. Yes or no?"

"Sure," I said. "As quick as you can."

I gave Marjorie more than enough money. She grabbed her purse and went to collect Nate. Turly, Arliss, and I went over the inventory of ammunition. Arliss had three additional maga-zines for his machine gun; there were two dozen .38 cartridges, but only four shotgun shells, plus the two in the chambers. Arliss was the only one with experience of handling a gun, and anyway, there wasn't enough ammunition to fight off as many thugs as Hanson would throw at us. A fast getaway was our only chance.

FORTY-FIVE MINUTES PASSED. TURLY, ARLISS, AND I WAITED IN the living room. Arliss paced, and Turly sat on the sofa, tapping his feet and rubbing his forehead while I browsed the books stacked on the mantel. I'd given up trying to reason with Rebecca. She kept the den doors closed and refused to talk.

"What's it like?" Turly asked Arliss. "You know, getting shot at and shooting at other guys."

I turned away to witness this meeting of the minds. Arliss sat down at the other end of the sofa.

"I don't know," he said. "Scary. But you're so hopped up that you keep firing. It's kind of like both things—scared shit-less and so damned mad 'cause they're shooting at you."

"I don't think I could shoot anybody."

"Don't worry. Stay low. You can't hit much with that

popgun anyway. Just wait until they're real close. Then you can't miss."

"I don't think you heard me. I don't want to shoot anyone."

"They start shooting, you'll shoot back."

"Not me, man."

"After the first few bullets fly by your head, you'll get goin'. Trust me." Arliss played with the straps of his duffel bag. "You get all boiled inside. At first, you just can't believe it, then something pops, and, bam, you're firing away and trying to kill somebody. Then you kind of pop back when the shootin's over with."

"Kind of?"

"Well, what do you expect when you got blood on you from the buddy next to you, who's got no face left? You don't ever go back completely. I've seen guys, they can't go back at all. You know what I mean? Like Roach."

"No," I said. "What do you mean, like Roach?"

"He never popped back, I guess. That's why Roach gets so edgy. He came back from Korea a little turned in the head. He spent four months in the psycho ward at the Letterman Army Hospital. That's why I couldn't be mad at him for running off the way he did. All this shooting got him off the edge again. I just feel sorry for him, you know? Sad."

"So, stuff like that doesn't set you off?" Turly asked. "You know ... pop?"

Arliss went back to thumbing the bag straps, then said, "Nah. I guess you noticed I blow off steam all the time. It gets all that poison out of my system so it don't back up like a clogged sewer line. Roach tried to keep cool, you know, keep it all in, find other ways of making it go away, but I don't think he ever really did, and it came back on him."

Everyone turned at the rumble of a car engine outside. I rushed to the window. Behind me, I heard Arliss pull back the bolt on his machine gun. I peeked through the gap in the curtain. An old, rusty Ford rolled up the driveway.

"It's Marjorie," I said.

I opened the front door. She and Nate walked across the yard. She smiled and said something to him I couldn't hear, her voice light on the breeze. It warmed me; in spite of losing George, she was there for her boy, hadn't allowed herself to withdraw into depression.

I opened the screen door for them as they crossed the porch, suppressing the urge to say something tender. That rusty Ford was our ticket out of there, and away from her. Marjorie and Nate smiled, but hers flattened an instant later. They stepped inside. She held out the keys.

"It isn't much," she said, "but it will get you where you want to go."

"You sure you don't want to come with us?"

"I think you know the answer to that."

"We could at least drop you off somewhere safe."

"I'll be staying with the neighbor I bought the car from. The rest of the houses around here are vacation homes, so no one's here for the moment."

I could only smile and try to convey the message with my eyes. She didn't give me anything in return. She handed me the keys and I thanked her. She walked away. I watched her go, feeling certain I would never see her again. I called after her. "We left some money for you on the table."

She didn't bother to stop. "I don't want it."

I walked after her.

Arliss stopped me. "We've gotta go."

"I know, but I can't leave without saying good-bye."

"We'll get the stuff to the car. Make it fast."

I was about to follow Marjorie into the kitchen when I saw movement on the road through the curtains.

"Shit, they're here!"

38

Turly, Arliss, and I rushed to the windows. Two black Cadillacs pulled to a stop on the dirt road in front of the house, one behind the other.

"Marjorie, they're here!" I yelled. "Get upstairs with Nate."

Marjorie rushed out of the kitchen with Nate and moved to the stairs. She stopped and looked at me.

"Keep away from the windows," I said.

She stayed, held her look for a second. I beheld everything I would forfeit. The two of them; they were what made sense in the madness. All the other garbage became meaningless. Too bad I had only learned it on the day I might die. Marjorie headed up. The smash of glass brought my attention back to the danger outside. Arliss had ripped down the curtains and busted the window with the butt of his gun.

"Do the rest of them," he said.

Turly and I attacked the other windows.

Outside, the car doors popped open. Four guys emerged from the front vehicle, guns at the ready. Two had shotguns;

two had semi-automatic .45s. The driver emerged from the other car, then another guy from the passenger's side. They both held tommy guns. The back door opened, and Hanson stepped out.

Behind me, the pocket door to the den slid open. I looked back. Rebecca stood in the entrance, holding herself as if from an icy wind. She wiped the tears from her red eyes.

"They've come for you, darlin'," I said.

Her face was ashen and her body shook. Pity and what remained of my love welled up inside.

"What do you want?" Arliss yelled out the window.

Hanson laughed and called back, "You know what we want."

"We have Rebecca," I said, "but we haven't got anything else. One of our partners ran off with everything."

Arliss cleared his throat loudly.

"Oh, really?" Hanson said. "That's interesting." He waved his hand.

The guy with the tommy gun reached into the back and pulled at something. Roach came out of the back seat. His hands were tied, he was bleeding, and his eyes were swollen and red.

"Guess who we have?" Hanson said.

Arliss growled and moved for the door.

"Arliss, wait!" I said.

He stopped and jumped back to the window. "Let him go, assholes!"

"We have something else," Hanson said. He leaned into the car and pulled out the suitcase that Arliss had loaded with the heroin. He popped the latches and threw it toward the house. It hit the ground with a hard bounce. The lid flew open and planting soil exploded from the case as it rolled. It landed with the open lid facing the house. The only thing inside was what remained of the soil. Turly and I looked at Arliss.

Arliss shrugged. "I couldn't let Roach have it. Besides, it would have made him come back to me. Sorry I didn't tell you guys."

"We'll do a little exchange," Hanson yelled. "Rebecca and the shipment for your double-crossing friend."

"Where is it?" I asked Arliss.

He walked over to the duffel bag he'd played with earlier, unzipped and pulled it apart. The packets lay inside.

"If we give him what he wants, he'll just come in here shooting," I said.

"I don't want any of that shit," Turly said. "We make the deal."

Arliss said, "If there's a chance that he'll give up Roach, we've gotta take it. We can't leave him hanging. It ain't right. I still love him, and you don't turn your back on your buddies."

I looked at Turly. He nodded. Arliss too.

Rebecca came forward, one deliberate step at a time, shaking as she moved. Her eyes never left mine. She came in close to me.

"Good-bye, Rebecca," I said.

She hesitated at first, then leaned in to me, her perfume mingling with the scent of her tears. We kissed. I felt the softness of her lips and tasted the salt on her cheeks. She trembled as we embraced. I pulled away and stepped back for her to pass. She moved for the door. Arliss lifted the duffel full of heroin and placed the straps over her shoulder; she bent sideways under the weight. Turly held the door open for her. She stopped, turned one last time, and mouthed "I love you," then kissed Turly on the cheek.

"Good-bye, Rebecca," Turly said. "Thanks for everything. I hope you have a good life."

Arliss yelled out the window, "She's coming out. We'll shoot her if you don't let Roach go now."

"Arliss," Turly said. "You can't shoot her."

"Don't worry. I wouldn't shoot a girl in the back. But I'll kill every one of those fuckers if they don't let him go."

Rebecca crossed the porch. Turly slammed the door shut and ran to his window. I rushed to mine. The thug holding Roach hadn't let him go.

"Let him go or we'll shoot the girl!"

Arliss raised his submachine gun and held his aim as Rebecca walked within twenty feet, then fifteen, of the cars. I watched, bracing for the sound of his gun. Nothing happened. I looked over at Arliss. His gun was still trained on Rebecca, but his eyes had dropped to the floor. He jerked his head back up.

"Let him go, you bastard," he said. More a plea than a threat.

The thug released Roach and he careened toward the house. Hanson raised his gun. The thug grabbed Rebecca. Hanson fired twice and she screamed.

Roach's back arched and he fell to the ground.

Arliss roared and let loose with the submachine gun. Bullets sprayed the cars as Hanson and the thugs dove for cover. One of Hanson's men flew across the hood with his shotgun, his chest taking at least three rounds. Another with a tommy gun grabbed his throat and fell. The remaining thugs opened fire.

Rebecca stood frozen and unharmed in the mayhem. She

took a step back toward the house, but Hanson grabbed her by the hair and pulled her into the car. He dove to the ground and opened fire.

Bullets shattered wood and glass inside the house. Turly flattened himself against the floor. Arliss stayed low and fired short bursts. His magazine emptied and he dove for a second one.

Two thugs fired as two others split up and moved for opposite sides of the house. More wood and glass exploded. Bullets ripped through the room and crashed into the wall behind. The picture window in the dining room blew apart. A perverse sense of dislocation overwhelmed me for a short moment as I listened to the crash of ocean surf rumbling faintly beneath the din of gunfire.

I stuck the shotgun out the window and aimed at one of the two thugs moving toward the sides of the house. I fired both barrels but missed. "They're splitting up!"

"You and Turly go to the back," Arliss said. "I'll stay here."

I crouched as I moved for the dining room, barely able to control the urge to throw myself onto the floor and stay there. Bullets flew by, and the hair on the back of my neck stood up. I looked back for Turly. He was still flat on the floor, under a front window. I crawled back, grabbed him by the shirt. Bursts of Arliss's machine gun roared near my ear, momentarily blanking out my hearing. Fragments of wood and glass splattered all around me. Turly finally came up groaning, his hands and face cut. I pulled him along the floor and into the dining room.

He went to the left, I to the right. We stopped at the base of the fractured picture window. I popped open the shotgun and reloaded. I peeked above the window frame. Turly imitated me. We ducked back down and waited for what felt like an eternity. Bullets slammed into the wall and zipped out the broken window. Arliss kept up his short bursts of fire. I looked over at Turly and our eyes met. He managed a smile and just for a moment, his wild eyes calmed, and I saw the Turly I'd known only a few weeks ago.

I heard the crunch of footsteps on the glass outside to my right and the moment disappeared. Turly's face twisted into something crazed. He stood, aimed, and fired rapidly at my side of the window. I leaped up, bringing the shotgun around. Outside a pistol fired. Turly cried out and fell backward. I fired blindly, and the recoil pushed me back.

A scream from outside pulled me back to the window. The guy spun, a chunk of his shoulder missing, his arm flopping at his side. He raised his pistol, and I let loose with the second barrel. The impact threw him to the ground. He no longer moved.

I dropped to the floor and cracked open the shotgun. My hands shook wildly as I fumbled for two more shells. I held back my sobs for Turly and concentrated on getting the shells in the gun. I snapped the barrels back in place and crawled along the floor toward my friend. All I could see were his legs convulsing.

"Turly's been shot!" I screamed.

I reached his feet. A red hole gaped in his chest. His eyes were wide, as if he were surprised. I grabbed his legs to stop them from shaking. "Turl!"

The back door to the kitchen burst open. I jumped up, my vision still blurred from my tears. A black shape flew across the kitchen. I aimed in the general direction, pulled the triggers and both barrels let loose with a deafening explosion. The shape tumbled to the floor.

Pain ripped through my left side and up toward my head. I sucked in air and my side spasmed. I screamed, forced myself to look down. Blood seeped across the fabric of my shirt. I fell against the wall and tried not to pass out.

"Frank!"

Arliss. I looked in the direction of his voice. He fired off one more burst and ran into the room, grabbed me, and dragged me to the picnic bench, where I had a decent view of the living room.

"You hurt bad?"

I bent under another spasm, this time less intense. "I'm okay. Watch the front. I've got a couple of shells left. I can watch the back."

"Maybe they'll give up after losing four guys. We got 'em didn't we, Frankie?"

The front door blew apart. A foot kicked the remains of the panel open. Arliss grabbed the submachine gun, took two steps toward it, and opened fire. The doorframe shattered; the screen disintegrated; plaster fell in chunks as the bullets ate at the wall.

Then it stopped.

The machine gun was empty.

Silence.

First an arm, then a shoulder appeared in the fractured doorframe as the body leaned to the right. It slid down and dropped onto the porch with a hollow thud.

Arliss threw the submachine gun to the ground.

From the road came cracks of tommy-gun fire. Arliss jerked as another assault of bullets flew into the house. He dove for my shotgun with a crazed look in his eyes. Blood seeped from a hole in his collarbone.

Everything went gray. Arliss shook me, and my vision cleared. He laid Turly's .38 on the table next to me, then took the switchblade from his belt and placed it next to the gun.

"When you run out of ammo," he said.

His voice sounded distant but clear. He picked up the shotgun, crouched down, and crept along the floor toward the front door, grunting as he moved. I wanted to yell for him to come back and stay with me, but I couldn't talk.

I tried to get up, but my left side screamed and I dropped to the floor. I sucked in a breath. A pair of legs appeared at the front door. Arliss never saw it coming. A shot rang out, his head snapped back, and he fell.

39

I crawled underneath the table. The shooter stood over Arliss's still body. He fired twice more. I fought flashes of pain as I reached up and patted the table top in search of the .38. I could actually smell my blood, that acrid, metallic smell. I pushed back the panic and nausea. My fingertips found the gun.

Slowly, carefully, I lifted it and brought it down. The shooter's legs swiveled. Stepped toward the table. Floorboards creaked over the crash of waves. I aimed. The man stopped, bent his knees.

I fired.

Three times.

His shin exploded. Then the knee. The last took out the hip.

He screamed and fell to the floor writhing.

I kept pulling the trigger, but there was only the click of the hammer.

Our eyes locked. He reached for his gun. There was nothing I could do except watch. He grunted as his fingers clawed at the floor. Blood pooled around his ruined leg. He thrust his hand toward his pistol but screamed and coiled into a ball.

I shook off the darkness that threatened to envelop me. Hanson was still out there, somewhere. I hoisted myself up.

"Fess?" I heard Hanson call. "Crowder!"

I grabbed the switchblade off the table and staggered for the back door. I collided with the wall, then the doorframe, and my head spun. A numbness overcame the blinding pain. The knee-jerking spasms subsided, making it easier to move, but my mind was slowly shutting down.

I stumbled down the back steps, leaned against the side of the house and slid along the back, putting one foot in front of the other. The cold and the fog enveloped me. The graying of my periphery blended with the fog. I felt nothing but the para-lyzing cold. I reached the arbor; Hanson was visible through the rosebushes, standing by the car and staring at the house.

"Crowder!"

I had to hurry. If I collapsed now, he would find me and surely put a bullet into my head. I staggered across the back of the garage and around the side. My feet became tangled and I fell hard. Nothing but loathing and adrenaline drove me back to my feet. I reached the front of the garage and leant against the side wall to catch my breath.

Hanson said something I couldn't hear.

Rebecca screamed from inside the car. "Frank! Frank, are you all right? Frank!"

"Shut up!" Hanson yelled.

I stepped around to the front of the garage.

Rebecca leaped out of the car and wrapped her arms around Hanson's neck.

I had to help her. I took two steps, then collapsed onto my knees.

"You killed them," she said, tears streaming. "You bastard, you killed them."

He slammed the pistol onto Rebecca's hands. She let go and scratched at his face. Hanson backhanded her with the gun. She fell back against the car. He shoved her into the backseat.

The burn of hate drove me onto my feet. I popped open the switchblade, and for a moment, all I saw was the shining blade. I staggered forward, still thirty feet from the Cadillac and Rebecca.

"Frank!" Rebecca screamed.

Hanson fired into the car; the fog flashed orange.

Two shots.

Silence.

I wanted to die right then and there. I'd lost everything, everyone. An internal voice spoke softly of giving up, lying down, letting go. The cold sucked me toward the gray ground. My knees gave way and I went down, my butt against my heels, willing my body to move but forced into prayer.

I heard the scrape of shoes on gravel.

"There you are," Hanson said. He walked toward me, his .38 aimed at my head. "It looks like it's just you and me."

He stopped beside me, and I felt the cold metal of the gun against my temple.

"Drop the knife."

I had no reason to—he'd kill me anyway—but survival overcame reason, and my mind clung to life, to the breath in my lungs.

And so I did. I dropped the knife.

Hanson grabbed my hair and yanked my head toward Rebecca. Her limp hand extended from the open car door.

"See what you've done?" he screamed through his tears. "I didn't want to kill her, but you made me! You corrupted her!" He wiped his eyes and jerked my head up to face him. "You accused me of killing Mrs. Ivers, but you're worse than me. I give to charity. I support the arts. I donated money for a new wing at a hospital. I've carved a place out in this diseased society and given back. What have you done? What have you given except waste? You're pathetic." He pushed the gun harder against my temple. "You're going to die, and I'll go home to my wife and kids, and go on with my life. I'll give you a few moments to think about how bad you've fucked up before I pull the trigger."

"Frank!"

Hanson and I looked up. Marjorie leant out of a second-story window, her hand over her mouth.

I grabbed the gun and pushed it away from my head. It went off with an explosion of blinding light and hot gas.

Hanson yanked and twisted the pistol, and my strength faded. He finally wrestled it from my hands and swung it back into my face. The force of the blow drove me to the ground.

Marjorie ran up behind Hanson, the shovel I'd left in the flower bed already arcing through the air. With a growl, she smashed it into the back of his head. He staggered backward, fell to his knees, and leaned against the lead Cadillac. His pistol clattered across the trunk lid and hit the ground on the other side of the car.

Marjorie lifted the shovel high above her head and brought it down. Hanson raised his left arm and deflected it away from his head. It smacked hard onto his forearm and glanced his shoulder. He cried out, shot to his feet, and charged her. He caught the shovel as she began her next swing, and hit her across the jaw. She fell backward.

I summoned strength I'd lacked to save myself. I grasped the knife and lunged, aiming for his chest. Hanson jumped back. The move caused me to stumble. In desperation, I thrust blindly. The blade sank deep into his thigh. With a scream, Hanson balled up and collapsed.

I fell onto my side and gasped for air. A flood of pain sent me reeling. Everything went gray, and the hurt gave way to numbness. Hanson whimpered and pulled out the knife with his bloody hands. He tried to stand, but fell back onto all fours, eyes wide as he fumbled the ground.

He inched toward the .38. I grabbed his foot. He squealed and kicked my hand away. I tried to push myself up, but another searing pain exploded in my side and I fell face-first into the dirt. I could only watch as he crawled between the two Cadillacs, my vision slowly constricting.

Through my fading consciousness, I heard hollow thuds and the ring of metal.

I looked up. The vision seemed surreal, nightmarish even. Saw innocence corrupted, man's fall from grace. A visceral sense of repulsion and regret was tempered by the primal satisfaction of witnessing justice being done: Marjorie—beautiful, blessed Marjorie with her sky-blue eyes and flower-print sundress—stood over Hanson, and slammed the shovel down on his head—or what was left of it—over and over and over.

S IX MONTHS LATER
     Those moments before I lost consciousness haunt me
still: Hanson lying in a river of blood; Rebecca's pale hand
jutting from the backseat of the car, her fingers splayed out as
if reaching for me; but mostly Marjorie, blood spattered on her
face and arms, the fury as she lashed at the man who'd taken
so much from her.

Then a bright, beautiful memory of Marjorie's face as she
hovered over me just before blackness descended.

I don't remember the doctor she bribed, or the first ten days
of my recovery. There are sounds and hazy images, but the rest
is locked away in a distant place. Healing, I guess. For as much
as my body needed to mend, my spirit needed it more.

Marjorie had stopped the bleeding, gotten me into the rusty
Ford, gathered Nate, a few clothes, and the money left on the
table. She drove the two hours to the outskirts of Stockton,
where she knew a doctor from the pharmacy she worked at
who'd patch me up, no questions asked.

Two days later we went across the Sierra Nevadas and into

the desert. After a four-month ordeal in a hotel room outside Tonopah, Nevada, I recovered. Between times, we read the newspaper accounts of what had unfolded after we'd escaped.

The police had arrived at the beach house and found twenty kilos of heroin in Hanson's car. The newspapers called it "the Moon Bay Massacre." An investigation was launched; indictments were handed out, creating a flood of accusations, recriminations, cover-ups, and distortions. A few lesser syndicate members took the fall, but most of the evidence that could have brought the entire thing down was swept under the carpet.

As for Rebecca, I will always think of her. Part of me still loves her, and I forgive her.

I grieve for my friends and will never forget them; the loss will always be there. But in time, I'll find a place for those memories ... somewhere they won't hurt so much, won't haunt me.

If there's anything I've learned, it's not the finding of truths that counts, but the searching for them, because the real ones are never discovered. They are peeled back in delicate layers that reveal but more layers beneath. The real truth is in the act of that peeling. You never get to the heart of it. That things reside in the corner of the eye or the tip of the tongue or the end of an unreachable rainbow that keeps on shining and changing and promising. It's in the running after all, the joy of running toward something rather than away from it.

Marjorie, Nate, and I are outside Clovis, New Mexico, driving south on Route 70. Nate has turned in the front seat. He watches me, his head rising above the seat back, his hands cradling his chin as I write all this down. His smile is broad. I grin and look at the intense blue of Marjorie's eyes in the rearview mirror. I examine the features of her face—the curve of her ears, the rise of her cheekbones—and follow the slope of her chin to her lips, which curve in a smile that always brightens my heart.

"Do you need another pill?" she asks.

I shake my head, look down at my shirt. There's a dull throb where I took the bullet. I don't want to take any more pills. I've been numb for too long. The sheer pleasure of sitting in the backseat of the car, going south with Marjorie and Nate, is something I would not diminish.

We haven't decided where we're heading yet: maybe El Paso, Lubbock, Guadalajara even. I know we'll never be able to stay in one place for long; I'm sure there's a contract out on my life. Bribing the doctor took half of our money, but we're doing okay. I'll find a job and start playing and composing music again.

We haven't spoken of love. It still hovers beside us while we grieve and heal. It will come in time, I know it. Regardless, we'll never see San Francisco again; never go where the summers are colder than the winters; and never, ever go back into the fog.

THE END

Did you enjoy this book? You can make a big difference in my career!

Reviews are the most powerful tools in my arsenal when it comes to getting attention for my books. Like most readers, I'm sure you weigh reviews heavily once you've seen the book's cover and read the description. And without reviews, a reader might move on without giving a new author a try.

That's where you can come in: An honest review of this novel —or any of my other novels—just might be the thing that convinces them to read and discover new stories and authors. Like me!

If you enjoyed this book, I would be very grateful if you could take five minutes to leave an honest review on the book's product page.

If you would like to sign up to my newsletter to receive news about upcoming releases, special offers, and insights into my writing life, you can go to: https://johnaconnell.com/subscribe
As a thank-you gift, I'll include a link in the welcome email for a free novella - the prequel to my Mason Collins series!

Thank you!

ALSO BY JOHN A. CONNELL

The post-WW2 Mason Collins crime thriller series

"A must-read series for me." Lee Child, bestselling author of the
Jack Reacher novels.

Madness in the Ruins

Winter, 1945. Munich is in ruins, and a savage killer is stalking the
city.

U.S. Army investigator Mason Collins enforces the law in the
American Zone of Occupation. This post is his last chance to do what
he loves most—being a homicide detective.

But he gets more than he's bargained for when the bodies start piling
up, the city devolves into panic, and the army brass start breathing
down his neck.

Then the murderer makes him a target. Now it's a high-stakes duel,
and to win it Mason must bring into deadly play all that he values:
his partner, his career—even his life.

Haven of Vipers

A fairytale town with gingerbread houses has become the Dodge City
of post-WW2 Germany, and the gang running things are ex-Nazis
and crooked U.S. Army officers.

Not the best place for U.S. Army detective Mason Collins to keep his head down, serve out his time, so he can go home.

While investigating a rash of murders, Mason discovers a web of coconspirators more dangerous than anything he's ever encountered.

Witnesses and evidence disappear, someone on high is stifling the investigation, and Mason must feel his way in the darkness if he is going to find out who in town has the most to gain—and the most to lose…

~

Bones of the Innocent

Summer, 1946. Just as assassins from a shadowy organization close in for the kill, a flamboyant stranger offers Mason a way out: He must accompany the stranger to Morocco to investigate the abductions of teenage girls. Girls that vanished without a trace.

Once Mason lands in Tangier, he discovers that nothing—or no one —is what it seems. This playground for the super rich is called the wickedest city in the world, and he realizes those who could help him the most harbor a terrible secret.

But just as Mason begins to unravel the mystery, the assassins have once again picked up his trail. Now, Mason must put his life on the line to find the girls before it's too late. If he lives that long…

~

To Kill A Devil

1946, Vienna. When a shadowy organization fails to assassinate Mason Collins, they go after his colleagues, his friends, and the love of his life. Mason knows the only way to stop the killings is to cut off the head of the snake.

Armed only with the alias, Valerius, Mason treks across Franco's Spain to war-torn Vienna to eliminate the man ordering the hits. But tracking him down seems to be an unsurmountable task; everyone speaks his name with awe and fear, but no one knows if he's real or a gangland myth.

Mason, desperate for answers, abandons his strict moral code, leading him down a very dark path, and to succeed in hunting one devil, he makes a pact with another.

But what Mason doesn't know is that, even if he does find his way in the darkness, the man they call Valerius has something special in store for him.

ABOUT THE AUTHOR

John A. Connell writes spellbinding crime thrillers with a historical twist. In addition to his standalone, Good Night, Sweet Daddy-O, he writes the post-WW2 Mason Collins series, which follows Mason to some of the most dangerous and turbulent places in the post-World War Two world. The first, Madness in the Ruins, was a 2016 Barry Award nominee, and the series has garnered praise from such bestselling authors as Lee Child and Steve Berry. In a previous life, John worked as a cameraman on films such as *Jurassic* Park and *Thelma and Louise* and on TV shows including *NYPD Blue* and *The Practice*. Atlanta-born, John spends his time between the U.S. and France.

facebook.com/johnconnellauthor1

twitter.com/johnaconnell

bookbub.com/authors/john-a-connell

goodreads.com/8623003.John_A_Connell